SARAH LEE

ABOUT THE AUTHOR

Marion McGilvary lives in London and has four grown-up children. She has written for *The Times*, the *Financial Times*, and *The Observer*, where she has been a regular contributor and columnist. *A Lost Wife's Tale* is her first novel.

A Lost Wife's Tale

A NOVEL

Marion McGilvary

HARPER

NEW YORK • LONDON • TORONTO • SYDNEY

HARPER

HarperCollins books may be purchased for educational, business, or sales promotional use. For information please write: Special Markets Department, HarperCollins Publishers, 10 East 53rd Street, New York, NY 10022.

FIRST U.S. EDITION

Designed by Cassandra J. Pappas

Library of Congress Cataloging-in-Publication Data is available upon request.

ISBN 978-0-06-176609-1

18 19 20 OV/RRD 10 9 8 7 6 5 4 3

To Judith Anne Corrente

1

MY NAME WAS Edith Lutz.

So what are you thinking? Thin? Earnest? Maybe Slavic, with blue eyes cut like tribal scars into the tight, bare canvas of her face and broad, streamlined cheekbones flaring like wings from a sharp nose? Or are you seeing feral wariness, muddy skin, and nondescript pale brown hair, yanked into a ragged ponytail with a rubber band? Or German, perhaps? A statuesque Jayne Mansfield blonde, with stout legs, an uncomplicated relationship with porn, and a wardrobe full of accessorized Birkenstocks?

It was open to interpretation.

In fact, once that summer, I met an earnest, underdressed college kid from Ohio reading the Bible on the bus downtown who, despite the Boston Celtics vest that hung like slack-jawed chins from his moist, hairy armpits, introduced himself with a formal, if damp, handshake, and made me spell it out for him as he held my bony fingers in his sweaty palm.

"So, like, do you drop stuff all the time?" he asked, smiling goofily at his own wit.

"You know—Lutz, klutz," he elaborated when I gave him the blank stare I used for idiots and men in shorts, which pretty much had my social life covered back then.

Yep. Just what you need sitting next to you on the bus down to the East Village, a fucking poet. He'd be whipping out his guitar any second and putting it to music. But anyway, ineptness hadn't occurred to me at the time. On the contrary.

To me, the name was always German. She would be staid, practical, fiercely capable, and a bit worn around the edges. The sort of person who favored sensible shoes, like the kind my mother used to wear when she was on her feet all day in the shop—with maybe a plain, knee-length, A-line skirt, and white cotton underpants bought a size too big for comfort. Like the real me, she was in her late thirties—not quite yet middle-aged, but in training for it; slim, average height, pale, and fairly uninteresting. She was a woman who did not care too much about appearances and who could fade easily into the background, like a thin wash of watercolor paint.

Without perfecting a goose step or manufacturing an accent with lots of *z*s in it, to get fully into character, I still had to dress the part. I drove to the mall and bought a simple, made-in-the-Philippines polyester skirt with a licorice-thin plastic belt looped through the narrow waistband and a cotton shirt in a sad shade of nursing-home lilac from a rack of several thousand of its identical sisters. The footwear wasn't much of a stretch since I always wore flat heels, but nevertheless I felt the leather flip-flops I had found the previous year in Guatemala, though fine for Harvard Square, were a little too ethnic for Fifth Avenue. I sifted through the cast-off shoes in a thrift store and, since it was summer, picked out a pair of shabby nurse's sandals with molded wedge heels and the ghosts of another person's toes imprinted on the insoles like the Turin shroud for feet. I thought about bleaching my fair hair several shades blonder, but on the salary I expected to become accustomed to, I knew there was no way I could maintain my roots. Of any sort. I did, however, thread my long hair into a braid and then wind it into an amateurish bun. All I needed were my glasses perched on the end of my long, straight nose, and I became the stereotype of the mousy office girl I had once been, except that then I had been young. And I had looked absolutely nothing like this.

So, would you hire this woman? I asked my reflection as I pirouetted in front of the jaundiced mirror in the women's bathroom at Penn Station after I had changed out of my own clothes in a stall. Well, I guess that depended how desperate you were for domestic help, and I really hoped the next person on my list would be frantic, because I was running out of time and options. I had not liked the woman at the last interview. I had dragged myself all the way to her hushed country mausoleum in upstate Connecticut only to discover that she and her husband already employed a cook, a nanny, and a housekeeper, and that what they wanted now was someone to take sole charge of the wife's bedridden mother. I had told the agency that I had no interest in looking after children, but it had never even crossed my mind that I might be expected to nurse the old. Had I been struck by a sudden urge to transform myself into a Mother Teresa of the Aged, I had a demented mother of my own back home whom I could care for.

I left without even meeting the invalid.

By ruling out both ends of the age spectrum, I'd whittled down both my options and the patience of Mrs. Garcia at the agency, who kept telling me in her nasal Latina twang that beggars couldn't be choosers when I was competing with a whole country full of undocumented workers out there who would work for less than minimum wage. I couldn't afford to be so picky, she said, all but snapping her fingers at me, and she was right. So far, I'd been offered only one position—as a receptionist in a small hotel in the theater district, run by a cartel of Nigerians, one of whom hired me without his bloodshot eyes ever meeting mine. But the front desk was too public and the hours closer to slavery than hard work. Also, the hotel was on the sort of street where you could earn more money by lying on a bed than from renting it out, and I wasn't convinced by the sign claiming that only guests were allowed past the lobby.

So, for the nineteenth time, I checked the appointment in the letter from the agency. The short job description said only that Adam Davenport lived alone and wanted a full-time, live-in cook/housekeeper who would work weekends and house-sit over the summer. The person who called from his office before the interview, an offhand, WASPy-sounding secretary who seemed about twelve with an IQ not much higher—fortunately—specified that he wanted someone honest, reliable, and organized.

Two out of three wasn't bad.

According to the street map that I had already folded and refolded into tattered squares, the Upper East Side would be easy to get to, but it was too far, too hot, and too humid to walk. I hated the subway, especially in summer, and had never been able to figure out its intricacies. Even when I lived here, it had defeated me. It was like being asked to do mental arithmetic in a foreign language, and the various routes still looked to me as though someone had been testing different colored markers on a scratch pad. So, since I was early, I decided I would take a cab up to the Met and bide my time in the museum. I rolled my cutoffs and T-shirt into a cigar and pushed them into a tote bag. Then, smoothing back my hair, hoping in vain that the humidity wouldn't do too much damage, I swapped my severe reading glasses—sadly, a necessity, not a prop—for a pair of sunglasses, crossed my fingers, and set off.

The cab scuffed the sidewalk, then headed north through the honking, wheezing traffic. An orange plastic skeleton hanging from the rearview mirror danced agitatedly in the blast of an air-conditioner that blew itself out before it reached the back seat, swinging widely to the right and left every time the driver swerved. I suddenly remembered why polyester wasn't a good fabric for the heat, as a trickle of sweat ran down between my breasts and tendrils of hair uncoiled in ferns around my face. I felt as though I had been steamed alive by the time the cab emerged on Eighty-second Street, like Alice from the rabbit hole, into a different world of the sleek and coiffured, airbrushed by money.

I idled in the lobby of the Met for half an hour, too cheap to pay the suggested donation, then I picked up someone's leftover *New York Times* and tried to care about Ross Perot's chances of being elected president. No matter that I had been in the States for more than ten years; I still couldn't really get interested in politics. It was all the same to me whether Clinton stayed or went, I thought, as I ate an ice cream in the shaded fringes of the park before walking over to Madison and down to Eightieth Street. Fortunately, the crepe-soled sandals were comfortable.

It was only a couple of blocks, and I was still too early. I hid in the chilly interior of Ann Taylor until the perky sales assistant's insistence that the baby pink cotton-cashmere-blend twin set would look wonderful with my complexion (yeah, sure, honey, because it coordinates with sweat) drove me back out into the heat. I found some shade at a nearby bus stop and perched there like a meerkat, craning my neck to keep my eye on the front door of the house. It was a dull UPS brown with a barred half-basement hidden behind a fence bearing a long planter. On the second floor was an elaborate bow-fronted window with Art Nouveau metal frames covered with verdigris, as intricately decorated as a cloisonné jewelry box. The doorman smoking outside the apartment building on the corner gave me a sour look before ascertaining that I was neither a hooker nor a vagrant and then slid back into his building like the rainy-day guy on a cuckoo clock. No one else came out of the house while I waited, which was, I told myself, surely a good sign. It meant Mrs. Garcia hadn't lined up a whole stream of other interviewees. The minutes wheezed wearily away in the heat until, at exactly three p.m., with a brisk step, I crossed the street, hesitated for a moment about which of the two entrances to use, then climbed the steps that fanned out like a bridal train and rang the main doorbell. It responded with a distinct lack of enthusiasm and apparent silence. I was just wondering whether I should go down and try the other bell in the basement when the street door slid open on buttered hinges, and there he was.

From the way his secretary had spoken about him, I had been expecting a fussy sixty-something bachelor, possibly gay, with cats, manicured fingernails, carefully clipped hair, and vowels to match, but the man who led me straight into what could have been either a boardroom or a formal dining room was younger and slightly disheveled in his linen pants and crumpled cotton shirt, in a weekend-in-the-Hamptons sort of way. He also seemed to be just as nervous as I was. He was, at most, fifty, with mad, barely tamed, Beethovenish dark brown wavy hair and the kind of even, square-jawed, fair-skinned good looks you got on knitting patterns in the 1950s.

Adam Davenport stared at me over the top of his black-framed Elvis Costello spectacles, the almost identical twin, separated-at-birth, from those hurriedly perched on my own nose. "So, Mrs. Lutz?" he queried after we had each introduced ourselves and discussed the ease of my journey at exhaustive length, ". . . where does your name come from? I presumed you must be Eastern European when my secretary gave me your details. Russian, or perhaps Czech, but your accent"—he coughed—"would hint otherwise. You're English?" There was a question mark signifying a great deal of doubt. So much for Mrs. Garcia's insistence that my toney "Briddish" accent would be a selling point.

"Scottish. Originally," I added and smiled, like it was a funny affectation I had acquired especially to amuse him.

He laughed obligingly, so I joined in, as though I was used to this sort of reaction, which, after all this time in the States, I kind of was. Though it still took all my self-control not to ram the gold cigar of his fountain pen up his aristocratic nose.

"More Glasgow than glasnost," I said. He laughed again.

Ha, fucking ha, I thought.

I should have realized that the Scottish accent was going to be a bit of a problem for any would-be fräulein. After all these years in the land of the Yanks, where even the academics I knew spoke Spanish with a flat American intonation, I still couldn't banish the Scottish slang that slipped into my sentences like the neighbor's cat whenever the door swung open. Five minutes into the interview and anxiety had grabbed my glottal stops and choked all diction right out of me. I was off script and improvising, nerves causing me to drop *ochs* into my sentences the way a bad cook over salts the stew. And now, dear God. Now, I was even doing stand-up.

Davenport was staring at the papers on his desk, reading and rereading my references with Talmudic concentration. It was as though someone had hit the PAUSE button in the middle of a long Swedish film. My finger twitched to press PLAY.

"I think the name might have originally been Lutzman," I babbled, trying to distract him, hurrying him along.

His eyes flicked up.

"But I'm not sure," I continued, careful not to trip up over the consonants, bouncing the *t*s smartly off the back of my teeth. "My husband Frank's family came over from Germany during the war, but they didn't like to dwell on the details."

I was already evicting Francisco's father from the tiny antique-stuffed town house they used to have in the East Sixties and relocating him to a dusty Upper West Side apartment filled with bad modern art, dusty pots, and macramé, and substituting his trophy wife for a septuagenarian with an untidy chignon and a part-time psychoanalytical practice in the spare room. What can I tell you? Too much Woody Allen at an early age.

In fact, apart from my old boyfriend Karl, the only German I had ever known was Henny, the greengrocer in the village where I lived in southern Scotland, who had been rounded up during the war and had spent it interned somewhere in the Highlands. After the war was over, he resumed his life selling cabbages and turnips to the local populace, who treated him as though he had just been away on a tour of Scotland's great golf courses instead of living as an enemy alien for five years. Not that anyone ever forgot he was a German. But they just called him "Henny the Hun" and left it at that.

Anyway, as I had hoped, the merest mention of war and the

whiff of a possibility that there might be a Jewish horror story hiding underneath my adopted family's reluctance to discuss the provenance of their name, and the subject was dropped. There was another painful pause while Adam, once again, scanned the papers spread across the table.

For fuck's sake, would he ever stop reading the references? There wasn't anything wrong with them. I knew that. I had written them myself.

I took the opportunity to glance at my surroundings. We were both poised awkwardly at one end of a long lacquer table running like a ruler down the length of the room, whose walls were painted blue to match the kitschy tiles in the fireplace and the Delft china which, I would come to know, was hidden in one of the dressers. The ceiling was trimmed with white cornicing iced around the tops of the walls like frosting. A huge pear-shaped chandelier dripped glass prisms from an ornate plaster ceiling rose, and two long walnut cabinets, each containing an army of glasses lined up in ranks, ready to march out over the table, stood on either side of a chalk-white marble fireplace. At the far end, a pair of spindly French windows cut the light into squares like a checkerboard across a faded wine-colored Turkish carpet revealing a balcony leading to a decked yard with a Japanese maple shading a small fountain. It was the kind of place God would live in if he moved to Manhattan and cheated on his taxes. It was by far the most expensive piece of real estate I had ever been in, even taking into account Francisco's family's Colonial house overlooking the sea outside Cartagena, in Márquez country. Francisco's summer home was vast and elaborate but simply furnished, not oozing money like sap from the hardwood floors the way this place was. I couldn't imagine living here. You could get lost simply by wearing Paisley and standing on the rug.

A cough and the briefest glint of eye contact brought me back to attention. "I see you've only worked as a housekeeper once before," he said. "In Boston?"

"Yes, my husband and I came over two years ago on a sabbatical from Oxford and I decided to stay on after . . ." I left the sentence unfinished and left the academic details vague.

"You said he was American?"

"Yes, his family live out in the Midwest. Fargo," I added, hurriedly substituting the Coen brothers for Woody Allen. I hoped this guy didn't watch a lot of movies. "But we're not close."

"And before you came to America you and your husband lived in Oxford?"

"Yes, that's where we met. Frank taught there."

"Really? Which college?" he barked.

"Balfour." I held my breath hoping that Davenport's mother's, sister's, priest's dog walker wasn't related to the college president in that peculiar way the transatlantic upper classes have of networking. It was tricky sticking so close to the truth, but I couldn't risk a lie that took me too far from what I knew, and Balfour was a big, unfashionable graduate school whose members were international and varied. It would be difficult to pin anyone down there.

I hoped.

"Ah, I don't think I know it. I've been to Oxford a couple of times, but I don't really know the university. It's a beautiful city."

"Very beautiful." I nodded, limp with relief, like one of those dogs you put on the dashboard of your car. I exhaled so loudly that the papers, which he had finally set down on his desk, fluttered.

"I guess I'm just wondering why you don't go home now that you're . . ."

"A widow," I supplied, then faltered deliberately and counted to three slowly; I had practiced this for hours: "My husband died a year ago . . ." I let my voice trail off and hesitated long enough for the expected sympathy to wad into the space before continuing. "But without Frank there are too many memories back in Oxford. There's nothing to go back to . . . It's easier here."

Interrupt, damn it, I thought. I was running out of lines. Then on cue, Davenport mumbled, "Oh, I am sorry, it must have been a very difficult time for you."

I inclined my head to acknowledge the weight of grief and my stoic acceptance of it, twisted the sliver of gold on my wedding finger, and smiled bravely.

"No children?" he asked.

I shook my head. "It never happened." I shrugged again, going for the Oscar in understated tragedy. I could see that this was yet another topic that Adam would treat like an outbreak of herpes.

"Um well, my own daughter might spend a fair bit of time here after the summer vacation, but she lives downtown with her mother at the moment. She's fifteen. She doesn't take too much looking after. Quite independent. Too independent, if you ask me. I also have a son who's at Groton—eighth grade—and he'll only come for the odd weekend. That wouldn't be a problem for you, would it?"

"Of course not," I lied, while silently damning that snippy bitch at the agency for not filling in all the details. I really had no interest in doing the whole Mary Poppins thing—especially not for a teenage girl. Panic gripped me as a store detective would a shoplifter. I wanted to get up out of the chair and leave, but I was held down by my collar.

"And your own family—are they still in Scotland?"

"No, my parents are both dead." I didn't elaborate but stared at him, daring him to inquire further.

He looked as though he wished he could evaporate. He dropped his glazed eyes back to a reexamination of the loop in the signature which I had rehearsed over and over again, like a beloved boy's name on a school textbook, until it had just the right flourish. He adjusted his glasses.

Poor soul, I almost felt sorry for him. He was interviewing Typhoid Mary in his dining room, and I expected him to give me a job, hand over his keys, and entrust me both with the care of his impressionable children and the smooth running of his household. In another century they might consider burning me at the stake.

"Cooking," he ventured, back on safe ground. "The woman you worked for in Boston, Mrs. McBride, speaks highly of you?"

There seemed to be yet another question hiding in the statement, so I hastily attested to my skill in the kitchen: "I can cope with most things. She used to entertain a lot and I ran the house and did all the cooking—mostly plain dishes—roasts, salads—but I can also do Spanish, Italian, French—I'm not a Cordon Bleu though."

"No German food? No oliebollen and appelflappen?"

I couldn't think what he was talking about and he saw my confusion. "I expect not; those are Dutch things my grandmother used to make—but I thought there might be similarities."

"Ah, I don't know." I smiled politely. "Frank was a Latin American expert and we spent a lot of time in Central and South America, so we got a taste for the food," I explained.

He opened his mouth to inquire further, then thought better

of it, doubtlessly fearing that curiosity would unearth an even more torturous story.

Nice lips, I thought as he closed them. Being very correct, he was too polite to pose any more personal questions and, as I had hoped, too desperate for some household help to care. I was the ideal employee. I could speak English, or at least a recognizable version of it; I had a green card, could cook, run a house, and, according to the estimable Mrs. McBride, was honest and efficient. I had no dependents and I could start immediately.

And so, after a few token inquiries about my husband's sabbatical and Boston life, which, as he had told me he was "a Yale man," were easy to dodge, I was hired on a month's trial, beginning on Monday, and given a set of keys to the basement, where I would have my own apartment.

I accepted so quickly that I didn't even ask how much he was paying me.

We shook hands. I took the Amtrak back to Boston and rode the T out to Porter Square, where, to the creak and groan of naked floorboards and the hollow sighs of bare cupboards, I packed up our little house on Beech Street.

I dumped the contents of the freezer, took out the trash, deleted all my files from the computer, turned off the gas, shut down the AC, and opened the door of the empty refrigerator. I wrote a note explaining how to turn on the furnace for hot water and stuck it on the cork board. I left a spare set of keys in a kitchen drawer ready for the new tenants, a visiting Swedish professor at the divinity school who had already arranged to rent the house for the autumn term, and dropped my own in an envelope with the Realtor on Hope Street.

Before I'd had time to register my loss, it was done. I was back in Manhattan, letting myself into the basement of what was supposedly an architectural jewel of the Upper East Side, with its carefully preserved original features, all decorated like an elaborate wedding cake. But the house was really just a rich man's folly built in a mishmash of styles in 1922, stubbed out among the red brick apartment buildings at the butt end of Eightieth Street between Madison and Park. It was as much a historic treasure as I was a German widow and had about the same amount of character.

And since neither of us was quite what we seemed, we suited each other just fine.

2

BUT THAT DOESN'T mean I liked it.

Downstairs in the basement, the house lost its gracious manners, as well as the air-conditioning. My suffocating bedroom was full of angry French reproduction furniture that missed no opportunity to nip spitefully at my shins and elbows as I walked past.

There was an overbearing mahogany wardrobe the size of a fat woman's coffin that tipped forward whenever I opened the door farther than a crack and threatened to swallow me. The bed was a narrow single Empire divan with an oak frame that buckled and yawned, showing the gaping teeth of the missing springs on its chain-link base, causing the mattress to collapse with exhaustion whenever I sat on it, which was often, since the room contained no chair. The single chest of chipped veneered drawers was backed against the wall behind the door like a cornered fugitive and dropped dandruff flakes of sawdust over all my clothes. At night I could hear woodworms chewing through the wood.

Whenever I walked into the bedroom, a tight sensation of unease pinched me like a secondhand dress that had belonged to someone much thinner. I couldn't help but long for the bright little room I had left behind, with its shaky brass bed and primary-colored tribal rugs on the painted floorboards. We liked to pretend we'd found the carpets while trekking through Peru, but the only things I picked up in Peru were bedbugs. The rugs had arrived, sight unseen, from a mail-order outlet I found in an ad in the *Boston Globe Magazine*. I thought I had graduated with honors in solitude when I left home as a raw teenager, but on Eightieth Street I soon came to realize that I hadn't even made it out of grade school. In the cramped bedroom I sat hunched in the hollow of the mattress and stared at the curling Scotch tape left by the posters of a previous tenant, listening to the rest of my life tick away on the bedside clock. What had I done to myself? I looked at the dust felted on top of every surface in the room and choked on something halfway between despair and asthma. But I had to make the best of it. This was my life now.

Around the time I realized that losing a husband spawned a corresponding need to make a living, fast, it also became blindingly clear that I didn't have employment opportunities ringing my bell like the Avon lady. Up until then, Francisco had supported us both on his modest but steady academic salary, supplemented by a small family trust fund that yielded enough to pay for travel during the summers. I made pin money here and there by editing overseas students' theses, but obviously that wasn't going to be enough to sustain me in the big, wide, expensive world of independence. My typing, never particularly accomplished at the best of times, was accurate but slow. I was used to paying more attention to syntax and accurate foreign spellings than to speed and spreadsheets. My office skills were hopelessly outdated, and even if I had only wanted a job as a sales assistant, I would need references and experience—neither of which I possessed. I did a quick stock-take and decided to build on my existing skills. I had rusty grade 3 piano, a gold medal for lifesaving, and a bronze medal for Highland dancing. I knew the Dewey decimal system backward and could speak enough Spanish to get by. I could cook, run a house, and smile prettily while looking riveted at dinner parties when I was bored to the point of catatonia. I was good at pastry and proficient at sex, but since I was probably too old for prostitution and not decorative enough for the escort business, it seemed as though I should concentrate on cooking. If I found a job with cooking that let me live in, it would also solve the problem of accommodation. That settled it: instead of summoning the maid, I would become one myself.

I picked up a copy of the *New York Times* and scanned the want ads, deciding that my best bet would be one of the agencies that specialized in supplying domestic help. I chose a small but respectable-looking company with a P.O. box in Manhattan that looked humble enough to be the front for a business run out of someone's garage in a New Jersey suburb—as it turned out, it was Yonkers. Then, posing as my own previous employer, I used some headed notepaper from Francisco's office to furnish myself with a glowing character reference. Those laborious word-processing skills finally came in handy. When Mrs. Garcia called the house to check me out, I adopted a vague North American drawl, hoping its inadequacies would pass as Canadian, playing accent-keepie-uppie for the few minutes I spoke to her, and praised my wonderful housekeeper highly. And so I became Edith Lutz.

The name took a bit of getting used to, especially since no

one ever spoke it aloud. At first, hoping to familiarize myself with the curt, sharp vowels, I began to recite it like a mantra, over and over again—a Buddhist chant echoing eerily around the rapidly emptying rooms, as painfully, picture by plate, I dismantled the traces of the years Francisco and I had spent together, packing my own belongings, and then his, into boxes: some for charity, some for storage. But I was still afraid that my new name would sneak up on me unannounced, hail me from across the street, and I would forget who I was.

Once installed in the basement on Eightieth Street, I was more or less living alone, with only fleeting glimpses of my employer, so it wasn't as though a whole host of people were calling out my name on a roll-call. The guys at the market addressed me as "ma'am," until overfamiliarity with Marco from the deli counter at Eli's, whose name was written in red Magic Marker on a badge pinned to his lapel, led me to correct it to "Edith," which only embarrassed us both. Meanwhile, Adam Davenport, who seemed to find it as awkward having me in the house as I felt being there, didn't call me much of anything at all. Mostly he assiduously avoided making eye contact. I began by calling him, deferentially, Mr. Davenport, but addressing a floating spot somewhere between my knees and my feet, he mumbled an unintelligible protest and insisted upon Adam, managing to make the name sound more like a curse than a plea for informality. I rarely saw more than the jacket of his linen suit, crumpled like a Kleenex at the bottom of the stairs, so it was a moot point. At least it meant I could throw away the polyester skirt and forget the uniform of the German drudge. There was no audience to dress the part for. Instead, I wore all the cotton dresses that I had intended to take with me to Colombia, where, in the life that had been so cruelly snatched from me, I had planned to spend most of the next six months sunning myself in a hammock on the beach. So, as July steamed into August, I was cool, at least, if not comfortable.

The days I could just about manage, but the nights were long exercises in barely suppressed terror. Like a good Stepford wife, I rose at six thirty and prepared breakfast for the master of the house. When he had gone to work, I polished and dusted and scoured and scrubbed the already spotless house until every piece of silverware lay, untarnished, in a drawer, the tines of the forks and the cups of the spoons all facing east, cuddled against one another in sets of twelve, while the plates gleamed in graduated tiers like porcelain ziggurats. I swept the stairs in shifts, although only Adam and I walked on them, and I dusted every unread book on every shelf. It was like being in my own self-inflicted Sisyphean hell, but with a toothbrush and a trigger spray bottle of Mr. Clean instead of an uphill struggle with a rock. I finally became the kind of housewife that my mother would have approved of. Pity she wasn't around to applaud.

In the swelter of the empty summer afternoons, I passed the time walking from Dean & Deluca up the block to Zabar's way across the park for only one item, taking two slow buses downtown to Chinatown for minute quantities of ginger and star anise when the stores on Lexington had everything displayed in a cloud of exhaust outside on the sidewalk. I wore a knock-off baseball cap and swapped my Ray-Bans for a hideous pair of rhinestone sunglasses, both bought from an African immigrant on the street, lest someone from my previous life should find and claim me loitering in the produce aisle at the Gristedes squeezing a lemon. Naturally I avoided galleries and exhibitions, where the chances of recognition were greatest, and imposed an exclusion zone around NYU and Columbia, where I might have encountered a stray academic who knew me from Boston. To cool off, I swam in the pool at the Y until my hair, which I had decided I couldn't afford to lighten, became bleached a radioactive shade of green-blond from the chemical combination of chlorine and sun, while my arms and shoulders grew good Eastern European shot-putter's muscles. In the afternoons I lay in Central Park until the cooing and crying of well-bred, overindulged babies being pushed around in strollers by dusky women who were not their mothers drove me back home to the dim, welcome silence of the house.

As long as I busied myself with unnecessary chores, I could keep my anxieties at bay. But they would circle round and round the edges of my mind like wolves round a campfire, waiting for that second of inactivity when I would drop my guard and they could slink right in and curl up at my feet, their teeth gleaming in the flames. I'd be in the middle of choosing something to pretend to read in the library on Ninety-sixth Street, fighting the urge to reshelf misplaced books, when sorrow would catch me and tears would course helplessly down my cheeks. I'd find myself at the end of a block in a stunned trance while the WALK turned to DON'T WALK and back again. Once or twice, passersby, usually old guys hugging grocery bags who looked as lost and untethered as me, stopped and asked me if I was feeling all right, as though they thought I might be about to do an Anna Karenina and throw myself under a car. But that would have shown a lack of imagination and required better underwear than I possessed. In any case it would have taken too much effort. Or at least a sharp push from behind.

But, still, there weren't enough hours in the day to worry; I had to borrow them from the night instead. As the woefully inadequate fan shuddered from left to right like an arthritic spectator, the enormity of what I had done would crouch at the end of my bed and pounce on my chest at two a.m. I would wake, already sweating in the stewing heat of my bedroom, my heart compressed with anxiety, blood drumming in my ears, and lie in bed frozen with terrors, both named and unthinkable. I took St John's wort and Bach Rescue Remedy, but both had as much effect on my anxiety as a deer pissing on a forest fire. For sleeplessness I tried a range of over-the-counter remedies from the Indian lady at the drugstore, but they made me disoriented and fuzzy headed, yet still wide awake. I drank a lot of herbal tea with names like SleepyHead and Nighteaze, then woke up from my precious few hours of slumber to go to the bathroom and pee. SleepyHead, my ass.

Eventually, I gave up and just got out of bed and paced. I listened to the tinny sound of talk radio until the depressing news bulletins of bombings and plane crashes made me hurriedly turn the dial to middle-of-the-night Music to Slit Your Throat By on stations where it was always 1965, and played old tapes from the Salvation Army store on a powder-blue children's cassette player that I found in one of the kids' bedrooms. I indulged in long laundry sessions, and as my arm slid back and forth over heat-shimmering planes of rippled Egyptian cotton, Leonard Cohen and I would groan in unison. At a whisper, in the flannel-lined tomb of the otherwise silent house, we sang: "*It's four in the morning* . . ." But by this point Leonard and I had been wretchedly harmonizing for long enough to tell the time. In a fit of unaccustomed female intimacy, the wife of my friend Karl had once told me that this was her favorite song. She said that if any man had played it while he was trying to seduce her, she would immediately have succumbed. Who would have thought it? I didn't know what was stranger: tuneless moaning acting as an aphrodisiac or the notion of Karl's wife having a libido. I thought the song was too full of regret to be erotic. Anyway, I doubted whether Karl had ever got into her sterile underwear with any help from Cohen. He was more into Laibach when I slept with him—thankfully not as an accompaniment to sex but to shot glasses brimming with peach schnapps. It was a novel concept: sexual discernment through song. I had always gone to bed with men regardless of their taste in music—regardless of their taste in anything, actually, as long as they had a liking for me. Even now I would happily have slept with the entire road crew of a Black Sabbath tribute band if afterward I could do just that—sleep.

I wondered if I would infect the whole house with insomnia through the concertinas of crisp white bedsheets. But then everyone was just "Damn" Davenport and myself, and he already had problems sleeping. I sometimes heard him walking around in the kitchen overhead, slow, light footsteps, and then the faucet running, the splash of water. With a little upswing of hope, I began listening for him. I took to leaving a jug of iced tea in the refrigerator, with one of his errant wife's frigid white china plates bearing a couple of cookies on the table, as if he were Santa Claus. But then, just like Santa, he stopped coming when I started to believe in him. I missed his footsteps. I often felt as if I were the only person in the whole world awake. A sudden flare of light from a bathroom window the size of a postage stamp in the apartment building on the opposite side of the yard would fill me with optimism—or as close as I got to the feeling, which was maybe a slight lift in my heart, one floor up from desolate.

My apartment was folded into the back of the basement. The door, obscured by the main stairs stacked like a pile of change and some fat, fleur-de-lis railings, led first to a room that, I assumed, had once been Adam's children's playroom. It had an old needle cord sofa, a wall of bereft shelves containing a few leftover kids' videos, tattered picture books—some very old classics that I remembered from my own childhood—and an ancient TV with a flop-eared antenna and a trailing cable that ended in a tripod of colored wires. In theory this room was my sitting room—but it was like the waiting area in a children's hospital where all the kids were dead. I went in there only when I had run out of other places to clean; the spots on the carpet alone held at least a week's possibility of fruitless scrubbing and shampooing. I was saving it for a rainy day. When the temperature was hitting ninety every day, rain was something I was really looking forward to. Next to the sitting room was a series of large closets in a line like cereal boxes, used for storing wine, a washer and dryer, and a large chest freezer. My small shower room came next, and finally, at the rear of the basement—with a view of eight broad, jagged, stone steps leading up to the garden above, and the briefest glimmer of blue sky and the square windows of the soaring buildings behind—lay my bedroom. Next to it was a small galley kitchenette and a mud room with a row of poignantly small rubber boots for children who had long outgrown them. When I could bear to look at them no longer, I hid them behind the similarly incrementally sized row of bicycles in one of the storerooms.

We fell quickly into a routine, Adam Davenport and myself. He worked in publishing, and I worked in the kitchen. I made him coffee in the morning, which he drank wordlessly, at the vast dining-room table where he'd interviewed me, marooned alone behind the *New York Times*. I offered him breakfast: wholegrain toast, eggs cooked in a Kama Sutra range of ways, homemade granola. Each he declined, saying that he was happy with coffee, but I squeezed him juice and made a fruit salad anyway—then usually consumed most of it myself, standing up at the sink, before scraping his untouched leftovers into a bowl for tomorrow's juice. He told me it was his custom to eat lunch and often dinner out, and so he instructed me to make sure there was some cheese and crackers in the refrigerator that he could take to his study if he was hungry or leave sweating in its Saran Wrap if he wasn't. He usually wasn't. But this didn't deter me from leaving him beautifully arranged plates night after night in the hope that he would eat.

I threw out the Canadian cheddar that he had favored before I arrived and gave him Manchego and Taleggio. I experimented with tortilla stuffed with spinach, and *pipérade* with truffle oil, but apparently he didn't like cold eggs, wherever they hailed from in continental Europe. I left out plates of grapes, a selection of charcuterie, and olives with rosemary, but they lay there till the ham turned up its toes and the olives grew fish-eyed. Sometimes I'd rescue the plate buried under papers in his study, jubilantly empty but for crumbs and crusts; at others I'd find it on the draining board, with the plastic peeled back a few inches, missing only a few bites. But most often he didn't even open the kitchen door. The waste disposal ate very well.

My frustration finally got the better of me. One day, after I had found fat Sicilian figs almost bursting out of their dusky purple skins at Eli's, I asked the wall-eyed assistant who waited on me since I'd scared off Marco to shave me some transparent slices of *jamón serrano*, which probably cost more than he earned in a day. That night, instead of closeting myself in my room, I sat upstairs pretending to attend to some unnecessary chore, like licking the chrome clean on the kettle, and waited until I heard Adam come in. Luckily it was not a dining-out night that he had forgotten to tell me about, and he arrived around eight thirty, a heavy exhalation and the rattle of his keys announcing his presence. The moment the street door swung closed behind him, I walked into the marble hall and held my hand out to take his jacket, which he usually threw like a drunk on to the gilt chair that sat daintily next to a table bearing a matching, monstrous clock, big enough to have its own hunchback. I smoothed the linen of his jacket and hung it in the coat closet, feeling like a fifties housewife. I would be asking him if he had had a good day at the office next, except that I could tell from the dark circles under his eyes, and the slump of his shoulders as he bolted the door behind him, that he almost certainly hadn't.

"Edith," he said, looking as shocked as if I had turned up wearing tassels on my nipples and barely restraining a man on a leash. "You shouldn't be working this late. Is everything all right?" He spoke to the blue-cheese veins in the marbled tiled floor and turned as though to climb the stairs. "Mr. Davenport—Adam," I emended. "I know that all you want me to do is leave you a plate of something in the refrigerator, but please, please, just for once, come and sit down and let me cook you a proper meal."

"I'm really not . . ." he began, foot poised on the bottom step.

"I just hate throwing away all this uneaten food night after night, but if I don't prepare anything, then I feel useless." I noticed he was getting thin. He was wearing a rumpled white shirt with a loosened striped tie; his sleeves were rolled halfway up his forearms and the elbows poked out of them like a skinny schoolboy's. He began to stammer excuses into his chest, his whole body twitching in eagerness to avoid me and get back to the business of climbing the stairs, but I wasn't letting him get away.

"Please, come into the kitchen and let me feed you," I said, and without another word, I walked through the hall toward the back of the house, hoping he would follow me. In anticipation, I had set a place for him at the kitchen table. There was a tureen of gazpacho, salty Sardinian flatbread, and a platter with the ham and the figs, torn apart and pursed up like the pouting lips of a silent-screen star. Without asking, I opened a bottle of beer, poured it into a tall glass, and handed it to him, pulling the chair out and indicating that he should sit.

"Really, it's unnecessary," he stammered. "You don't need to go to all this trouble. I don't have much of an appetite these days."

"I can see. You're fading away. But it would be a kindness to me if you would sit down. I haven't spoken to a soul in three days, except to say, 'six ounces of ham, thinly sliced,' and even that was in Spanish. Bad Spanish. So, please, please, indulge me. Have a drink. Talk to me." I smiled to show I was kidding, but I wasn't. I was pleading.

Francisco would have sighed, long-sufferingly, and rolled his eyes. He would have complained wearily, saying that he had been talking to people all day, and that now all he wanted to do was relax and be left in peace. I had only the sketchiest idea what Adam did at his office. For all I knew he led corporate bonding sessions all day and was exhausted from standing at a white board with a flip chart, sick of the sound of his own voice. Maybe he was just like Francisco had been: keen to keep his own thoughts and withdraw into a distracted silence. But I didn't care. I had begun to strike up conversations with the cold callers who rang trying to get me to change from AT&T to MCI. I was only one toll-free number away from calling the Samaritans. I needed some company.

To my relief, Adam started to laugh. He removed his glasses, rubbed his eyes, and took a long, long swallow of the beer. "That sounds wonderful; you have no idea quite how wonderful. I'm going to need another one of these, though"—he gestured to the bottle of beer—"and there's a condition," he added, drawing out a chair and sitting down. I looked at him. Actual eye contact. They were green, I noticed. "Get a glass and a plate, and join me."

I hate beer, but this wasn't the time to quibble. I snapped off a few shards of bread, cut some tomatoes, took out another bottle of Beck's and sat opposite him.

"I didn't know you spoke Spanish," he said.

"I don't, not really. But we traveled around South America a lot. Frank was . . ." I rummaged through the index cards in my head, which I had supposedly prepared for just this moment. They were blank. "He loved South America. We spent a lot of time there, because of his research." Had I told him this? I couldn't remember. "I picked up a bit—just kitchen Spanish. And we had a few friends back in Oxford from Argentina and Colombia." I just kept spitting out word after word, digging myself in deeper, instead of shutting up.

"What did he do, your husband?"

"Development studies," I said vaguely. "And he taught at Oxford."

"And then he was at Harvard?"

I nodded.

"It's bound to be a bit of a change being in New York after living all those years in Oxford. You must miss it," he said more than asked.

I shook the question off casually. "Not really," I answered.

"Did you get up to London much?"

I shook my head, claiming that we liked the quiet life, sucking my cheeks in anxiously.

"You said you met your husband at the university?" he asked. Now, this I could do. I had a ready-made answer. "I was a secretary and he was a student. Not very original, I'm afraid. What about you and your wife?" I asked, trying to deflect further curiosity. "Who? Gay?" he asked, as though he had a few wives stashed in a cupboard that he'd outgrown and wasn't quite sure which one I meant. "Oh, Lord, that wasn't original either. It was just sort of inevitable, I guess. We were at Yale together, but I knew her before. Her sister went out with my brother Timothy, and my parents and hers had a place near each other in the Berkshires. We used to go to the same summer camp in Maine when we were kids." I murmured something encouraging, though I couldn't think of anything worse than marrying your childhood sweetheart. "We started going out when we were freshmen, and when we graduated, getting married just seemed the next step. It was as if someone had filed the flight plan for my life when I was about six and I merely went ahead and followed it. It was all so predictable. I always saw that as an advantage, but now I'm not so sure, though I guess that predictability would have been something of a luxury for you."

"Why?" I wondered.

"Well, I mean with your husband, um . . ." He wanted to say *dying*, but the word stuck in his throat like a piece of dry bread. His face flushed with mortification. "I am so sorry, what a tactless idiot I am." I shook my head wordlessly. I couldn't go there. Sirens were flashing, slow down, pull over, turn back. "Gay always used to tell me I was the least sensitive man alive." He grimaced as he bit off the last word.

"It's fine, really . . ." I said, hoping to preempt yet another apology. "Tell me about your work," I said quickly, trying to steer him into safer waters.

"Only if you promise to shoot me first," he said and laughed again. A joke. We were making progress. "It's very boring: booksellers, budgets, sales forecasts, meeting targets. Believe me, it's not interesting. I'm very dull company, I'm afraid. Gay used to say that too," he added wryly.

I poured my beer inexpertly into a tall glass, then sipped my way through five inches of foam, wiped off my mustache, and listened while he talked about his house in Nantucket, where he was planning to spend most of August, and then, on his third beer, about how Gay had left him six months previously. It wasn't exactly easy listening to the catch in his voice as he described her sudden departure. By this point, rather than a beer, I could have done with a vodka myself. Preferably intravenous.

The subject of the kids seemed a better bet, though I really wasn't looking forward to getting into a doting discussion on the joys of parenthood. I did a hurried U-turn. "Your children are cute." (Since both were away at summer camp I had yet to meet them, but judging by the forests of photographs arranged throughout the house, they weren't, but I could hardly say, "Your kids are a testament to the dangers of inbreeding.") "You must miss them."

"Yes. But of course it was better for them to go to live with Gay. I couldn't separate her from the children, could I?" I wrapped my arms tightly across my chest and nodded my agreement. I felt as though I had a broom handle welded to my spine.

"What are their names?" I asked, when I got enough breath.

"Ned, my son, is thirteen," he replied, his face breaking into a smile. "He's at Groton." I was glad he had his attention fixed on the last drops of gazpacho so that he didn't see the look of disbelief in my eyes. Ned—what kind of name was that? I had an imaginary donkey called Ned when I was about eight. But it's surely not something you would call a real-life, almost buck-toothed kid. "And your daughter?" I prompted.

"Oh, Lennie—Leonora—she's fifteen going on thirty-five. She didn't want to board; she's at Spence. You'll meet her soon. She'll come to visit when I get back in the fall. Her mother wasn't happy about her being here while I was alone. As you will have appreciated, I'm not home often enough to look after a child—I work such long hours." I smiled in vague agreement while thinking, my God—Ned and Lennie. What a pair. These WASPy Americans never failed to amaze me with their capacity to inflict unnecessary handicaps on their otherwise privileged children. Poor girl. What sort of parent calls a baby girl Leonora? It sounded like she should be living with the March sisters in *Little Women.* I felt an unexpected surge of sympathy for the blond, orthodonticized teenager whose latest school mug shot I had just that morning dusted in its square silver frame. We had something in common after all—myself and this teenager, whose arrival I was already dreading. I may not have known much about kids, but I knew exactly what it was like to be saddled with a hideously awful name. My own real name was Agnes.

3

But at least mine was inherited, not capriciously bestowed on me at birth by the bad-name fairy.

There's a whole dynasty of us—withered, mousy Protestant women—with two things in common: fragile complexions and the first name Agnes. My mother was called Agnes, and my grandmothers, coincidentally, on both sides, were called Agnes, then there was one great-grandmother, another even greater, two aunts, four cousins, a small niece, and—well, you get the point. The women in my family either had remarkably little imagination or they considered Agnes to be their own particular brand-name—like Coke is to cola.

But the Agnes was an unpopular brand. As a girl I couldn't understand why my mother hadn't chosen a modern name—like Michelle, Vanessa, or Samantha (though in retrospect I can see that there are good reasons why no eight-year-old should be allowed to choose her own name). I wouldn't even have minded being one of the five girls in my elementary school called Linda.

At least they had something to bond over. But, instead, I was Agnes, pronounced with a Lowland snarl to sound like something between a dry sneeze and the yip of a small, irascible dog just before it sinks its sharp little teeth into your leg.

However, I learned early that there was no point in complaining about having to bear the family mark of Cain. It could have been worse. In a moment of brief postpartum madness, my mother had toyed with the idea of bucking family tradition and calling me Bridie. Bridie McBride . . . ?

I rest my case.

So I spent the first part of my life as the uncompromisingly stern Agnes McBride. And, later, when I married Francisco and replaced the McBride like a pair of baggy old knickers with his much frillier, flouncier surname, I couldn't help but marvel at my lucky escape. I liked being Agnes Morales, but if I had been stuck with Bridie Morales I would have sounded like a cancan girl in a Wild West saloon or a pet beautician who specializes in shampooing poodles.

Sometimes you have to be grateful for small mercies.

But even Agnes Morales wasn't great. From the mouth of my husband Francisco the harshness of Agnes was transformed into a sex-laden endearment. He swallowed the *g* like an oyster and sucked on the *s* till it swelled into a short breathy *a.* But on English lips I sounded like a Spanish maid, which, as things turned out, was ominously prescient. I grew into it, you might say, except that just as it began to fit me, I had to shrug it off and find another.

After much deliberation the first name I gave myself when job-seeking was Ruth. I had decided that this, finally, was my chance to have a gentle, feminine name that would soften my edges. Yet when I began filling in application forms for jobs, I just couldn't think myself into it. I didn't know her. I tried it on, but it didn't fit. I found Ruth's meek, biblical prettiness too delicate and forgiving. A lifetime as Agnes had conditioned me to something with a snap at the end of it, like a rolled-up towel on a bare leg. So I chose another ugly name, to match my nature.

I picked Edith from the hatchet-profiled frontispiece in a beaten-up copy of a book on the Bloomsbury Group and added it to the Lutz I had already decided on. I went to the departmental library and looked myself up on LexisNexis and yes, my instincts had been right, there was an Edith Lutz living in Germany—a fifty-something Freudian analyst and the author of several long monographs with compound German titles, not a word of which I could understand.

Edith Lutz.

It settled on me like a hard-wearing, scratchy tweed suit, and soon it came to grace my artfully self-composed references and testimonials, my new New York Public Library membership, and the front of the envelope Adam left for me at the end of the month with my wages inside, in cash.

I couldn't do anything about a bank account, driver's license, or passport, but the possibility of foreign travel was unlikely to arise, at least for a while.

Working for Adam quickly appeared to be not unlike the day-to-day business of marriage to Francisco, right down to the absence of sex, which in our relationship had been slowly replaced by diffidently polite goodnight kisses and low-voltage his-and-hers bedside lamps that allowed each of us to read without disturbing the other. Granted, while I was married, I hadn't done a great deal of housework either, but then I hadn't realized that if it wasn't included in the package, you could actually get paid for it.

With Adam my duties were not onerous and were mostly self-inflicted. He worked long hours and rarely returned home before eight p.m., still eating only when I forced him. He traveled occasionally, a night or two here and there, for which he packed himself.

He told me that in the autumn he would go to Frankfurt for the book fair and to London in March. He would go to the East Coast for meetings and hoped to entertain occasionally, promising it would not be extravagant and that I could hire extra help if necessary.

He expected his shirts to be sent to the laundry, but I did them myself by choice. Yet, though I may have ironed his striped boxer shorts and made his bed, housekeeping still allowed for an element of mystery that marriage did not accommodate.

His estranged wife, Gay—who apparently wasn't, in either sense of the word—worked as an editor in a rival publishing house. His son, Ned, was safely confined at boarding school, and his daughter, Lennie, lived with her mother in her smart, minimalist penthouse apartment in TriBeCa. Since I had been installed in the basement and was able to function as a ready-made proxy housemother, I knew it was only a matter of time before she began coming here on weekends—a prospect that I anticipated with about as much relish as a root canal without anesthetic.

So far I knew the rest of his family only from the two rows of silver-framed studio photographs on the top of Adam's grand piano, seemingly placed in the middle of the elegant parlor upstairs for the sole purpose of displaying snapshots.

There was a speckled black-and-white one of his grandfather, founder of both the fortune and the publishing business that accessorized it, and another taken in the forties of his glowering father posed beside a stout, boot-faced woman who was, unfortunately for everyone doomed to inherit her genes, his mother. I could see no resemblance between this stern, well-upholstered, mustachioed man and the slim, gaunt face of his son.

There were brothers, all heavier variations of Adam, like balloons with more air in them. I couldn't tell Tim from Stanley, but both were older.

In the back row there was a single, glamorous professional portrait of Gay signed TO GAYNOR WITH BEST REGARDS by Richard Avedon, taken in the early eighties, judging by the ruffled neckline of her dress. But no wedding pictures. She was beautiful in a chubby, Westchester, country club sort of way, I grudgingly allowed, but the New Romantics did no one any fashion favors, least of all the plump.

At the front there was a chronological selection of each of his two children taken at various stages of their school careers, obviously chosen by a fond, if willfully blind, parent. Certainly Adam's daughter would not thank him for displaying the picture of her, around age nine, looking like a bespectacled Jack Russell terrier, while Ned's latest photograph in his soccer uniform could have graced a wanted poster.

Behind these ranged a great number of black-and-white publicity shots in which, treading perilously close to subvulgarity, Adam was flanked by famous authors, a few B-list actors, Barbara Walters, and even Salman Rushdie. A peculiar vanity, I thought—as if he were in danger of forgetting his place in the world without a photograph to remind him. But then he wasn't the one chanting his name out loud to cultivate an identity, so who was I to talk?

Sometimes, on a good day, I would go upstairs with my duster and footle around the parlor, adjusting paintings and straightening cushions, knocking them into shape with such military precision that even my mother would have saluted them. I would sit at the piano and play my grade 3 examination pieces, plodding gracelessly through a Viennese waltz, before carefully replacing the damask cloth and rearranging the photographs one by one, marveling at Adam's ability to live so peacefully surrounded by all these people from his past.

In Scotland we kept our family photographs under lock and key—like the last strains of a deadly virus, isolated from the general population—crammed inside a battered tan leather suitcase that was, in turn, crammed at the back of my mother's closet.

I am around nine or ten, and bored. Being an afterthought has its advantages, not least that arriving thirteen years after my closest sibling means that I am usually home alone. My mother works in the village pharmacy, counting Seconal into smoked plastic bottles for the sleepless and Librium for the depressed.

My father is the manager in the local bank, giving out Masonic handshakes and short-term loans. My sister, Maisie, has married a Roman Catholic, her former ballroom dancing partner, and—whether to escape the Presbyterian censure heaped on those who married out or in search of better opportunities—has emigrated to Australia. And my brother, Geordie, is at University in Glasgow being smart.

I have already found and read the Christmas catalogs hidden under the bed and trawled through my mother's dressing table looking for anything of interest. But given my mother's obsession with hoarding, storing, secreting away, you can always find something to look at.

Nothing is thrown away; everything is neatly stored—as if the secret drawer police might make a dawn inspection without warning, cresting the mountain range of ludicrously large brassiere cups pointing up like the Alps. Most of the drawers contain piles of clothes being kept for Sunday best. We have whole rooms for best. A best front bedroom that no one ever sleeps in, a best front parlor for visitors who never come, and a best front door through which the visitors who never come can make their arrival. So naturally, best clothes for visits that never occur are absolutely necessary.

She also likes to keep some new clothes aside to be buried in just in case death should call unexpectedly, without calling first. Not content with maybe a nice nightgown and a clean set of underwear, my mother seems to regard death as a two-week vacation on a cruise ship and has several collections of burial clothes—a costume for every occasion. Whether at a cocktail party, an impromptu summons to afternoon tea with the Queen Mother in Balmoral Castle, or a walking tour of the Hebrides in particularly cold weather, she will be the best-dressed corpse in the graveyard.

With a hat and gloves to match.

The suitcase is a rare prize. I shake it gingerly. I've learned the facts of life from a childbirth manual that I once found inside an ottoman, and I am not overeager for any more information. One twist and the locks on either side of the case spring back smartly to reveal a treasure trove of photographs: hundreds of them, held together by rubber bands shriveled like souvenir umbilical cords.

Some are in albums, others still in the yellow Kodak envelopes they were born in, but most are heaped amid a mess of loose negatives curling like fortune-telling fish.

Old people, seen as young people in old-fashioned surroundings. Photographs of my mother looking impossibly skinny and pretty and happy. My father tall and lanky, owning the same kind of body that in my adolescence I will have to learn to grow into.

Baby Geordie, baby Maisie, baby me, and even, I am sure, baby mother and father, though I can't recognize them. Instead, there are gray-faced, mottled strangers galore, dead people dripping through my fingers, color prints already losing their definition, and frozen smiles fading to dirty nicotine shadows.

When I at last brave my mother's admonishment not to poke my nose into things that don't concern me and ask her about them, she sits on the armchair with me sprawled on the floor beside her, lights a cigarette, and starts to pick through the contents.

She strokes my sister's ballroom dancing portrait. Deep, deep sighs from mother. Moving swiftly on. Maisie's wedding album. White embossed paper with tissue paper and professional photographs taken mostly in the chapel. The book hastily put aside. More and heavier sighs. Instead, we sift through generations of Agneses until we hit on Maisie with an oversized bow in her hair. "Aye, but she was a bonny bairn." My mother's eyes grow all misty, for once not because of cigarette smoke. I am fed up with hearing about Maisie's superior childhood and adolescent beauty. Neither she nor my brother takes after my mother's side of the family in anything except height. They are both short. Petite, according to my mother; trolls, according to anyone else. But in all other respects they resemble my father: glossy dark curls, brown eyes. Nature has reversed her gifts for me. I got the Agnesy wishy-washy complexion and the kinky fair hair, but am tall and thin like my dad.

I have his nature, too, my mother maintains. I don't really know what that means. Just that it isn't good.

So I tune out my mother's soggy reminiscences and help myself to some of the pictures of Maisie when she was a teenager, posing with her head on one side and black sixties eyeliner curling at the corner of her eyes. She was very pretty, like a model. I wish I looked more like her. I wish she were closer. She seems to have been gone for so long that I can hardly remember what it feels like to have a sister.

Of course, it isn't to evade the past that my mother hides the suitcase at the back of the wardrobe in the best front bedroom.

It is dust more than death, dirt, not disgrace, that my mother fears at this stage. Ornaments and picture frames attract it, she says, lying idly around wantonly beckoning to it like the Pamela Anderson of the dust world. To combat this and thus wage her personal war against filth, everything is packed away in the name of hygiene. Cleanliness is not merely next to godliness but a whole cult of its own. But I didn't understand my mother's fetish for keeping things nice until we started hiding the real filth under the carpet.

ADAM'S HOUSE WOULD give my mother a coronary if she wasn't already demented, half dead from not-so-Lucky Strike emphysema, and so immobile in a nursing home that dust settles on her as if she were a Dresden shepherdess while she waits out her days. Unlike the more modern starkness to be found elsewhere in the house, Adam's parlor was a shrine to inherited consumerism. Everything was on display. Each surface came with its own particular sitting tenant: Delft figures from the family collection arrayed like a chorus line on the shoulder-high mantelpiece, silver candlesticks on the sideboard, Tiffany lamps, and Royal Danish porcelain sweet dishes, different clocks chiming different hours on different shelves as if the house had several time zones.

Worst of all was Adam's study at the top of the house, which had a whole metropolis of papers and manuscripts piled up around the floor, each topped with a Post-it note.

That, at least, was familiar to me. Francisco had a little room on Beech Street that looked much the same. His props, he used to call them. The detritus of academia, which made him feel learned and secure. A man of letters and teeny bits of paper covered with indecipherable references.

My mother would have tidied both places in a matter of seconds with everything boxed up and locked in the cellar, where she would first have vacuumed the wine bottles, washed the bottles with Clorox, and rearranged the labels alphabetically. Damn it, she would probably even have thrown the oldest bottles out.

However, if she were to see me with Adam, the real horror would not have been the attraction of his dirt but that I was working in service.

As I had come from a long line of women who had clawed their way out of other people's kitchens, my life as a maid would have been greeted with long looks and sharp intakes of breath.

But it didn't matter now. My mother had not spoken to, or even recognized, me for years.

Now, with Francisco gone, I was finally alone. It was terrifying.

Enough time had gone past for me to have grown accustomed to his absence, but I still missed him as if he were an amputated limb that, every now and again, you try to use, to stand on, because you forget that it's gone. You can still feel pain in all the nerve endings, even though you're massaging the air.

Loneliness was a pillow pressed to my face. After the discovery of a black-and-white portable television in the room with the bikes, I switched my allegiance from the public radio to afternoon soap operas and late-night made-for-TV films. I'd watch the craggy, perma-tanned hero kiss the pretty, barely adolescent heroine, and crumble like a cheap cracker, sure that no one would ever kiss me like that ever again. Over the years there had been the occasional lover to fill some of the white space left by Francisco's frequent foreign conferences and long field trips from which I was invariably excluded, but now it was all gone. I couldn't call on anyone for affection, and the only men I was likely to meet in Adam's house worked for Federal Express or steam-cleaned the carpets.

That kind of passion had been dead between Francisco and me for a long time. Since he stopped hoping for children, sex had dwindled to a celebratory obligation undertaken on birthdays and Christmas that we both pretended to enjoy, the way you do an unwanted gift. But it didn't mean that I stopped loving him.

In bed I lay curled against his back like an animal sheltering from the wind, my palms pressed against his waist as though to brace myself against an imagined onslaught, knowing that he would cushion me. And, loyally, he had been my barrier against the world, even when disappointment had burrowed in between us and I hadn't been able to give him the family he longed for.

But now the bed was empty. What had it mattered? All the plans we had made for a life that seemed set to run before us plain and straight—like one of those roads in the prairies, sometimes frighteningly so—were gone.

And so, long after I heard the hiss of the toilet flush on the third floor that heralded Adam's last visit to the bathroom before he slept, I would open the back door and pockmark my thighs on the top garden step overlooking the yard and stare up at the black shadows of the oppressive apartment buildings that surrounded it, watching as their illuminated windows were extinguished one by one.

I listened to the occasional stream of gentle laughter trickle out of a neighbor's open bedroom window, or to the ever-present music from the desiccated rock star who lived in a mansion farther down the street and who I sometimes saw walking his dog, and probed, tentatively, at an even more distant past, wondering what Kirsty would think if she knew I was living five houses away from her teenage heartthrob. She had waited in line for hours to see his concert in Edinburgh when she was fifteen, while I, a year younger, was left behind at home to marvel jealously at the story of his every gyration. Now I saw him most days, sitting in the coffee shop on Madison with his two tiny daughters, his once luxuriant locks replaced by a shiny, silver-fringed tonsure. His real name was Brian Hogg. You could see why he had changed it.

I would think of the two of us, sitting giggling in her bedroom, the window open a crack so we could blow smoke out of it, before leaping back from the memory, with a cattle prod of pain.

Then I'd hear the howling of the stray dogs which everyone denied prowled through Central Park at night, on and on and on, and the piercing, unearthly sound would follow me back inside and ring shrilly in my ears, long through the night.

If I had a gun, I would have gone over there and shot them.

4

I AM TWELVE.

Kirsty is a year older and she's ahead of me, running up the street, her yellow hair flapping in sheets across her face, when she turns to urge me to follow her. We stop to peer in wee Tam's shop window, past the pyramids of yellowing Tide boxes and the dead bluebottles. But it's his wife that's serving, leaning against the counter to take the weight off her feet. Her legs are all swollen and look like two glistening pork sausages in her shiny surgical stockings—the crease at her ankle just needs a bit of string. If we go in and say hello, wee Tam sometimes gives us a popsicle to share, but not Mrs. Tam. She always hunts us.

We don't like her.

Kirsty goes skipping along the sidewalk, her legs wobbling like undercooked French fries. "Step on a crack and you'll break your mammy's back," she shouts, pulling a string of hair out of the corner of her mouth.

But I don't like playing that game. My mother's back is bad

enough already. She's always rubbing it and groaning, saying, "Oh, I'm fair done. I'm fit for nothing," and then asking me to get her two painkillers and a cup of tea.

"Step on a crack and you break your mammy's china," I call instead. "Look, that's her teapot away, and her sugar bowl." But it's a bit of a boring game, because really it's easy to avoid the cracks, and if I broke my mother's china she'd kill me.

We stop at the bottom of the steps next to the Running Dog Bar.

Kirsty asks me if she should go and get Margaret out to play, but I say no. My mother doesn't care for Margaret, not since that time she came to sleep the night and didn't wash her feet before going to bed. "What can you expect with her folks downstairs in that bar all night?" she'd said. "Dragged up, that bairn is, no better than a gypsy." But I wouldn't mind being dragged up. You always got soda and potato chips at Margaret's house, any flavor you wanted. You just went to the Running Dog, knocked on the bar's back door, and asked. Salted peanuts too.

We run round the war memorial, cross the street, and see Mrs. Ponte from the café walking up toward the hardware store. Her coat makes swishing noises as she marches up the road, a fan of black hair flattened by her tights running down the front of each leg. American tan, they are. A horrible orangey-brown color.

When I got my first pair of pantyhose to go to Kirsty's last birthday party, I asked my mother if there were other colors of tan. Was Scottish tan different? In the end I got golden rose, and they turned my legs a funny red, as if I'd been sitting too near the fire, like the lazy tartan that Kirsty's mother has. She sits in the chair all day reading romances from the library and doing the crossword in the newspaper. She never goes out. Kirsty even has to change her library books for her. She puts a little code in the back of all the ones that she's read, so that Kirsty knows not to get the same ones out again. Kirsty says her mother is feart to go outside. But that's daft. It's because her dad is rich.

Mrs. Cameron doesn't need to go to work or even do the cleaning. She has a woman who comes in and does it all. Mr. Cameron is quite old. He has hair growing out of his nose. He is a funeral director, so he has a big black hearse and his own private gas pump. When my mother started working at the chemist at the far end of the village, I used to ask her why she couldn't work for Mr. Cameron instead and be just over the road, but she said those coffins in the back room gave her the creeps. Maybe they give Kirsty's mother the creeps too and that's what she's feart of. I asked Kirsty if they ever had dead bodies in the house, but she just gave me a look that would have curdled milk and told me I was ignorant. Kirsty can be a bit superior sometimes, but I like her mother. She always wears bright red lipstick, which people say isn't decent on the undertaker's wife, but I think it's nice. And anyway nobody sees it since she stays in all the time.

"Mrs. Ponte . . . Hello, Mrs. Ponte," calls Kirsty in a singsong voice, running up beside her.

"Aye, Kirsty," she answers, nodding as if she were heading a ball. "How are you, hen—how's your mother?"

"Fine . . . she's in the house," she adds, as if she'd be anywhere else. And besides it's me Mrs. Ponte is talking to. She was best friends with my mother when she was young, before she married Mr. Ponte and her name was still Cissie McLean. I'm going to answer, but Kirsty butts in. "What about your Dan—where's he today?" asks Kirsty. She's got a brass neck, that girl.

"He's out on his bike, hen—I think he went fishing."

"Aw." Kirsty's face falls. So he wouldn't be serving in the café.

Sometimes, even when we don't have money, we go in and pretend we can't make up our mind what we want just so we can speak to him. He's gorgeous.

Mrs. Ponte stops at the hardware store and says cheerio, but Kirsty has already lost interest now that she won't be seeing Dan, so I wave an answer for her. She's dancing along the side of the road, heading up toward the church on the corner, where we can see a crowd of people hanging around.

"Look," she says. "It might be a wedding." A wedding means a scramble. The best man throws bags of pennies and thrup-pennies out of the car window as the bride's car drives away. You can get quite a lot of money if you're lucky, especially if you wait for the bag of sixpences. We can't see any other children at the church, so we rush forward expectantly, thinking we'll get all the money, but the vestry door is shut. It isn't a wedding.

Kirsty pulls herself up on the railings and sits on the church wall, kicking her legs. I jump up beside her, my knees pressing forward on my Bri-Nylon slacks with their little stirrups tucked inside my shoes, pulling so tight that they start to drop away at the back, showing my bum. I stand up quickly, hitching them up to the place where my waist should be. The knees still stick out as if I've got two apples down the front of my slacks.

There's a faint skirling of bagpipes somewhere in the dis-tance.

"It's a band," says Kirsty.

I wish I could disappear. I hate parades. I know that every time there's a band, sooner or later the subject will get on to Kirsty being crowned last year's queen at the village fete, when she rode through the streets, waving at everyone, on top of a lorry covered with flowers made out of toilet paper.

"Do you remember when I was the queen and there were

three pipe bands walking behind me? I was nearly deaf from them." Like I said, the man with the big drum was hardly over the head of the brae and already it's queen, queen, queen. I say nothing.

"And do you remember when they came to the house in the morning and stood outside in the road and played 'Flower of Scotland'?" I feel like one of the slugs in the back garden when my mother throws salt on them and they just sizzle and dissolve into slime.

I can remember only too well when she came down the front path with her elbow-length white gloves and her long train.

"Do you know I can see right up your skirt?" I tell her. "You've got flowery underpants on and your bum's hanging out of one side."

"Well, they're clean and paid for," she snaps at me, but she gets down off the wall anyway and shuts up about being the queen.

She takes my hand, and we run off down to the river, along the railway tracks and back home. She lives in a huge house up the street from me—you could get lost in it. There's a sitting room and three bedrooms upstairs, all just for her. Her mum and dad sleep downstairs, where there are another two big sitting rooms. The mum and dad sleep in twin beds, like Rock Hudson and Doris Day—though Kirsty warned me not to tell anyone that. But anyway the woman who cleans for them already told my mother when she was in at the chemist, so everybody knows. The cleaner also said that Mrs. Cameron never lifts a finger or does a stroke of work. I don't know what she's complaining about. If Mrs. Cameron did the washing and dusting herself, then the cleaner wouldn't have a job.

"I'm going in to see if I can get some money for ice cream.

Wait here—I'll be back in a minute," orders Kirsty, as she squeezes herself through a hole in the fence.

I wait for ten minutes, but she doesn't appear, so I wander up to my own house. I know there's no point in asking my mother for money. She isn't working today and is sitting in the back kitchen, legs apart with her bum on the storage heater, even though it isn't on. Her arms are resting on each knee and she is puffing smoke into the carpet.

"What are you up to?" she asks, drawing her rapt attention away from the floor.

I see her eyeing the knees of my pants.

"Have you been out dressed like that?"

"Aye," I say, backing away out of reach of the pointed finger of her lit cigarette, which she turns and grinds out in a saucer.

"What's wrong?"

She shakes her head in despair. "You're a disgrace. I don't know why you can't keep yourself looking clean and tidy like Kirsty." I sigh, fed up. Better to brush past this one.

"Can I get a drink?" I ask with a rush of optimism over experience, hoping for a soda.

"Aye—there's plenty of water in the tap." She sighs and resumes her examination of the carpet as though she were being paid by the hour to watch it.

In the back lobby, I sneak open the cupboard, pull off my old plimsolls and put on the shoes that are in the back, hidden inside the box the toaster came in, quietly, without my mother's hearing. The shoes are leather slip-ons with straggly bows at the side.

They're hand-me-downs from Kirsty, though I don't think she's ever had them on. They're too big for her, but her mother sent for them from a mail-order catalogue and didn't bother to return them. She doesn't like to go to the shops and so she doesn't like to go to the post office either. I have bigger feet than Kirsty, but the shoes are a bit loose on me too. I've stuck a fleecy insole inside to make them fit my long, thin feet. If my mother sees them, she'll make me give them back. We don't need their charity, she'll say, even though she's always moaning when things don't fit me. She says she can't keep me in shoes because I'm growing too fast.

Sometimes I get things from the youngest Agnes, and that's great because at least she's fashionable. Young Agnes told me I could be a model, that I had the right cheekbones for it. I don't really know what she means—I'm just skinny. Anyway, everybody's got cheekbones; otherwise their face would collapse.

I stroll down to the front gate dragging my feet through the gravel, getting wee pebbles in my shoes and watching for Kirsty.

She's lucky: she's cuddly, with dimples. Her hair is straight as a poker and it floats like a bride's veil when she walks. She doesn't have pointy hip bones and her legs aren't all gangly like mine. I don't know why I got made the wrong way, like scones without the bicarbonate of soda so nothing rises.

I see her coming back through the fence and I walk wearily toward her.

"I had to make my mother a cup of tea, but then she gave me a shilling," she says, opening her hand, lined with dirt across the palm, and showing me the coin. Typical: I get cold water out the tap and she gets money. "We can get ice cream at Ponte's." That cheers us both up. She's so lucky, that Kirsty—honest, if she fell in the river she'd float like shit.

We walk along the grass border by the side of the road and kick stones across the cracked tarmac that looks like a big sheet of licorice that's been split down the middle.

Then Kirsty whirls round, skirt billowing. "Come on, Agnes," she says. "Maybe the band comes back down the street again and we can catch it going the other way." And she links her arm through mine, hooking my elbow. "*Come on!*" she shouts. "Or we'll miss it." My shoes are half falling off and make clapping noises, like slow applause, behind me on the sidewalk. But still, I run up the street. Behind her.

5

SO, HOW ARE you coping with all this, Edith?" asked Adam.

He cast his arm around twenty square feet of blank-faced oak cabinets as though worried that the dishwasher might lead a sudden revolt, bidding the German kitchen appliances to rise from the walls and overwhelm me, but I knew what he meant. I had been working for him for just over two months, much of that time spent alone with only a shifting gang of Polish decorators for diversion.

I had been wrong about my prospects for meeting members of the opposite sex. I could have had my pick of squat, paint-splattered men in overalls.

"Oh, it's fine. No problems at all," I said airily. "The house runs like clockwork."

"It must have been lonely here on your own."

"Not at all. I like my own company," I lied and smiled reassuringly.

Adam and Gay had a place in Nantucket that, despite their imminent divorce, they continued to share: she took her vacation in July and he had his in August. When he offered me the job, he had told me that he would be away most weekends over the summer and that all I would have to do was stay in the house and supervise the contractors who were coming to redecorate the labyrinth of corridors and stairways.

"Let them in, make sure they don't steal the silver, and keep on their backs all the time," he instructed—unnecessarily, as it turned out. The men found the silver as ugly as I did and were so hard-working that I had to remind them to stop. The Poles and I mostly communicated in mime, much of it me pointing at my watch or proffering refreshments with lots of agreeable nodding. We struck up a relationship using the international language of cake and beer, which they spoke fluently.

Thankfully everything in the house was to be painted the same shade of corpse blue-white, so at least there was no discussion about color swatches.

During August, Adam had spent only a few nights in the house, returning in the middle of the week for meetings and, once, to make a short trip to visit an author in Dallas. He went to stay with friends in upstate New York for Labor Day and offered to buy me an airline ticket if I wanted to fly off to visit Frank's family in Fargo. I nearly laughed in his face, but I managed to resist the impulse, wishing that I had said they lived in Palm Beach or California, which might have been nicer places to have pretended to visit my fictional in-laws.

He said he hated leaving me alone over the holidays, but I assured him it made no difference to me. I left the AC on full blast in the rest of the house, which eventually permeated downstairs and brought the temperature in the basement to a bearable level, and at night, I barricaded myself in the bedroom, stifling the moans and groans of the old house with the drone of my fan.

However, since his return, at his insistence, we had fallen into the habit of sharing supper most evenings. By the time he came back from Nantucket, tanned and antsy with the forced suppression of all the energy he usually channeled into his work, I had begun to feel as if my mouth had been stapled closed, and now I waited for him to come home at night with the eagerness of a young bride. I was frantic with excitement that there was another living, breathing English speaker who actually responded to my voice.

Francisco and I had fallen into the sort of nonspeak that I guessed all couples did after a decade or so of happy enough married-dom. I chattered about anything that came into my head, and he pretended to hear me, grunting assent with an offhand benevolence that faltered only with the challenge that he wasn't listening, which could rouse him to exasperation because it was true. I could have asked him for a boy toy and he would probably just have nodded pleasantly and said: "Of course, darling, whatever you like."

"You know I'm no good at small talk," he would protest, giving my cheek a distracted pat, followed by a kiss on the top of the head, which usually heralded his walking backward into his study.

He had not always been so reticent. When we first met, we used to lie awake long into the night talking about our very different childhoods, each of us drawing pictures in the dark to entertain the other. I never tired of hearing his stories of growing up with his grandmother Olinda in Cartagena, coming here with his father as a teenager, his summers on the farm in

Colombia, all more colorful and exotic than my own gray, shadowy anecdotes, so that my past faded modestly into the background of his. But eventually the only thing we discussed in bed was who had locked the back door.

Of course in the early years of our marriage he didn't have tutorial groups and lecture halls to service with the sound of his voice, nor had he an ever-changing stream of students regurgitating the same essay topics term after term. He wasn't obsessed with research grants and fieldwork and agriculture development programs. I could occasionally engage him by feigning a sudden desire to debate the toothlessness of the United Nations or Third World debt, but most of the time I let him be.

I was sure that some of his emotional reserve stemmed from losing his mother at such a young age, but the years of childlessness hadn't helped. If we had had babies, I guess we would have been infatuated with their every word and gesture, but we merely had the disappointment of their absence, and each other. My inability to have children was the great unspoken subject, never alluded to, never discussed. It was my failing. And so I simply resigned myself to the house's being a talk-free zone and got my fix of frivolity from his students.

But with Adam there was no taboo subject to carve a line across the dinner table, and, furthermore, I did my homework. I started scanning the *Washington Post* so that I could pass myself off as an enthusiastic Clinton supporter and sound knowledgeable about the upcoming elections. I knew more about the Unabomber than the court stenographer and left the *New York Times* crossword, half finished, ostentatiously strewn across the kitchen table. I read up on his authors in the book review section, until I could have given him an essay on the modern American short story. Well—the price of heirloom tomatoes and the brevity of the asparagus season could take you only so far.

Adam, to my astonishment, couldn't give a damn about the latest economic crisis in Argentina. To my joy he was much more interested in discussing his authors' private lives than the plots of their novels. I discovered who was gay, impotent, alcoholic, and immoral. As the recipients of secrets, publishers, apparently, are just like priests—except not nearly so discreet.

We usually ate together on weeknights while a heap of engraved cards inviting him to openings and book launches piled up, unopened and unanswered, stuffed into the drawer in the hall table. On weekends he went to catered dinner parties and smart restaurants where, he complained, he was always lined up with a series of well-groomed, blond, overexercised divorcees straight from desperation central casting, while I stayed home for my string of hot dates with *Wheel of Fortune* or *Masterpiece Theatre.* But tonight was a Sunday, and he was home—an unexpected bonus. I had been planning on watching *The X-Files*, but now I would be standing up Mulder and Scully for my own perfect partnership.

At first he had made the bold suggestion that we walk over to Serafina for dinner, but I thought that this was taking good labor relations a step too far. How would he introduce me if we ran into someone he knew—oh, this is Edith . . . my maid? And what if? But then my mouth dried up. It was safer to stay home.

And so I did what I did best. I cooked.

The remains of supper lay ravaged between us. Half a cold roast chicken with Persian apricot and pistachio stuffing splayed, legs akimbo, next to a bowl of curdling, garlicky paprika mayonnaise and a Greek salad. I cooked as I had once fucked, across cultures, influenced by years of homesick boyfriends who each had his own idea of what constituted comfort food. Even the German potato salad was a memory of beds gone by. It had been Karl's one culinary flourish, usually accompanied by roughly hewn salami and served between the sex and the cigarette, but I told Adam that the recipe came from my *mutter*-in-law Lutz.

Francisco's mother had been dead since he was seven and probably had not even known where her kitchen was. His grandmother lived with seven servants in a faded but beautiful Colonial house within salt spray of the sea and hadn't lifted more than a teacup in her life. Back on the family's farm, there was a black mud-packed farmyard full of sinewy, coffee-colored Colombian peasants hand-grinding corn for her tamales, while his Brazilian stepmother, who, when she lived in New York, thought cooking meant dialing for takeout (and, generally, had the houseboy do it), now lived with his father in Rio and a staff of two who slept in a cupboard behind the elevator shaft.

I began rinsing the serving dishes, scraping the limp, floury potatoes into the sink, and covering the chicken carcass with foil.

I would use it for stock tomorrow.

"Was your mother a good cook?" asked Adam. "I guess you must have taken it in with your mother's milk . . ." I laughed so hard that I could hear myself begin to snort. "My mother's milk. Are you mad? The only thing I inhaled from my mother was second-hand smoke and Clorox. God, no. My mother's twin contributions to world gastronomy were boiled hamburger and pot roast. The main ingredient of everything she made was salt. Until I was fifteen I thought canned lima beans were a green vegetable, and I'm still strangely addicted to the smell of ammonia."

"So what happened when you were fifteen?" That brought my laughter quickly under control. I hesitated.

"Oh, then I was initiated into the dark, satanic arts of broccoli and string beans. I moved south and was corrupted by the English. Before that, I thought red peppers came in packets, dried into flakes like fish food. Even the local Chinese restaurant had been corrupted. If you called up for takeout, Mrs. Yang would say, 'Aye, Taiwan Hoose, do you want French fries with that?'"

"You moved to England when you went to college?"

"Um, no, I didn't go to college. I traveled round Europe; after that I got a job in Oxford, met Frank, and then I just became an academic wife."

"So where did the interest in food come from?"

"Necessity, I guess. Franc—I mean, Frank liked food that reminded him of home; he had to have rice at every meal, rice and beans, he even ate rice with potatoes. I guess beans are a vegetable in South America." I made a face. "Anyway, I guess I started to learn to make the sorts of things he liked."

"I'm confused—France? South America? I thought your husband was German. Are beans and rice a big German thing? My family's Dutch originally, did you know that—hideous stodgy food but no beans, I think?"

"Oh, no, Dutch, I didn't know," I stalled.

"Yes, Van der Port, when the family first arrived, but somehow it got corrupted and my grandfather Matty decided it was better, sounded more American. He built this house—that's why there are tulips on the iron work on the parlor window upstairs, and on the railings—did you notice?" I hadn't. But it made sense. As did the blue and white china and the Delft tiles in the fireplace. I asked him some questions about the painted wood paneling in his study, but he shrugged, not particularly interested in the house's history. He seemed more interested in winkling out mine.

"So Frank was a *Küche, Kirche, Kinder* kind of guy?"

"Of course not. I mean, there were no *Kinder*." I smiled weakly. My palms were sweating. I wiped them on my napkin. "And absolutely no *Kirche*, just a lot of *Küche*. He was very hard working, so I just took over all the domestic stuff. He was a Latin American expert." I took a deep breath; I was getting this all wrong. I needed to shut up, but Adam was still looking at me attentively.

I began to long for Francisco's indifference. "So, we spent time there because of his job, and the food sort of stuck. I'm not thinking straight—too much wine." I tapped the side of the glass with my fingernail: it rang out like a firehouse bell. Then I hurried on. "We had to do a lot of entertaining in Oxford—there were always people staying with us and I got sidetracked into being a sort of career wife, moving around with . . . Frank." I said the name somewhat overdeliberately, as though I were on a game show and had to be sure to get the right answer before the buzzer went off. "Then it got too late and he had this research fellowship at Harvard I didn't know where to start." I was losing it here. Time to stop drinking. My tongue didn't seem to have any connection to my brain.

"Actually, I worried about you, here all alone in the city over the summer." He made it sound like a confession. "It must have been very strange and lonely after all you've suffered."

"Noooo, it really was rather peaceful," I said brightly, as the waste disposal finished grinding its leftovers like a good child cleaning its plate. "Really. It was probably just what I needed. Some recovery time." He protested when I bent to pick up his plate and silverware and told me to sit back down and relax. "Just leave it, Edith; the washing up isn't going anywhere, and that bloody dishwasher sounds like Apollo 8 taking off. I'll never be able to hear you if you turn it on." He poured the last inch of pinot noir into my glass: a pink Venetian goblet that he had brought, together with the wine, from the elegant dining room next door.

The kitchen, though lavishly appointed with every glimmering example of German domestic engineering, was not stocked with any sort of luxury. Concealed behind the oak doors was enough stylishly uniform flatware to host a sit-down supper for twenty-four and three sizes of wafer-thin water glasses that threatened to shatter if you hit a high note singing over the washing up. But there was nothing frivolous or beautiful. Adam's ex-wife was obviously a woman who liked to keep everything in its proper place, for its proper function, including the hired help. My own tiny kitchenette in the basement had only two each of Kmart's finest soup bowls, side plates, dinner plates, and earthenware coffee cups, as if they were marching together into a Soviet minimalist ark. She hadn't anticipated that the maid would be doing much entertaining.

"You didn't find the house intimidating, here all by yourself?" Adam persisted, in a tone that hinted he was not unfamiliar with the feeling.

I took a sip of the wine to delay answering. It tasted like soft fruit, with the fragile velvet fur of overripe raspberries slipping down my throat. My half-pint mugs of the Bulgarian cabernet sauvignon that I bought at the liquor store, chilled to the point of merciful tastelessness, were never going to hit the spot after this.

"Well, I did think I might be a wee bit scared, so I slept with that big Victorian chest of drawers pushed against my bedroom door." I smiled, to show how ridiculous I knew this was, though the truth was that I had made one of the Polish handymen unscrew the shutters on my bedroom window, even though the security bars were no less intimidating, and then affix new bolts onto the inside every internal door downstairs in the basement, and I kept the back door locked shut even when it was a hundred degrees outside.

"I know how awful this house can feel when it's empty," Adam said, playing with the blue-striped cuffs of a shirt that I knew from my laundering had tiny pink tips on the underside.

He had very elegant hands, which I noticed as he fiddled with his cuff links: clean, square fingernails and long, clever fingers, thin and tense like the rest of him, a dull gold wedding ring still worn on his left hand.

"When Gay first moved out, I hated coming back in the evening. The house was like a morgue, especially with both kids gone. I told Gay that I would leave and she could stay—but she said she hated the place. I don't know why, quite." His eyes darted to the space beside the refrigerator where his children's heights, noted from the age of three, climbed the wall. He looked around the kitchen helplessly, as though the toaster might pop out an answer to his wife's discontentment. Poor man: I didn't know what Gay had found so oppressive about the Dutch mansion, but I was in no position to judge what made a woman pack her bags and disappear. Nevertheless Adam's pain was palpable. I could hardly bear to examine it. He was holding a mirror up to my face.

"You didn't find it too quiet?" he asked.

"Oh, you get used to it," I replied, as casually as if solitary confinement were a leisure activity you got on Club Med holidays as an alternative to scuba diving.

"Well, I'm back now, except for a few short business trips—the Frankfurt Book Fair, which is a bore; it's such a hectic week and by the end of it I feel punch drunk and don't know what the hell I've bought or sold. I'm also hoping that the children will be spending some time with me on weekends, so it will be a little busier from now on."

Gay still hadn't deigned to let the kids sleep over and I had yet to meet either of them—something that didn't trouble me much. The boy, Ned, had gone back to boarding school at the beginning of September, but I wasn't going to be spared the girl much longer.

"Lennie is finally coming over next weekend—you'll meet Gay too. I think she wants to check you out. She even asked about your references." He laughed awkwardly, and my stomach somersaulted. "I showed them to her; I hope you don't mind. Nervous mother and all that." I did mind, but I was in no position to say so. A cold feeling of unease ran through me at the idea of her scrutinizing my faked testimonials. Nervous mother? I hoped she wasn't nervous enough to check with the fabled Mrs. McBride.

"Do you want some dessert?" I asked. "I have tarte tatin—or there's Manchego from that cheese place in Soho." We were like two strangers out on a first date.

He shook his head. "Thank you, Edith, but I'll stick with the liquid sustenance." He raised his glass in a mock toast. "And anyway it's too hot to eat much." Even in mid-September it was still stuffy enough at nine o'clock in the evening for us to be sitting with the kitchen doors thrown open on to the wrought-iron staircase that led down to the yard and out into the inky evening beyond. A few voices tumbled in from people sitting outside on their balconies, and some children's voices screeched gleefully from somewhere high on the building on the left. We had the lights turned off so as not to attract moths, and at Adam's urging I had lit the candelabra that usually festooned the walnut table in the dining room. From the outside, we probably looked like just another happily married couple sitting in the dancing candlelight, but, inside, the awkwardness between us was almost a third presence at the table. I could have set it a place. After just a couple of weeks of a formal employer-employee relationship, it was still strange to be sitting sharing a meal with a stranger who paid my wages. Especially a stranger whom I looked forward to seeing and who had just admitted he had been worrying about me.

"It must have been great for your kids growing up here with all this space and the park nearby," I said, as another skirl of secondhand excitement whipped through the night followed by an adult's laughter.

"I guess," he said doubtfully. "To tell the truth, I was never here. We had nannies and Magdalena took care of the house; Gay dealt with all of that."

"I would have loved it. When I was a kid in Scotland, we lived outside in the summer months—you didn't come home until you heard your mother calling for you. We used to pee in the bushes, because if you went home to use the bathroom and your mother noticed the time, she might keep you in; otherwise you could get away with playing outside until ten o'clock." I got a little carried away with my reminiscences. "One summer, my friend Kirsty and I decided to camp out in the back garden and . . ."

"And?" Adam had a happy, go-on-and-entertain-me smile on his face, but my voice dried up. Where had that come from?

"Oh, nothing, really." I shook my head.

"Do you still see her?"

"Who?" I asked, though I knew perfectly well who he meant.

"Kirsty, your friend. Is she still in Scotland? If you ever want to have a guest, you only have to ask. You must consider the house yours whenever I'm away."

"Oh, no. Kirsty . . ." I began, but I didn't know what to say. "I haven't seen her since we were teenagers. We don't keep in touch."

"A shame," said Adam. "But if you want to ask any of your other friends?"

"There isn't anyone."

"Surely there's somebody. You must have been bored out of your skull being cooped up with the humidity and pollution of Manhattan for August. It's unbearable. It can't have been much fun," he insisted.

"Adam, you forget that I lived most of my adult life in Oxford," I reminded him, keeping up the fiction I had invented for myself. "If you want rain, tourists, and boredom, try spending August in England."

"What did you usually do for the holidays? Didn't you say you and your husband traveled? Didn't you want to take a few days off yourself and go somewhere this summer?" he asked, no doubt overlooking the fact that people who worked as hired help probably weren't in the habit of weekending with the jet set on the French Riviera and that, in any case, the recently bereaved and penniless wouldn't have vacations at the top of their list of priorities.

"In the early days we used to spend a lot of our summers in Rhode Island, with my husband's family." This much was true—but I was hoping, nevertheless, that the words *we* and *used to* would be enough to kill the rest of the conversation as dead as the husband. But no.

"But I thought they lived in Fargo?"

"Yes, but they had a summer place, on the beach in a little town outside Newport."

"Newport—I know Newport very well, I used to sail there when I was a kid. We have an author who lives there and I often visit him. Do you sail?"

"No. No sailing. I took a few lessons, but I discovered, several miles into the Atlantic, that I'm scared of water." I laughed. "And Franc—I mean, Frank's family, well, they didn't socialize much, and they definitely didn't sail." I hurried on before he could start to ask for details. I had probably met the author he had visited. Newport society was worryingly incestuous. "We also went to Colombia several times—for Frank's research. Once to Guatemala, Peru, Argentina, Brazil, Central America, a *lot.*" This was also—more or less, give or take the odd cousin—quite true. I had allowed the fictional husband the same area of expertise as Francisco, as my powers of invention could go only so far—I couldn't conjure up a whole new specialist subject—and threw in a few vague words such as *aid* and *development*, masquerading as details, and hoped Adam knew as little about it as I did. We all know the cardinal rule of a successful lie is to stick as close to the truth as possible, and not to elaborate.

"Um, Colombia must be nice," he ventured doubtfully.

So I elaborated: "Oh, yes. What with drug cartels, the kidnapping, the crime, the mosquitoes bigger than cats—you know—it's not exactly Tuscany, Adam." He looked shocked, and I jumped in to correct myself. "Actually, it's not nearly anything as bad as people say it is. As long as you stay in the big cities, life goes on pretty much as it does anywhere else. Very pleasantly." I stopped myself from blabbing about the armed bodyguards that any trip to the country necessitated, and the fortresslike security surrounding granny in her isolated bubble of privilege and old money.

He laughed—for a long time, even as he walked into the dining room and came back with another, already open bottle of pinot noir.

The fortunate thing about Adam was that he was usually so afraid of prying into the circumstances of my widowhood that even the most oblique mention of it had him backing off like a vampire confronted with a crucifix. He was not alone in that. Most people shied away from the shroud of misery that was wrapped around me like a dress that summer, prêt-à-porter from the Bereaved Collection by Edith Lutz. I wore it well.

But tonight the alcohol had put Adam in touch with his warm and fuzzy side. He was intent on empathy. "You must miss your husband, Frank." He touched the name as though it were a poisonous spider, nudging it tentatively with a long stick. "It must have been unbearable for you." I didn't respond, but he stuck at the subject, nervously but doggedly. "I can only imagine how terrible it is to lose someone you love."

"Yes."

"Do you mind talking about him?" After a pause, I shook my head no, but I waited until he had refilled my glass from the new bottle and took a long gulp before answering. "Of course I miss him. But I talk to him all the time in my head, which is silly, really, because it's not as though he ever really listened to me when he was alive. But you know, it's that audience you have to your life: the one other person who applauds your victories and overlooks your mistakes. Then, suddenly—poof—it's gone. You're alone." I had another swallow of wine before continuing. "And it doesn't get any better; it just persists, like a pain that only occasionally responds to morphine. He was my only family, my history. Being without him is like walking around without any skin, except that every morning I wake up and have it stripped off me afresh. Just before I open my eyes, I sometimes forget where I am. I think, for that moment just before I swim up into consciousness, that I'm still living my old life, and that he's going to be lying there on the other side of the bed; that I can reach my hand across the sheets and feel his chest or the curl of his hair between my fingers. And then I remember he's gone—and lose him all over again." I swirled the purple liquid around the pink-tinged glass and took another long drink. Jesus fucking Christ. I closed my eyes and took a deep breath. First Kirsty and now Francisco. Let's do babies, and he can hit the jackpot. If I kept on talking, the tears that were filling my eyes would start cascading down my cheeks in torrents. And with half a bottle of wine inside me, once I started I could flood the basement.

He saw I was fighting for composure, and his green eyes clouded with concern. He pulled his long fingers through his rumpled hair. "I'm an insensitive oaf. I should shut up. I didn't mean to upset you, Edith; I'm so sorry." His thin fingers reached across the table and held mine in a surprisingly firm grip. I drew in my breath with a sudden gasp. It seemed like years since someone had touched me, and centuries since I had welcomed that touch.

I closed my other hand over his.

"It's fine. I'm fine." How many times had I said that this evening? I was like one of those dolls that repeated stock phrases every time you pulled a string in her neck. "Too, *too* much to drink," I said. I pulled my hands away and pushed the chair out, ready to start clearing up. I told him that it was getting late, that I should put things away because I had lots of chores to do and had to get up early. We both knew I was making excuses. The place shone like the show house on an OCD timeshare.

"Oh, leave the bloody housework, Edith, please sit down. I'm a stupid, crass, stumbling fool. I shouldn't have said anything. It's just that I see you sitting there in the candlelight and you look so"—his voice dropped an octave—"sad." He paused. "And, well, it seems so wrong that I've got you slaving away in my kitchen, keeping an old fool company when you should have a happy life with someone you care about. This shouldn't have happened to you." Now I felt like a worm. My self-pity evaporated into salty, crusty puddles of self-loathing. "Please, Adam, leave it. It's not like that. It's really not what you think. No one knows what goes on inside another's marriage. Relationships are complicated. Ours certainly wasn't perfect. Far from it. I don't think Frank was always very happy with me, but, you know, when you look back, there's always a tendency to remember the good times, not the bad. Maybe it's self-preservation."

"Tell me about it." He sighed. He stood and leaned across the table and put both hands on my shoulders, guiding me gently back toward the chair. "Here, have another drink. Please. Look, I know you must be lonely, because I'm lonely myself. I've spent three weeks in a shingle cottage on an island hidden among the dunes on the most beautiful beach, surrounded by pine groves, with two uninterested kids who barely took their eyes away from MTV, entertaining so-called friends to whom I had nothing to say, buying meals at overpriced restaurants for authors to whom I already pay a great deal of money, telling them how wonderful they are when they are mostly sociopaths with massive egos, wishing I could just sit quietly, like this, with someone who made me feel comfortable. So don't let me chase you away with my loutish prying. I hate drinking alone about as much as I hate eating alone. It makes me feel like the sort of sad old fart whose wife has tired of him and left him rattling round in a too-large house with no one to talk to . . ." He grinned weakly, and I felt yet another twinge of guilt strong enough to make my throat burn.

He looked so defeated, so solemn and vulnerable, slumped in the kitchen chair, rubbing the edge of his fist against the grain of the wood as though he could polish up his sorrow and make it more palatable. I couldn't help myself. I stood up, seeing a fleeting glimmer of anxiety in his eyes as I walked around the table toward him. Maybe he thought I was going to slap him, but nothing could have been further from my mind. I wanted to gather him up and do to him what I longed for someone to do to me. I curled my hands over his balled-up fists, bent over and kissed him on the forehead. His unruly hair snaked across my face and stuck to my lips. I smoothed it back over his temples, but it sprang through my fingers.

He was the first person I had touched for months. His skin felt cool, like the underside of a pillow on a hot night.

"Mad hair. It was the first thing I noticed about you." He pushed his chair back, the sound a scream of alarm in the otherwise silent house, drew me down into his arms until I was crouching on the floor between his knees, and kissed my mouth.

"You probably didn't want me to do that," he said. In answer, I tilted my head up toward him and kissed him back. He pressed his thumb against the corner of my lips. "You have a smile," he said. "From the wine." His fingers traced the curl of the wine across my cheek and slipped into my mouth—and maybe two, or twenty, minutes later, with my loose cotton embroidered shirt unbuttoned, hanging from my bare shoulders, I stopped to wonder, briefly, if the kiss had been one of my better ideas.

My body said yes.

My head said get the fuck out of there and push that chest of drawers in front of your body so it doesn't swing open for the first intruder who walks past.

"Adam, this is a bad idea. We don't really know each other. You have no idea what you're getting yourself into," I murmured, as he began to peel off the rest of my clothes. But he wasn't listening, and, in truth, I didn't say it very loudly.

For once I really didn't want to be heard.

6

EVEN BEFORE I slept with Adam, I had already fallen in love with his bedroom. When he first showed me around, I had managed only the briefest glimpse of a thick palette-knife nude with nipples the size of small planets swirling in a constellation of flesh on a canvas above the bed. Adam seemed to be embarrassed by the painting and closed the door almost as soon as he had opened it, then led me up past the empty guest bedroom to the mournfully abandoned children's rooms on the fourth floor. But after he left for work and I was alone in the house, I went back to explore.

The room was large enough to contain the whole floor plan of the house I used to live in. As elsewhere in the house, there were slim, shuttered casement windows, floor to ceiling, overlooking the street, and a pair of dressing rooms opposite, side by side, like two sentry boxes, each leading into its own separate bathroom. Unlike the rest of the overstuffed house, it was sparse and modern with several impressions in the deep cream carpet where large objects had once stood and left behind their indelible footprints.

As the Poles worked their way methodically around the house, obliterating golden yellow from the parlor and unblueing the dining room, I waited expectantly for the bedroom's transformation. It was such a peaceful, anonymous place, like the best suite in a well-appointed lunatic asylum.

Maybe that's why it so appealed to me.

The nude was bubble-wrapped and relegated to the wine cellar, and the grimy ghosts of other, departed paintings were covered with the same brittle shade of arctic white as the rest of the house. Now the surfaces gleamed like mother of pearl—or polished snow. You would swear they would melt if you turned up the heater.

The whole house resembled a Breugel winter scene without the tiny people. It reminded me of the Scotland of my childhood, when I still liked snowy days and would wake in the morning after a big silent storm to find everything fresh and clean, with a blindingly white covering of snow—and before winter became an oppressive test of endurance.

Gay's bathroom, however, was more or less as she had left it, with assorted toiletries arranged around the marble sink and stored inside her medicine cabinet with the precision of a department-store stock cupboard. These were, presumably, the products she had no use for in her new *Architectural Digest* loft in wherever the hell it was she lived. Inquisitively, I sifted through her shelves, smelling the towers of expensive French and Italian soap still in their pristine wrappers. From the boxes of unopened cosmetics in shiny black Chanel packaging, I broke the cellophane and saw she wore sheer pink lipstick and pale, fragile porcelain face powder—and contact lenses, judging by the numerous products for cleaning them.

There was also a row of perfume bottles arranged by height, each almost full: Guerlain, Chanel, and Dior—heavy floral, middle-aged French scents that would make my throat itch and my eyes water. I can wear only one or two fragrances without turning into a walking asthma attack, which is a nuisance, as I used to have a similar row of perfume bottles in my own bathroom back on Beech Street, whose names more or less spelled out the emotional trajectory of my sex life. Young men, I had discovered from experience, could not resist the cliché of perfume as the furtive gift of choice. Over the years I had been given the whole Calvin Klein range from Obsession to Eternity, each of these from a student who had a crush on me that lasted about as long as the flu, and on our wedding day Francisco gave me a huge flagon of Joy, which was probably the closest I really ever came to experiencing it. As far as I know, there isn't a scent called Contentment or Security, but if there had been, it would have been more apt.

Ironically, the most recent addition to the snaking conga line on my bathroom shelf was a bottle of Escape that had been slipped shyly into my handbag by a vertically challenged Lebanese doctor after I had finished typing up his research paper. A year on, and Escape was still confined to its box when I packed my belongings.

I threw it into a garbage bag, where it chattered fretfully to the rest of the bottles. It wasn't part of my exit plan, but I still didn't want to leave any trace of my previous selves behind.

Gay had had no such compunction. There was an ivory silk-trimmed flannel nightgown hanging in the dressing room and some lightweight cashmere sweaters wrapped in tissue paper in one of the drawers.

Several pairs of dated but unworn shoes and sandals listed

forlornly on the cedar racks, artfully constructed especially for the purpose. What did she do with all this footwear? I wondered.

Alone of all the women I knew, I had no affinity with high heels and girly shoes. I had outgrown dressing up long ago. I hated shoes I couldn't walk in; I liked shoes built for speed. But Gay didn't share my Presbyterian foot fetish. Some of her underwear remained folded into neat triangles in a line in one drawer, and some bras in another. I opened them and inspected the size: 34D. I felt inadequate.

It was as if she were the one who had died, and Adam the bereaved husband, leaving her untouched belongings as some sort of shrine to her memory. It was only a pair of silver hairbrushes short of being sinister. Every time I walked through the dressing room to her bathroom beyond I felt like the second Mrs. de Winter, pressing my nose against the glass of Rebecca's impeccably preserved territory, dreaming of bathing in her tub and wrapping myself in her monogrammed towels.

Of course, *Rebecca* was the wrong comparison. I had been expected to play the Mrs. Danvers character, with my hoop of keys and all-area access pass, not that of the new bride. It had been up to me to change and smooth Adam's virgin white sheets, to knead the dumplings of his goose-feather pillows into fluffy perfection every morning, and to shake out the cumulus clouds of his duvet. I had picked up his book, facedown, from the carpet beside his bed and, after adding a bookmark, replaced it, but until now I hadn't as much as brushed against him as I passed him at the breakfast table.

And now I was waking up with his lips on my shoulder and his long tapering fingers lying possessively across my stomach.

Dear God. What have you done, you silly cow? I thought. So

what if he was upset? So what if you felt sorry for him? Wouldn't a sympathetic pat on the back have been enough?

I felt Adam breathe softly against my skin. He smelled of wine and lemons and sex. I tried to extricate myself gently, slithering out from underneath his arms. The clock beside him seemed to say two thirty, or at the very least, half past something unreasonably early in the morning. I needed to pee. I needed to go back to my own room.

I crept out of bed, trying to gather up my clothes, which, illuminated by the streetlights flooding in through the open shutters, lay in a trail scattered across the silvery carpet and out into the gloomy cavern of the hall. My shoes were agape, surprised, by the door, my plain schoolgirl bra dropped on the threshold inside the puddle of my skirt. The rest of my underwear I would no doubt find when I made the bed the next morning.

As I tiptoed, almost crawling, across the white rectangles on the carpet, disentangling my garments from Adam's, I wondered anxiously how awkward it would be serving him coffee in the morning when his mouth, surprisingly soft and yet strong, had spent most of the past three hours between my legs.

I had almost reached the door, painfully aware of the whiteness of my backside picking up the glow from the streetlights behind me, when I felt his skinny but muscled forearm snake around my waist.

"Edie, where are you going? Don't leave. Come back to bed," he whispered sleepily into my neck. "Shall I get you something—water, tea, wine?"

"Don't you think it would be better if I went downstairs to my own room?" I answered, with as much dignity as it was possible to muster while floodlit and stark naked before my etiolated shadow, a bra and a crumpled skirt hooked over my arm.

Even my nipples looked embarrassed and hangdog.

In answer, he gently took the clothes from me, dropped them back onto the floor, and tugged me inside the white blur of his sheets.

"It would be wonderful to wake up with you," he murmured. "As long as that doesn't make you feel uncomfortable. I know it might be hard for you after what you said earlier."

"It would be lovely not to wake up alone, Adam, but to wake up," I reminded him as his hands slid across my body, "you first have to get to sleep. You have things to do tomorrow, as do I."

"Take the day off," he whispered. "As your employer, I insist. Hell, as my employer, I insist I take the day off with you." I was surprised by his ardency. To be honest, although my lovers have been many and varied, on the whole they had been consistently inept. College boys of the kind I was once attracted to were inexperienced and shy, but since on the whole it wasn't their sexual skill I was really interested in, it didn't matter. I liked the attention—and the penis, swaying slightly under its own weight because of a desire, totally, for me. Oh, yes, I knew that this was a delusion; it wasn't really me. The penis is its own master and shows the same appreciation for a pair of twin blow-up balloons flickering on a computer screen as it does for any available orifice, but when you are in the room with it, ask not for whom the bell tolls, it tolls for you.

I wasn't looking for love or tenderness. Sex for me was often just an exercise in self-loathing carried out by proxy. I wanted the fucking, the purely mindless fucking and the chance to check out of my body and float to the rhythm of their thrusts while they filled me up inside. But staying power wasn't every student's strong point, and they usually came quicker than wasps to a picnic, and then wouldn't go away again until you swatted them.

Adam, however—though nervous, or perhaps because of the nerves—had amazing stamina, and the potential for recovery of a man half his age. He acted as though he had been put on earth for the single purpose of devoting himself slavishly to my body.

I was, frankly, astounded. Francisco had always been a utilitarian lover. He ticked all the boxes, in the same order every time, patted my back, kissed my cheek, and fell asleep facing in whichever direction I wasn't. I used to see him slap the flank of his horse on the farm with the same offhand affection he showed when he rubbed my shoulder blades. I was only surprised he didn't toss me a sugar lump. He wasn't much for the touchy-feely, unless it was ritualized foreplay. His after-game consisted mostly of handing me a towel to blot my body.

But Adam lost all his emotional reserve in bed. He kissed and stroked and petted me like an expensive, long-haired lapdog, and in return I almost begged like one. He kissed the back of my neck while I was sleeping, and, when he was inside me, I opened my eyes to find him just looking at me, as though I had been specially ordered from a celestial mail-order catalog and arrived before I was expected, looking even nicer than I had in the picture. I felt like Cinderella—risen from rags and transformed into a sex goddess.

I liked looking at him, too. The irises of his eyes swelled with the rest of him when he watched me, and whereas Francisco, who made love with his eyes closed, had been small and compact, Adam was long and lithe. He had only a scattering of dark hairs on his chest and was otherwise smooth and sinewy. His chest and upper arms were broad and knotted from tennis, his penis thick and heavy in my hands. When I bent over to kiss him, we banged noses.

"I have such a big nose," he whispered, running his finger ruefully down the length of his profile.

I laughed, before drawing my tongue down to its tip. "It's absolutely perfect, Adam. You have no sense of spatial awareness," I told him. "And that's supposed to be a woman's failing." He pulled me toward him and kissed me, then I laid my head against his chest, drinking in the scent of skin, closed my eyes, and fell into a thick, padded sleep—the first I had enjoyed in months.

7

THE CAR SERVICE dropped Gay and Lennie off at around seven the following Friday evening.

I was hiding downstairs in my bedroom, almost the first time in days that I had been in the room for longer than it took to change my clothes.

The previous week Adam had begun to dally in the morning, eating the breakfast he had resisted for so long, never leaving for the office before ten thirty, claiming an early meeting but really having three cups of coffee with me. He arrived home by six every evening, once with flowers that he left, wordlessly, on the kitchen table—whether they were a gift or a housekeeping chore, to be arranged and displayed, was never quite spelled out. Dinner took on less and less significance, and each night, before the food had time to cool on the plate, I abandoned the table and let Adam lead me back upstairs to his bedroom.

I counted the seconds until he took my hand.

I was sleeping better, but because my demons now had less

time to drive me, they began to hunt me throughout the day, hunching behind doors, ready to spring out the minute I found myself alone. With no night shift, I had less time for the housework and sped through the rooms in a flurry of activity, but this only made the guilt all the hungrier to consume me whenever the chance presented itself. I stopped looking in the mirror. I didn't like the bright gold-leaf flecks in my eyes. I didn't like the way my skin, tanned after months of forced marches through the scorched Manhattan streets, suddenly glowed as though the sun were rising within. I was dizzy with lust.

So Lennie's imminent arrival for the weekend, in some ways, was a relief. I would sleep in my own bed and get back to the kitchen sink where I belonged.

I heard the front door slam shut. Gay obviously still had her keys. Heels tapped across the marble floor overhead, followed by some indeterminate scuffing and dragging. The word *Adam*, pronounced with an imperious upswing, sliced the silence. He was upstairs in his study, but he had also been listening for her, and within seconds, amid a muddle of voices, I heard the muffled sound of numerous footsteps on the stairs.

My stomach tied itself into elaborate macramé knots of tension. I could have fashioned pot holders out of it. Should I go upstairs and offer tea? Or maybe I should open a bottle of wine? Adam had not given me any pointers, and it seemed presumptuous to put myself in the role of hostess, proffering drinks in what had been, in fact still was, the woman's own house.

I tried to make myself look calm and distracted. I grabbed one of the paperback proof copies that Adam had given me to read, stuck my glasses on the end of my nose, and curled up on the cord sofa in the old playroom. I put the fan on to drown out any threads of secondhand conversation and fixed my eyes on the print until it danced around the page like ants, and read not a word. There was a clatter on the basement stairs. Adam poked his head round the door.

"Edith, would you mind coming up and meeting Gay?" I hurriedly folded my glasses inside the book and jammed it down the side of the sofa. Then I smoothed down my hair, realizing too late that I probably looked as though I had driven twenty blocks in an open convertible, and switched off the fan. My hands were shaking, but Adam was standing in the middle of the room, looking at the scabby walls and the stained carpet that no amount of shampoo had shifted.

"Good grief, has it been like this since you arrived?" he asked, then shook himself, muttering under his breath. "How stupid, of course it has. I haven't been in here for years. Doesn't the AC work?" I shook my head no. He winced. "What a dump."

I couldn't agree more, but nevertheless I felt slightly defensive about the shortcomings of my personal space, though at the same time relieved that he had not seen my bedroom. He thought this room was bad—at least it had natural light. The bedroom was the sort of place where you locked up your mad aunt and pushed dog food under the door.

The comparison made me cold with dread.

"It's not so bad," I began, but he cut me off with an expression that I had not seen before, somewhere between anger and disgust.

I wondered how much of it was directed toward me. Instinctively I crossed my arms protectively across my breasts and stuffed my hands under my armpits like a street urchin trying to keep warm. This was not looking good. I followed him upstairs to the first floor.

Gay was sprawled elegantly on one of the cream sofas in the parlor, her arms spread across the back of the cushions, which I noticed she had rearranged, her oversized bust pushed upward, as though she were sitting in a showroom modeling yachts. Apart from the water wings, she was pin-thin but with an underfed, too-many-cigarettes, too-much-coffee pallor. No trace of the chubby country-club girl of her early studio portrait remained—unless you counted the jawbreaker pearls round her throat. She was even slimmer than I was, but with an unhealthy pinch to her cheeks and a scrawniness to her neck.

She looked as if she hadn't had a good meal in her life. But those amazingly prominent breasts. They seemed too cushioned to be fake. I could see the faint outline of peach lace through her shirt.

I immediately felt defensive. He must be a big-tit man. What did he see in me? Convenience, I suspected.

Her hair was a mix of champagne blond and white that I thought probably owed more to the hairdresser than to nature and was cut in a short, ruler-straight, Mary Quant–style page boy that fell a millimeter under her ears. She blinked a lot, I noticed, as she gave me the once-over, as though she couldn't quite believe her eyes and was trying to clear her vision. After rooting through her bathroom cabinet, I thought she would wear contact lenses, but today she had on very serious half-frame spectacles. She looked like a late-model Andy Warhol in drag, if Andy Warhol's mother had been Garbo and had worn good lingerie.

She didn't get up. I pried my right hand from its clenched position, hoping that it wasn't covered in sweat, and shook the limp tips of her little manicured fingers. She looked at me over her headmistress glasses, blinked, and said nothing. I wished I had kept on my own specs, just to provide some competition. I felt as though she were going to give me detention.

"Edith—Gay, Gay—Edith," snapped Adam. A slight narrowing in the other woman's eyes told me that she had been expecting to be introduced formally, with her surname, and probably some forelock tugging. Years of inherited pique rose in my throat.

Adam scowled at her. "I can't imagine how you let this house get into such a state. That apartment of Edith's downstairs is a disgrace—it's a hovel. You can't expect anyone to live in it." Apparently Gay wasn't the only one who was mightily pissed off.

"Excuse me, Adam, but *I* don't expect anyone to live in it. The state of *your* house is entirely *your* affair. You can organize your own life—that's why it's called Do It Yourself. Anyway," said Gay, her eyes studiously avoiding me, "isn't that what you have the housekeeper for—to keep house? Shouldn't she clean it?" Bitch. I was very near slapping her ugly specs right off her nose.

"*She* does clean it, Mrs. Davenport," I replied with ice in my voice.

She blinked again, several times.

I blinked back, hard, for emphasis.

Gay looked flustered, and for a second I could see that she was as disconcerted as I was and merely trying to bully her way out of an awkward situation.

"The house does look well taken care of," she allowed tersely, her lips barely moving. "You've obviously been doing a good job. Adam let it go to hell after I left." Adam poured himself half a glassful of whiskey and threw himself into an armchair.

"Well, to be fair, Gay, you did take Magdalena with you and only left me with her 401(k)." I hovered uncomfortably, Gay and

I both quivering like a pair of scorpions facing up for a fight. "What are you standing up for, Edith? Sit down, for God's sake. You're not on trial." I sat on the opposite armchair as Gay compulsively smoothed down the legs of her trouser suit, and then opened her Gucci handbag with a loud snap. She took out a small Cartier diary from inside the leather cover and extracted a business card.

She handed it to me. Her perfect pink fingernails gleamed like opals. I took the card and tucked my rough, unkempt hands back under my arms, suddenly remembering another reason why I had absolutely no women friends. They were too bloody hard to live up to.

"This has all my numbers on it. Anything, and I mean anything, that Lennie needs, check with me, whatever time it is, day or night." Her eyes blinked on every other word. She bit her lip, and I could see the signs of strain on her face. "This has all been a bit difficult for her . . ."

"Don't worry, Gay. Edie will take care of her as though she were her own child," said Adam.

"Do you have children?" she asked, almost hopefully.

"No," I said, and looked away. I couldn't meet her eyes. I just couldn't take any more of that blinking.

"I know, I'm being a bit overanxious, but she's asthmatic and you have to be careful that she doesn't exert herself too much in this heat, or that her allergies don't get worse. This is her pediatrician, this is the number for her allergist, and this is her medication; I've made a list of it. Make sure you read it." She handed me a small toiletries bag together with a folded sheet of paper. "You can speak English, can't you?"

"I can just about manage it," I replied stiffly.

"You do have a very strong accent, I thought Russian . . ."

she said, as though I might not have noticed it had she not taken the time to point it out.

"I'm Scottish, originally."

"Quite," she said.

I looked at Adam. He rolled his eyes, then winked. I couldn't stop myself from laughing, but Gay went on as though I had opened my mouth merely to let my teeth air. "She's allergic to dairy and feathers, and wheat bloats her; try to keep her away from leaf mold, and she shouldn't have sugar because she's becoming far too porky." Great—leaf freaking mold when we live two blocks from Central Park—how was I going to manage to keep her away from that? By filtering the air? I also thought it was a bit harsh of her to refer to her daughter as porky, but just then the door opened and Porky herself stood before me.

Actually, Gay had a point.

She was a plump sunflower blonde with the sort of pink skin that looked as though it had been scrubbed with a nail brush.

She was also rather spotty around the chin, which didn't help, nor did the purple train tracks adhering to both upper and lower teeth. She had on a scruffy plaid sweater, a rumpled blue skirt which I hoped was her school uniform, and an expression of abject misery, both of which looked as though they had been worn for a very long time.

"Hi, you must be Edith," she said, brightening when she saw her mother and father were not alone. Her face lit up as she gave me a handshake and a full five thousand dollars' worth of purple-plastic-and-metal smile. "I like what you did to my room." She walked across and perched one cheek of her bottom on the armchair occupied by Adam, but she addressed her mother. "Mom, the walls have been painted and I have a new bed with one of those really cute satin quilts we saw in Bloomingdale's, and there's a huge desk. It's so grown up and sophisticated, like a whole new room." She kissed her father's head and toppled onto his lap like a sack of tennis balls. A heavy sack of tennis balls.

"Thanks," she said again to me, as though I had paid for the bed myself instead of just ordering it from Crate and Barrel when Adam told me to furnish both kids' bedrooms.

"And I *love* your hair," she said.

She had to be kidding. I had cut it with the poultry scissors halfway through August and instead of straggling down my back it now tangled around my shoulders, twenty-six different shades of chlorine-bleached blond with jade-green highlights, and ends like an untrimmed hedge. But no.

"It'th really cool," she enthused, lisping slightly through the metal. Getting her tongue round Edith Lutz was going to be something of a problem for her.

Getting my head round Lennie Davenport was going to be an even bigger problem for me. Yes, she was overweight and had pimples and braces, but the girl was heart-stoppingly beautiful.

She had Adam's direct green eyes but with the addition of startling little orange flecks and full Cupid's-bow lips.

She looked like a blond pedigreed cat.

She sucked the ends of her buttery-yellow hair and all the doors in the rickety house of lies I had built for myself swung wide open. The ghosts of my past walked out of the shadows, drew out the chairs, sat down, and drummed their fingers on their rattling skeleton legs, waiting for an audience. I would have to get to them one by one. But absolutely the last one I wanted to deal with was the teenage girl.

Some women would probably turn into June Cleaver at this

point, rapidly taking the tubby teenager under their wing and into their squishy big hearts. But that wasn't going to happen here. She wrapped her soft arms around her father's neck and kissed his cheek, laughingly complaining about the scratchiness of his face.

And I loathed her on sight.

8

I AM FOURTEEN.

Kirsty was fifteen last week. She got her own television in her room and a gold locket. This Saturday she is going to her first dance in the Weaver's Hall. I beg to go with her, but I am too young, my mother tells me brusquely, as though I had asked for something obscene, like red stilettos and a bondage mask instead of fifty pence for the entrance fee.

"I am not too young," I protest, but she won't even entertain the idea.

"You are not going, and that's that." There is no point in persevering—my mother is like quick-drying cement when she makes a decision—but her refusal is not going to cause me much of a problem. Kirsty and I simply initiate the first in a long string of successful scams—I say I am staying at her house and go to the dance anyway. By this point, Kirsty's mother not only never leaves the house but rarely ventures out of her bedroom. She stays in bed most of the day in a pink satin dressing gown and reads with the blinds down.

"It's her nerves," says Kirsty.

"She's a lazy trollop," says my mother. Either way, she is never going to tell on us because no one ever sees her. Kirsty's dad isn't much better. He only speaks to you if you have a corpse that needs to be buried, and even then you have to snuff it before the nine o'clock news. Any later and he's well into his whiskey.

As we grow older, the scam becomes more complex: we each claim we are staying with the other and spend the night with whichever school friend has the most lenient or neglectful parents.

We are confident that we will never be found out, and until the policeman arrives on my parents' doorstep in the middle of the night a little over a year later, we never are. And by that time it doesn't really matter, because Kirsty isn't speaking to me anymore and there's nowhere else I can go.

And so we're squeezing through the swinging saloon doors of the Weaver's Hall to a fanfare of strobe lights and Alice Cooper banging out of the speakers. Kirsty's eyes flash white in the stuttering darkness, mad with excitement. Her halter top is fluorescent. Her teeth gleam. She tucks her perfect honey-blond hair behind her perfect small ears with their perfect silver heart-shaped earrings and grabs my hand.

"Come on and dance," she urges, but I shake my head, suddenly shy. I want to go to the bathroom. I want to go home. I feel useless and awkward and gangly—like a lighthouse with a big yellow beacon on my head that flashes on and off telling everybody that I'm at my first disco and don't know what to do. But worse is yet to come.

Kirsty ignores my protests and drags me to the center of the crowded floor and there, to an enthusiastic chorus of "School's Out," I learn something new and totally unexpected about myself.

While Kirsty's breasts bounce like they're being tumble dried under her Tide-white halter top and draw the attention of every pair of male eyes in the room, I discover I can't fucking dance.

How come no? I ask myself in a flurry of panic and flailing arms as I try, in vain, to move my limbs in time to the beat of the record that is pulsing out across the dance floor. I stumble, I trip, I slap someone standing close to me, who doesn't even blink. His eyes are so intent on the orbs threatening to escape from Kirsty's shirt that I could probably have taken his wallet.

My legs feel as though the circulation is just returning to them after four years in a coma. They wobble and drag themselves across the floor five seconds after my brain gives them the instruction to move. I am shaking like someone with cerebral palsy.

I still can't understand why this is happening. Don't I know the song? Yes—I've danced to it in my bedroom at home. I've sung to it with the electric plug of the vacuum cleaner as my microphone.

I can feel the bass thudding in my chest like slow hiccups, but I just can't find it with my feet.

Kirsty is standing next to me, her hair swishing back in front of her face as if she is in some kind of manic shampoo commercial, her feet tapping in tall heels, her smooth arms waving to and fro, her breasts swaying. How is she doing it? I slow everything down until I am barely moving. I shake my shoulders and shuffle my feet from side to side. This is better. At least I am not hitting anybody, but you can hardly call it dancing. It's more like when you're dying to go to the toilet but there's a line.

Mercifully, the record plays out, and in the brief pause before the next song starts I edge through the sweating bodies to the fringes of the hall. Feigning fatigue, I plonk myself onto the row of folding chairs, linked together in an unruly conga line around the perimeter of the room like wee schoolgirls on a class outing, and contemplate the collapse of any hope I may have had of a normal adolescence.

What happened to my feet? Hadn't I spent years drilling my heels and toes into the rough planks of the floor of this very same hall? Didn't my Highland fling send the Johnnie Walker ashtrays into wide glass *o*s of astonishment? And hadn't my sword dance dazzled the disco ball—if not the judges—at the youth county finals in Selkirk last year, when I had failed to win a medal but had come home, nevertheless, with a HIGHLY COMMENDED ribbon?

I suddenly realize, as I listen to Sweet singing "Blockbuster," that the reason Miss Matheson had repeatedly clapped out the beat, calling one-two-three-four when I heel-toed it across the boards, was because otherwise I couldn't keep time to the music.

I had not, in fact, learned to dance; I had learned to count and to move in formation like a hen-toed shire horse doing dressage.

"Why are you sitting down there?" yelps Kirsty. "You can't be tired already," she moans, looking around the room to be sure she isn't missing anything. Fifty pairs of eyes stare back at her for exactly the same reason. She shoulders me out of the seat and yanks me back onto the dance floor.

"But, Kirsty, I can't dance," I hiss in her ear. "I look stupid."

"Just jiggle about. Nobody's even looking at you," she says, immediately beginning to rock from the waist, the male population of the room swaying with her as though they were watching Wimbledon.

She is right: absolutely nobody is looking at me. I am invisible.

At least she has a waist, I think to myself, watching her shimmy about, and good legs. Not only does her chest spray across the room like a volley of automatic gunfire whenever she turns around, but having seen her in a swimsuit, I know that her legs meet at strategic points all the way down from the top of her thighs to the bones of her ankles. This, my mother told me, is how you know you have a perfect figure. My hip bones stick out at angles. I have a washboard chest. I don't need my mother to outline my limitations. I am nothing compared to Kirsty. I mean, all that blond hair, never out of place but hanging straight down her back like a knife. While my hair is short and of an indeterminate color somewhere between boring and fucking boring, which no amount of shine-enhancing shampoo will enliven. And since my mother works in the local pharmacy, I have tried every brand.

Thankfully, the next song spins into silence with a final guitar chorus and a diminishing drum solo. "Move," says Kirsty, pushing me toward the stage, where a row of boys holding bottles of Coke sit hunched and draped over the edge, like vultures waiting for roadkill.

"Where are we going?" I whisper.

"Peter Nelson is sitting over there. Let's go and stand in front of him; maybe he'll ask me to dance." Kirsty knows that Peter, the doctor's son, has a monumental crush on her. If they start going out, it'll be a match made in Women's Guild heaven, where your daughter kisses only boys of her own social class. In our village there is a very small pool in which to dip. Because my dad is the bank manager, I get to be in it, but I'm down at the muddy end, owing to being skinny.

Then, apart from Kirsty, there's Peter, then Derek, the pharmacist's son, and Dan Ponte, whose parents have the café. I have already been warned off him because Kirsty likes him, and anyway he's what my mother calls "wild," which is just another way of saying Italian and Catholic and to be avoided. Fat chance. He'd never look at me. I am a head and a half taller than everyone my own age, but I am still hoping that some of the other boys will grow. I also hope I'll wake up one morning and find I have turned into Mia Farrow or that I'm in the Partridge Family and David Cassidy's my brother.

I follow Kirsty to the back of the hall, feeling ridiculous. I wish I had worn my new shoes, which have a stacked heel and a little crossover strap with a pearl, but Kirsty wouldn't let me. She said they made me too tall.

So she's wearing them, the toes padded with cotton wool so they fit her.

She drags me back onto the dance floor. I do what's expected.

I came, I saw, I danced to Glam Rock.

Older boys ask us to dance, but I can see them arguing about who gets Kirsty before they walk over and tap our shoulders. I am the spare. I wish I could slip through the jaggy cracks in the planks or maybe hide in the bathroom, where girls draw lines around their eyes and lips as though they needed to find their own edges before they could color themselves in.

The girls say "hiya" and tell her they like her shoes. Everybody always smiles at Kirsty; even Dan Ponte, who is gorgeous, no matter what my mother says, always hangs around Kirsty whenever he sees her on the street. He has tanned skin and dark curly hair. He looks like Donny Osmond.

Peter Nelson jumps off the stage and holds a long conversation with the front of her shirt. A slow song comes on and the two of them start dancing as I stand there like a pint of milk left to sour on the step. It's just like being back at school, practicing for the Christmas party, and everyone gets picked except me and I have to dance with the laddie from the dairy farm who always smells of cow. I look around and see Dan Ponte watching Kirsty and Peter with a bitter expression on his face, his jaw dropping like a bottle opener.

He glances over at me, looks me up and down, and then turns away. I make a show of rummaging through my handbag, but there's nothing in there except a purple lipstick and a safety pin. I slip away to the bathroom and hide in a stall. I hate this dance.

I wish I could go home, but I'm spending the night at Kirsty's and I can hardly go to her place without her. I feel like crying, but if I do, all my mascara and eyeliner will run down my face. I only put it on because Kirsty told me to. I look like a boiled egg with a face painted on it for Easter.

I stay in the stall even when someone starts banging on the door. I don't care. But eventually I have to come out and go to look for Kirsty. She is standing in a corner with Peter and a couple of other girls who are in her class at school. I wonder why she didn't go to the dance with them instead of me. She's really popular. I wave at her. She waves back but doesn't move. I wiggle my fingers and make for the door. I think I would rather wait outside her house than hang around here like a bad smell.

She runs after me.

"You can't go home now."

"I'm fed up."

"But I'm not ready—we just got here."

"I'll wait for you round the back—in your summerhouse," I

say, pretending a casualness that I don't feel. "You've got your other pals."

"Okay." She looks at her watch. "We have to be home by ten o'clock, but it's not even nine yet." I realize I have been hiding in the bathroom for nearly an hour.

"Peter is going to walk me home." She smiles conspiratorially.

I smile back, even though I think that the skin around my mouth is going to crack like the leather on her dad's car seats.

She dances away. I am dismissed.

Outside, it is nearly dark. It's been raining and it's cold. I shiver as I run quickly down the short road, past the war memorial, past the Running Dog Pub, and round the corner to Kirsty's house. I have to be careful just in case I see my dad out for a walk, but the street is deserted. I splash through the black clouds shining up at me from the puddled street, then, just when I get to the side passage near her house, I hear the swoosh of a bike on the wet asphalt. I turn and am surprised when I see that it's Dan Ponte, his bicycle cutting the street into twin fountains of water.

He's always running up and down our street on his bike, mostly looking for Kirsty, I think.

He pedals the bike round in a circle, spraying water everywhere.

"Agnes," he shouts, making a hissing sound on the *s*, as though he's trying to charm a snake or calling a cat. I didn't think he even knew my name. It's Kirsty that he always pays attention to.

He never speaks to me; even when I go into the café where he often works after school and buy cups of coffee, he looks right through me. He's a couple of years ahead of us—at the Catholic school—and he'll be leaving in the summer. He told Kirsty that when he turns eighteen, he's going to take over the café and run the store full-time.

"Shh," I say back. "I'm not supposed to be here until later on."

"Where's your pal?" he asks.

"She's still at the dance—with Peter," I add, mostly out of spite, really. Just to rub it in. "But I'm staying with her the night, so I have to wait here until she comes home."

"I saw you leaving the hall; I thought she'd be with you," he says, getting off the bike and standing awfully close to me.

"Nah." I shake my head. I'm nervous. I haven't spoken to any boy for this long, ever—not unless I am doing a science project with him or we are related or something.

"Do you want to come for a walk with me?" he asks.

I am stunned. "Who, me?" I ask. My mouth is open; raindrops fall into it. I forget to close it.

He nods, shrugs his shoulder, and scans the street. "I can leave my bike, and we can walk along by the railway bridge."

"No." I find myself shaking my head vigorously, though inside I'm digging my elbow deep into my ribs and saying, go, go, go, Agnes—for God's sake. It's Dan Ponte. "I said I'd wait for her round the back in the summerhouse, and I better watch that my dad doesn't see me. I live just over there." I point over at the square sandstone house on the other side of the road with the lime-green paint trim that my color-blind dad insists is maroon.

"Nice house," Dan says. "So, did your dad rob that bank he works in?"

"No, he did not," I say indignantly. But he's not really listening.

He lights a cigarette.

"I'll wait and keep you company, then," he says, and with

a final look over his shoulder he follows me up the side path, through the creaky back gate, and along the side of Kirsty's overgrown garden to the rotting gazebo at the far end of what would be her lawn if anyone ever cut the waist-high grass.

It's pitch black except for the light coming from her mother's bedroom window. I put my fingers to my lips and point. "Shh," I say.

"It's a mess around here," he says when we get to the end of the garden. There's smoke curling out of his mouth that makes him look like a dragon. "Where do they keep the stiffs?" I point to the yard on the left, where a long shiny hearse sits outside a building with small blacked-out windowpanes.

"It gives me the creeps," he says.

I agree. "But there's nobody there now," I tell him confidently. I wouldn't spend the night in the house if there were any dead bodies waiting to be embalmed.

"It's a funny thing to do for a job, burying dead people. I'd rather serve coffee to the living any day," says Dan, settling himself down next to me on the green mossy slats of the bench in the summerhouse.

"Your jacket is lovely," I gush inanely.

Dan is wearing a leather jacket and a pair of Levi's that fit his long legs like sticky-back plastic. He puts out his cigarette on the concrete and gives me another look like the one he ran over me at the dance. It makes me squirm.

"Do you smoke?" I shake my head.

"Drink?" Again, another no.

"You're a good wee girl, then."

"I'm not so wee," I reply.

He grabs my arm and pulls me closer to him, and I realize with a half-excited sort of dread that he's going to kiss me. I've been practicing, on the inside of my elbow, and on my pillow, and Kirsty showed me how you move your mouth, though to be honest she looked like a complete idiot, gaping away like a guppy looking for fish food. But Dan's mouth, when it lands on mine, is nothing like what I expect. He tastes sour and smoky, and before I can even think what to do, he's stuffing his tongue into my mouth. I nearly gag.

He cracks up laughing. "Did nobody ever kiss you before?" he says, snorting through his nose. The smell of stale cigarettes blasts across my face.

He kisses me again, and this time he puts his hand on top of my chest. I try to pull back, but he keeps hold of me. "You can open your mouth a bit," he says. "And maybe breathe or you'll be in one of those boxes over there in the hearse." Tears are jabbing at my eyes. I don't know what I should do.

First I can't dance and now I can't kiss either. And I don't think he should be squeezing me and touching me like this.

"You have to stop," I say, but not too loudly, as I'm scared that someone will hear me.

"I don't have to do anything I don't want to," he says. "You should be begging me for it. How old are you anyway—fifteen, sixteen?"

"I'm fourteen," I whisper.

"Jeez, I'm baby snatching." He pulls back like he's been burned, stands up, lights another cigarette, and starts to walk away. "I'll see you," he says without meeting my eye. "Tell Kirsty I said hiya." I hear the gate slam behind him. The bolt tinkles as it hits the catch, then the night blots up the noise and it all goes quiet.

Kirsty doesn't turn up till half past ten, and she has a soppy expression on her face and no lipstick. Her chin is red and scurvy-looking.

"Oh, Peter Nelson kissed me," she crows in a sing-song voice, shutting her bedroom door behind me after she's wheedled her mother into not caring that we are late. "He kissed me loads," she shrieks, throwing herself into a starfish on her frilly eiderdown and kicking off *my* shoes, which are all scuffed.

"Well, Dan Ponte kissed me, too," I shoot back, aiming right for her back.

"What?" she says, sitting up and looking at me with disbelief.

You'd think I told her there were Martians in her kitchen helping themselves to the Gypsy Creams.

"I'm telling you—he came down on his bike and sat with me in your summerhouse, where he kissed me. Twice. With tongues." I want to say that he even tried to get his hand into my bra. I might have let him if it hadn't been for the toilet paper already there, but I realize that this might make me into a slag, so I shut my mouth.

"Nonsense," she says.

"Is not. It happened." Kirsty's almond eyes, hard with navy-blue eye shadow, narrow into nasty little slits. "Oh, Agnes, you are so jealous. You're just making it up." I am so annoyed I could slap her fat face. "I am not making it up," I sob. "He sat with me round the back. You'll see his cigarette butt stamped out on the ground if you look." She is skeptical. "Yeah, right, tell me another one," she snorts. "Everybody knows that Dan Ponte likes me; he's not going to bother with a wee lassie like you." She struts along the hall and slams the bathroom door shut.

"He did, Kirsty." I am crying now. But she isn't listening. She's back out of the bathroom with her nightdress on and is getting into her bed, pointedly putting the light off. I have to get changed in the dark, and when I get in beside her, she slips right over to the other side of the bed. She ignores me, and then I hear soft snores coming from her pillow. I get up and wipe my nose on a bit of toilet paper, but it has lipstick on it that I don't see in the dark, so when I wake up I have a purple stripe on my face.

Next morning I am going back to my house. Kirsty is annoyed, but her mother has told her to walk me home. We are just crossing the road when I see Dan Ponte speeding along the sidewalk on his bike, and I wave at him. He ignores me.

"What did I tell you?" says Kirsty, her mouth twisted and her voice snide with satisfaction.

"Look, he did so kiss me," I insist.

"Hey, Dan," she shouts really loudly, right across the middle of the street for everybody to hear. "Agnes says you and her were snogging round the back of my house last night."

"Aye, that'll be right," Dan shouts back. My heart swoops up through the cloud and does a flip.

"See." I look at her for an apology, but Dan is still talking. "Who do you think you're kidding? What would I be doing sitting fiddling with a wee lassie? I'd need to be desperate. But I'll take you round there any time you're ready," he says, with a big smug grin.

"You're a liar, Dan Ponte," I gasp.

"Have you been telling stories, hen?" he tuts loudly.

"You know I haven't," I say, but he's already cycling off up the hill, his bum wiggling in the air, ugly laughter trailing after him, rancid, like the smell of tobacco.

"You're rotten with jealousy, that's what it is, Agnes," says Kirsty, flouncing back into her house and leaving me by myself on the sidewalk.

I tuck my nightdress under my arm and drag my feet as I walk along the street. Even on a Sunday there's nobody in when I open the back door. The house is cold and, as usual, the fire isn't lit.

9

LENNIE BEGAN TO come every other weekend, walking the few blocks down from Spence on Friday afternoon and leaving late Sunday night, when either a car service or her mother, usually without ever taking her expensively shod foot off the accelerator, collected her. Slowing to a crawl, she'd sound the horn, and Lennie would run out to the car. The whack of the front door slamming behind her was the high spot in my week.

While she was in the house, she stuck to me like Saran Wrap.

Whenever I turned around, she seemed to be behind me. I'd go up to the kitchen to start dinner and there she would be, leaning against one of the counters, peering into the refrigerator or sitting on the edge of one of the pine chairs pulled out from the table, waiting expectantly for me—as though I were going to start doing magic tricks or handstands across the floor. Mooching, my mother used to call it. It made me edgy and irritable. I couldn't shake her off.

What are you cooking? What are you making? What's that? Where does this go? What was your husband's name? What was it like in Oxford? Was it far from London? Did you ever go to Harrods? Have you met the queen? Do you know Princess Diana? She had an insatiable curiosity about my previous life and no compunction about indulging it. The questions went on and on—and, yes, I could manage the ones about the Royal Family since Charles and Diana's divorce had been splashed all over the papers that summer, and explain the finer points of bread making when I was up to my elbows in dough, but I started to struggle when she wanted me to give her a virtual tour of Carnaby Street. It was like being interrogated by the shopping Gestapo. I thought I was going to have to deal with Ned as well over the fall weekend, but, thankfully, Gay took both kids to visit her mother in Miami.

I thought having Lennie around couldn't get worse, but occasionally, such as when Adam went to Frankfurt and Gay was also out of town, I was left to entertain her alone.

Entertaining? It most certainly was not.

I hadn't planned on being used to facilitate Gay's social life, but with her brother banged up in boarding school—even though she drove me crazy—at least I had only Lennie to contend with. She rarely left the house unless I walked down to the market, when she invariably accompanied me. In the evenings I often found her lying on the sofa in the sitting room that was supposed to be mine, immediately reclaimed as hers, watching the television that had miraculously grown a working plug and acquired three hundred cable channels and a VCR. But whenever she heard my footsteps on the stairs, she would follow me, almost to my bedroom door, asking me if I wanted to watch a movie with her.

I didn't.

I tried to encourage her to call her friends from Spence and go hang out with them, but she claimed they were all "lame" and said she got enough of them at school. She had quarreled with her friend Leila, who lived in the apartment building on the corner and whose Irish doorman, Fred, I was, by now, on back-in-the-auld-country terms with. I had hopes of some respite when they finally made up, but Leila's mother worked most weekends, and, instead of getting parole, I found myself under virtual house arrest with two fifteen-year-old inmates, who lolled around the kitchen asking for sandwiches and then not eating them.

If this was motherhood, I hadn't missed much, I thought, as giggles and shrieks filled up the space in the house, and CDs, potato chip bags, magazines, open bottles of nail polish, soiled towels, and squished sachets of face cream bred indiscriminately in the downstairs sitting room, which also acquired new posters, a bead curtain, and a lava lamp. I didn't see any point in having the painters come back to redecorate it, as Adam had instructed, since I had effectively been banished to the three square yards of my bedroom. All it meant was more work, more upheaval, and less privacy.

I came to long for the time when my weekend activity consisted of watching the dust motes drift through the air.

In the midst of it, Adam retreated to his study with the cheerful resignation of a man who knows when he's beaten and eagerly hands you the cane so you can whack him some more. He loved Lennie's noisy presence, and when she wasn't pestering me with questions about Harrods, she was cupped in the tiny sofa opposite his desk, surrounded by displaced manuscripts and papers, chattering to him about her grades and her teachers—with whom, I'm afraid to say, I was also on first-name terms. I had met Ned briefly when he had come into the city to see a doctor after a sports injury and he had spent the afternoon at the house with me after Gay went back the office, but he was due to come for his first proper visit at the end of the week. I was dreading it. I didn't know how much more of this *Full House* sitcom I could take.

Adam came home from Frankfurt on Saturday night, red-eyed and exhausted, and then disappeared into his study after breakfast on Sunday morning with the correspondence that had piled up while he was away. Lennie, for once, was upstairs in her bedroom, doing homework. Her preferred location was the kitchen table, but I had tried to drive her out by colonizing it with sheets of pasta. I knew it would take me nearly an hour to crank out enough tagliatelle for the four of us—Leila was staying for supper—when I could have opened a box of the many already provided by Dean & Deluca in three seconds, but I thought that this was one way to get rid of her. I should have known better. The minute I dragged the pasta machine out of the cupboard, she sprang up like a weed from behind the refrigerator door, her eyes bright with curiosity. Before I had the dough mixed, she was aimlessly turning the handle, asking for instructions, and the chore that should have been accomplished in peaceful Zen-like silence took all morning and acquainted me with twenty-seven things I never wanted to know about Mariah Carey.

Did you know she was born in Huntington, Long Island?

I'm sure you are as thrilled as I was with that information.

The pasta should really have been moved to an airtight container, but having finally levered Lennie out of the room by leading her upstairs with a trail of brownies, I covered it with damp dishtowels and left it hanging over the back of every available chair. I decided I'd run the risk of salmonella and was even willing to toss the whole lot out and use dried spaghetti if it would keep Lennie away from me. I made tea, put two cups on a tray, and tiptoed up to Adam's study. I poked my head round the corner of the door and was greeted by a smile on his face that made the new paintwork look dingy.

"Can I come in?" I whispered. We had hardly managed to have a moment alone together since he came back the day before.

"Yes," he mouthed back, rising to help me with the tray. He closed the door behind me and turned the key in the lock.

"Where's Lennie?" he asked, still whispering.

I pointed my finger upward. "Homework and carbohydrates," I said wryly.

"Is she driving you crazy? She really likes you, you know. She was in here singing your praises earlier." I shrugged. The feeling wasn't mutual, but I didn't have to write that out in capitals. I poured each of us a cup of tea and nursed mine, leaning on the edge of Adam's desk.

"I think she likes having a woman around the house. Gay always worked and the nannies were never much use in the kitchen. Magdalena cleaned but she didn't cook. It's good for her to have proper meals. I think that Gay just nags her all the time for eating too much." I made no reply, but Adam didn't notice: he was too happily wrapped up in his little domestic dream of the woman barefoot in the kitchen, and the child fat and rosy and fast asleep in a crib by the hearth. Okay, the woman in the kitchen was his mistress, but who was I to spoil the fantasy? "It's a pity you never had children, Edith," he said. "You're so good with Lennie. She wants to stay longer. She asked if she could stay here more often during the week. I mean, it's only ten blocks from Spence—it would be so much closer than Gay's apartment." I nearly choked. The Earl Grey burned my throat like arsenic. "But Gay won't agree. She wants her with her downtown. We compromised by letting her stay till Monday morning. Can you drive her down to Gay's to get her clean school things? I never asked whether you had a license. You could take my car. It's in the garage on Eighty-first. I hardly use it."

"I don't drive. I never learned," I lied. I didn't want to get into the sticky question of insurance details.

"Don't worry about it. I'll just get Gay to send it up with the car service." Then he ran his hands up the inside of my thigh. "I missed you. I'll be glad to have you to myself again," he said, smiling, his eyes narrowing with concentration as his fingers rose higher. I felt myself begin to melt, almost sliding off the desk, the cup clattering in its saucer.

He just had to look at me and I wanted to tear my clothes off.

He pulled me onto his knee and began kissing me, the skirt pulled up around my waist. In seconds I would be fucking him on the chair, but I drew away, tugged down the fabric of my skirt and wriggled from his grip.

"Mr. Davenport," I protested. "You must learn to keep your hands out of the help's underwear. Lennie will hear." And as though my voice were connected directly to God, her shoes clattered downstairs and she ran past his door. A few minutes later I heard Leila's voice join hers in the kitchen.

I gave a resigned sigh, as I knew I should go to clear up the pasta.

When I went back downstairs, both girls were hunched over the dining table, flicking through a magazine.

I shut the kitchen door, but Lennie opened it again.

"Edie, you speak Spanish, don't you?" She turned to me for confirmation, before dropping her eyes back to the magazine when I protested that I knew only a few words.

"She lived all over Spain and Brazil, my dad told me," she announced, glaring at me as though daring me to contradict her.

"I spent a couple of months in Latin America, is all, not Spain. And they speak Portuguese in Brazil," I said insistently, but she merely shrugged as though this were an unimportant detail.

"Latino men are so fit. Look at . . ." Her mouth moved and words tumbled out as her squat fingernail, half of it painted with green polish, pressed into the matte face of a muscled man dressed in a wife-beater.

"But he's gay," said Leila, turning the paper idly.

"He's not; he's going out with some model."

"I was telling Leila that you could help her with her Spanish if she was stuck, couldn't you, Edie?"

"I can speak only a little bit. I have no idea about the grammar, sorry," I said tersely. Bloody, bloody hell. What was I—the homework elf?

I started to gather up the flat ribbons of pasta and drop them into a Tupperware container. I wiped the table, clearing the flour into little white peaks, then swept them into my hand. The moment I made my final swipe with the cloth, the girls swooped across the surface. *Vogue* and *Glamour* lay spread-eagled on the table, their pages already wrinkled and dog-eared.

Lennie was smearing a free sample of face cream over her cheeks.

"Did you ever see Princess Diana when you lived in

London?" she asked. "It must have been really glamorous living there. Where did you live exactly? Did you live near Big Ben?" I froze.

Good question—where the hell had I lived? "I told you already, it wasn't London, it was Oxford. It's like Princeton is to New York. Far away."

"But you did go to London? You like, shopped there and stuff?" Did I? I couldn't remember. Maybe I should have kept crib notes. I hardly remembered how to take the bus. Bogotá was more familiar to me that London.

"I've been to London lots of times," said Leila. "My mother has friends there. We stay in Kensington, near the palace, you know?" I didn't. "But my dad always drags us to all the museums—it's really boring. I just like Harvey Nicks, and Hamleys is like this really great toy store—I loved that when I was a kid. And at Christmas they decorate the street with lights and you can see Santa in this cool kinda grotto thing—do you know it?" How the hell was I supposed to know anything about toy stores when I had no kids? I thought hard. Where was it, Oxford Street, Regent Street . . . ? My mind went as blank as the white board on the front of the refrigerator. All I could think about was that we needed eggs and sea salt.

"I told you, I didn't live in London, so I don't know my way round—and anyway, I don't really like talking about England," I eventually stammered.

"But it's so exciting. I want to go there when I'm older. And Paris. I want to live in my own apartment, and be thin, and have lots of boyfriends—just like her." She caressed the page in the magazine lovingly where a tastefully nude model unfolded to reveal a perfume sample.

"Well, I hope you would be wearing more clothes, and have

a bit more flesh on your bones. You would have to be anorexic to look like that, Lennie. It's not real life."

"No, I wouldn't. My mom's thin. You're thin. You've got a great figure."

"And neither am I lying across a page, naked, making come-hither eyes at the camera. I'm a woman with a dead husband standing at your sink washing your plates, making your bed, and cooking your supper. That might be your idea of a fucking fairy tale, but it's not mine." Lennie and Leila both looked at me as though waiting for my head to spin.

I might just as well have vomited across the waxed oak floorboards. That sort of mess would have been easier to clean up. Instead, my words sat and steamed, the "fucking" buzzing round and round in my ears like a fly.

Lennie had tears in her eyes that she hastily wiped into a snail's trail across one of her newly moisturized cheeks. Leila dropped her gaze and stared avidly at the magazine, as if it held the secrets of the universe and not just of how to get really great skin in three weeks.

"Hey, chill, I'm sorry, I didn't mean to upset you," stammered Lennie, her voice teetering like a glass on the edge of a table, ready to fall and shatter into a thousand pieces.

"I know you didn't. I'm sorry. I shouldn't have snapped," I replied, already hearing the story being repeated to Gay. Or, even worse, Adam. I shuddered. I felt bad, but as I dried my hands hurriedly on the dishtowel and ran downstairs to my bedroom, I knew only a sense of relief, the way you do when you've been banging your head for ages on a brick wall and suddenly you stop. Or, at least, how I imagined that would feel.

But all too soon I was back to butting the wall with my forehead.

I didn't go up for dinner. I said I had a lot of letters to write. I returned to the kitchen just long enough to throw out the pasta and leave them a salad and cold cuts. Then I sat on the edge of my bed and bit my knuckles, wondering how long I could keep this big-sister charade going.

After two and a half months of insomnia, I had finally managed to fall asleep when I spent the night upstairs with Adam. Even better, the hours before sleep passed in mostly mindless, adolescent sex—or at least the kind of sex I should have had when I was an adolescent. We seemed to fall asleep having sex and wake up in mid-thrust, ready to take up where we had left off.

The return to the dank room in the basement every Friday night brought the sexual idyll to an abrupt end. It was like being banished to a subterranean Siberia, and I usually spent the time with the lights blazing, staring out through the barred windows, thinking about the future as though it were a lump in my breast that I was frightened to acknowledge.

So, of course I had no letters to write. There wasn't one single person in the world who knew where I was. I hadn't seen my mother in years. I had hardly spoken to my sister in twenty years.

My cousin Agnes, the only person from home whom I vaguely kept in touch with, thought I was in South America, and I communicated with my brother, Geordie, in Singapore only when necessary, and then only in dollars and cents. He paid all of my mother's nursing-home bills but questioned every last packet of cough drops she sucked. I had no girlfriends. I couldn't contact Karl. I couldn't seek out any of Francisco's old colleagues, and his family was as dead to me as he was. It was frightening how small your life could suddenly become—no more than a tiny soot stain that a wet finger could erase. Just like that.

Now all I had was a secondhand name, a secondhand bed, and a secondhand husband, all of them temporary.

Which, after tonight's neurotic outburst, might be more temporary than I had imagined.

I did my mental arithmetic. I had saved almost every cent I had earned. I had accumulated a couple thousand dollars, which I had stuffed into an envelope inside a pillowcase at the back of the linen closet upstairs. The share of the money I had withdrawn from our joint account was hidden in bank-fresh bundles of twenty-dollar bills in the downstairs freezer, inside a Tupperware container marked CHICKEN STOCK. I had something saved from my previous life in a savings account at the Citizen's Bank in Harvard Square, also untouched. If I had to leave in a hurry, I could live for six frugal months without working. The thought made me retch. I needed air.

I opened the back door and crept to the top of the garden steps, where I wrapped my jacket around my shoulders and looked out across the yard. It was almost the end of October. I had been here for nearly four months. Summer was over. The leaves from the apple tree next door had curled up and died, the rotting fruit scattered like dog turds across the decking, and the maple was bare. I could see into the kitchens of the apartments opposite, one atop the other, a head popping occasionally into view. How much longer would I be here to watch them?

The kitchen light in the house behind me went out, plunging me into darkness and sending me back indoors. As I negotiated the dark cavern of the stairs, I heard the dishwasher kick into action overhead.

There were heavy footsteps and the clicking of interior light switches. Lennie's voice danced across the ceiling, out into the hall and up the stairs like Tinkerbell. I lay on my bed with the jacket still draped over my shoulders and listened to the house settling down for sleep. I closed my eyes.

I woke up to feel the jacket being tugged off my face.

"What the fuck," I screamed, but nothing came out of my mouth. I grappled with the hands that were round my throat and drew myself into a ball in the corner of the bed.

My vocal cords would not work, billiard balls of panic ricocheting around in my brain.

"Don't," I finally whimpered. Great—after eventually getting the words out, all I could manage was "don't," and even that sounded like it was coming from a long way away—like Jeanette MacDonald calling out for Nelson Eddy from out across the valley.

My heart was beating so loudly it muffled everything. I focused my eyes and saw the outline of a body hunched over me, and heavy-framed glasses revealing eyes that looked even more shocked than I felt.

"Edie, you had it wrapped round your neck," he said. It was Adam; his hands held out my jacket, twisted into a cloth croissant.

For a second I couldn't think who he was, or who he was talking to.

"Edie, Edie, it's okay—it's me," he murmured.

"What in the name of holy fuck are you doing creeping round my bedroom in the middle of the fucking night?" I half coughed, half cried, swatting him away, even though he was only trying to calm me. I started rifling for the serrated bread knife that I had hidden under my pillow and yanked it out, waving it in the air.

"I could have fucking killed you. Are you off your fucking head?" Too late I remembered that I was brandishing a knife at the man who was paying my wages. Adam carefully took the knife and laid it on the floor, giving it a kick underneath the bed, and I started to sob, noisily and with an unattractive amount of snot.

It was not my finest moment.

"I'm so sorry." He patted my hair, smoothing it down. "I didn't mean to scare you. I just wanted to see if you were all right. Lennie told me you were a bit tense this afternoon, and then you didn't come up for supper. I've told her to apologize, but now I seem to have done a pretty good job of upsetting you myself," he added.

Tense. Does threatening to knife your boss make you seem tense?

"Adam, I—am—not—your—fucking—wife." I enunciated the words precisely, as if I had been taking elocution lessons for Pissed Off 101. "I'm the housekeeper. I'm supposed to clean up your crap and do your laundry, not sit at the top of your table dispensing food and womanly wisdom like I live here with a little bell that I ring for the servants. I—am—the—fucking—servant. I don't come to supper; I fucking cook it. I can't deal with this. You seem to have some kind of *Brady Bunch* thing going on in your head and have forgotten that I only work here. We're not a couple." It was a good speech, but, except for the cursing, most of it was unintelligible.

"Oh, shh," said Adam, his face white and aghast. "You must know you mean more to me than that?" he said and began to kiss me, stopping to wipe my face tenderly with the corner of his shirt, then kissing me again. He kissed my eyes, my cheeks, the corners of my lips, and, open-mouthed, I wound my arms around his neck and pulled him closer. He began to drag my clothes off, but I stopped him and just tugged them aside. My head was crushed between his shoulders and the rickety headboard with its uneven lumps of padding, the springs of the geriatric mattress wheezing like an old man, as I pulled him into me and he pushed me hard against the wall until my cheek slapping the plaster made him stop.

"Shit, this is no good." He looked at the red mark spreading up one side of my face, which had an imprint of the wallpaper embossed into it, as though in shock. "What the hell am I doing?" I didn't care, I just hoped he would keep on doing it.

"Here I am trying to tell you I care about you and I'm hurting you." Hurriedly, he stood up and fastened his belt over his still gaping jeans before gathering me into his arms. He looked around the bedroom. His eyes took in the shutters with their loose hinges leaning against the wall, each with what I now realized was supposed to be a tulip-shaped keyhole cut out of its center. "My God," he muttered, "you don't even have curtains, and the shutters are broken. Look, get up and come upstairs. Let's get out of here. This place is depressing. I had no idea." He surveyed the tattered wallpaper, the bare walls, the barred windows as though he'd opened his eyes and found himself in a Bangkok prison cell.

"I took them off myself—I get a bit claustrophobic, but I know, it's fucking awful, isn't it?" I started to laugh through the tears. And I couldn't stop: it suddenly all seemed so ridiculous.

"It's a wonder Amnesty International hasn't started a letter writing campaign for you. You should have told me how bad it was," Adam said, pulling me up the stairs behind him.

"I've been in worse," I replied, without elaborating.

Upstairs, he brought me a brandy and an Ambien, dressed me in one of his T-shirts, and put me into his bed.

I never even felt him get in beside me; nor, in the morning, did I hear him get up. When I woke, it was already eight o'clock.

My head felt like birds had been nesting in it, and my eyes looked as though they had been pecked out of their puffy sockets.

I crept into Gay's bathroom to look for something from her pharmacopoeia for my headache, but the bathroom cabinet was empty. It took me a second to realize that the perfume had also gone, as had the soap and the bath oil. There was nothing except a lone white towel with a little seashell embroidered on the corner.

I went into her dressing room and found it had been similarly ransacked. A pair of black trash bags lay sprawled on the floor like drunks. I was just peering into their depths when Adam walked up behind me.

He folded me inside his arms. I could smell his lemony cologne and feel the wiriness of him underneath the crisp cotton of his shirt. He looked like the captain of cricket from one of those old British boarding school stories I used to read as a child, ready to go in and bat for the team.

"I was just coming to get these," he said, kissing my ear. "I left you a cup of coffee beside the bed. Stay there. I mean it," he added forcefully. "We're going out to dinner tonight, and if you cook something, I promise, I'm going to throw it into the garbage myself." He picked up the bags. "I'm going to stick these downstairs and drop them off at Gay's the next time I take Lennie home." I peered over his bent shoulder and looked inside the first bag. The heel of one of Gay's Prada sandals pointed right up at me like an insult from a passing cab driver.

"I'm going to drop Lennie at school on my way to the office, but I'll call you later to see how you are and I'm going to have my secretary make an appointment for you with our doctor. I think you're rundown."

"No, no, I'll be fine, don't do that, I'll see my own guy," I blurted, jolted out of my daze. I had managed to skirt the whole question of health insurance by saying I already had a plan, which I did, but not one that I could access. "I'm sorry about my meltdown last night. It was just a big fuss about nothi—" He put his fingers on my lips, then kissed me.

"I'm the one who should be sorry. I've been a fool. I should have realized that I was putting you in an awful position and that you would be feeling insecure. Things will be different, I promise, but I have to go now. Rest and we'll talk later."

"What have you done with all of Gay's stuff?"

"I moved it out," he answered. "So that there's enough room for your clothes. I want you to bring them upstairs today." It was the most direct order he had ever given me.

"I can't move up here. I can't. I can't use her bathroom. It's weird."

"Well, we'll swap if you like: you can have mine. Whatever you like, just put things where you want them."

"What about Lennie?" I asked.

"What about her?" he replied, holding my eyes in an unwavering gaze. "Last time I checked Lennie didn't decide where people slept in this house. She'll just have to deal with it." If we'd been wrestling, I would have been pinned to the floor in a shoulder lock, and panting.

As it was, I was just panting.

"I'm not moving into your bedroom, Adam. It doesn't seem right," I said.

"Suit yourself. Take the guest room, then. But you are not going back into that fetid hole in the basement, and we are not going to sneak around like a pair of kids anymore." He grabbed the bags, kissed me again, inaccurately, on the lips, and left.

I ran my fingers lovingly across the marble edge of the sink.

There was nothing I would have liked more than to run myself a bath and languish in it like Cleopatra, but I couldn't.

I walked back into the bedroom and lifted the coffee cup to my lips. Adam's shirt swiveled around my hips. I sat on the edge of the bed, spread my legs, and examined my toes. I would wait for Adam and Lennie to leave and then go downstairs and have a shower.

A second too late I noticed the bedroom door was still open and Lennie was standing on the landing watching me, her eyes taking in the indelicate amount of flesh I was displaying.

"Hi," she said.

"Hi, Lennie," I replied, as though I were Martha Stewart with a bowl of pancake batter in my hand, not the hired help sitting on her father's bed with no underpants on. I tugged the corner of the shirt in an attempt to cover my knees but only got as far as the top of my thigh.

"You're wearing my dad's shirt," she said unnecessarily, since it had the name of his health club emblazoned on the front.

I couldn't think of any explanation that would sound convincing, even to myself.

Adam's voice called out, urging her to hurry or they'd be late.

She didn't move but just stood watching me.

"But what are you doing here?" she asked, sounding suddenly like a little girl who has just lost her favorite doll.

Adam called out again.

Her expression changed from disbelief to faint disgust, as

though the implications of finding me sitting on her father's bed had just begun so sink in.

"Did you sleep here?" she gasped in a tiny voice.

I wanted to say "no" and tell her that it wasn't what it looked like. But I couldn't. Because it was. In fact, it was even worse than it looked.

But thankfully nobody knew that but me.

10

"SO, WHAT? ARE you and my dad, like, shacking up now?" Lennie said the following weekend, giving me a sly look from underneath her long, curling lashes.

The painters had finally come back and were in the process of turning the basement into a blue-white ice palace and more contractors had been summoned to extend the air-conditioning. In the meantime I had moved in to the upstairs guest room—right across the hall from her dad's study—but the girl wasn't stupid. Or particularly forgiving. There was a sneer in her voice.

I wasn't sure what Adam had told her. He could do really interesting things with his tongue, but dissembling wasn't one of them.

But, however he had explained my half-naked presence, it hadn't made Lennie any less interested in pursuing me. If I thought she had stuck to me like static before, I was now discovering a whole new meaning to the word *attachment*.

It was like having a chaperone, a blind chaperone, to whom everything had to be explained, step by step. I felt as if I were in a fly-on-the-wall documentary and providing my own running commentary. Even when I hid in the bathroom, she knocked on the door asking me for everything from nail-polish remover to advice on menstrual cramps.

"What about your husband—have you got over him? I thought you were going to be, like, tragic forever. Are you going to marry my dad? Will you be my stepmother? I hope you don't think you can shove me out of the way if you get married." I didn't know which question to rebut first, so I made a list and worked my way through them.

"Well, we're definitely not getting married, so you can forget that, and where you live has nothing to do with me—that's up to your father and mother, and always will be. I know you saw me in his room, but that has nothing to do with the fact that I still just work here. I'm not going to be making any decisions beyond whether I buy Snuggle or Wisk. I'm not going to interfere in your life. I would not and never shall presume to make decisions for you—that's your business. That's the last thing I have any interest in. As for getting over my husband—well, that's my business." She looked disappointed that there was not more drama to be milked from the situation. "It's weird, Dad having a girlfriend. In some ways it's kind of gross, but Leila says you're cool, so I shouldn't really mind. I mean, I liked you before, so what's the biggie now?" I sighed—so now even the neighbors knew about my sleeping arrangements. If Fred knew, he might at least stop trying to fix me up with his illegal buddies in other buildings who wanted a green card bride, but he would also blab it to everyone from the guys in the garage to the other maids all down the block.

"I mean, as long as you don't move to, like, the country or anything. Or have babies—jeez, I'm not interested in the whole stepsister thing. That would be sooo disgusting."

"I'm not his girlfriend, Lennie. And I'm definitely not in the baby-making business. However, you shouldn't be discussing your dad's private life. Not without talking to him first."

"But I did talk to him first." She cast me another sly look. I felt like a teenager gossiping about boys: my friend has a crush on your friend. Not that anyone had ever had a crush on me when I was that age.

"I don't know why you have to be so sneaky about it, is all . . . Lots of my friends' parents are divorced and they all have girlfriends and boyfriends."

"Oh, please, Lennie," I remonstrated, "I don't want to talk about it."

"Whatever, anyway—it's not me that you have to worry about—it's my mom. She's going to freak when she finds out. It was bad enough when Dad was on holiday in Nantucket without her, and he had all their friends staying there. She didn't like that at all. She kept calling all the time. I think she was waiting for Dad to ask her to fly up, you know, and be, like, civilized . . . But this—ha, this is going to turn her into queen psycho bitch, big time."

And the girl wasn't far wrong.

It was not pretty.

On Sunday evening Adam drove Lennie home with Gay's clothes and cosmetics packed into two suitcases, my having persuaded him that the trash bags did not send the right kind of message.

He didn't arrive back until two a.m., tight-lipped and rigid with anger. I was sitting up in his bed, where I had been reading the same sentence for the previous hour, when he walked in.

He began to undress, pacing in and out of his bathroom, punctuating his sentences with his toothbrush, and appearing each time wearing successively fewer clothes, until he stood only in his boxers.

"You know," he railed, "I thought that my wife had walked out on *me* but apparently not," he said. "Suddenly we're still married, and she has a right to determine how I live my life, who I live with, and when and where I see my children. She won't let Ned come here and visit, and she wants me to sell the house." He laughed without humor.

"Will you? Lennie says she doesn't want you to move."

"Oh, she can't touch the house. It's not even mine. It's all tied up in some kind of family trust. We only came to live here because neither of my brothers wanted it. She's probably entitled to about a tenth of the value—I can buy her out. She can have the house in Nantucket if she wants and half what I have in the bank, whatever little that is. What she can't have is the last word about my private life." He climbed in beside me and gave me a spearmint-flavored kiss, sliding his hand across my stomach and knocking the book from its resting place to the floor.

"Adam, you mustn't let this get in the way of your family—it's not worth it."

"Oh, don't be ridiculous. In the first place, I want you here—in my bed, in my life—and everyone will just have to suck it up and get used to it. And in the second place, it's not about you, it's about Gay wanting to control everything. It would be the same whoever I started to see; it just gives her a particular pain in the neck that I've replaced her so easily with—I think her exact words were my 'own live-in kitchen whore.'" I flinched as though he had slapped me.

"Sorry, that was harsh, but you might as well know what

you're dealing with. I think she thought that my life would just stay on hold while she was the one having all the new beginnings." He reached across me and turned out the light, pulling me against him as he lay down.

"But why did you have to tell her? Why does it have anything to do with her?" I asked the hollow of his neck. "As you said—she left you."

"I didn't want to put Lennie in the position of having to keep secrets. It's better to get it out in the open. I hate subterfuge. So you might as well move in here with me—there's no point in keeping up the fiction that we're not a couple. Whatever you say, we are a couple, and it makes me very happy."

"I don't feel right about it, Adam. I can't sleep with you when your daughter's in the house. You're right about not wanting her to keep secrets. She can't. She's already told Leila and God knows who else. They're probably giving out flyers at Eli's."

He shrugged. "If Gay gets her way, Lennie's not going to be a problem. She doesn't want her to set foot inside the house again."

"All I seem to be doing is causing trouble for you. What will you do?"

"Don't worry about it. I'm not going to give in to her." But I did worry, and for the first time in months it wasn't about myself.

Long after Adam had fallen asleep, I lay awake, sobered with that awful three a.m. clarity in which, despite the gloom, everything is illuminated, and you get brutal truth, straight up, without a twist.

I was making Adam's life worse, and for what? There was no future for me here, and I knew that I should be extricating myself before he got even more comfortable with the idea of me as a benign Mrs. Suzy Homemaker. I would have to leave, and soon, but how? Where? I turned to look at him, at his face, half covered by his left hand, where the wedding band still gleamed on his ring finger. He slept with a child's fierce concentration, his eyes squeezed shut as though unconsciousness was a serious business that demanded all his energy.

His features had none of Francisco's angelic sensuousness: the lips were narrower, the cheeks thinner, and, of course, he was older. The eyes, without Francisco's thick, fringed lashes, radiated lines across his pale cheek like a five-year-old's drawing of the sun. But when he smiled, his whole appearance transformed: his cheeks fell into merry folds like one of those funny dogs with the pleated faces. It entranced me, that change, which I could bring about with only a word or a gesture or a touch. I loved it.

Comparisons are odious, my mother used to say, before making them anyway, always to my detriment. And I made them too, measuring Francisco against Adam, then hastily wiping out the differences I found. But, inside, the two men were a lot alike. Both had the same relaxed kindness, which they offered generously, even casually, although Adam was a lighter soul and much less self-contained and detached than Francisco had been.

He had more ardency, more intent—at least where I was concerned. He saw me. Or at least he saw who he thought I was.

I stroked his already roughening cheek, resisting the urge to kiss him awake. I promised myself that I would find some way out of this mess. I owed it to him.

But no matter what people say about the cold light of morning, it's still a lot warmer than the stark, surgical chill of the night, and as usual, when I finally woke, a little after seven, I reneged on all the deals I had brokered with myself four hours earlier. I rose, brushed my teeth, made Adam coffee, and kicked my good intentions to the side with the rest of the lies, then shoved them in the hamper for another day.

But I was tired.

I couldn't get moving. Adam sprang out of the door soon after eight, bristling with purpose. I watched him go with the same wistfulness I had always felt when Francisco rushed off to his office at the university, leaving me dangling, cut adrift, looking at a long, formless morning until he came back and pulled me in to shore. I needed something to do, but instead I dallied. I drank several cups of coffee, until my ears sang with static. I stripped Lennie's bed, washed her sheets, and practically breathed on them until they were dry enough to iron. It was almost a relief when I heard Adam's key in the door just after lunch. I wasn't expecting him home in the middle of the day, but the chance to stop working, stop thinking, stop agonizing, was welcome. I set the iron down on the ironing board, snorting steam like a dragon above the sheets I had been ironing creases into for the previous half-hour, and walked out to meet him, a smile ready on my face like that of a chat-show host, waiting to cue in my next guest.

It faded when I saw Gay standing in the hall. Apparently we had company.

"Ah, Mrs. Doubtfire," she said, swinging her keys round manicured fingernails. They were painted pale lilac today, I noticed, and the glasses had been banished. "I hear your job description has been expanded somewhat." She was wearing a dark suit with heather-colored cashmere underneath. She tapped her high heel on the marble floor, though she still only came up to my chin, and blinked several times.

"I thought we should have a little chat. Set a few things straight." I stood and looked at her for a long time, then tossed my head haughtily and strolled slowly back into the kitchen. Rat's tails coiled around my neck, but I acted as though I had just spent three hours at the hairdresser's. Fuck her, I thought. If she was expecting a cowed little Victorian scullery maid, she was in for a surprise.

"I'm talking to you," she piped after me.

I ignored her and unplugged the iron. I hoped she didn't see my hands shaking.

"Don't walk away from me when I'm talking to you."

"You're not talking to me; you're yelling at someone you think you can order around, and that definitely isn't me. Whatever you seem to think is or isn't part of my job description, Mrs. Davenport, doing what you say certainly isn't on the list." I spoke without looking at her, calmly winding the cord round and round the iron, so tightly that I strapped my hand to the handle and had to undo it.

"But fucking the boss is?"

"No, fucking the boss I do in my spare time. For fun. I don't get paid overtime for it. It's a pleasure, not a duty. Though, obviously, you approached the task rather differently when it was part of your job description," I added, turning now to face her and being confronted with more of that bloody blinking. "You didn't give me much of an act to follow."

"You've got a nerve. Who do you think you are, you slutty little gold-digging bitch? You're forgetting that you're an employee, and that this is still my house. And that"—she pointed her thin index finger upward—"is still my bedroom, so don't get too comfortable up there."

"For your information, I'm sleeping in the guest room. When

I spend the night in your bed, I don't actually sleep." I paused for effect, as her eyes fluttered. "Much." All this, delivered in my best Edinburgh accent. Miss Jean Brodie couldn't have done it better herself.

I understood a little more about Gay than she realized.

Whether by accident or design, she had left the blue paper innards of last year's Cartier diary in the drawer of her bedside table.

Naturally, I had read it. There was little of interest. It was mostly lunches, dinners, meetings, dentists, functions at both children's schools, and a series of appointments for facials, a plastic surgeon at Manhattan ENT, and another for varicose veins. I noticed the last two with a little thrill of spite that only a woman who cannot see into her future would feel.

Adam hardly got a name check, but the initials RF next to lunch appeared with notable frequency, and even blocked out a few weekends that coincided with entries for Adam visiting Sydney and Miami. I wondered if there was more behind her decision to leave than boredom with marital bliss.

"If you think Adam's going to choose you over his children, then you're even more stupid than you seem. Obviously, he's not going to be influenced by the sort of person who gives free blow jobs and scrubs lavatories for a living." I wanted to push the iron into her face and hold it there until her hair singed.

"Well, obviously," I parroted, "you don't know just how good I am at blow jobs." Her pale face flushed, and for once the eyes widened—yes, I thought, remembering my earlier comparison, she did look exactly like Andy Warhol, screen-printed crimson. I wondered if there were another three copies of her elsewhere in yellow, blue, and green.

"I don't expect to influence Adam. As you say, I just scrub

toilets for a living. But if I'm no threat to you, why are you here? Why did you walk out in the first place if you're in such a hurry to come back and mark out your territory? Remind me—didn't you choose to leave?" I folded the ironing board, jammed it back like a gangling skeleton into a cupboard, pulled out a kitchen chair, sat down, and crossed my legs as elegantly as you can when you're wearing old sneakers, cut-offs, and a man's Ralph Lauren shirt that is several sizes too big for you. By sitting, I had lost the height advantage, but my legs were shaking so much I was afraid they would collapse like the ironing board. "And since you've done it once, I'm sure you can manage to find the door again. I'll let you see yourself out." She opened her mouth to answer but was interrupted by the rumbling of several men in overalls, lumbering up from the basement. A stepladder appeared from the narrow stairwell like a rabbit being pulled from a magician's hat.

The Poles had been replaced by a team from Ecuador, shy, grinning, gap-toothed men who worshipped the empanadas I made especially for them.

"*Disculpe. ¿Qué hago ahorra, señora? Hemos acabado de pintar el cuarto de frente. ¿Comienzo a preparar su cuarto de baño?*" asked Jesus, the shortest, squattest, smiliest of them.

"*Sí, sí, pero primero, tengo que librarme de esta perra,*" I responded.

Then, without pause, I launched into a long and unnecessary barrage of Spanish, none of which had anything to do with their chore of redecorating Gay's bathroom upstairs, but had a lot to do with Shakira's last album. In my previous life I had never directed workmen; I only knew how to order food, thank maids, ask about children, husbands, and wives, and talk dirty. I thought that fulsome congratulations on their *pingas grandes* might have taken them, somewhat, by surprise, so instead I rattled on about the weather and their grandmothers, recited a few song lyrics, and asked them if they wanted to drink something, using all the wrong tenses.

Gay's thin, pink mouth quivered with uncertainty. The painters looked perplexed. They were used to my being friendly, but until now I hadn't been quite so effusive. Or personal.

"Was there anything else, Mrs. Davenport?" I asked her. "We employees have jobs to do and the men want to get started on your bathroom. I'm having it painted in a beautiful shade of green," I hoped she would leave soon because my well of Spanish was rapidly running dry and my cheeks twitched from the rictus of fake smiling.

I led the painters up two flights of stairs and heard the door slam. I had just enough time to tell the men where to go before I sprinted next door and vomited into Adam's sink.

I could talk a good talk. Those many midafternoon reruns of *Dynasty* had obviously had some subliminal influence on my inner bitch, but the outer coward was still sick to her stomach.

All these bloody locks in the house, and who could have known that the first bogeyman would arrive in the daylight and have her own key.

I came out of the bathroom and lay down on the bed. One of the Ecuadorans peeped out of the door with a roller in his hand and asked me if I needed anything. I said no.

Nothing that yet another new identity wouldn't fix, anyway.

I hoped I hadn't just made sure that the next time Adam saw his children would be when they graduated from college.

I hoped he had a good lawyer.

I hoped I wouldn't be looking for a new place to live.

But Adam only laughed in rather delighted disbelief when he heard what I had said to his wife. He laughed even harder when the painters began nodding at him and smiling, while patting imaginary bumps on the front of their stomachs.

"Are they hungry?" he asked me.

"No, they heard me throwing up. Now they obviously think I'm pregnant. They're congratulating you."

"You're not, are you?"

"I already told you: I can't have kids."

"I know. I know. Bad joke. It's a shame. You would have beautiful children." He sounded almost sad.

"Yeah, yeah." I pushed him away with a shrug of pretend amusement; I had already been through this with one man and wasn't looking to reprise the role.

Adam had already been to his lawyers, and while I had been lying on the bed mentally counting out my running-away money, Gay had obviously been doing her own accounts.

Most of his money was locked up in a family trust. His kids were taken care of well into their dotage, but his personal fortune was tiny and tightly entailed. Gay could afford to retain the lifestyle she had grown accustomed to only if she toed the line in the Manolos that her husband's generous allowance subsidized.

Ned finally came the next weekend, as planned, with two friends, three sets of filthy soccer clothes, and a small ecosystem of head lice that were harder to get rid of than Gay. Then. Lennie threw a tantrum until her mother let her stay on for Halloween, when she jubilantly stood at the door and single-handedly gave out five thousand pieces of candy to the ghouls and ghosts of the Upper East Side.

Meanwhile Adam's lawyers quickly arranged a custody agreement. He would have both kids for alternate holidays. This year he got Christmas and Easter. Gay got New Year's, spring break, an undisclosed lump sum, all her living expenses paid, and the deed to the house in Nantucket as a sweetener.

However, she also kept her front-door keys.

Adam immediately changed the locks.

And suddenly, just like that, I was a step-mistress.

11

I USED TO LIVE in Oxford." As soon as the words jumped out of my mouth and across the table like unruly toads, I realized that I had made a mistake.

Baxter, Adam's oldest friend, had come in from Long Island with his family to gloat about Clinton's win and watch the Macy's parade from Adam's office downtown. This was followed by Thanksgiving turkey and all the trimmings back at the house, but, really, I was the one being roasted.

The turkey was a stripped arc of backbone and dessert was crumbs and piecrust. Outside, the kids were having s'mores and second-degree burns on the barbecue in the yard, supervised by Lennie and Ned.

Baxter swiveled in his chair and looked at me curiously.

"Really? Which part?"

"Woodstock Road," I added quietly.

"Oh, yes?" He waited for me to say more, but I merely concurred, wishing that he would drop it.

"I know Oxford quite well. My brother went there. Keble? He was a rower. Do you know the college?"

"Well, I know where it is, if that's what you mean."

"Where were you exactly?" I felt as if I were being cross-examined under oath. I wished I had kept my mouth shut, but it was too late: Baxter had his teeth into me now and wasn't letting go.

"I wasn't at the university. Frank was the academic."

"I mean, where did you live?"

"Near South Parade."

"Ah, yes, there was a pub there or a restaurant or something that we used to go to. Wasn't it near the river where you could hire rowboats?"

I shrugged noncommittally. "I guess . . . it was a little ways from the river."

"I'm trying to think of the name."

"Sorry, I don't know; we didn't really go out much."

"Didn't go out much?" he parroted, as though I had just confessed to being a member of the Ku Klux Klan. "Good God, that sounds very dull. What did you do with yourself? No cinemas, no concerts, no restaurants? Oxford's such an interesting place. You must have done something, surely?"

"This from Mr. McCulture himself. When was the last time you went to a concert? You haven't seen a film since you took the girls to *Pocahontas*," said his wife, Jenny, a sloe-eyed Canadian with Brillo-pad hair that made you think of only one thing: conditioner. She looked like she ran a psychic tearoom and wore lots of layered vintage clothes in velvet and lace, and she had a permanent smile pasted on her face that was impossible to resist.

"You'll have to excuse him, Edith; he's obviously been doing some sort of Vietcong interrogation course in his lunch hour." She turned to her husband. "I wish you were half as interested in anything I tell you . . ." But Baxter persisted: "So what were you doing there?"

"I was married, Frank was always working . . ."

"Goodness, you don't have a lot to say for yourself, do you?"

"Not everyone has your charming way with words, honey." Jenny laughed. "Really, I do apologize. I don't know what's got into him."

"Red wine," said Caroline, a literary agent who looked like a young, already overweight Elizabeth Taylor with high coloring and obscenely red lips. "Have another glass and leave the poor woman alone," she said, lighting a cigarette.

"I'm only saying that it sounds like a very dull life," Baxter said, shaking his head in a bewildered schoolmasterly fashion, as you might if one of your pupils told you that Al Gore was a form of extended metaphor.

"I didn't have a lot of free time," I mumbled by way of explanation. I felt as though I had shown myself to be only one notch up the evolutionary ladder from a talking chimp in a tea commercial.

Baxter did not look convinced. He had long furrows etched into his cheeks like the creases on a pair of cheap pants, and his teeth were stained purple from Adam's good burgundy.

I smiled to show I didn't care. I was drinking white wine, so I had the chardonnay ring of confidence, and anyway my tolerance had been honed by years of being addressed as "my dear girl" by a decade's worth of patronizing elderly professors.

Adam leaned over and took my hand. "Baxter doesn't understand that some people have to work for a living. For him, being a prick is a full-time occupation. Edith lost her husband a year ago," he added, throwing Baxter a hard look that implied the subject was closed.

Caroline and Jenny both murmured in sympathy.

"Someone put the blanket over his cage, please." Jenny sighed wearily and flapped her husband with her napkin. "Ignore him, Edith; he's professionally bitter. You're lucky—I have to take the idiot home with me and hope that he doesn't infect any of the children." Baxter threw his hands up in mock surrender, while Caroline, mercifully, changed the subject and began enthusing about her latest find: a Lithuanian biochemist from Stanford who was going to popularize bacteria for the masses. He could start with Baxter, I thought sourly.

"He's going to be the Jacques Cousteau of germs," she protested enthusiastically, above the hoots of cheerful derision.

"I'm telling you, Adam, you really should get him to do a book. I've already got him signed up for a series on Discovery." But Adam paid her scant attention. He was too busy watching me.

I caught his eye and the rest of the room vanished. He smiled.

I smiled back. I couldn't wait for them all to leave and for it to be just the two of us.

I rose and began to clear the last of the dessert plates. Jenny heaved her ruffled bulk out of the dining chair and followed me into the kitchen.

"I'm sorry to hear about your loss, Edith." I felt she was waiting for further elaboration, but I just kept stacking dishes. "I hope you don't take my pig of a husband seriously. His abrasive personality is part of his charm," she said archly, "or so he keeps telling me. If it's any comfort, he warms on further acquaintance. He's very loyal to Adam and he really couldn't stand Gay, even after all those years." She chuckled.

In reply, I kicked open the dishwasher. Caroline appeared with a pile of coffee cups and saucers teetering Pisa-like in her plump, polish-tipped fingers. "I know it's insulting after all that lovely food, but I don't suppose you have any candy lying around?" I produced a bar of dark Valrhona from the back of the refrigerator, where I had hidden it inside an empty egg carton to keep the kids from eating it. Caroline accepted it gleefully. "Fan-freaking-tastic. I love chocolate—did you know it's supposed to be an aphrodisiac?" She pronounced it like the old name for Zimbabwe. "I just like it because it's fattening." She smiled lasciviously. "Gay wouldn't have candy in the house. I used to have to stop at the Duane Reade on the way home and buy a Snickers bar."

Jenny reached her hands out and snapped her fingers, demanding a piece. "Caroline, I was just telling Edith that Baxter never got on with Gay."

"Heck, no. He used to call her Gary. Behind her back, obviously," said Caroline through a mouthful of chocolate.

I wondered fleetingly what names he would be calling me.

"So how long have you two known each other?" Caroline asked, a little slyly, breaking off a square of chocolate and putting it into her smiling mouth. "I must say, Adam's kept you very secret. We hadn't a clue until Adam told Baxter that he'd met this 'amazing woman.' Gay is spitting, apparently." I stuck my face into the dishwasher to avoid answering and got a blast of hot, damp air leftover from the last batch of plates.

My glasses steamed up.

"Everyone says she's livid. I think she thought she could swan back whenever she felt like it. Have you met her? You haven't turned to stone, so I assume not." The two women sniggered.

"Oh, she dropped by," I muttered, piling clean crockery into a space in the nearest cupboard. It wasn't where they went, but I rammed the door shut, sending the mugs rattling to the back of the cupboard as if they'd just been confronted by a fat man in a crowded elevator, knowing that I'd be sneaking back to rearrange them later.

"Well, the food has certainly improved since you arrived—not to mention Adam's mood. I don't know what you're putting in his tea, honey, but it's done wonders for him. He looks really happy for the first time in years." Caroline patted my arm.

"You should give me some for Baxter; he could do with a bit of tenderizing," Jenny added.

"Honey, don't you thump meat with a mallet to tenderize it?" said Caroline.

"Oh, poor baby, he can be such a pain in the ass." She rolled the *r* as though it was going to unfurl from her mouth like a party streamer. "The truth is that he's just being stupidly protective of Adam, who is obviously completely crazy about you. I think Baxter just wanted to make sure you weren't a Gay II, the sequel, which of course you're not. He'll be eating out of your hand like a pampered pug by the next time you meet. I promise." It was kind of the women to try to reassure me, but I sincerely doubted that Baxter and I would ever bond.

Furthermore, he had been absolutely right about Oxford.

My life in the droopy, dilapidated house on Plantation Road, pigeon-chested with ornate wrought-iron balconies and squeezed like a sharp intake of breath between a block of apartments and the Carpenter's Arms, had indeed been dull and uneventful.

That's exactly why I had loved it.

However, it had been fifteen years since Francisco and I lived there.

12

I DROVE THROUGH HARVARD Square and headed for Garden Street, where I was lucky enough to find a parking meter only a block away from the institute. I crunched up the gravel path to the blond-bricked building. The entrance hall, normally milling with bodies, was deserted, as you would expect in early June when almost everyone had gone for the summer and those few still on campus were sleeping off hangovers. Even my flip-flops, slapping the flagstone floor, seemed intrusively noisy.

A couple of inadequately pinned papers and posters fluttered as the door swung closed behind me, sucking the air out of the already stifling corridor. I pressed the buzzer, and James let me in to the air-conditioned reception area, where he sat barricaded behind a desk in a starched dark-blue uniform like a militiaman at an African border crossing. The air was thick with ozone from the row of slit-eyed Xerox machines lined up like sleeping alligators all along one wall.

"Good morning, Miz Morales," he wheezed, dragging his eyes away from the paperback novel he was holding like a sandwich in one big brown fist. "You still here?" he asked, somewhat unnecessarily, since I was standing there in front of him.

I explained that Francisco had left already for Colombia so I was spending my evenings at home with Ray Charles, Tom Wolfe, and Jack Daniel. I think he thought these were the names of three college students, so my attempt at humor was lost on him. He couldn't have been less interested in my activities if I'd started reciting the chord sequences from "Georgia on My Mind." His rheumy eyes glazed over. If he had been fifty years younger, he would have said, "Whatever." As the director's wife, I had no function or identity of my own. I seriously doubted whether anyone in the college even knew my own surname. I was merely a plus one to Francisco, and without him I became a virtual nobody, a minister without portfolio.

With Francisco on sabbatical next term, the odious John Willis was taking over as director until Christmas and it would be John's long-faced wife, Sylvia, who would be decanting the Costco wine boxes and hosting the welcome parties. It would be she who reassured the Muslim students that the pork cocktail sausages were a hundred percent halal beef, at the same time telling the vegetarians they were tofu.

If I wouldn't have to endure one more meet-and-mingle lunch while reining my Scottish accent into slow sentences with all the syllables fully articulated, I'd be a happy woman.

This would almost make up for the fact that I would be stuck in Cambridge over the summer, but it was a very, very small consolation. The original plan had been that we would both go to Colombia until December, but at the last minute Francisco had announced that he needed to go alone. His grandmother had died in the spring, and as well as taking a trip to inspect the program he was running in Panama, he would have to sort out her estate and take a trip to the farm, which she had left him in her will. He claimed he needed some time "to think" and that he had too much to do. How could he hope to get any writing done? He despaired. In short: I would be in the way.

He suggested that I wait until the end of September and join him at the university in Bogotá, which was a bit like winning a weekend on Alcatraz instead of a Caribbean cruise, but nevertheless, I bowed to the inevitable. With Francisco, I was so used to bowing to the inevitable I had calluses on my knees.

I let myself into Francisco's office and checked through his papers to see if there was anything urgent, then went back to reception and collected the mail jammed into the director's pigeonhole, which I would sort and forward if necessary. Then, as usual, I flicked through the *M* slot, where some of our mail invariably ended up. Mendez, Maconde, Mahboubi, Mohammad, Miller, Mistook, but nothing for Morales.

And then my fingers froze on a long, pale-blue envelope, tucked away at the back, addressed to MS. AGNES MCBRIDE, C/O THE LATIN AMERICAN INSTITUTE FOR ENVIRONMENT STUDIES. The words took up most of two lines.

Damn it. What now? I didn't have to look at the postmark with its array of foreign stamps to know it was from Edinburgh. My heart plummeted like a suicide off a bridge. What did they want? More money, probably. They usually contacted the lawyer or Geordie about the financial stuff. Geordie was the family cash cow these days, but if there had been any other problem, surely they would have got in touch with Maisie, who would then have rung me. The envelope bulged, pregnant with unknown dread. Whatever was inside, it couldn't be good. I glanced over my shoulder to see if James was watching, but he was licking his finger and painstakingly turning a page.

Quickly I slipped the envelope into the middle of the rest of my mail and turned swiftly back into the hallway, calling goodbye over my shoulder to James, who merely harrumphed in reply. My voice shook as if it were walking in heels.

Outside in the street, the sun smacked me flat in the face like a flashbulb.

A lone girl in a lilac dress with a dazed, still drunk, sleep-creased expression was drifting across the campus like a crushed flower, carrying her shoes in her hands.

Not one of our students, I decided, examining her face, the remains of last night's mascara lying in a grubby crescent under her eyes; probably a casualty from a late-night party going back to her dorm after waking up in the wrong bed.

I watched as she approached, lost in her own dreamy thoughts, bending to unchain a bicycle from the tangle of others crammed into the rack. As she left, I saw my younger self, winding back to my room in Summertown with blisters on my feet the morning after another party, at another college, in another town, on another continent. Three thousand miles and twenty years away.

Francisco and I met in Oxford when he was writing up his thesis on the effects of deforestation on indigenous people in some obscure South American country. Well, I say obscure, but back then I thought Colombia was a TV detective and Honduras a small Japanese car, so it probably wasn't quite as rarefied as it seemed. We met in the Centre for Latin American Studies on Woodstock Road. This, in itself, was not unusual: I met everyone in my office, since it was merely a desk with a sit-up-and-beg manual typewriter right in the middle of the main reading room, like an aid package dropped onto a desert island. Here I drank coffee, smoked cigarettes in those far-off halcyon days when you could light up inside and nobody shot you, made change for the Xerox machine, typed two-fingered letters heavy with white-out fluid, and chatted to students as they arrived for their tutorials. Back then, he was just another scruffy student with too much facial hair and not the distinguished professor he later became. He was not tall, only a little taller than myself, but with a halo of dark, luxuriant curls that added a couple of inches to his height. The first thing that struck me was that he had the coldest, bluest eyes I'd ever seen. The second thing was his voice. Though he'd lived in America off and on since he was in his teens, he had retained the lilting cadence of an accent that, at will, he could sprinkle through his speech like the cinnamon on a cappuccino. The building where I worked, part of a seventeenth-century convent, had once been a chapel before a reverence for books and learning overtook that which was held for God, but a respectful hush still pressed its palm over the place, making loud conversation an affront. There was something sinfully furtive and intimate about the quiet, exotic way he spoke, the stained-glass windows raising their shocked eyebrows at us from the altar now covered in reference books, and within half an hour I was totally hooked. I discovered that he had done his undergraduate degree at Yale and that he had a black-eyed brunette with an overbite back home to whom he was practically engaged. I couldn't have cared less—I was concerned only with the long-distance part of the story, not with the relationship. I had already time-shared Karl with his high school *liebchen* and the woman who would eventually be his wife, so what difference did a girlfriend three thousand miles away make to me? Opposite my office on the other side of the Woodstock Road was a row of glowering, double-fronted houses set back from the street. At number 62 there was a heavily laden flowering almond tree, hunched underneath the weight of its pink crepe blossoms, where Karl lived. We had dated on and off for a couple of years while his girlfriend, a diminutive, overexercised jockess with perfect teeth and a surgically enhanced nose, was finishing her own Ph.D. somewhere in Virginia. Across the hall from him there had been Bruce Grossman, a pretty-boy Australian whom I went out with the previous winter until he left for a job in Sydney, and at 64, a diminutive Egyptian whom I had poached from an American economist named Nancy, until he went to work for the UN. Finally, at 66, until a couple of weeks before Francisco arrived, there had been an Italian anthropologist who, roughly in the same time frame, had wanted to marry me. Unfortunately, his mother had other ideas, and he was now back living at home in Rome with a doctorate but no fiancée. I slept with them all, serially and concurrently. I did them like declining verbs. What can I tell you? I was a regular one-woman United Nations of sex.

So, with the Italian gone, I now had a vacancy. And weekends to fill. And, most important, no central heating. I was always cold in those days. Oxford was a damp place in the winter. I often wished I had chosen somewhere warmer to live, but then I hadn't really chosen Oxford in the first place. It had chosen me. I was sixteen and wretched beyond words. I had been back home for the last of several brief and deeply uncomfortable meetings with my parents and the lawyer and had not been encouraged to linger. I wasn't eager to return to my aunt's boardinghouse in Scarborough, which, by now, was perpetually full of querulous and demanding senior citizens on bus tours who had me running up and down the stairs like a demented bluebottle. So whether it was chance or subconscious design that I got on the wrong train in York, fell asleep, and ended up chugging my way to Oxford, I'm not sure. But when I arrived, instead of crossing to platform 2 and retracing my steps, I was washed out of the station in the flood of young people gushing through the open arms of the doors, each dashing off in their own purposeful direction. For the first time in almost a year, I felt a wonderful invisibility fit over me like a well-tailored coat. No one noticed me; no one looked at me; I felt like a wartime evacuee whose label had fallen off. On impulse, I stopped a taxi driver and asked him if there was a youth hostel nearby, and he drove me to the bottom end of the Abingdon Road, where I moved into a dormitory in the YWCA. It was five days before I thought to let my aunt know I intended to stay there. I had done a typing course over the winter in Scarborough until the scrutiny of the other girls became unbearable, and, though slow, I managed to get an interview at a temp agency on the High Street. The first job they sent me to was that of a temporary receptionist in the admissions office at Balfour College, but, with my accent requiring subtitles, it was decided that I would be much better suited to a post where vocal interaction wasn't essential. When a position came up as a typist in the Centre for Latin American Studies, I carried my coffee cup three doors north, set it down at another desk, and began a perfectly calm, quiet, and anonymous life surrounded by men, all only to happy to absorb me. My living arrangements were less comfortable. I couldn't wait to get away from the intrusive estrogen of the dormitory, where the presence of so many meddlesome and opinionated girls made me feel claustrophobic. The minute I found something I could afford on my meager wages, I moved into a room in the inaptly named Summertown, where it always seemed to be damp.

Privacy was all well and good, but my room was freezing, with only an electric blanket between me and hypothermia. In common with all the men I made a habit of dating since I arrived in Oxford, Francisco lived in college accommodations and had radiators that were always on—even in June—and a maid who vacuumed once a week. I'm not altogether sure if the warm feeling I got whenever I thought of him had to do with his personality or his access to constant hot water. He used to joke that I had only married him for his central heating, but he was only half wrong. He also had a house on Plantation Road. By the time we had swapped small talk and tea in the college refectory, I was already penciling Francisco Eduardo Alvaro Morales, all the way from Colombia by way of Manhattan, in to my life.

He was shy and low key, and though his eyes were icy sharp, he exuded a calm unruffledness and an irresistible I-can't-believe-you're-really-flirting-with-me modesty. By October I was his unofficial roommate, by December the girlfriend was an ex, and in May when he submitted his thesis, he also accepted a junior teaching post at Balfour. Francisco's job not only gave him full dining privileges and a fat pension plan. It also came with its own subsidized accommodation with three floors, a cellar, and a front door that I could lock behind me at night. And that's when I married him.

13

AT THE BEGINNING of December, just over eighteen months after we first met, I had been presented with Francisco's dead mother's extremely old-fashioned engagement ring. He sneaked into my office before I arrived in the morning and, in a sentimental gesture not since repeated, typed out on an index card in uneven, one-fingered courier "Will you marry me?" and left the ring on the space bar of my typewriter. I was halfway through my first cigarette before I noticed it glinting on its Bakelite ledge and, when I reached for it, knocked it tumbling into the tinny, clawing levers of X, C, V, and B. By the time I rescued it and slipped it onto my finger, the index card was matted with overtyping.

It was a square emerald set in gold the color of oranges in syrup, with sharp-faceted diamonds on either side. I couldn't quite believe how big it was, nor could my mother. Her small, blotting-paper eyes darted toward my finger as I lifted a cigarette to my mouth.

"Is it not heavy?" she asked. Relations, though strained, had been maintained over the years by painful three-day visits at Christmas, mostly made because students also had a tendency to go home at that time of year, and even I didn't have the stomach for a TV dinner in my room by myself. But this preseasonal trip had been taken to break the news that I was getting married, and my mother, in her own restrained, lugubrious, and critical way, was delighted. Finally, I had done something right.

In the place of bunting, balloons, and family celebrations, we had store-bought cake and mother-and-daughter smoking sessions.

She even shared her Lucky Strikes.

"There's a bit of money in that ring. Unlucky, though—green," she added. "Green for envy."

"Well, I don't think I'll have much trouble with that, will I?"

She lifted her chin in disagreement, offended. "I don't know. You've got a good job, a good life. Things turned out all right for *you*," she said accusingly.

I kept my mouth shut. I didn't really want to pursue this subject.

"Are you planning on bringing him up to meet us at Christmas?"

"No. We're going to see his family. His dad's an ambassador at the UN."

"Ambassador?" she harrumphed. I wasn't sure this constituted a proper job in my mother's eyes.

"You'll see him at the wedding. He's very nice," I mumbled inadequately.

"But you're not planning on getting married here, are you?" Her eyes snapped open like poppers.

"No, we'll do it in Oxford."

"That's good, because I told you—there's nothing left of your wedding money. It's all spent. And more. We're living on a pension now."

"We'll pay for it ourselves. We're not planning anything grand."

"As long as you're sure he'll be good to you," she said; then, satisfied that he wasn't going to cost her anything, she asked for another look at the photograph I had brought.

"Touch of the tar brush about him, though."

"Mum, he's tanned. He's from South America."

"Aye, whatever you say. Still—your bairns will look like darkies."

"There won't be bairns," I said.

"Oh get away with you, Agnes. You say that now." I didn't waste my breath contradicting her; I saved it for the smoke. She gave her scruffy slippers with the sheepskin trim a minute inspection, turning her heel as though she were trying on a pair of dancing shoes. "Does he know about your wee bit of trouble?"

"No."

"That's right. He doesn't need to know. Don't bother saying anything." Eventually I rose. I didn't want to pursue this. I headed for the kitchen, hoping to escape, but wincing and groaning, she inched herself out of her chair and hobbled after me.

"Agnes, it's not too late to have children of your own. Life is long. You've got every chance." She slid her words like a knife through butter.

"No, Mum. Don't go on about it."

"You did the right thing at the time."

"I didn't get a choice, if you remember," I snapped, lifting my eyes to stare at her, daring her to contradict me.

She didn't.

I filled up the kettle, plugged it in, and spooned Nescafé into a couple of mugs. My mother leaned against the washing machine, her hip indenting on the Formica worktop as she settled herself to wait for the water to boil. There was a long silence as the kettle cleared its throat and whined into life.

I pretended to be interested in the row of frozen cabbages in the back garden, while my mother tapped her cigarette into the sink. The hot ash made a satisfyingly spiteful hiss as it landed in the drain. I couldn't think why I had ever thought it was a good idea to come home. I could have done all this on the phone, but I had wanted to show my mother that I could make a success of my life my own way. I should have known she wouldn't be happy until I had two point four Protestant children, one of whom was called Agnes. That alone was a sufficient excuse for birth control.

To my relief, when it came to the actual wedding, my parents declined to attend, and I convinced Francisco that their reasons had to do with their health rather than indifference, and he didn't press the matter.

We were married in a register office with only Francisco's closest friend from college as best man and my ex-lover Karl, who, in the absence of anyone more qualified for the job, stood in as the bridesmaid. Though we tried to convince ourselves it was an impulsive, romantic event, the register office was situated on the upper levels of a brutal concrete shopping center in the middle of Oxford, and the occasion was about as close to a picture-book wedding as I was to a virgin bride. A damp caul of fog hung over the city, and it rained expressively all day long. I wore a long black lace skirt that I had bought at a flea market and had my bicycle slicker draped over my head like a veil for the dash from the car to the ceremony. In the afternoon we ate sausage rolls and chocolate éclairs at an informal party in what had once been the vestry and was now the conference room at the Centre for Latin American Studies. The toast to the bride was an enthusiastic one, especially among the seventy-five percent of the guests who had slept with her. It was more like a stag party than a wedding.

The next evening we boarded a flight to New York, where we played the final date on Francisco and Agnes's let's-get-hitched tour. Unfortunately, the Manhattan audience was lukewarm and less inclined to celebrate with high-calorie snacks.

Over on the other side of the pond, Señor Morales embraced his new daughter-in-law with slightly less warmth than you might show to a three-days-dead fish. The banishing of Miss Preppy Princess, Francisco's original intended, had been the first punch to land on the elder Morales' shoulders. The sudden appearance on the scene of Miss Scotland, who not only came from the wrong side of the tracks but the wrong side of the Atlantic Ocean, with the family heirloom already wedged on her finger, was the final knockout blow.

But in his stilted Spanish accent he managed to formally welcome me to the family. He did the honorable thing and swallowed his objections like a piece of gristle he was too polite to spit into his napkin, praying that I would be merely the practice wife. He himself had rehearsed at length, finally getting it right with number four, Herminia. There was every hope that Francisco would follow suit. I was so far from his idea of a match for his brilliant son that he didn't even know where to begin his protest—and anyway it was too late, since the ring was already mine. So he summoned a bottle of Krug, hijacked from another, more warmly anticipated occasion, and we drank ourselves catatonically drunk in close to ten minutes.

So that was meet-the-folks, done and dusted. The family, such as it was, consisted of Señor Morales, madrastra Herminia—who had a fulfilling career visiting the hairdresser, the dermatologist, and the manicurist—and a matching pair of ever-changing Hispanic housemaids who were always called Maria something. It saved Herminia, bless her, the bother of having to learn new names. She had something in common with my family after all.

For my part, my sister, Maisie, had put herself into voluntary exile by emigrating to a suburb outside Adelaide twenty years earlier, while my brother Geordie, the success of the family, was off playing poker with other people's money in an investment bank in the Far East.

He had never married, but according to the annual Christmas card, now had a girlfriend who worked in the same department and worshipped the same stocks and bonds. My mother and father saw no need to hang banners in the hallway for the new husband. We would communicate by phone and photograph until they felt like braving the long railway journey to Oxford and visiting us, which they never, in any of the succeeding years, attempted to do. They had already limited their physical contact with me and were happy to extend the same courtesy to Francisco.

So, as far as I was concerned, it was really just me and Francisco, the house on Plantation Road, and this brand-new surname that I could adopt and disappear into. Finally, I could rise from the ashes into a brand-new life and bury the incinerated remains of the old one.

14

UNTIL CHANCE RAKED them up again.

In Manhattan, autumn chewed up the months, and the glitz of Christmas itched only a few weeks away. It wasn't my favorite time of year, but, despite everything, I couldn't help being infected by the frenzied excitement that quivered around Lennie's increasingly elevated heels as the holy festival of consumerism approached. It was something of a novelty.

Since his father left the UN a couple of years after Francisco was offered the directorship of the institute at Harvard, we were excused family Christmases. Señor Morales had had enough of both me and New England winters by then and preferred the warmth of the Southern Hemisphere. If we weren't traveling ourselves, Francisco and I would either drive over to visit friends who had a little house in Amherst or stay quietly in Cambridge for the holidays. We never bothered with a tree and made do with a Mexican nativity scene and one simple gift exchanged on Christmas Eve, which was usually a book for Francisco and a scarf for me. I didn't wear scarves, but that fact didn't concern Francisco, who obviously thought he was married to a different kind of woman, which also accounted for the several pairs of earrings I had accumulated, all of which were for pierced ears, while my lobes remained smooth and unpunctured.

In Manhattan a cheerfully uncomplicated Ned had come home twice, each time accompanied by a series of shape-shifting friends with voices as shrill as Windex on glass, who ate their way through the refrigerator like locusts in football shirts.

The phone rang constantly for Lennie, while plans for parties and sleepovers and a list of must-have presents appeared on the refrigerator, with items crossed off and reinstated according to whichever magazine was most recent on the newsstand.

Outside on Lexington, Christmas lights glittered atop the pyramids of satsumas and pomegranates in every store, while flaming poinsettias lined the stalls outside on the street, and conifers leaned against the walls at the Boy Scouts' lot like unemployed migrant workers waiting for a pickup. The windows of the stores on Madison sparkled silver and gold, crammed with stuff I didn't want and certainly didn't need, but which nevertheless entranced me. I had a wonderful, heady feeling of happy anticipation—a sense that everything was possible and attainable.

The children were flying to London with Gay for New Year's, and Lennie had already extracted from me a whole list of things she should see while there, all of which I had cribbed from a guidebook I found in the Corner Bookstore. This left Adam and me blissfully alone and checking in to the Ritz-Carlton Hotel, where he had booked a suite for three nights. "It will be our new start for the new year," he maintained.

I squashed the voice in my head screaming at me from across the desk in the headmistress's study, where I had been dragged to account for myself: What new start, McBride? Just let me have this, I pleaded. Just this, and then I promise, cross my heart, swear, that I'll get back on track. The headmistress was unimpressed. I told her to fuck off. I was so excited that my stomach filled with butterflies and my toes curled. Ankle-deep carpeting that I didn't have to vacuum, adolescent sex, eye-shades, a tub big enough to swim in, and twenty-four-hour room service. The prospect hung there in the future like the star on top of my own personal Christmas tree, the last unopened door on my Advent calendar.

However, until then I still had to deal with the hormones that hit you in the face like a blast of Poison in the perfume hall at Bloomingdale's. Lennie had had her retainer removed at the end of November, and most of her brain at the same time. Her school uniform was rapidly modified. The skirts got shorter, the socks became pantyhose, the shoes, bought after much wheedling, with my help and grave misgivings, grew several inches higher, the pretty hair was expensively cut and gelled into jagged peaks, and her green eyes acquired rings of black eyeliner that leaked down her cheeks as if she were going to tour with a KISS tribute band.

She came and went through the house as it suited her. She and Leila, often in a clump of similarly scantily clad girls with sullen, underfed expressions and high-pitched, overdramatic and underwhelmed voices, trailed back from school later and later, until I found myself lingering by the window in the parlor, peering through the curlicues of iron tulips, waiting anxiously for her to get back. On Saturdays she wanted to hang around at unspecified locations with her friends and come home late, unaccompanied, in a cab off the street. I nearly choked on the prospect.

Adam had no idea who her friends were or who she was with, but he was happy as long as she was out enjoying herself. Boys' names fell from her newly glossed lips as if she had Tourette's, her neckline plunged with her mood, and what had once been a bovine, sweetly agreeable nature became full-scale attitude.

"You're not my mom," she said, when I suggested she should wear something a bit less revealing than a cropped T-shirt to stalk the aisles of the store du jour.

I was torn. There was nothing I wanted more than to back off, but I couldn't. It was bringing back too many uncomfortable memories. In spite of myself, I kept after her.

"But doesn't Gay mind your going out in only a sweater in the middle of winter?" I was being kind calling the two pieces of string and the dinner napkin Lennie was wearing a sweater.

"She doesn't care, and neither does my dad, so I don't see that it's any of your business. You're hardly one to talk about looking cheap."

I swallowed my terrier urge to rip her throat out. Calmly, I said: "Lennie, I'm not saying anything about looking cheap; I just think you have to be aware of the kind of message you're sending out. You're only fifteen. You look twenty. Men will think you're more experienced than you are. You don't know how their brains work."

"Yeah, but you do. You must know how men think, since it didn't take you long to get your hooks into my dad. Maybe you should be giving me lessons."

"I just don't want you to make the same mistakes I did," I stammered, but the words were difficult to say; dragging them out of my mouth felt like pulling a cork with my teeth.

"What?"

"I just wish you'd be more careful about attracting the wrong kind of attention. I do know what I'm talking about. Believe me. I had to learn the hard way."

"Whatever. Leave me alone—it's none of your goddamn business."

"Len . . ." I remonstrated, but she was gone.

I took hold of my temper with both hands and held it down till it surrendered. Otherwise I would have kicked her legs out from under her and asked her who the hell she thought she was talking to. When dealing with Lennie for those difficult weeks, I regularly informed the God I didn't believe in that he ought to be canceling out some of my sins for having enough self-restraint not to wallop the nasty little beast.

I got no further when I tried to reason with Adam.

"She's young—she'll grow out of it. Weren't you the same when you were a teenager?"

"Exactly the same," I agreed.

"Well," he said, shrugging in a helpless what's-the-biggie sort of way.

"But I didn't grow out of it; it just got to be a habit," I muttered.

"What do you mean?" But I pretended not to hear. I could still turn a teenager's deaf ear when the mood took me.

"She looks like a ho," added Ned from inside the cupboard, where he was looking for cookies. I had found an unexpected ally in the anti-sluttification of his sister. "I told her she was turning into a slut, but she just told me to suck it."

"Don't call your sister a slut—in fact, don't call anyone that word. And don't say 'suck it'—it's crude."

"She did."

"Surely not."

"Oh, Edie, you're so naive," said Ned, with all the world-weariness of a thirteen-year-old who has toast crumbs around his mouth and is wearing a shrunken Spider-Man T-shirt.

I gave him a wry look. "I'm not the naive one; it's your father who needs convincing. Hasn't Gay said anything to you about it, Adam?"

"Mom thinks it's all your fault, Edie," Ned supplied matter-of-factly. ' "What can you expect when she's living with Slutsky and Bitch?' " he repeated in a reedy voice that was apparently supposed to mimic Gay's snooty accent.

"Ned . . ." cautioned Adam, but Ned shrugged, a fistful of cashew nuts in each hand. " 'S not my fault—I'm just telling you what she says. I don't call you that." Adam looked as though he was trying not to laugh as Ned disappeared back into the basement. "Ah, well, Gay . . ." He blew out his lips. "I haven't heard that one—I'm usually privy to the less witty epithets—but, yes, now that you mention it, there have been mutterings that your presence has been inciting the craven use of eyeliner. But bear in mind that Gay was still wearing navy-blue school underwear—with name tapes—when I first met her—and I was in my senior year at Yale before I got near them."

"But it's not me, or Gay, we're talking about here: it's Lennie. You should always be sure you know where she is, Adam. Speak to Gay—make sure you both have some idea what she's up to. At least make her leave the telephone number of where she's going—and if she's supposed to be spending the night somewhere, speak to the parents and check it out."

"She has a pager."

"And she claims she *forgets* to turn it on, but most of the time I think she just doesn't bother to answer it."

"I don't know why you're so worried. She's not duplicitous enough to actually lie, surely?"

"I was."

"I can't believe that," he said, smiling and grabbing me round the waist and dancing me round. "Not my sensible, goodie-two-shoes Edith. I bet you rescued kittens and helped old ladies cross the street. You couldn't tell a lie if you tried. You're an angel. Sent from heaven to make me—what are we having tonight?" He stopped and sniffed the air.

"Roast lamb," I supplied.

"See—practically perfect in every way." I scoffed. Men. Feed them, fuck them, they think you walk on water. Thank God.

Eventually, he did agree to be more attentive, but I could tell it was only to please me and not because he thought it was necessary. However, I had to drop the subject for the time being because I had other things to fret about. We were having people for supper—with the emphasis on the *we*. I was now fully installed as mistress of the house—in all senses of the word.

Baxter was coming with his horsehair wife. He had warmed to me a little over the past weeks, but he still had a tendency to snipe every now and again from up there in the control tower of Bastardtown. Adam insisted that it was merely an affectation and that Baxter had a heart of gold. The two had gone to Yale together, and Adam maintained a stubborn fondness for Baxter that couldn't be shaken, and, to be honest, I didn't try. He was a loyal friend, if not a particularly sweet-natured one, so I gave him the benefit of the doubt.

I had yet to meet the other guests. They had been Gay's friends but had defected to Adam after the breakup. The man was a banker, but I didn't know what the woman did. It didn't matter; I hardly expected her to be president of the housewives' union. We'd probably get stuck on theater and movies. I hadn't been to either in recent memory, but I read the reviews so I could manage to sound knowledgeable.

With Baxter in mind, planning the menu I had decided to forgo "that foreign crap," as he had so winningly referred to some of my past offerings while nevertheless having several helpings of everything. So we were having a traditional roast, and a boarding-school steamed pudding made with persimmons, which, just like Baxter, had a tendency to dry the mouth if not ripe.

The kitchen I could manage. Even the prospect of entertaining with a smile I positively embraced. What I couldn't deal with, increasingly, was Lennie. Every decision I made about the day-to-day running of the house was questioned and contradicted.

First it was the food fads, then it was the mess—the careless flotsam left strewn in her wake. I didn't want to give Gay the satisfaction of knowing her daughter had me on the ropes begging for mercy. So I bore it as best I could. Nevertheless, the girl drove me so high up the fucking newly painted walls that I was surprised to see there weren't claw marks on the ceiling.

Truly, there weren't enough orgasms in the world to make this teenage crap worth shoveling.

I had thought Lennie was staying in for the evening, but she suddenly declared that she had plans. She came downstairs at five o'clock wearing jeans, for which I got down on my knees and personally thanked the patron saint of denim. I was less delighted with the divinity in charge of the low-cut, sparkly top that clung, barely, to her chest.

I eyed a pair of pushed-up breasts that would have put a pair of Cornish hens to shame. She was definitely her mother's daughter. I made wide eyes at Adam, who was busying himself in the dining room, putting water glasses on the table and trying to look like a man who did this sort of thing every day instead of employing people to do it for him.

"I'm going out," she announced, swinging her purse. "I need money."

"Honey, don't you think that's a bit too much?" Adam protested, looking at her neckline and wincing.

I coughed, pointedly.

"Where exactly are you going?" he added.

"To Doug's place, on Park Avenue." Doug—I hadn't heard this name before. I willed him to ask questions.

"And Doug would be . . ." inquired Adam.

"From school." He seemed to accept that.

"But Lennie, you go to an all-girls school," I added.

"I know." She gave me a look of annoyance. "But—I—met—him—on—the—way—home—from—school, didn't I? He goes to Regis. A group of us are going to his house." What group? I screamed silently.

"Where on Park?" Adam asked.

"At Sixty-third."

"And how are you getting there?"

"I'll walk."

"It's twenty blocks."

"Okay, I'll take a cab."

"You are not walking down the street *or* hailing a cab looking like that."

"I'll have my coat on, Dad."

"And how are you getting back?"

"We're all spending the night." Adam looked at me for guidance. I shook my head, trying to disguise it as a crick in the neck and failing.

"It's got nothing to do with you, Edie, so butt out."

"Leonora—cut it out. You will not talk to Edith like that. And anyway, it's not Edith you have to convince; it's me. I want you back home. By midnight. We don't even know this guy. Give me the address, and I'll have the car service pick you up." Adam began to pat his pockets for a pen.

Lennie looked thunderous. "That's so lame."

"You either come home or you don't go." Lennie seemed to know she was beaten. A few further halfhearted protests followed before, finally, she flounced upstairs, fighting tears. Adam and I exchanged glances, both feeling as though we had narrowly missed being hit by a speeding car.

"Will you talk to her?" Adam asked.

"Not me; you should go. I never seem to say the right thing." I wasn't overeager to step into the lion's den. I was fed up getting my hand bitten off. Let her do what she wanted. What did I care? She wasn't my responsibility.

"Please, Edie, I'm out of my depth here." Okay, so it was my responsibility . . .

I waited a second and followed her. By the time I got upstairs to her gaping bedroom door, her face was already smudged with eyeliner, spilled like ink all across her face.

She looked up at me pitifully. "All I want to do is go out and see my friends," she said in a broken voice. "What's so bad about that?" I sat on the bed and waited for her to stop emptying the contents of her purse, theatrically, all over the floor. There was a pack of cigarettes among the lipstick and crumpled tissues, one of which she wadded into her fist and used to dab her eyes.

The cigarettes terrified me. Her mother would kill her and me if she knew she was smoking. How the hell did she get anyone to sell them to her? I knew that I had to say something, but I didn't know what and I didn't want to make an even bigger scene. I had no experience dealing with teenage girls. I didn't even have any girlfriends. The silence stewed. And then it occurred to me: just try being Mrs. Director. When Francisco's research students came to me crying because they thought they would never finish their theses, or worrying about pregnancies, parental expectations, and problems back home in a rural part of Latin America that just didn't translate into Harvardese, I knew just what was needed: briskness and common sense.

"Look, Lennie, it's not that bad . . . Your dad is just worried about you." She sniffed and glared at me as though I'd just ripped the leg off a baby and stuck it on a spit.

Empathy, then, I thought.

"I do know how you feel. When I was a kid, my parents were so strict that I could hardly move. Once my father even came and dragged me out of a youth-club dance because I was ten minutes late."

"I'm not a kid."

"Okay, point taken." I tried again. Sincerity this time.

"Nobody wants to spoil your fun, but when I was about your age I got myself into tons of trouble, and it makes me a bit nervous watching you—oh, I don't know—being young, I guess. I'm sorry—I can't help it."

"What kind of trouble?" She stopped kicking clothes around and sat next to me on the bed.

"Bad, bad trouble . . ." I made a dismissive gesture, but, at last, I had her attention.

"No, tell me."

"Well . . ." I hesitated, ready, even now, to just smooth it over, but I went on. "One night my friend Kirsty and I sneaked off to a party that my parents had told me I couldn't go to, and while I was there, a fight broke out, and I was hit on the head with a chair."

"No! Really? That's awesome! What happened?" She had swapped purses and was cramming makeup into the new one. The cigarettes, hidden inside a cosmetic bag, were quickly concealed in its depths. I wondered whether I should pretend not to notice. You have to pick your battles—and this probably wasn't the best time for this one.

"Not that awesome—the chair knocked me out, and I came to on the floor with blood on my face and everybody looking at me."

"Oh my God, that's unbelievable—how cool!" she said.

"Actually, it was ugly. Really ugly." In spite of myself, I shuddered.

She relaxed and threw herself back on her pillows, waiting for the rest of the story.

"So there I was, legs in the air, black eye, flat on my back on the floor, covered in blood, and the next thing the police were called, and I found I'd lost all my money, and we were about six miles from home. It was a really long walk—you know, deserted country lanes—middle of the night? My parents hadn't a clue where I was, so I could hardly call them up from a phone booth and say, come and get me." Lennie laughed, but nervously.

"I was too scared to go to hospital, because then they would have found out that I'd sneaked off."

"So what did you do?"

"Walked it—but don't go getting any ideas . . . "

"Walked home in the middle of the night? You must have had rocks in your head. Were you crazy? Weren't you scared?"

"No, that's the point. I wasn't, and I should have been, but it just never occurred to me at the time. I was so innocent, I just didn't think it through."

"But I'd never do anything like that."

"I'm not saying you would. I'm just saying that not every mistake you make seems like a bad idea at the time. You have to be sensible. Your dad isn't saying don't go; just let him send a car for you."

"But I'm not going to get bashed on the head. I'm only going to my friend's house—it's hardly running around with scissors, is it?" She started picking the nail polish off her fingers. I could have put on flamenco shoes and tapped it out in Morse code for all the impact I had made. I almost gave in.

"And while we're on the subject of being sensible, I don't want another fight, but I do want the pack of cigarettes."

I picked up her purse and offered it to her.

Her face quivered and flushed as she began to protest that they weren't hers, but I cut her short.

"Look, no explanations, no arguments, no lectures—not now, anyway—just hand them over."

Reluctantly she threw them onto the bed without looking at me.

"Don't tell my dad."

"We'll talk about it later. You're not stupid; you know what these things do to you. Now, okay—go and enjoy yourself, but come home afterward and don't let—whatsisname?"

"Doug."

"Don't let Doug get too much of a preview. You've got a great figure. You're gorgeous—you're too pretty to be that obvious." I nodded at her cleavage.

"Can I come home at two?"

"Midnight."

"One o'clock?" Since I figured there was a good chance that Baxter and wife would still be sitting around slugging liqueurs at one in the morning, I agreed and got her to write down the address and telephone number so we could send a car. "Let me help you clean your face up." I soaked a cotton pad in cleanser and carefully wiped off the black gloop.

"Models are supposed to put hemorrhoid cream on their eyes to stop the puffiness," I volunteered.

"What's hemorrhoid cream?"

I explained.

"Yuck—I think I'll keep the bags. Look, I'm sorry for being such a bitch, Edie," she muttered hastily. "You're okay, really."

"Don't worry about it—it's in the teenage job description." I gave her the stiff pat on the back that was my closest approximation to a maternal hug.

"Watch my hair," she said, giving me an equally pro forma hug back.

I gazed at the jagged fright of rigid mousse that stuck out in seven directions from her scalp. "It looks good," I said. She pulled a skimpy silk cardigan over her top and gently rearranged the fronds of her hair until they looked like the leaves on an aspidistra.

I don't know why I was so worried about her. Any male would have had his eye poked out if he went within six inches of her face.

"I need to call my mom," she said, grabbing a quick look at her watch. "Did I tell you she's going to take me to a spa next week? She's going to take a day off work, and we're going to have manicures and facials." She named a frighteningly expensive place that even a style-challenged shut-in like myself had heard of. I left the room as she dialed the number.

"Hey, Mom," she crowed, "you'll never guess. Remember that guy Doug I told you about? He actually called me—can you believe it? And Dad's letting me go to the party . . . I know!" She laughed delightedly.

My shoulders slumped as I closed her bedroom door and headed reluctantly back downstairs to the kitchen.

The smell of roasting meat and garlic assailed me, and this, I reminded myself, was really all I should have been concerning myself with.

It was just that sometimes—well, sometimes I forgot my place.

15

IT WAS HOUSEWIFE heaven. The dishwasher was running, the table was set, the candles were lit, and the stove would be pinging within the next half hour to signal that it was time to begin roasting the vegetables. It was really the simplest of meals. I had left myself only the task of soft polenta, which was unnecessary but would give me the excuse to hide in the kitchen between the butternut squash velouté and the roast.

Adam was wearing a cream shirt and a pair of jeans. I didn't have to dress up; I couldn't, in fact, dress up, since I didn't actually own a winter dress. But I thought I should change so that the first impression I made wasn't that of singed meat.

My few clothes hung somewhat forlornly in Gay's vacated closet. I almost wished Herminia would spring out of the shoe rack and invite me on a shopping trip. I had brought only my summer things, most of which were useless as winter engulfed me. We hadn't yet had the first snowstorm, but I knew I would have to buy some boots and sweaters if I wasn't going to die of hypothermia when the New York winter kicked in. So far I had survived by teaming a few of the skirts with pantyhose and two of Lennie's cast-off cardigans. I had also inherited a down coat that had once been hers. It protected me from the elements, but it also swamped me. She was at least two sizes larger. But I was grateful for her sudden interest in fashion, as without those items she rejected I would have had nothing to wear.

As it was, my choices were few: I could wear the black skirt with the white shirt or the clean jeans and the shrunken cashmere sweater with the snags at the cuffs that I had a horrible feeling had once belonged to Gay even before it had been gnawed upon by Lennie. I rejected the first choice as too utilitarian. I would look like a waiter. So, by default, it was the cashmere sweater and the clean jeans. I pushed up the sleeves to hide the frayed edges, rubbed my hair with a wet washcloth to flatten down the wisps that were flying around my face, frizzing dementedly with static electricity, and smiled at myself in the mirror.

"How nice to meet you," I said, several times in several keys. "*How-kind-of-you-to-let-me-come*," I hummed, transported briefly to the junior production of *My Fair Lady*, in which I had played, in turn, a dustman, a street urchin, and, because of my height, a nonspeaking male consort. Kirsty, of course, had been Eliza. I learned every one of her lines with her.

"*Now once again, where does it rain?*" I trilled. "*On the plain. On the plain.*" I bowed and curtsied. I wiggled my bottom. I sprayed myself with one of the least noxious of Lennie's perfumes to rid myself of Eau de Scullery, and waited with trepidation to see if it would make me sneeze. Miraculously it didn't; I hadn't had even the slightest wheeze in months. I looped the legs of my specs behind my ears, wearing them over my hair like a preppy headband, then slapped some color into my cheeks that I didn't really need. The kitchen was like a furnace, and my face was already flushed and slightly damp. I hoped I wouldn't be too hot in the sweater.

The doorbell rang. I looked at my watch. Quarter of eight. It would be the Baxters. They were always early.

Sure enough, downstairs Jenny was removing her voluminous crushed-velvet coat. I held out my hand for it. Baxter was wearing a Burberry raincoat that smelled of cigarettes and damp and a misplaced belief that his own status could be elevated by wearing overpriced designer clothing. It was pouring outside.

"Edith," he grunted, dropping his coat on the chair and giving me a frosty air kiss before walking straight upstairs to the drawing room. Jenny, however, her ubiquitous smile stretched from ear to ear on her broad, pixie face, raised her neck out of a roll of silk crepe ruffles and touched her cold cheek to mine, handed me a bottle of wine, and gave my arm a squeeze.

"Edie, you look incredibly well. Life must be agreeing with you. Something smells wonderful—what are you cooking? Is there anything I can do?" I declined her offer of help and sent her upstairs, where Adam was undoubtedly already tipping his good whiskey into Baxter's eager gullet.

"I'll be up in a second; I just have to get something from the kitchen," I said to her broad backside.

Inside, I peered into the oven, poured myself a few inches of vodka chilled from the freezer, and knocked it back. I lifted a tray laden with canapés—tiny blini with smoked salmon, each with a limp sprig of dill draped over it like an exhausted contortionist—and carried it upstairs.

The doorbell rang again as I reached the hallway. This time

it was an extremely tall man with a tiny black-clad wraith of a wife with too many too-white teeth and not enough skin, so slim that she could have slipped into her husband's breast pocket in place of the three-cornered pocket square it currently held. These would be the old friends. I didn't catch their names, as I was juggling coats, dripping umbrellas, a cellophane-wrapped bouquet from a smart florist that probably cost more than I earned in a week, and the tray of canapés, but I led them up to the parlor floor and busied myself rearranging plates and napkins on the low table while further introductions were made. Hands were gripped in turn, flaccidly and then bone-crunchingly, and careful kisses were bestowed. A distant ding-ding-ding reverberated below in the kitchen. I whispered in Adam's ear that I had to go tend to the food—and fled gratefully to the safety and delightful dearth of polite social discourse than can be found in a tray of roast parsnips.

I had just shut the crossword in a drawer and was stirring the soup when Adam poked his head round the door some twenty minutes later. "Is everything okay? Aren't you going to come up and have a drink?"

"In a second—I have to finish a few things here." He made a kissy face and, satisfied, disappeared bearing a bottle of Evian and another of champagne.

I stirred the soup again. But I hadn't even turned on the gas.

Ned sidled upstairs from the basement, where he was beating up hookers and drug dealers in a video game, and started to forage for peanut butter, as you do when you're a teenage drug lord in Miami. I made him a sandwich and sat at the table, watching him eat, until the timer sounded again. I couldn't delay things any longer. I had to take the meat out of the oven.

I sent Ned to tell Adam that dinner was served, splashed

some truffle oil into the soup, which I'd warmed, ladled it into bowls, and carried it out to the dining room.

Lights, camera, action. *How-kind-of-you-to-let-me-come*: I was on.

I sat on Adam's right. Jenny was opposite. Baxter, damn it, plonked himself next to me before I could direct him elsewhere.

I smiled companionably at the other guests at the nether reaches of the table, the way you do when your train breaks down in a tunnel, or you're stuck in some unforeseen situation that requires stoic good nature. Behind them, a lopsided, half-dressed Christmas tree that Adam had brought in that morning from the Boy Scouts, which Fred the doorman had helped him drag out of the car, hunched apologetically in the window like a handicapped flunky.

All it needed was a white napkin draped over one of its branches.

Jenny began to tell us, in almost forensic detail, about her family's plans for the holidays. Baxter grudgingly complimented me on the soup, which set off a round of appreciative sounds.

"It's delicious," said the small, dark woman—Sadie, Sandy, Saffy? I never did learn her name. "I love truffle oil. I would put it on my muesli if I could." One look at the woman was enough to reveal that she hadn't ever eaten muesli in her life. The oat flakes would have overwhelmed her.

Baxter had begun a long conversation about an earnest British rock band whose latest CD he had just bought. I heard him say: "Yes, they're astonishing, quite astonishing." Twat, I thought, as I nodded in agreement in case he started asking me if I knew them personally.

Jenny, meanwhile, had got to the twenty-seventh of December and was halfway to her sister's in Montreal—you know, there's a reason why those folks hide underground in winter. It was like listening to the time of day service: *At the tone I will lose—beep—my fucking—beep—mind.* I tuned her out and immersed myself in pleasurable thoughts of the forthcoming carnal feast at the Ritz-Carlton. Adam had promised there would be no enforced outings. We could spend as much time as we wanted, alone, in the room. I could have anything I wanted, he told me, as long as it began with *c.*

"Champagne, caviar, crab, chocolate," he recited.

"Or cornichons, chutney, cold coffee, and cheese doodles," I teased. The possibilities were endless. I amused myself with mental pictures of a huge, old-fashioned bathroom with marble fittings, a steamed-up mirror, little candles, ice buckets, crumbs in the bed, and blindfolded sex.

But even with room service on New Year's Eve, there would still be at least two formal dinners to be eaten in a restaurant. I would, occasionally, have to get dressed. With only one pilled sweater, a couple of schoolgirl cardigans, and a maître d's outfit in my wardrobe, this would be difficult. As well as grown-up shoes and some boots that wouldn't kill me on the sidewalk, I would have to buy real clothes, I realized.

The dark-haired woman was claiming my attention. "Edith, you used to live in Oxford, Adam tells us. We spent eighteen months in London. In Chelsea . . ." I nodded like I had a street map of it drawn inside my skull and would be able to zoom in on the house by satellite. Couldn't these freaking people with their Ivy League education and perfect teeth who run the whole damn world get it into their head that Oxford was fifty miles away from bloody London? She was still talking: "Charles"—she motioned to her husband—"was with Merrill Lynch for a while."

"Oh, really?" I said, trying to look interested. I was guessing that this was a bank, but I couldn't be sure. It could be a relative or the names of their kids. She chattered on about where they lived and where their kids went to school: no Merrill, no Lynch, so I was probably right about the bank. I smiled energetically and made a few general remarks about London being historic, exciting, great for shopping, wonderful museums. Hell, if she'd slipped in that they had been involved in a gangland drug bust, I probably would have enthused about that too. Oh why oh why hadn't I put myself somewhere like fucking Stockholm, where it was dark all the time and everybody committed suicide?

The moment there was a lapse in the conversation I stood up and excused myself.

The phone rang while I was beating a vat of boiling polenta that hissed and bubbled like a hell mouth. I heard Adam pick up the extension in the dining room, but I was too busy evading spitting globs of cornmeal to hear what he said. It was probably Lennie petitioning for a later curfew.

But no, it was Caroline, the literary agent who had also been a regular visitor over the past weeks. She said she had been having a drink at the Carlyle with some new author she wanted Adam to meet—could she bring him round?

"We have enough food, don't we, darling?" he asked, kissing my flushed cheek. "I told her it would be fine. We'll just set another couple of places." I agreed, only really hearing the "darling"—darling—an endearment. A public endearment. He sometimes whispered this sort of thing when we were in bed together, and I saved them up, like a miser hoarding coins, and got them out when I was alone to gloat over without ever believing they were really mine. This was a first: a "darling" in plain hearing without being prefaced or accompanied by an erection. Or at least, not visibly so.

"It's not the germ man, is it?" I asked idly, still silently stroking the darling and tucking it into my back pocket for later examination.

"German?" He looked blank.

"No, germ man. You know, the person she was talking about last month; the microbiologist who's going to be big in bacteria? I hope he won't regale us all night about viruses and spores."

"Could be. I'm not sure. She mentioned his name, but I can only listen to Caroline for about five minutes before I get worried she's going to eat me up with those big red lips of hers."

"You wish."

"I prefer yours," he said, as he drew me toward him for a long kiss, which I broke off with difficulty.

I left him to carve the lamb while I put another pair of plates on the table. I moved myself down to the end and stuck the germ man next to Baxter. Serves him right, I thought.

I put the rest of the food on serving platters and followed as Adam hefted it onto the table.

The doorbell rang again. I was dizzy from the noise of buzzers.

It was like being on a quiz show and not knowing any of the answers.

And your starter, for ten, is: Where are Jenny and Baxter planning to spend Christmas Eve and what will Jenny be wearing—the blue velvet or the pink?

"That'll be Caroline," Adam announced and rose to let her in.

My God, that was quick; I know the Carlyle was close by, but the waiters were all so slow it usually took an hour just to get the check. She must have called when they were already outside the door. I hadn't even managed to put a forkful of lamb into my mouth. Wearily, I noticed that I hadn't brought any extra wineglasses. Damn it. I had polished them and left them sitting on the kitchen worktop. I went back to get them.

In the dining room I could hear Caroline kissing and hugging and being brightly effusive. "Brilliant," "clever," "interesting," I heard her gush at intervals like Katharine Hepburn doing Tennessee Williams, when I knew she came from Long Island. Heck, just the sound of her voice exhausted me. I pushed open the swinging doors carrying the two goblets ahead of me like weapons.

Charles was halfway out of his seat with his hand outstretched. Caroline had her fat little arm, resplendent with twenty or so gold bracelets, circled around Jenny's shoulder and was singing her praises to the germ man. Lucky bastard—he hasn't had to listen to her recite her life like a railroad timetable, I thought.

And then my feet bolted themselves onto the floorboards. My heart stopped its steady beat and began struggling to climb out through my rib cage. Someone pulled a drawer out of my stomach.

The man she had brought was standing on the threshold. He looked ill at ease, dragging his hand out of the pocket of his tweed jacket and grimacing tersely in lieu of smiling. His hair was cropped close to his scalp, with tightly clipped curls flattened by the rain, and his eyes were like little bird tracks on his face, which, though tanned, had an unhealthy waxiness to it. I noticed his beard was also trimmed very short—no more than a shadow on his chin, which had a little dimple carved into it. Why hadn't I ever known he had a dimple?

He was speaking very quietly, something about Caroline insisting—being sorry to intrude—very rude, terribly kind. I could barely hear him above Caroline's babbling. Poor thing. His eyes seemed reddened, as though he had spent too long staring at a computer screen, although now it was me he was staring at, but with disbelief. His face collapsed like a condemned building being hit by a demolition ball.

"Ah, and this is . . ." Adam began, drawing me forward.

"*Ag-nes,*" gasped the man, the two syllables the sort of sigh you might make after a long climb uphill. His fists fell uselessly to his sides and hung there like plumb lines from the sleeves of the jacket we had bought together at Brooks Brothers, back when we were happy.

"Francisco," I replied bleakly. It had been so long since I had spoken his name aloud that the fudge of it stuck in my mouth.

I watched Adam's face drain to the same blank shade as his shirt. He turned to me apprehensively. "You two already know each other?" he asked.

"Adam, I'm so so so so sorry," I whispered, as though I were soothing a baby. Then I took a deep ragged breath before plunging into the icy depths of the next sentence.

"This is Frank. Francisco Morales." There was a long, yawning, echoing, screaming silence.

"My husband," I explained, just in case he was confused and thought there were any other walking corpses in the room.

And then I dropped the glasses.

Francisco's fist struck the side of my face and knocked me backward into the door frame. Around me, shards of glass chimed all across the polished floor.

"You bitch," he whispered, weakly, as I slid down the dining-room wall, ". . . and what have you done to your hair?"

ON BEECH STREET, ice cubes snapped like gunshots in the freshly brewed mint tea cooling on the gas stove. I only needed to drop the needle onto the waiting record to hear Ray croon that Georgia was, once again, on his mind; but I was more concerned with the pale-blue envelope I had found among the mail at the institute. It was still lurking in the buried depths of the manila circulars and flyers for conferences that I had dumped on the kitchen table.

I tried to ignore it, but the body was beginning to smell. There was no way to avoid the fact that, soon, I would have to exhume it. Why on earth was the nursing home writing to me? My mother had lived alone for several years after my father had died, becoming more and more isolated and disoriented until she began calling me in the middle of the night not being able to figure out the time difference, asking where the fridge was, or why God had turned all the lights off. After she almost blew herself up trying to put the milk inside the central-heating boiler, I was forced to make my second visit to Scotland in two decades.

With Maisie and Geordie both overseas, although some of the cousins continued to look in on her, I was the closest next of kin, and so four years earlier I had flown back to Scotland and made all the arrangements. I emptied my childhood out of the cabin trunk, filled it with some of my mother's clothes and ornaments, and moved her into a nursing home I found in Edinburgh, where she had remained ever since, slipping ever more surely into the milky waters of her own dementia.

She passed her time in a high-backed chair, staring into the middle distance under the illusion, on her good days, that she was sitting on a runway in Jakarta, waiting to take off on a long-haul flight to Adelaide. On my monthly phone call the nurses told me she was rarely lucid and hardly spoke, but then who would she speak to? Nobody but a few of the old Agneses visited her.

Since the money from the sale of her house had run out, Geordie was the only one of us who had the means to take care of the bills, but he usually dealt directly with her lawyer, and Maisie, being the eldest, made all the major decisions about her general care. If there had been a medical emergency, the nursing home would have telephoned to let me know, but otherwise there was absolutely no need for them to get in touch; all of which only made the letter addressed to me from the Bluebell Rest Home even more disturbing.

I poured myself a glass of tepid tea, turned on the record, which coughed out static until the scratchy bars of the first track kicked in, and then, unable to put the dreaded moment off any longer, I reached for the envelope.

I sliced it open with a vegetable knife and shook out the contents. To my surprise there was just a note card from the matron's office with a couple of lines scrawled across it in ballpoint, and another, mauve envelope that had been opened and inexpertly resealed with Scotch tape.

"Dear Agnes," said the loopy black handwriting on the note card with the corny little bluebell on the right-hand corner, "I am sorry that this letter has been opened, but we thought it was for your mother. Obviously there was some mistake—many apologies." I picked up the cheap envelope hidden inside like a Russian doll. Sure enough, it was addressed to Agnes McBride and had been forwarded on to my parents' last address from our old house in the village. From there it had been sent on to the nursing home.

There was no return address, but the postmark said Yorkshire. It had covered a lot of miles to get here. I took a long swallow of tea, with hands suddenly clumsy and trembling, and turned the envelope over and over as though it would reveal its secrets through touch. To hell with the tea. I looked first at the empty bottle of Jack Daniel's, then scrabbled through the cupboards under the sink, pulling out three cans of lima beans, until I found some apple schnapps that Karl had brought as a hostess present on one of his visits. I poured a huge slug into the grassy, green- colored tea and took a tentative sip. It burned like creosote and tasted like shit—mint-flavored shit.

I took another swig anyway, sat down on a kitchen chair, and carefully peeled back the long ribbon of Scotch tape. Two sheets of lined dime-store notepaper, rolled over on themselves several times, sprang out of the opening. The paper was so thin I could see scars like Braille that the pressure of the pen had made on the blank side. I smoothed the pages out on the table.

"Dear Agnes," I read for the second time that morning. This time the handwriting was round and careful, as if it had been copied out several times to ensure it was word perfect. I guess I knew who had sent it even before I opened the envelope, but I didn't want to admit that I could possibly be right. I read the address at the top left-hand corner. It had come, as the post-mark had forewarned, from a town in Yorkshire in the north of England.

Unable to delay a moment longer, I turned straight to the signature at the bottom of the last page.

It was like a slug in the brain. I read the name, repeating it a few times under my breath.

How in hell had they come up with that? I wondered. A few words were added in brackets—both as unnecessary as screaming at a deaf man.

Hurriedly, I read the nine neatly blocked paragraphs in

between before rolling the sheets into a long cigar and placing them on the table, where I watched them curl to and fro, as though waiting for them to burst into flames.

Oh God, oh God, oh God, I thought. In the background, Ray crackled into silence, the record whirring round and round until it swung into the next track. The band struck up and soared into the chorus. "*Hit the road, Jack,*" Ray sang. "*And don't you come back no more, no more, no more, no more.*" The words snagged in my brain. I didn't usually take advice from song lyrics, but this time Ray had a point.

All these years, and now this. I had come so far but not far enough. What now? I was at a loss about what to do.

I had an overwhelming urge to just get the fuck out of there as fast as I could, but where should I go? I couldn't join Francisco in Colombia until September, and I certainly couldn't hang around here for the summer. Not now. Perhaps not ever. How could I tell Francisco? The idea of having to face him with this news and all its implications overwhelmed me. I couldn't do it. I had to leave. I had to leave quickly.

And so I did.

It took me two weeks, a handful of phone calls, and two short letters to vanish. Not much to wind up twenty years of your life, but I was too numb to grieve for my own dispensability.

The first phone call was to Geordie.

"What have you done this time, Aggie?" His smooth, transatlantic accent immediately dropped down an octave and a hokey Scottish drawl kicked in. "Have you started smuggling in prostitutes from Eastern Europe? Formed a drug cartel? Robbed a bank?" Geordie had always been impatient with anything that threatened his tightly budgeted balance sheet of a life.

"Don't be a dickhead, Geordie." I explained what had happened; there was no point in beating about the bush. I wanted him on my side and silenced.

"But what's the problem? Wouldn't it be simpler for you to just tell him about it? It's not a hanging offense. Not outside of Scotland, anyway. Do the yanks have an extradition policy?" He laughed at his own wit.

"I can't. He doesn't know a thing. Nobody does."

"Fair enough, Ag," he said. "On your own head be it. I just hope he doesn't start pestering me—I don't need it. I'm in the middle of a big merger and I can't spare the energy for your domestics. Are you okay for money? Tell me where you are and I'll wire you some." I promised I would, but I never did get around to giving him my address.

Next I called Maisie and told her I needed to disappear. I knew Francisco would call her, so I gave no details of where I intended to go. She would have told him in a heartbeat.

The past, however, was mine alone to divulge. She promised that she wouldn't say a word.

The last phone call was to my younger cousin Agnes, who now lived in Glasgow and with whom I had some sporadic correspondence. I didn't have to explain anything to her. She was as horrified as I was. She promised she would go and visit my mother and try and smooth things over at the nursing home, but just to be on the safe side I also wrote to them, saying that I was now living in South America. I asked them to forward all further correspondence to my sister in Australia until I had a fixed address. I would have told them I had spontaneously combusted if I thought it would stop them sending anything else to Cambridge. But, sooner or later, there was a strong possibility that I could be tracked down there, and I certainly didn't want to be found.

Finally I wrote to Francisco. It was a short note, to the point and only four lines long.

Four lines for almost twenty years together.

Poor soul.

No wonder he hit me.

16

FOR A SPLIT second I had been almost joyfully pleased to see him, but a smack in the face has the knack of clearing the head, as well as emptying it of any misplaced sentimentality.

Over the preceding months, I had often wondered what I would do if I ever ran into him somewhere. At first, before sex and sentiment stupefied me, I'd be daydreaming, dawdling by the flower store on the corner of Lex or idling at Eli's choosing a mango, and I'd suddenly think of him. I'd look behind me, imagining that he could be there, somewhere in the crowd. I'd conjure him up and see him distracted, rummaging around in his jean pockets for loose change before glancing up and catching sight of me, overjoyed to find me again.

So, yes, I overplayed the wishful thinking, forgetting the reality.

Before Francisco left for Colombia, things between us had been cool for so long there was a skin forming on our relationship, but with his absence, I retreated to an idealized version of our life together that belonged to the far-distant past. I wanted the old Francisco to come back, eager and happy at the sight of me, not the disappointed man I had made him into. I toyed with the memory of him as he used to be, dangling it in front of my eyes the way you do a ball of wool to an old cat that is too sophisticated to chase after snaking yarn, but which, nevertheless, pounces. As would I. I'd resurrect his curly head in the crowded Manhattan streets and run after him, calling his name.

But then there was Adam, and, in the messy hole I had dug myself into, Francisco was better off dead. As far as I was concerned, he was fulfilling his contract as a visiting professor at the University of Bogotá and the house on Beech Street where we had lived on and off since we moved from Oxford fifteen years earlier was occupied by some Professor Prim from a boondocks university in Wilderness, Wisconsin, doing a study on climate change. I knew that Francisco would be back in January, but I had put it out of my mind, like everything else that happened outside the cozy little fantasy I had found for myself.

The punch was a wake-up call.

It was also déjà vu, of a sort. Though this time around I didn't actually lose consciousness: I just slithered down the wall, banged against the speed bump of the dado rail, and crumpled into a heap by the skirting board.

But, once again, there was blood in my teeth and, more surprisingly, blood dripping from my ear. More seeped up between the fingers of my right hand from landing on the broken glass, and my left leg was bent like a checkmark on the lined page of the floor.

It took me a while to realize that I was speechless because I couldn't open my mouth, and that this and the screeching pain were related.

What a shame I had dropped those wonderful goblets—now there would only be ten, I thought vaguely, trying to remove a splinter of burgundy crystal from my palm and finding myself unable to make my fingers work. Kaleidoscopic faces peered down at me in fragments: Adam, his face so white that only his concerned and confused eyes seemed to loom out of the starkness of the paintwork; Baxter, red-cheeked with the exertion of struggling up from the table, gently holding my shoulders, attempting to pull me upright; Jenny, uselessly trying to wrap my hands in a napkin soaked in water from the jug on the table, which only diluted it and spread it further. I had put several slices of lemon in the jug, and it stung like the bejesus. Tears oozed from my eyes. The other two faces came and went. Charles half carried me to a chair. His wife patted the hand that wasn't bleeding.

"Shall we take her up to the drawing room and lay her down?" fussed Jenny. No, I thought but didn't say. I'll bleed all over the white carpet. It'll never come out.

Adam was screaming at Francisco. "You mad son of a bitch. What in the name of God do you think you're doing? You can't go around hitting people." Don't shout; remember Ned . . . I murmured mutely in my head. I didn't want the child to hear and come upstairs to see this.

"You should leave." Adam turned to Caroline. "Get him out of here. Now." But Francisco just stood there, stunned, immobile, behind the group of kneeling figures crouching around me like the three shepherds come to visit the Virgin Mary, except whoever I was, that certainly wasn't one of my aliases. He clenched and unclenched his fist as though waiting for another chance to take a swing at me.

"So this is what you mean by 'needing to get away'—this!" He spat out the word like dirt from his mouth. "You didn't even have the decency to tell me the truth. What kind of person are you? You fucking bloody disgusting lying bitch," he said, all in a rush without even bothering with the commas.

I couldn't have explained even if my mouth had worked, but it wasn't until months later that I told him to go and stuff that *need to get away* up his ass, right after he'd removed his own *there's really no point in your coming to Colombia with me because you'll just get in the way* to make space for it. Just then I had no room for self-righteousness. I merely hung my head in shame and dropped blood into the black cashmere, which accommodatingly absorbed it.

Caroline, looking as though her crocodile purse had turned round and taken a bite out of her face, put her arm around his shoulders, trying to usher him into the hallway, but he shrugged her off. He reached into his inside pocket, wrote something on a piece of paper with harsh jabs of his pen, and threw it onto the table.

"You had a visitor," he said; then, without another word, he turned and walked out the door.

I felt like the sort of creature that just moves through life leaving a long trail of slime.

The front door swung open on its hinges until Caroline bustled out, closing it gently behind her. The women began gathering plates and glasses. Baxter had found a dustpan and brush and was sweeping up glass. Charles disappeared into the kitchen.

I heard water splutter into the sink.

"You might need stitches in that," said Adam, gesturing to

my hand, where Marimekko poppies of blood were blooming on the napkin. "Come on. I'll drive you to up to the emergency room at Lenox Hill."

"Adam . . ." I began, then cried out in agony, which only made the pain worse.

His face was rigid. "Let's just get the wounds dressed."

"But . . ." It came out as blood.

"Save it," he said, turning his face away from my gory attempts at speech. "What do you think you could say to me now that I might possibly want to hear?" I closed my eyes. I couldn't bring myself to look at him.

He drove me the few blocks to the hospital, though I could have walked quicker than it took him to get the car out of the garage, where I struggled unaided out of the car and then watched it disappear from sight.

After I had waited for what seemed like a century with the Upper East Side rich drunks and junkies' club, a male nurse cleaned up my face and sent me for an X-ray, where they told me I was lucky. I would have laughed if it hadn't hurt so much. A doctor plugged me full of local anesthetic and told me to use ice to stop the swelling. The nurse then checked my various cuts and abrasions for glass, glued my skin together, and handed me a leaflet with the number for a domestic violence hotline and another for Alcoholics Anonymous.

"It's not like that," I protested. "I fell against a door." I might as well have been saying *wah, wah, wah* for all the notice the doctor took of me, but that was hardly surprising.

I was saying *wah, wah, wah.*

"You don't have to put up with some jerk treating you like this," counseled the nurse. He was about twenty-five, with long dyed-blond hair showing several inches of dark roots, tied back and folded over on itself until it looked like a knot at the back of his neck, and like me, he was not from around these parts.

"Call them." He gestured to the number that had been rubber stamped on to the bottom of the leaflet.

I shook my head, briefly. It hurt too much to argue further.

Let me take advice from a boy with his hair tied up into a bun.

I had a few butterfly stitches on my hand, and another on a gash behind my knee. He checked me for concussion, handed me a care sheet for head injuries, and warned me to call 911 if I started to feel dizzy or sick. As though it were possible to feel any more nauseated than I already did.

I was exhausted, but I walked home. It took me only ten minutes. I passed a couple in the doorway of an apartment building, wrapped around each other and oblivious to the car that skimmed the sidewalk, as though looking for hookers. I gave them a wide berth with only my long-legged shadow splayed out like a sixties cartoon in front of me, leading the way, but I wasn't afraid. Where's a passing psychopath when you need one? If anyone had tried to cut me into steaks for the freezer, I'd have opened the trunk myself and climbed right on in. Anything was better than going home.

Wherever that was.

17

WHEN I WAS fifteen, there was no broken glass. Only an orange plastic kitchen chair, dimpled with cellulite and radiating four heavy steel legs at unforgiving angles, one of which caught me on the side of the temple and knocked me out and over, taking the tip of my left incisor with it.

My lip split open, my cheek was grazed and bleeding, and by the next morning the whole left side of my face was swollen and my eye was purple.

As I fell, the world seemed to slow. The coil of kicking, punching bodies rolling toward me seemed to stop and start, jerking forward in slow increments like a child's flip book. There were screams, though the music played on in the background: Elton John singing "*Saturday night's alright for fighting.*"

He was right on the money.

The lights had just dimmed, and couples were everywhere, lying on the sofas, curled up in the chairs, while the dancers were clinging to each other and kissing like washing machines on a fast spin. Kirsty was already gripped in the vise-like arms of Dan Ponte, her blond hair in a long ponytail, swishing indolently to and fro as they rocked, off beat, heedless of the music.

That was my cue. As usual, I was heading upstairs for the bathroom to sit out the smoochy records they started to play at the end of the evening. If nobody had locked themselves inside, I would smoke a cigarette and wait for it to be time to go home.

The fight broke out as I crossed the sitting-room floor, and I intercepted the chair just as I walked past the open door to the kitchen, where it was kicking off.

Kirsty was embarrassed—annoyed that I had the bad taste to allow myself to be knocked unconscious, especially when somebody switched the lights back on and the full wreckage was revealed. Cans of beer were spilled and crushed on the floor, and the offending chair now lay on its back like an upturned turtle.

"What a sight you look, lying there like an eedgit—get up and stop making a show of yourself. Thank God nobody knows us," she hissed, glancing across the room trying to catch sight of Dan, who, in common with almost every other male in the room, had scampered out like a cockroach the minute the lights came up while their abandoned girlfriends hung around dazed and crying. She couldn't see him and was furious that she had to link arms with me and shoulder me up off the carpet and out into the freezing night rather than being able to go look for him.

Outside, we could see our breath, little puffs of ectoplasm drifting through the air. Frost bloomed across the roofs and glittered on fences, crunching underfoot like sandpaper. We walked out of the cul-de-sac and up the main road as the windows of the houses slowly went dark, one by one, until only the acid-yellow pus of the streetlights remained, glowing like sores in the night sky. We sat on the wall by the deserted bus stop and shivered, our bums turning cold and clammy on the icy granite.

A taxi idled at the curb, but we waved it away. We didn't have enough money: the money that was supposed to get us home had disappeared from my pocket. A police siren wailed in the distance, and then the car appeared at the end of the road. Kirsty dragged me behind the bus shelter so they wouldn't see us.

"Where has Dan gone?" she said, looking up and down. He was supposed to get us a ride back to the village with one of his friends, but he had vanished. He had been in some trouble with the cops the year before, when he had punched a drunk in the café, so he wouldn't be hanging around to be picked up again.

"Maybe he'll come back and look for you when it's quieter?" I suggested.

"I'll kill him if he does," she said. "Imagine just going off and dumping us." She was offended, and there was a nasty glint in her eye. Kirsty wasn't used to boys letting her down.

"Can't you call for your dad to come and get us?" I asked.

"As if—with you looking like that? He'll never let me out the house again. I'll be keeping my mother company by the fire for the rest of my life. Anyway, he's not there. He's golfing this weekend."

"Golfing? In the snow?"

"Maybe it's not snowing in Aviemore?"

"It's where people go skiing—where else would there be snow?"

She narrowed her eyes, the way my mother did, just before she swatted me with the back of her hand. "You're a right know-it-all. But if you're that bloody clever, why didn't you duck?" she scolded, giving me a disdainful glance. "You looked a complete spastic spread out on the floor. And how could you have lost all the money? You're hopeless, Aggie."

"I didn't do it on purpose," I snapped, but halfheartedly, because it hurt to speak. I had a wad of paper towel in my hand, which, despite all claims to the contrary, was not absorbent, and blood was beginning to congeal on my cheek. My lip throbbed; my tongue hurt where I had bitten it; my leg ached from the fall.

She clicked her tongue, not exactly accusing me of attention seeking but letting it be known that she considered I had been.

"It's a rotten shame. I was looking forward to that party for ages. It's the first time Dan's ever taken me anywhere out of the village." I resisted the urge to remind her that we had actually gone ourselves on the bus and met him there after he had been to the pub. The distinction would have been lost on her, but now it was too late. "Trust you. And now we're stuck here with no money—and no fags." She shook out her empty packet and tossed it into the gutter. "We'll have to walk home." I was annoyed. We were in a little town several miles distant from our own village, all because Dan Ponte had wanted to go there, and frankly, even without the fight, it hadn't been worth the bus fare.

"I only came because you asked me to—do you think this is the way I want to spend my Friday night—knocked out at a stupid, lame party in a stupid house, in the middle of stupid nowhere? I'm not that desperate for a half-pint of cider. I've got better things to do."

"Aye, like what?"

"Well, for a start I'm going training tomorrow afternoon."

"Och, training," she huffed. "No wonder you fell over—it

must have been the excitement of being out in the big world getting too much for you!"

"I didn't fall over—I got hit on the head."

"I don't know how you can be bothered, up and down, up and down—what's the point? It's that boring." I had recently joined the school swim team, but Kirsty didn't think much of it. Swimming was the only sport I had ever been any good at, and there was a big competition coming up the following weekend. I needed to keep up my times. How was I going to manage with my leg hurting like this?

"I like it," I said stubbornly.

It was okay for Kirsty, who seemed to drift through life, good enough at everything to keep her bobbing like a perky little cork, but I had few opportunities to shine. On dry land and dance floors, I possessed neither skill nor grace, but with the opening of a pool in the school sports center the previous year I had discovered that in the water I was sleek and fast. Amazingly, I had won race after race in the annual swimming gala and had recently been asked to join the county swimming team. It meant training three nights a week after school and on weekends, but it wasn't as though I had any other commitments in my social diary.

My face felt as though it had been hit by a tennis racket, but I wasn't worrying about that. Instead, I rubbed my bruised thigh anxiously. My new white pants were smeared with blood and dirt. Not only had I lost my taxi money, but now I didn't have enough to get the bus to the pool. And there were still miles and miles to walk home. I hoped the walk wouldn't make my leg seize up and stiffen. I flexed and pointed my ankle, and groaned at the pain. The flesh was swelling through the straps of my sandals. My toes were blue.

"I'd hate to have to do all that swimming. You'll get shoulders like a man if you don't watch out. Mind you, I like Mr. Anderson. I wouldn't mind seeing him in his swimming trunks." She gave me a sly look, but she wasn't telling me anything I didn't know.

Mr. Anderson was gorgeous. A bit odd, the way he kind of looked through you without really seeing you, but really good-looking and muscled, with white teeth and broad shoulders.

He was a sports teacher at school and trained us for track, field, and swimming. Even Kirsty, who didn't like running because of her big boobs, started turning up for gym, in tiny little shorts. I knew she was envious that I got to spend so much extra time with him.

Not that he so much as glanced in my direction when she was around. At fifteen I still had no bust. I had stopped stuffing toilet paper down my bra since Kirsty had thoughtfully pointed out at the crowded bus stop that there was a strand of perforated white paper snaking out of my sweater. I tried pretending that I had stuck it up my sleeve like a hankie, and it had got lost. But nobody was fooled, and the boys had all sniggered. It's a shame I hadn't persevered. It would have come in useful now, I thought, spitting up blood onto the sidewalk and dabbing my lip with peaks of paper towel that only stabbed more pain into the cut.

In a swimsuit, however, there was no shape to stuff. I had nothing but a skinny sausage of Lycra to hide behind. When I had my cap on, I looked like a Spanish exclamation point—as long and slim as an eel with a tiny black spot for a head. My bones shone through the thin nylon of the Speedo suit, and my hips jutted out like single quotation marks on either side of the full stop of my navel. "Good child-bearing hips," my mother, erroneously, informed me when I complained. I sucked everything in, but the bones remained on guard—pointing out at twenty past eight like a gun-toting cowboy, ready to take down anyone who came too close.

I longed for Kirsty's curves. Sometimes she would come to the swimming sessions with me, just to flaunt herself in front of Mr. Anderson. She'd get into her pretty blue polka-dot suit with the frill round the neckline that she sent away for from *Cosmo*, and dangle her round, pink feet in the pool, looking exactly like the girl in the mail-order ad. I wished she would let me have just this one thing for myself, especially as Mr. Anderson ignored me and sat next to her instead, chatting away to her with that glazed, slack expression on his face, oblivious to my laps.

Eventually I'd stand up at the end of the lane and remind him that I'd finished, but he'd just look at his stopwatch as if he were wondering why it was in his hands and absentmindedly tell me to get dressed. Once he even called me Alice.

But Kirsty would be leaving school in the summer, and I would have my life to myself. She was going to get a job in an office in the city and live in her own flat. I couldn't leave school until I'd finished my exams next year, and by that time I knew Kirsty, with a whole new set of smart friends and new clothes, would have left me behind. But it didn't matter. I wasn't in a hurry to go anywhere. I had swimming to look forward to, and next weekend we were going to Glasgow for the competition. Just Mr. Anderson and the swim team—me, a couple of freshman girls and two boys who were seniors.

One of the boys, Jamie, was as skinny as me, but quite nice.

His dad was a milkman, and he had red hair. Hardly the catch of the century, but neither was I. He always congratulated me when I won, and sometimes, after training, we got the bus back home together and went and had a coffee at Ponte's. Dan Ponte had left school and was always there behind the counter in his white jacket with his name embroidered in red on the pocket, smirking at me, calling Jamie "Carrots." Dan wasn't quite as good-looking anymore now that he spent all day making soapy coffee and slinging burgers, but Kirsty still liked him. Jamie was cheery, always smiling, and he always bought the coffees. Mind you, Kirsty thought he was pot ugly and geeky so I never mentioned him to her; and when she started going out with Dan, she was always hanging around the café, so I stopped taking him there. Not that I would ever have gone on a date with him, even if he asked. No matter how nice he was, there was no way I would commit social suicide with a carrottop.

I just hoped that my leg didn't stop me from swimming.

"Your face is all mashed up, you know." I knew.

"Your eye looks like raw mince." She laughed a bit, but then gave my hand a squeeze to show she was sorry.

"Thanks."

"Is it sore?" It stung like hell, and my tooth was thumping to the beat of an hour in a dentist's chair. I felt like crying, but when I had come round after the fight, bawling like a baby, Kirsty had warned me to shut up in case somebody called for an ambulance.

"How are we going to explain it to your mother and mine if the hospital calls them? When you see her tomorrow, you can just tell her you fell. Nothing's broken, is it?"

"No," I agreed. I clutched vainly at the hollow of my throat, where the locket I had got for my birthday just the week before had nestled earlier in the evening. It must have fallen off somewhere. It was exactly like Kirsty's. My mother would be livid that I had lost it, but I didn't say anything. I licked the missing tip of my tooth, swallowed the tears and the bloody saliva, and did as I was told.

But now it was really cold outside, and my fluffy jacket, though it looked like sheepskin, was polyester fake fur. I was freezing, and my fingers were numb. I was wearing strappy sandals, and my feet, in pantyhose, were slipping up and down on the silver platform soles. I didn't want my muscles to get too cold or I'd definitely get a sprain. We should move, I suggested.

"Aye, come on," she agreed. "We can hitch a lift, but we'll have to walk for a while first." She managed to both drag me along the street and poke me with her elbow at the same time. "The police might still come, and they'll pick us up if they see us hitching. They all know my dad from when he comes to get the bodies after there's been an accident. We'll have to wait till we're right outside on the road." I stumbled forward as though on stilts. Kirsty, in brand-new black leather boots, strode out like an officer in the SS. I looked at them enviously—it was me who had pointed them out to her in a store in Galashiels the week before. I loved them and had tried them on, but I couldn't afford them. Not so Kirsty—her purse was padded out with cash like it was on display in a department store. She was into the store beside me and had them bought before I could even peel the zipper down. And now there she was, strutting about in the stacked heels with her piggy-wee legs while I was getting frostbite.

"For God's sake—come awn," she shrieked, snapping me out of my jealousy. "Move! We'll be here all night if you don't give yourself a shake." She had one cigarette left, tucked behind her ear, and we shared it; mine had been squashed in the packet when I fell. We took two draws each until the filter tip was soggy.

"Yuck, you've got it all bloody," she said, throwing it away into the dark hedges that cowered furtively on either side of the country lane. Outside the town the string of streetlights came to an abrupt end, but the crescent moon hung low in the sky and lit our way, making the frost shimmer like glitter on a Christmas card. No cars passed us until we reached the crossroads with the main road going off to Selkirk, but even then the first thing to pass was a cargo truck. It rumbled past us, making the road shake.

Neither of us stuck up our thumbs. We weren't that stupid; we would never get into a cargo truck with a stranger.

My feet in the high heels were killing me. I was dying to take them off, but it was too cold to walk on the frozen asphalt in just pantyhose. Kirsty was humming away to herself, an Abba song, the metal tacks in the heels of her boots keeping time to the music, my feet staggering in semiquavers. I would normally have joined in, the two of us linking arms and singing together, but my mouth was sore and my tongue swollen. I didn't want my lip to start bleeding again.

We heard the swish and crunch of another car coming along the road. Its headlights made the white of my pants seem like two long, skinny flags waving in the blackness and threw my etiolated shadow across the tarmac. It was a little Ford Escort.

Kirsty held out her thumb and turned to face the glare of the lights as the car drew closer. It slowed a bit, but it was a young couple inside who probably didn't want a pair of battered teenagers in their back seat. The car looped around us and accelerated away.

"Oh, fuck you," shouted Kirsty after them, giving them the finger.

"Don't do that; they might get mad at us," I warned.

"So what if they do? It's not as if they can kick us out of the car since they never bothered to let us into it in the first place." She stuck her hands in her pockets and trudged ahead, leaving me limping behind.

The next car didn't stop either, though Kirsty was practically dancing in front of it. It swerved and continued to speed off into the distance.

"They probably think we're drunk, watching you falling all over the place. Can you not walk straight—what's the matter with you?"

"My leg is really sore," I complained, "and my ankle is swollen."

"Oh, Agnes, you're such a greeting face—stop moaning—if it wasn't for you, we wouldn't be in this mess." I couldn't work out how it had all got around to being my fault: it had been Kirsty's idea to go to the bloody party, and then we had stayed late waiting for Dan when I wanted to go home.

She had been the one who convinced me to lie to my mother when I had been told I couldn't go out. I would rather have stayed in and watched television. But it was too late to carry on about it. Now I just had to concentrate on putting one foot in front of the other.

"Will your ma not miss us and be worried?" I wondered hesitantly, half hoping that her father's dark green Humber would appear and whisk us off home to the sweet purgatory of scoldings.

"Nah, she'll have had her cherry brandy, a Valium, and a Ponderax chaser. She'll be out for the count until twelve o'clock tomorrow. Not that she'll tell my dad that." It was true. Her mother ate pills like sweets. I knew this because my mother was the one who filled her prescriptions at the chemist. Sleeping pills, tranquilizers, water pills, and laxatives.

"It's no wonder she doesn't go out; she would rattle like a tube of Smarties," my mother had said.

We had turned off the main road where a back lane cut through the fields and wound over the hills to the first scattering of houses on the necklace of small villages that led to ours. There was another lone bus stop at the crossroads. I sat on the frame of the shelter where the glass had been kicked out, complaining of being tired. I told Kirsty I needed a rest.

She had joined me, shivering, when we heard another car. Kirsty darted out onto the road and put her thumb in the air. I leaned out of the bus shelter and did the same. "Watch out," I called out nervously, thinking that maybe we should be more cautious, but she just kept hitching.

The car slowed to a crawl. I couldn't see through the windscreen; the headlights dazzled me. I shielded my eyes as I waited for the car to stop, but Kirsty was already walking toward it, pulling her short, squat shadow behind her until it pooled around her feet.

"Oh." She laughed, leaning over to peer into the open window, her hair where it had escaped from her ponytail falling across her face until she pushed it back behind her ear in a showy gesture.

"Hiya, sir. What are you doing here?" she asked, all casual, leaning one hand against the bodywork. It was a shiny red Volkswagen.

"Look, Aggie—it's Mr. Anderson." She flicked her eyes toward me and raised her eyebrows in a can-you-believe-it expression of delight.

I came up beside her, reluctant. Goddamn it, I was thinking—this was going to land me right in the shite. Why did it have to be him?

"I should be asking you two the same thing. Agnes McBride—I wouldn't have expected to see you out at this time of night. Do your mothers know you're trailing around the countryside?"

"No," I muttered, trying to keep the bad side of my face hidden.

If he saw me all bashed to bits, he would be sure to force me to go home. And what if he knew about my leg? He definitely wouldn't let me compete. I wished we had stuck to the main road. This was bad news for me, but Kirsty was almost squealing with giddy joy.

"Are you giving us a lift, then?" She was sliding from one leather-shod foot to the other, her heels crunching as she undulated like a genie let out of a bottle. "Will you drive us back to my house? Please . . . please," she wheedled, all fake sweetness and light.

He had already opened the passenger door, and Kirsty was skipping round to get into the car. But then it was my turn for his full attention. "What happened to you, Agnes? Are you all right?" He had seen my bruises.

"She got in a fight," Kirsty supplied, climbing into the front seat and leaving me to clamber into the back.

"You were fighting?" He was shocked and beckoned for me to come on.

I wasn't sure about getting a ride from a teacher. Maybe we would get into trouble at school for hitchhiking, but Kirsty's face was set in a sullen expression and brooked no argument. She told me to stop hanging about and get in. I turned toward the window, trying to keep the bad side of my face hidden.

"You're a lifesaver, sir," said Kirsty. "We were at a party, but this idiot here got in that fight, and lost all our money, so we ended up having to walk."

"What are you doing getting yourself involved in fights for? It doesn't seem like you." I caught his eyes in the rearview mirror.

Damn that Kirsty. "I wasn't fighting, honest, sir, I wasn't. I got caught in the middle of a fight at the party, then her cretin of a boyfriend went off and left us, and I'd lost all my money, so we had to walk home."

"Well, at least I've got a boyfriend . . ." Kirsty was chattering away. "You should have seen her—all over the floor, but you won't tell, will you? Her mother will go apeshit if she finds out." I saw Anderson's peculiar glassy eyes watching me. "You look pale, Agnes. Are you sure you're all right, hen? Maybe you need a doctor. Poor thing, you've had a bit of a battering."

"Oh, Agnes is all right. She'll do anything to be the star of the show, won't you, Aggie?" She laughed. I shut my eyes.

Mr. Anderson said something else, but I wasn't really listening.

He was being nice, and his kind voice was coming and going like bad radio reception. My stomach began to lurch.

"I think I'm going to be sick," I managed weakly, before I started to retch.

Mr. Anderson hurriedly stopped the car, and I toppled out and threw up into the frozen ditch by the side of the road. My knees gave way. I couldn't stand up again.

"God, now she's puking—and she's staying at my house. I can't take her back like this." Kirsty was almost in tears, legs and arms both crossed, her composure cracking now that the script wasn't reading the way she'd written it.

I felt Mr. Anderson lift me under the arms, then gently half carry me onto the back seat. "Lie down, lass," he said, "you're not well." Like that was breaking news.

Kirsty was blathering on, her voice trembling, telling him

where we lived, but I couldn't keep my eyes open. I was melting, giving in to the desire to close my eyes. The car was rocking me as if I were an infant in a stroller. All I wanted to do was sleep.

My eyes drooped until I just let go and drifted off into the black. I heard Kirsty's voice bubbling away in my head, on and on and on in her usual Kirsty-World sort of way, until I woke up with pain chiseling into my jaw. The car had rumbled to a standstill. Thank God, I thought, we're home. Kirsty grinned at me from the front seat. We were back in the village.

"Mr. Anderson says you can sort yourself out here first."

"What?" I gaped at her. What was she talking about? I rubbed the condensation away from the back window and through the water, trickling in rivulets down the glass, I saw we had drawn up outside a whitewashed little cottage with darkened windows and a high hedge huddled around it, all dusted with frost. It looked like something from a fairy tale, like Hansel and Gretel, but made of chunks of iced limestone instead of gingerbread.

"But, Kirsty, where are we?" I croaked.

I was talking to her back; she was already picking her way over icy puddles to the front door.

Mr. Anderson disappeared into the porch and switched the light on. Then he stood on the step and beckoned me forward with a wave.

I breathed on the window and watched his face mist over.

But he was still there when the glass cleared.

18

I HALF EXPECTED MY bags to be packed and dumped on the sidewalk when I arrived back at the house, but only a garbage can that I had forgotten to take downstairs welcomed me, its lid askew in a rakish salute.

It was four a.m., and all the lights were out except for the orange glow of the desk lamp in Adam's study. I hoped he wasn't still sitting up there waiting for me, but I guessed I would have to face him sooner or later.

A toy town of clean crockery lined the kitchen table. I sent a silent thank you to Jenny as I relocated everything as carefully and quietly as I could with one hand, knowing I wouldn't get a chance to tell her myself.

The piece of paper that Francisco had left on the table remained propped up on the sideboard. I picked it up and read it. You don't think things can get any worse and then they do. I crumpled it inside the pocket of Lennie's old coat, which I guessed I would have to take with me, as I didn't have another one to wear.

I took the Tupperware container full of cash out of the freezer in the basement, then wearily climbed the stairs, listening for footsteps that didn't come.

On the third flight, I crept up and peered cautiously into Lennie's room, where, to my relief, a dark lump was visible underneath the covers. Across the landing Ned was asleep with his bottom in the air and his cheek jammed against the mattress as though he had been dropped from space at a great height. I pulled the duvet over his shoulders and stooped to pick up the glass of water on the carpet that he always kicked over in the morning. Outside his room, I opened the linen cupboard and slid my good hand underneath the folded pillowcases until I found the fat envelope concealed at the bottom. Inside, I had managed to accumulate about ten thousand dollars. My passport was also there, taped into a little parcel together with the bank card and checkbook for my old savings account, and, wrapped in cotton wadding, Francisco's mother's engagement ring.

I tiptoed downstairs to Adam's bedroom. The door was closed and I hesitated, but I needed to get my clothes, so there was no alternative but to enter. However, when I turned the handle and went inside, as I had half expected, the bed was empty and hadn't been slept in. I dragged my eyes away from the pillows I had smoothed that morning, a lifetime ago, then went into Gay's dressing room and rewound my life back into the same suitcase I had arrived with, plus a brace of larger shopping bags for the few extra things I had acquired since my arrival.

Adam appeared, his face ravaged and his eyes bloodshot, leaning against the door frame as I rummaged through the laundry hamper for my few items of unwashed clothing. I pretended I didn't know he was standing behind me until he spoke.

"You're leaving already," he announced more than asked.

I nodded my agreement, rolling up a pair of underpants and jamming them into one of the shopping bags.

"Where will you go?" he said, trying to sound as though he didn't really care about the answer. His words were a little slurred. He had been drinking.

"I don't know—back to Cambridge maybe?" I spoke the words with difficulty, only to realize the foolishness of that idea and the downright stupidity of voicing it.

"You'll go back to him?"

"No. Absolutely not. I doubt he'd have me in any case." Damn it, another wrong thing to say. "I just mean I guess I will try to talk to him. Eventually." As I gathered up my things, he sat on the bed, following me with hard eyes, the pupils hammered into his head like steel nails.

"Do you want to go back to him?" he asked aggressively.

"No, but even if I did, I think it's gone a bit past what I want, don't you?"

"How's your face?"

"It's fine; just bruised." His mouth opened and closed soundlessly. "I just can't fucking believe you. What the hell kind of game have you been playing with me these last months? Why all the lies? And your fucking dead German husband—you disgust me."

"It wasn't a game." I shook my head. How to begin? "I'm sorry, Adam. I . . ." He slapped the words away with an expression of repugnance.

"He called you Agnes . . . ?" I lifted the suitcase and hooked the carrier bags carefully over my bad hand to avoid touching the stitches.

"Yes, that's my name," I said simply.

"Who the fuck have I been living with all this time? What kind of a person are you?" I started to cry, but I kept my voice even.

"If it's any consolation, I liked being Edith a lot better than I ever liked being Agnes." His mouth looked as though it had been sewn shut and the thread pulled tightly at one end. I could practically smell the stench of my own lies. I wanted to crawl across the carpet on my knees and beg him to listen to me, to look at me, to believe me, but what would be the point? What could I say?

I walked toward the door. The silence spread across the floor between us like sealing wax, hard and brittle, until Adam broke it. "Just tell me one thing," he called after me, with a little lilt of hope in his voice. "Was he violent? Did he threaten you? Is that why you left him—is that why you changed your name?" Until that moment I think he was still willing me to give him some sort of justification that he could have accepted. He was longing for me to say something, anything, that would redeem me. What was one more lie after so many?

But I didn't have any more energy left for fiction, so I kicked the corpse one more time. "No, nothing like that. You can't judge him on this evening; he's a tremendously sweet, gentle man. I don't think I ever saw him lose his temper, not once. He never even raised his voice. That was part of the problem. It was as if he faded away. Tonight was just a shock, his seeing me here. It was too much for him. He snapped."

"Then why did you leave him?" he asked, his eyes imploring me to give him an answer that he could make sense of. I wished I had one.

I put down the suitcase and fumbled in my pocket for the piece of paper that I knew bore an alien name and telephone number written out in Francisco's jagged, elegant script.

"Did you see the note that Francisco left behind?"

"No. Why, what is it?" He was too drunk even to register the significance of the question.

I opened it and closed it again. "Oh, just some contact details. It's not important." I stared at Adam. He looked like a man who had walked across the Antarctic without his overcoat and had his skin flayed off by the elements.

I screwed the paper up into a ball the size of my heart and walked to the bathroom, where it fell eagerly into the tangled embrace of a skein of dental floss at the bottom of the wastebasket.

But when I came back to the bedroom, he had gone. There was only the hollow of his body on the bed. I took the nightdress that I kept, for show, underneath the pillow and winced as a door upstairs slammed and bounced on its hinges.

19

ADAM HAD SAID that there was no need for me to leave immediately, which seemed almost insultingly decent of him. However, I knew that I couldn't be there when the children woke up in the morning, so I sat downstairs alone on the hard hump of the Federal sofa in the dining room in my too-big, borrowed coat, surrounded by my collection of orphaned bags, and waited for morning to call my name.

At seven o'clock, before it was properly light, I let myself out as quietly and efficiently as I had arrived. I straightened up the house as best I could with one arm, took out the garbage, and set the breakfast table for the children. I put my keys in an envelope and left it beside the clock in the hall. The clock was still chiming as I closed the door.

Fred was already outside his apartment building on the corner, so I turned left and went down Park to a café where I drank polystyrene coffee, looking like the homeless person I had just become, and examined the number on the flyer that the nurse had given me. I wasn't so sure that I deserved a "nonjudgmental, safe environment," although, technically, I could have made a case for being a battered wife. Maybe I ought to give them a call and see if they had a shelter I could go to?

But then, as I looked in my wallet to see if I had enough change to make the call, I remembered the shabby hotel where I had once been offered a job. It was still marked with a red asterisk on the map I had in my purse.

It seemed like the obvious answer. Nobody would ask me any awkward questions, and, more important, I wouldn't have to make up any more lies.

Thirty minutes later a sleepy Nigerian was showing me into a room with barely a foot of color-blind, patterned carpet even more incandescently angry than Adam had been, shouting at gold brocade wallpaper on either side of a large double bed. But it had tea- and coffee-making facilities, a television screwed to the wall, and its own bathroom with two towels the size of a facecloth. I paid extra for a window even though it only faced another filthy pane of glass less than six inches away, and the sheets looked clean. It was perfect. I paid a week in advance and settled down to lick my wounds, or at least to leave them to fester quietly.

By the end of the week my stitches had dissolved, the swelling in my jaw had gone down, and the bruise had faded to the same shade of dark disappointment as the shadows under my eyes.

With the help of nude beige concealer from Maybelline, I ventured into the back office and renegotiated with the manager, an impassive African immigrant who had three scars on each cheek, as though his face had been marked up by an editor attempting to capitalize his yellow-rimmed eyes. Deal struck, I moved into an even uglier room on the eighth floor of a building a block away, where I paid for another window and the further luxury of not sharing with another three illegal hotel workers, and, for a loss of about fifty dollars a week, I sat at the office computer all day. Then from six to midnight I let rooms to gullible tourists and desperate backpackers with rucksacks the size of compact cars, or to a stream of mismatched couples who rarely stayed longer than an hour and who always paid in cash.

I volunteered to work all through the holidays, though at first the manager was dismayed that I didn't have plans to go to church over Christmas. He spent ten dutiful minutes telling me about making room for Jesus in my life before I told him I was Jewish, at which point he gracefully conceded that I could work for minimum wage on Christmas Day while he and his extended family went to a Pentecostal temple in Queens.

I watched the ball drop in Times Square on TV in the reception office, reading a tattered *Cosmo* from June 1994 with a cheeseburger and Coke that Adi, one of the lesser Nigerian cousins, brought me from McDonald's. A drunken Australian called me a cunt when I told him we didn't have a bathroom, public or otherwise, he could use and then he pissed on the steps. So, one way or another, I got all the *c*'s Adam had promised me.

I stayed there through January, until I found a respectable job as a receptionist at a holistic medicine practice in the East Village, about ten blocks from Adam's office in Union Square. Now that I could finally use my Harvard credentials, it was easy to impress the two men who interviewed me, and they hired me on the spot. When I mentioned that I would also need to find somewhere to live, they had the perfect solution. Within a week I found myself installed as a roommate in the fairly tragic apartment of one of the practitioners: a divorced homeopath who had a dusty spare room on the low side of Park Slope in Brooklyn and a blind cat, both of which revived, rather spectacularly, my latent asthma.

I gave my references as the hotel manager, Adam, and the dean of Cabot House, who had fed me most of my editorial work while I was living in Cambridge. As far as I am aware, not one of them was ever contacted. People are surprisingly slack about these things.

I took another job near where I lived cleaning the office of a dentist on Seventh Avenue in Brooklyn between seven and nine every morning, and worked for the socks-and-sandals brigade, answering the telephone and making appointments, between two and eight in the evening, Monday through Saturday. The rest of the time, I waited.

Do you know that feeling when you're longing for a letter, when you're almost itching for it to arrive? When, every morning, you find a dozen reasons to dart down to the mailbox just to check to see if there's anything locked away that isn't a flyer for a pizza delivery?

This was the vigil I kept for the first long, slow months after I left Adam's place.

The moment I was settled, I wrote to him with my new address and telephone number, "just in case I get any mail," I said.

I knew there would be no mail to forward, and anyway the only person I wanted to hear from was him.

Every morning, I took a widow's walk, to and fro across the window of the homeopath's bedroom at the front of the apartment where, naturally, I should not have intruded. But I wasn't interested in her pots of arnica and rosewater face creams, or in the tapestry pillows of cats and dogs that she rearranged meticulously every morning on top of her patchwork quilt. I was only interested in the street, staring through the metal-frame windows, willing the mailman to pull up in his little truck, then jog up the steps while his skinny mandarin pigtail flapped in the breeze behind.

Officially, I could use the box-sized kitchen only between certain prescribed hours, as detailed on a typed, three-page sheet of rules and regulations. These included: no use of the phone except in emergencies (it was in the main sitting room, which I was also barred from); no television in my room (the noise disturbed her); no using the waste disposal (apparently it encouraged rats); no using the microwave (negative rays and carcinogens); no kicking the cat (this being the only one I broke with any regularity); and no smoking on the fire escape. Nevertheless, after I came back from my cleaning job I dallied in the tiny kitchen, squinting through the turret window in the corner, like a man outside a sex shop, pretending to read the parts of the newspaper that contained jobs I was unqualified for. I turned the pages, concentrating on the type, seeing nothing, and all the time longing for it to be time to go and unhinge the jaw of the mailbox, then splay out the envelopes on the table like a peacock's tail, hoping for something from Adam.

Every afternoon I put on my increasingly oversized coat and walked to work with the same sinking feeling of defeat as I realized that, once again, the mailman had been and gone, passing me by with his treasure of low-cost insurance for the possessions I didn't own, and a life I didn't care about, all addressed to people who didn't even live here anymore.

My landlady was as postally bereft as I, but at least she existed in the shadowy world of manila-encased copies of *Homeopathy Today* and Publishers Clearing House sweepstakes with their promises of large cash prizes if only she would tick the box, subscribe to *Kreative Krafts*, and return the envelope within fourteen days.

At the practice I daydreamed at my desk, counting off the days in my head since I had written to Adam, and finding an excuse to extend the deadline for a reply by another twenty-four hours. I booked clients for cranial osteopathy and acupuncture and felt dejected and deflated as I wondered how I would pass the interminable chasm of time until the next morning, when I would wake up and plead with the fates again, ah, yes—maybe today.

Then, as two weeks turned into four, it became: maybe next week, maybe next month, maybe never, almost certainly never, and then just never.

20

FRANCISCO HAD ALWAYS been a lax correspondent, even when we had been on good terms. Once, before we were married, he had gone home to Colombia for Christmas and sent me a two-page missive on lined yellow legal paper that arrived in Oxford three weeks after he did.

That letter alone should have told me everything I needed to know about the future trajectory of our relationship. I have it now, folded into a precise triptych, the thick, spiky-black handwriting soaring up the page like the New York skyline or teams of Modigliani figures waiting for a bus. It reads like the travelogue of Dulles McDull and is a description of the view from his grandmother's balcony. It's New Year's Eve, and the night sky is ablaze with fireworks being set off from hundreds of craft in the harbor, the barrage of explosions punctuated with the odd round of gunfire. "Every year," he writes, "some poor bastard gets shot by a drunk who forgets to aim upward." I skimmed over the words, searching for something personal and found it, at last, on the line before he signed his name. It said: "Take care, Francisco." Hardly a love sonnet—no mention of love at all, in fact.

But then there were greeting cards for birthdays and Valentine's Day, some of which survived the years and nestle with the letter, still in their envelopes with a bite out of each corner where I had torn them open as they arrived, one by one, propped on the breakfast table, the fireplace, or accompanying an ill-wrapped gift.

He brought all this redundant love with him when we met to pick over the ruins of our marriage. I sat opposite him like a failed Ph.D. student with the papers he had found in his file cabinet and brought with him tossed on the butler's table in front of me.

I had arranged the meeting soon after I started working in the East Village. I expected that he would have moved back to Beech Street when our tenants left at the end of semester, so I called him one evening, long after everyone at work had gone home and I had the office to myself. A woman with a heavily aspirated foreign accent answered the phone on the first ring. He must have been sitting close by, as, one wordless second later, he came on the line, his few curt words sounding more Spanish than usual, as though language were a sexually transmitted disease and he had caught it from the woman beside him. He didn't mention who she was, and I didn't need to ask. She was probably me, but twenty years younger and with a graduate degree in development studies and an interest in do-gooding. By mutual consent we agreed that I shouldn't go up to Cambridge. He didn't want me in the house, and since it sounded like somebody was already sleeping in my bed, neither was I eager to return.

Instead, we met on a snowy Sunday in the third week of February, in a place better suited to taking tea with an elderly aunt of whom you weren't very fond than to cauterizing a runaway wife. I had finally gotten around to buying boots, but my feet were still cold, and the hat I wore did the same for my hair as going for two weeks without shampoo. I was the only woman not in a fur and straight-from-a-cab heels. I was a wreck.

We ordered a pot of jasmine tea that we poured with great ceremony worthy of a geisha and crippling solicitousness, and then, with none of the care that had been lavished on the tea, he emptied out the contents of his briefcase.

He laid out the details of my share of his university pension plan—my few years of employment at Balfour College back in Oxford would entitle me to the princely sum of about five dollars a week when I retired—but Francisco's from Harvard was generous; and a letter that my father had sent me before he died, the sight of which stung me as much as it had the first time I read it, when he had congratulated me on what he considered to be the single shining achievement of my life—marrying Francisco. Then there were reams of statements from my savings account addressed to Mrs. A. Morales, which had continued to arrive at monthly intervals after I left. Francisco had opened them and stapled them together in chronological order.

"You didn't take any cash out of your account," he said bitterly. "I thought you must be dead," he said; "otherwise, what were you living on? The couple of hundred dollars that you withdrew from our joint checking account wouldn't have lasted long. Of course I jumped to the wrong conclusion. I should have wondered *who* you were living on."

"It wasn't like that." I started to tell him that I could explain, but, as I couldn't, I just winced, mutely, while he threw paper darts at me.

Underneath the statements were three mauve envelopes

identical to the one that had been forwarded from the nursing home, but addressed this time to Agnes Morales in care of the institute at Harvard. Each one had been opened. The floor lurched as though I had hit a sudden belt of turbulence. I wanted to vomit.

"You know what these are. Obviously," he said, as he threw them on the table.

Oh my God. I braced myself. The plane was hurtling toward a pencil-line runway two thousand feet below me.

I scanned his face. It was hard to imagine that he could be more livid than he was, but I was sure it was possible. However, he dropped the envelopes without further comment, his jaw clenched, as though being silent under torture.

I felt as though I had been strip-searched.

The last letter he produced like a switchblade, waving it under my nose before handing it over. It was a faded cream envelope in a square hand with a preprinted queen's head embossed on the front.

Jamie. I smiled in spite of myself, taking it from him and caressing the crown with my thumb.

"You bitch—you sit there and smile?" Francisco was watching me the way you watch a rat in a corner. "It was quite illuminating going through your letters," he said, spelling it out in little chips of ice.

"You've read them all?" I covered the envelopes with my hands, as though I could still keep everything inside unknown.

"Agnes, you disappeared for nearly six months without a word. Of course I read them. I went through the boxes you put in storage and read every piece of paper I could find. I called your mother's nursing home, where the matron—the fucking matron—told me they'd heard you'd 'gone away for a while.' I spent hours trying to track down your brother, hoping you'd be there with him, but when I finally got through, he wouldn't tell me a thing. Then he just wouldn't even take my calls, the piece of shit. And as for Maisie"—he pronounced the *z* sound like a razor—"you know, you used to complain about Herminia, but your family makes the fucking Vietcong seem gracious. She just put her oaf of a husband on the phone, who treated me as though I were a bug." He spat the word into my face.

I jumped back. I wouldn't blame him if he beat me to a bloody pulp.

"But not one of them would tell me a thing."

I closed my eyes.

"Not one of them would tell me a thing about you and the bloody little bastard you told me you couldn't have . . . the bastard you've been hiding from me for twenty years." And then the plane hit the ground, but, unfortunately, I was still alive.

Where are all the bloody trigger-happy Colombians when you need them?

21

My mother sent me off to an Agnes who ran a boardinghouse by the shore in North Yorkshire when I was four and a half months pregnant.

Spending ten minutes with my feet up in stirrups would have solved the problem easily, but my mother wouldn't even say the word *abortion*, let alone allow one. It didn't help that I was already three months gone before I plucked up the courage to tell her, so time was short.

She was outraged. "It's murder," she had hissed when I meekly suggested that maybe I didn't have to have the baby. Stapling me with her eyes, she paused for a long breath and then said, in a whisper like vapor escaping from an icebox: "Do you think you would be here if I believed in abortion? Two grown-up children and you think I wanted another bairn at my time of life? But I had to knuckle down to it, and so will you." I felt as though I'd just trudged home through a snowstorm without my skin. I couldn't feel my fingers; the saliva on my tongue froze.

"There have already been too many people hurt with your stupidity . . . and if this gets out . . ." She looked at me meaningfully, leaving me to fill in the blanks, which I did.

All of them.

And I didn't mention it again.

She brought home a test she had smuggled out of the drugstore where she worked, but she wouldn't take me to the doctor. In a village the size of ours, she was worried that everybody would know. Everyone already knew far too much about me, and my family had been shamed enough. I was more talked about than Patty Hearst. My face and name had been shown on the evening news, and I'd been reviled in both the local and national press. A school photograph with my head circled to single me out from my classmates had been shown on *Reporting Scotland*. Jean Rook had mentioned me, dismissively, in the *Scottish Daily Express*. My mother couldn't take any more gossip and wanted rid of both of us, but fortunately there was an even more convenient way to deal with the problem. After a few hurried long-distance calls, it was decided the baby, and me, would be removed geographically.

After she recovered from the sight of the blue spot in the test tube and the flame of her handprint had faded to a palm-shaped blush on my jaw, she made plans for my exile. "Don't tell another soul," she warned, her mouth a thick pencil scribble of dislike.

Who would I tell? Nobody was talking to me.

"They think you're enough of a little tart as it is, without this." For several weeks all but obligatory public appearances were suspended, then, as soon as circumstances would allow, my mother put on her black Mussolini mohair cape and her Fair Isle tea-cozy hat, and marched into action with Fascistic zeal.

Like a general leading her troops into battle, she goose-stepped me along the railway platform with the tip of her furled umbrella and deposited me on a train in Carlisle. Finally, she had something she could control.

I put up my hands and surrendered. I had nowhere else to go.

I didn't pack much on the basis that most of my clothes soon wouldn't fit me. I had a couple of pairs of nylon pants with elasticized waists and a few sweaters in the brown leather case.

A trunk full of schoolbooks, which I would be expected to study on my own, was to follow. I wouldn't need much else. "Agnes is stout," said my mother; "you can borrow something of hers as you get bigger. You'll not be giving any fashion shows." I helped out a bit with the boardinghouse, though there wasn't too much work to do. It was off-season, and there were only a few paying guests. I washed up, helped with the beds, wrestled the wet sheets onto the washing line and ironed the ice out of them when they had frozen solid. Otherwise, Agnes took pity on me and let me rest.

I spent most of my time pretending to study, earnestly poring over chapter three in *Bienvenue*, which involved asking people in small Provençal villages where I could find the nearest tennis court, while really reading Westerns and romances set in the Australian outback that I found on the shelves in the boarders' sitting room.

When not wishing myself wooed by a sheep farmer or rustling cattle in Oregon, I walked by the sea, watching the waves roll in and smash themselves into exasperated spit on the beach, while seagulls screamed furiously overhead. The vast North Sea terrified me. If I stood too close to the shore, I was afraid of the wrath of the water—that it would sweep in, swallow me up, and drag me away. But sometimes I went right up to the water's edge in my Woolworth's gum boots and stood there anyway. I'd listen to the gulp of the hungry waves, and feel the sand collapse beneath my heels as the tide curled over my toes and sucked on them, coaxing me further. Come on; come on; just another step more. It made me think of Kirsty.

And then I stepped back.

I called Agnes my aunt, but she was one of my mother's distant cousins in one of those twice-removed, elongated family relations that I had never understood. Her kindness, though brusque and often baffled, was a balm after my mother's steel-knuckled scorn. She rarely sat still and was always tired, worn down as she was by hard work and taciturn men, but she gave me an easy ride, plying me with greasy bacon sandwiches to "keep my strength up" and the sweet, milky tea that I've never been able to drink since. Her own children were grown and married off to sensible Northerners, or at least sensible enough not to let any of their kids be called Agnes. Until she was saddled with me, she hadn't ever had to deal with a wayward teenager, let alone one who was also pregnant.

Occasionally we talked about the baby, but only as though it were some rather unwieldy ornament that, one day, when I went back home, could be shoved into the back of the cupboard under the stairs when visitors came.

We both knew it would never be on show.

It was she who arranged for me to take classes at the secretarial college, a room above a bakery that was redolent with the scent of custard slices and the casual spite of slow-witted girls with fast fingers.

"Don't upset yourself, lovey. Just ignore the silly mares. You're a smart girl. Life goes on," she assured me. "You'll put all this behind you, and the typing will be just the thing to fall back on after it's all passed," she told me.

There was no question of my ever returning to school. I did my O-Levels as a moderately pregnant external student at the local school. I looked as if I had a beach ball stuck up the front of my blouse, and none of the other kids spoke to me. I hoped to do just well enough to scrape a pass in math and English but was so woolly-headed that I couldn't concentrate on anything: I could spend hours lying on my bed watching feathers fly through the air, but I couldn't get information to stick in my brain.

"Never mind, pet," Agnes said. "That's how it goes when you're expecting. You should be sitting quietly, thinking lovely thoughts so that you have a happy baby." That was a novel concept. I didn't have room in my mind for any sort of thought. I had closed all the doors and windows, so that there was no space for French verbs, no space for Hamlet's soliloquy, no space for bovine reverie, and certainly no space for happy babies.

But the typing proved to be therapeutic, so I tapped out lines and lines of senseless gibberish, and week after week I squeezed my stomach behind the desk above the bakery until my fingers could hardly reach the keyboard. Then I practiced blind on the breakfast table, clattering away at invisible keys on a copy of the *Yorkshire Post*: *sadly hasty kid is there; sadly hasty kid is there; sadly hasty kid is there.*

Yep: sometimes the gibberish was uncannily apt.

22

SHE LOOKS JUST like you, you know."

"You've met her?"

"Oh, yes, walked up the path to the front door on Beech Street and rang the bell. A lot more forthcoming than you."

"Oh, God, I . . ."

"She got your address from your mother's nursing home, flew over to Boston, turned up at the institute, and the doorman directed her the rest of the way. She had been on quite the voyage of discovery. Taken a week's vacation to come over and look for you." If my shoulders had buckled any more, they would have been on the table.

"She thought I was her father, but I soon disabused her of that idea."

"I'm—"

"So who is?" I looked at Francisco in a daze. "Was it him? I can't find anything else from a man, and the dates fit. The girl says she's nearly twenty-one now," he added.

I couldn't follow. "Who are you talking about?"

"The—man—in—the—letter. Are you being deliberately obtuse? Because, if so, it's not going to work." Oh, the mists cleared, the man in the letter. I caressed the envelope tenderly. "No, Francisco, he was just a guy at school. I hardly knew him."

"You hardly knew the father of your own child?" His voice grew so loud the teaspoons shook in their delicate saucers and moved pointedly away from us. "A child I didn't know existed; a child you denied me?" He rubbed his hands on the legs of his jeans, as though he were trying to wipe them clean.

I didn't know how to begin to tell him. I didn't want it to get any uglier than it was, but we were talking at cross-purposes.

"No, Francisco—I hardly knew Jamie, the person who sent the letter. He was a couple of years older than me. He wasn't the father. He wasn't even my boyfriend. He just wrote to me . . . well, to be kind, I guess."

"So who was the father?"

"It was someone who didn't want anything to do with me or the baby."

"And why didn't you tell me about him or about the baby? I mean, didn't it occur to you at any of those times we talked about having a family?"

"It wasn't anything to do with you and me." I addressed the sugar bowl. It seemed to take the statement quite well.

Not so Francisco.

"How can you dare sit there and say that?" The teaspoons quaked again.

I squirmed like a kid caught stealing sweets.

The letter I now held in my hand had arrived before I left for Scarborough, when the scare had turned to scandal and my life had exploded like the dust bag on an overstuffed vacuum cleaner.

Just seeing the handwriting made the past rise up like the smell of camphor in a long-undisturbed pile of clothes.

My parents and I were still living in the village, in the big house, before shame downsized us and drove us out. It was a shrine devoted to starched antimacassars and Dralon furniture, with three sitting rooms, each used according to the status of the visitor. The hierarchy was mostly untested—generally people sat by the kitchen fire and flicked their cigarette ashes into the coals. It saved dirtying an ashtray. As I may have mentioned, we didn't get many visitors.

Especially then.

I was upstairs with the curtains closed, listening to a pop music station on a black transistor held together with brittle, yellowing Scotch tape. The sound faded and crackled, sometimes disappearing altogether until I gave it a sharp kick with my foot, when it would surge back to life with a sudden increase of volume. "*Why don't you write me / I'm out in the jungle / I'm hungry to hear you . . .*" I tapped my toes encased in my father's thick fisherman's socks in time to the music, surprised to learn from Simon and Garfunkel that men too sat around alone, longing for comfort and solace.

I had thought it was just me.

I was a leper. Agneses came and went through the kitchen but fell into embarrassed silence if I entered the room. My father hadn't addressed a word to me in weeks other than to instruct me to change the channel on the television set, usually to avoid the local news. My mother pushed pills on me from her own secret stash: Librium broken into microscopic pieces to calm me down, iron for my wan face, cod liver oil to pad my bones, and alternately slivers of Mogadon to send me to sleep when she found me reading on her two a.m. bathroom run and

Dexedrine to wake me up when I couldn't be roused from my bed until the afternoon. If I had stayed at home much longer, the happy baby my aunt would later anticipate would have had every chance of being born a junkie.

My mother spoke to me in plates of lumps of mashed potato and ground meat in oceans of cooling gravy, thumped on a tray on the ottoman at the foot of my bed, whose inevitable and rapid regurgitation, we had not yet realized, was caused by something more than merely the stress of public humiliation. I had no friends. Kirsty had been moved to a special hospital in Glasgow, but no one suggested I visit her. I hadn't so much as walked up to the village shops for weeks.

So I listened to the radio and sat shivah for the death of disco, gorging myself on golden oldies. I sequestered myself with the *Children of the New Forest* and reread *Heidi* and *Jane Eyre*, wondering, not for the first time, what she saw in the miserable old bastard married to the lunatic in the attic, and how being saddled with a blind geriatric could possibly constitute a happy ending.

I counted the weeks on my fingers and got to August with a horrible chill that had nothing to do with the freezing fog hanging over the village like a giant net curtain that needed a wash.

Sprawled across my rumpled bed, surrounded by pop posters and fashion-magazine cutouts, I pulled the eiderdown up to my chin and wished there was someone I could talk to. My few school friends had deserted me. The cousin Agnes nearest my age wasn't allowed in the house lest she catch slack morals from the toilet seat. I could write to Maisie, but my mother had told me not to, and the solicitor had warned me against putting anything down on paper. Anyway—she was so far away. What could she do? I lit a cigarette from my secret hoard, stolen earlier from my mother's open packet, and blew the smoke through a crack in the skylight window so she wouldn't smell it. Despite doping me with every pharmaceutical she could persuade the doctor to prescribe for her, she balked at allowing me cigarettes.

I closed my eyes against the biting wind blowing the smoke back into my face, trying to clear my mind of unwelcome thoughts with every exhalation, relaxing my limbs, just as the psychiatrist at the hospital had taught me. The sweet combination of nicotine and hyperventilation had just begun to make my head swim when my mother's voice snaked into the room like a whip.

She rasped over the static of the radio: "Ag-nes, there's a letter here for you." I jumped up, sending the ashtray ricocheting under the bed, spilling bent fingers of cigarette butts among the dust balls. I flailed at the smoke that hung lazily in the air before running downstairs.

There it was, standing against the clock on the lace-topped sideboard, this nondescript cream envelope. I turned it over, while my mother hovered.

"Should I open it, hen?" she asked. Pregnancy had not yet turned her totally against me, and I was still treated to the odd chicken endearment.

"It might not be nice." Not nice was my mother's way of saying that it might be from a raving fucking lunatic. We had received a handful of hostile anonymous letters over the previous month.

We had been instructed to hand them all over to the police.

"And if it's from him, don't even touch it."

"It's not going to be from him, Mum, all his mail gets read before he sends it," I said, responding with more conviction than actual knowledge.

She pulled at her lip and smoked, meaning both hands were in her mouth at the same time.

I held the envelope out to her. "You open it, then." She balanced her cigarette on the edge of the fireplace and peeled back the envelope as though she planned on reusing it at Christmas.

"Looks like a bairn's writing," she said doubtfully, which was not reassuring. A lot of the crazy letters had the appearance of having been written by people who could hardly form their letters and often resorted to capitals.

"Oh," she sighed in surprise. "It's from Jamie somebody? There's no second name."

I grabbed the paper out of her hands. "Jamie Frazer?"

"Just says Jamie. I don't even know if it's a laddie or a lassie. Very neat writing for a laddie. Crawfoot Drive's the address."

"Och, it's nobody. A boy at school with me. In swimming," I said, before she started doing a census of Crawfoot Drive so as to discover his pedigree. My mother knew the stud line of the entire village.

"Don't read it if it bothers you, hen," she called after me.

I dashed back upstairs and threw myself down on the bed.

Wintery sunlight filtered through the almost opaque glass of the skylight as I began to read.

He was doing his final year exams at school and bogged down with studying. He wondered if I would be going back to school. He said that I shouldn't worry about what people were saying. He knew it wasn't true. He asked if I was all right, and if I would write back to him and let him know. Maybe he could come and visit?

He was the first person who had expressed any interest in seeing me, but, even without a precedent, I knew I wasn't allowed visitors. Neither could I send anything through the post without censorship from either my mother or the solicitor. I may not have been the one in jail, but I still couldn't get bail.

I replied to my mother's subsequent twenty questions with shrugs and monosyllables, and left the letter lying around in triplicate on my kidney-shaped dressing table with its wrap-around mirrors, so she could read it and reassure herself that he was a harmless schoolboy. But when the house was deserted—my mother at work; my father in his greenhouse; whichever Agnes left to guard me gone up the street to buy milk—I called the telephone number he had printed underneath his address. I kept hanging up at the sound of his mother's voice until, at last, several days later, he answered.

We managed a couple of snatched calls over the next month or so. When I told him I was leaving for Scarborough, he thought it was for a holiday in the sea air. But after I arrived at my aunt's house, there was no more need for secrecy. He began writing again, and this time I could answer.

I don't think we ever discussed anything more personal than musical preferences or books. I remembered he was a big Pink Floyd and early Bowie fan, whereas I liked Carole King and Roberta Flack. He was reading *The Catcher in the Rye*, and I was spending most of my time in a parallel universe dipping sheep and being rescued by a man in a slouch hat called Tex. Well, that and flicking, reluctantly, through the pages of *Mother and Baby*—ironically, the twin aspects of my condition that I would never experience.

I failed to mention either.

He complained about his exams. I complained about my solitary studying, which was so dull it would bore the fillings out of your teeth. I never referred to the expanding waistband on my skirt or the checkups at the prenatal clinic.

His father, the milkman, was proud of, and eagerly ambitious for, his clever son. Jamie was planning to go to Glasgow

University to train as an engineer. I was planning to go to a home for unmarried mothers run by some sort of religious organization in York. In my mind the future was a picture, frozen like a movie still, with me forever clutching a cardboard suitcase on the threshold of an imagined convent, like Maria in *The Sound of Music*.

He wanted to come to see me when school finished in July, but I knew that by then I would already be living with the Sisters of Perpetual Disapproval. I couldn't let him see me swollen and pregnant, wearing my uncle's shirt like a smock. I therefore had to perfect the first of my unaided disappearing acts.

So I stopped writing.

Undaunted, he continued to send the letters every two or three days for a while. Then they dwindled to once a week, hitting the mat every Saturday, as regular as married sex.

But even though I never replied, I couldn't resist reading them. In later years, I found it easier to give up smoking than it had been to ignore Jamie's letters.

And still, even as I packed the baby sweater I had painstakingly knitted and a doll-sized nightdress supplied by my aunt into a duffel bag, they kept on coming. Finally, dread engulfed me every time my aunt passed me another pale cream envelope and they lay, unopened, collecting like grime, under my bed.

At the end of June I gathered the whole bundle of letters, both those I had read and those that remained sealed, all with the same embossed stamps and Jamie's girlish cursive handwriting, ripped them in two, and sent everything back in a jiffy bag—and of course, I never heard from him again.

He deserved better, so I gave it to him. I thought I was doing him a favor, but I guess he didn't see it that way at the time.

If I'd known then the torture of waiting for a letter like the postscript at the bottom of someone else's life, maybe I would have been kinder.

I often wondered what happened to him. He could be building bridges with giant Erector Sets, or whatever it was that engineers did. He could have a bungalow in a scenic spot and a second home in Spain where he plays golf in the winter with his wife.

Or maybe he's a tired, disillusioned man with a beer belly, his red hair bleached prematurely white, counting out his days in bubble packs of Atenolol and Amlodopine.

All I had left was the letter in my hands, the sole survivor of the purge, hidden, as it was, inside the copy of *Lorna Doone* in the footlocker in my mother's attic, and rescued when I put my mother into the home.

"So who was he—or is that information given out only on a need-to-know basis?" Francisco persisted sarcastically.

I groaned, feeling like a Ping-Pong ball, batted to and fro between the past and the present.

"Who?"

"The father of this prodigal child who's been trying to smoke you out for the past year? Damn it, do I have to screw this out of you? Agnes, can you even begin to imagine what I felt like when I found out?"

"I didn't want you to find out," I said weakly. "That's why I left."

"Well, how kind of you to spare me. Am I to feel grateful? Should I congratulate you for your thoughtful consideration? Now I know. So cut the crap and tell me the rest." I took a deep breath. "I got pregnant, I had a baby, it happens. What's to tell?"

"But you must have been very young, impossibly young."

"I was fifteen."

"Fifteen? But Agnes, you were still a kid yourself. You were only a schoolgirl." He didn't seem to be able to bring himself to believe it. "And what about the father—who was he?" Okay, I thought, you asked for it, you can have it: "He was my teacher."

"Your teacher?"

I thought I knew what shock looked like, but it had even more manifestations than I had imagined. Francisco's face went blank.

It was like watching one of those toy slates that you draw on and then pull across to make the picture clear.

"In the name of God, Agnes." Shock had kicked a Spanish cadence into his sentence. "You were a child and you had an affair with your teacher?" I heard disgust mix with disbelief.

"I didn't have an affair with him." Francisco tapped his fingers and his knee jiggled, as if he were on edge, waiting for a starter's pistol to urge him into flight.

"But what happened?"

"You want the whole story, chapter and verse? You insist on knowing absolutely everything?" My words crested on a wave of annoyance. "Fine, here it is. We were hitchhiking home from a dance and he picked us up. He gave my friend and me a ride back home, except that he didn't take us home, he drove us to this place in the countryside, and he kept us there. And yes, I was a bloody schoolgirl." He cradled his head in his hands. The sudden weight on his elbow clattered a saucer aside and spilled an oil slick of tea across the bottom of one of my bank statements. I noticed he was wearing the same tattered jacket with the frayed sleeves he had on the last time I saw him. Both the shirt and the sweater he wore underneath were things I had bought for him, washed for him, folded for him, packed in a suitcase, laid in his dresser.

He gasped and almost reached for my hand before he thought better of it. He kneaded the stubble on his chin instead.

"And that's how I got pregnant." There was a moment after I had told the story that I could have had him back. I had his sympathy, and his horror, and of course the element of surprise. He softened. His eyes melted.

His shoulders lost their rigidity. If I had reached out and touched him, I believe, I think, I could have turned it all around, poured my heart out, put my coat on, and gone straight back home to displace the girl from my bed on Beech Street.

He was contrite, ashamed even, as though he were the one who had done something wrong, who had abandoned me in my time of need.

"But Agnes, fuck, why didn't you tell me? All the time that we've been together. You never mentioned a word. Nobody did." I could see him roll back the years and reinterpret my family's distance, their reluctance to visit, their reticence, the silences, my lack of interest in home, all of it seen through different eyes.

"Did everyone know?"

"I didn't tell anyone, Francisco. My mother didn't even tell my sister and brother until after the baby was adopted. It was hushed up. It had to be. You have no idea how much worse it would have made things. I haven't spoken to a soul about it, not a single person. I just wanted to forget it all."

"But what about the baby? That isn't over and done with. The 'baby' is six feet tall and eager to track you down. Don't you want to meet her? It must have been terrible giving up a child. Didn't you want to keep her?" I checked his face for signs of insanity.

"Why would I? Of course I didn't want to keep it. I didn't want any memories of what had happened. I gave it away. That was the end of the story. Then suddenly, out of the blue, there's this person trying to claim me, wanting to come to see me, wanting to drag it all up again. But I don't want to be seen. Why do you think I took off when I did? I thought I'd escaped it all when we left Oxford and moved to America. Your being offered the job at the institute was the answer to my prayers. I loved my wonderful, quiet, anonymous, nobody little life—our life, Francisco. I didn't walk out on it because I got out on the wrong side of the bed one day and fancied a change of scenery. I didn't want to tell you any of this. Things between us were bad enough."

He began to protest: "They weren't that bad . . ."

"Oh, come on, pleeeeease, let's not pretend. It was awful. You hardly spoke to me. If I had set fire to myself, you would only have asked me to turn the heat down. You arranged your whole sabbatical without consulting me even once. You went away to Colombia and your precious program in Panama for three fucking months and left me behind by myself because I was surplus to requirements. Tell me which part of this comes out of the happy marriage handbook? I knew that a long-lost kid turning up out of the blue would be the final straw. I panicked."

"Yeah . . . you looked like you were panicking," he scoffed, disbelievingly.

My eyes began to tear up: "You don't know how much I missed you. When I first left, there wasn't a day that went past that I didn't wish I could turn back time and go home, do things differently. But I was scared. When the letter came, I just flipped. I could not go back over all that again. Not even with you. Especially not with you."

"I thought you had left me for the man in Manhattan."

I raised my eyebrows. "I never met the man in Manhattan until I started working in his kitchen, and he was away most of the time. He thought I was a widow." Francisco recoiled. "I had to say something to explain why I was walking around like a zombie. In the beginning, it was just a job."

"In the beginning? And in the end?"

"In the end it wasn't just a job," I admitted.

"Did you love him? Caroline described the two of you as a couple."

"Oh, Christ, Francisco, I used him, okay? I used him to hide away, to stop being me for a while. I lied to him about everything. He didn't even know my real name." Even then, I still had him, just a fingertip away.

"But Agnes"—Francisco's voice grew tender, the subject of Adam swept aside like old confetti on the steps of a church—"why run away? You could have told me this. How much of a bastard do you think I am? Surely you knew that I would support you. I would have understood that you wanted to see your only child. We could never have any. This was your only chance."

I ducked that one. There were other reasons for not being able to have children than the mere physical inability to conceive. I couldn't contemplate another pregnancy. Ever. Francisco hadn't begun to make vague noises about parenthood until I was in my early thirties, but then, when nothing happened, we didn't discuss it. He never asked for a definition; I never spelled it out for him.

"I can't believe you didn't want to meet her," he prodded again.

I closed my eyes and drew air into my lungs as if I were about to make a deep dive into a cold pool. He just wasn't getting it. As usual, he wasn't listening to a single word I said. It was like trying to explain algebra to a polar bear.

"But you aren't hearing me. I did not and still don't want to meet my only child. To say what? 'Hello, dear, um, your father was a nutjob and you were a horrible mistake. Nobody wanted you—not your grandparents, not me'? I didn't even bother to give her a name. Do you think it's going to be three verses and a chorus of 'Mother and Child Reunion' with a full gospel choir and three-part harmony?"

He fell silent, thoughtful. "I know it won't be easy," he faltered.

Under-fucking-statement.

"Not only will it not be easy, but it won't be happening."

"You could explain things."

I gave him an impatient look. As though I hadn't gone over it in my mind a million times. "There is no explanation. The whole point is that I can't explain . . . It's not only my secret to tell. Other people are involved. The adoptive parents, for instance . . ." I broke off. I was growing impatient. I knew what I knew. He didn't have all the details.

"It's not an academic treatise, you know. You can't just lay it out rationally in paragraphs and say, 'Discuss.' It's a mess."

"I know, you want to spare the child's feelings . . ."

"No, I wanted to spare my own. It was my pregnancy, my baby, my child, and my decision. Can't you accept that, just for once, this is about me?"

"But the girl . . . You don't want to upset her, I can see that."

"Oh, the fucking girl—it's not about her. People got damaged here. I damaged them," I said in a small voice.

"I understand. It must have been awful, unthinkable. But, Agnes, you couldn't help being . . ." He searched around for the right word, settling finally for the wrong one. He dropped his voice. "It's not your fault you were raped."

"Oh, Francisco." I shook my head wearily, my own words a corresponding whisper. "Who said he raped me?" And that was the end of it. I saw the brief flicker of light in his eyes disappear.

His grip loosened, and let go. Almost twenty years of my life slipped away, downstream on a fast current. The moment for reconciliation had passed. I could have grabbed it, but I didn't want to. The life I wanted back wasn't this one.

I collected my papers and rolled them into the shopping bag I was still using as luggage. I pleaded with him not to tell the girl where I was if she turned up looking for me and, eventually, he agreed. In any case, as he pointed out, he didn't know where I was. I hadn't actually told him when I called.

He said he would get his lawyer to draw up a settlement of our property. I wasn't aware we had any. Lawyers or property.

The house on Beech Street was paid for by the institute, and everything else—the apartment in Bogotá, the villa near Cartagena, the farm, the place in Bahia, the Newport saltbox by the shore that we used to summer in—belonged to his family. But he insisted I should have something to live on. I told him I had a new job and an apartment, without mentioning that it was a back bedroom with a tiny closet and a single futon that dug its lumpy elbows into the small of my back, but he said it was only fair that I had half the assets. He asked if I wanted any of the furniture. I said no. He could give me whatever he thought was fair, or not. I was easy.

"Apparently," he said. "Are you still seeing that guy—the one you were living with?" he asked.

"No, that's over." I was proud of myself. I managed to get the words out evenly, without the crack in my heart rending the short sentence apart.

He nodded as if it was no less than he expected or I deserved, wrapped his scarf round his neck, shrugged on an overcoat, and clicked the lock on his now empty briefcase.

"I know that you've made it patently clear that it's none of my business, but I think you should definitely meet your child. You can't keep avoiding it just because it's uncomfortable. It will give you some sort of closure." Closure. What psychobabble planet was he on? Where was the self-help stuff coming from?

I didn't need any more closure. I just needed to be left the fuck alone.

He said goodbye, but disguised it in legal speak: "I don't have your address, so get an attorney—you will need one—and tell him to get in touch with mine." He gave me a card with the name of a legal firm in Boston. "How should I address you these days? Are you still Morales, or are you McBride, or what was it you were calling yourself in that house? Loost? Liszt? Wagner? I can't keep up."

"It was Lutz, but no—McBride will be fine."

"Lutz. Where the hell did you come up with that?" He shook his head.

"I made it up," I said to the nape of his neck, as he walked away.

"Ah, well, you're good at that," he said to the floor. His tired shoulders buckled under the weight of his coat. Lord & Taylor, winter 1993, I remembered. I hoped the girl on Beech Street would take better care of him than I had.

I sat for a second after he'd gone, trying to look calm, stirring the scum in a cup of cold tea as though I were two thoughts away from working out the rate at which the universe was expanding. But, inside, I felt like one of those characters in the computer game that Ned used to play, with a big bubble over my head that, instead of TIRED or HUNGRY, just said FUCKED and flashed on and off, visible to anyone who cared to look.

23

BY THE END of March there was still no response to the letter I had sent Adam when I moved into homoeopathy hell in Brooklyn. I had gone to Union Square some mornings after I finished work at the dentist's and hung out near his office, hoping I might run into him, but it was freezing and too cold to stand around for long. In any case, I looked like a vagrant, so that even if he had walked out of his building he would probably have looked at my hands for a coffee cup so he could drop change into it.

I didn't dare use the phone in the apartment because my landlady went through each AT&T bill marking off calls against the pad she kept beside the handset, and I had no privacy at my desk in the waiting room at the practice. Too late it occurred to me to do what the rest of the modern world was just beginning to do and get a cell phone or send him an e-mail which we had at work. I was a little behind when it came to technology. Thank goodness the people in the practice were Luddites: their computer was almost as outdated as I was, their accounting program only a little more sophisticated than carving notches on a stick, and their appointment system a highly innovative method consisting of a large date book and a pencil.

Still, I was in no position to feel superior. I could use a word processor, but when it came to the information superhighway, I was still trying to find my way out of the parking lot. I read manuals. I made mistakes. I spent more time making backups of my backups than I did making originals. Eventually I compiled a database and mastered a simple layout in a desk-top publishing program in order to put together basic information sheets for our customers on each treatment. In time, I even managed a monthly newsletter that I sent to every client together with their bill.

I discovered that what one of the younger partners (shiatsu and Swedish sports massage) called "all that office bitchwork" was much more mind-numbingly absorbing than cleaning had ever been, but, just like an anesthetic, it wore off when you stopped topping it up. And for that there was vodka. I found the predictability of my daily routine to be comfortingly reliable. I was surrounded by people, but they stayed off at a safe distance, usually reading old copies of *People* magazine.

Jocelyn, my landlady, a quiet, microscopic speck, not unlike the much-distilled remedies she prescribed for her clients, crept quietly around the edges of my life. She ate tiny meals of boiled eggs and quartered tofu-paste sandwiches on flaxseed bread.

She bought goat's milk in miniature cartons, and single-portion chicken breasts that lasted her two days and that she accompanied with a solitary boiled potato or one tomato sliced into four lewdly grinning quarters. She insistently invited me to join her for dinner, until I had no choice but to surrender my allotted time in the kitchen and stop cooking altogether. I ate at a nearby Chinese restaurant or subsisted on bananas, instant noodles, and chocolate. Only the crudeness of the sugar and salt cut through my indifference to flavor. I weighed no more than I had when I was a teenager. The muscles I had cut when I was swimming laps mushed into marshmallows on my arms; the toned thighs, tensed from months of fucking, turned into string cheese; and then the fat melted away.

"You're getting terribly thin, Agnes," she said one day when I passed her on my way to the kettle, where I was going to add hot water to my supper—Japanese noodles with extra monosodium glutamate and pink rinds the size of toenail parings that were supposed to be prawns. "Are you feeling all right? You don't eat enough, you know," she said, peering though her Jewfro. Ring, ring, I said to myself, as I smiled benignly in response. Pot here; is that you, kettle? Look, sorry, but I was just calling to tell you that you're black.

"I've never had much of an appetite," I replied, when the answering machine in my head clicked off.

"Your asthma seems to be getting worse, too." She had noticed that I walked round with an inhaler more or less permanently attached to either my hand or my mouth, like a Ventolin chain smoker, but it didn't seem to have occurred to her that this had anything to do with the patina of cat hair and dust, not to mention her own free-flowing locks, that covered everything in the house.

"Allergies," I explained.

"Well, you know, homoeopathy is ideal for that. I'll give you a free consultation if you want." Hmm, I thought, before declining, cleaning the house more than once a decade might also be quite effective. I had enough of the belladonna inside me without adding to it in tincture.

But then Graham, the putty-faced nutritionist, joined the balanced-diet refrain and proffered several jars of supplements that he urged me to take with meals. I didn't ask, what meals? as I thanked him profusely, and later I deposited them in the dustbins outside Kentucky Fried Chicken on East Fourteenth Street while I was eating fries and waiting for the bus home.

I resisted all further interference until Krishna, the Indian acupuncturist, newly arrived in the States from a five-year apprenticeship in Mumbai, took me aside after the Saturday-evening surgery and told me there was concern in the practice.

He was slender, brown, and incredibly pretty, with dark-fringed eyes as rich as Nutella. I could imagine him naked—small and smooth and perfectly formed—but that was as far as I got: imagining. There was, I knew, no Mrs. Krishna. He was single and lived alone. He had even asked me out to dinner once, but I refused. I didn't do dinner, and I didn't do Krishna. I looked, but I didn't touch. I kept my eyes on my appointment book and called out patients' names.

Until one night, as I was laying all my sharpened pencils out in nice straight lines, he drew a chair in front of my desk and sat on it expectantly. "You work like a Trojan, Agnes, and we all appreciate it, but, you see, you're really not taking care of yourself." His voice had a hypnotic rick-rack cadence to it. It made me feel like a child being bounced on someone's knee.

"Let me treat you," he urged. I thought he meant another offer of chicken tikka and popadams up in Greenwich Village, and I was already shaking my head, but he went on. "We'll get your chi back in balance in no time, open your passages, get you breathing properly." He gestured to the inhaler lying on my desk. "One session, and then you see how much better you feel." I said that my chi was just dandy and my passages best left closed, but nevertheless, at six o'clock the following Monday, when his last patient, Mrs. Solomon (migraines), had left in a cloud of Chanel, I found myself lying on his couch like a cadaver waiting for an autopsy, wearing a pair of paper panties and a white sheet while he took my pulse.

Well. What the hell, I figured. I'd already had the amalgam stripped from my fillings at a fifty percent discount by an alarmed Jim Goldmann in the dentist's office when he gave me a complimentary checkup, muttering all the time about "British teeth"; what was the biggie about having Krishna acupuncture me?

He examined my tongue and told me I had too much heat, muttered something about spleen and liver, then he casually stuck needles into my scalp, my forehead, my earlobes, and my kneecaps, until I felt as if I should be wearing white makeup and standing outside some teenage babysitter's window on Elm Street wearing a fedora and carrying an axe in my hand.

He lit a bunch of herbs that looked like a large joint and started heating the needles. Acrid white smoke billowed around me. I half expected him to start making *wa-wa-wa* war-cry sounds, and dance, keening, around the table. Though I kept that thought to myself on the grounds of racism.

"Is this supposed to do anything?" I asked, the movement of my jaw making the pins in my scalp and brow wiggle. That hurt.

"Shh," he said, stroking my hand and giving it a squeeze, my skin the milk on his coffee-colored fingers. He smelled of cedar and cinnamon. It sounds more romantic than it was. My only previous exposure to cedar had been in Gay's closet, and the wood in her shoe rack, but it was both compelling and awkward to be so close to a male body after such a long while.

"You relax," he said, sitting down beside me and holding my

hand. It was the unaccustomed intimacy that did it. Tears slid sideways out of my eyes and ran in channels through the crows' feet into a reservoir in each ear.

"Agnes, ah, yes—you're crying. Don't worry. You see, it's releasing all the negative energy. It will cleanse you." It'll take more than waving a large Marlboro Red at a few hat pins to cleanse me, I thought. There's not enough Tide in the world.

I didn't need someone torturing me by sticking needles into my flesh; I could manage that perfectly well by myself. But I didn't speak. I just let Lake Superior bleed itself out while I lay flat on my back on a plastic massage table looking at the magnolia paint on the stippled ceiling. We would need to do something about that, I decided. You couldn't expect patients to feel positive when they were forced to look into the impasto of swirling bas-relief.

I can't say it did me any good. It just put me in touch with my inner misery, whose address I had been quite pleased to have misplaced. But I said thank you very much like a good girl who has been given a piece of birthday cake at a party, even though she doesn't like marzipan, and took heart from the fact that the other practitioners in the surgery seemed to heave a collective sigh of relief. Each stopped proffering his or her own particular brand of snake oil and backed off, satisfied that I had been taken in hand.

And, still, the postman never rang twice.

Yes, Francisco was as good as his word and sent me an offer via my newly acquired attorney, a cousin of Krishna, whom I had never met but who had an office in the Bronx. A manila envelope arrived by Federal Express containing a full inventory of our joint possessions, which I was required to sign in order to waive any further claim on our estate. An estate—huh. We had a three-bedroom clapboard with a warped stoop that belonged to Francisco's institute, hardly an estate. The document listed every painting, every print, every chair in the house on Beech Street, which, in total, couldn't have amounted to more than ten thousand dollars' worth and that was taking into account the new washer and dryer I had bought the previous spring.

I felt enormously sad reading the inventory. I could still close my eyes and walk through each room in the house, from the basement to the attic. I had loved that house from the moment, fifteen years ago, that I got out of the car and stood outside holding Francisco's hand. I could recite from memory the store in which we had bought each cushion and document the strata of the wallpaper on the bedroom wall; I knew the history of every single chipped plate, dragged back from various corners of the globe, set out on the dresser that I bought at Pier 1 then bashed with a hammer until it looked as old and worn as the rest of our furniture. I could read the story of my marriage in the lines and checks of Francisco's winter flannel shirts hanging up in his wardrobe. And now I had the final page of the story, with everything drawn up into a balance sheet and its very small sum underlined.

But if our possessions were worth nothing, I also discovered that Francisco had invested more than half his salary ever since we met, and that, furthermore, his trust fund was more generous than I had realized. I knew we had savings, but nothing had prepared me for this. Apparently Francisco had kept some secrets of his own: he was, to be blunt, rolling in money like a pig in shit. I was stunned by the figure at the bottom of the printout.

My share of the spoils would be six hundred thousand dollars, payable whenever I wanted it. He had started the ball rolling on the divorce—irretrievable breakdown of marriage relationship. Fair enough—better than pathological lying and serial adultery. Once again, I was urged to indicate my acceptance and to have it witnessed and notarized before returning it to his attorney. He hadn't planned this overnight, I realized. The settlement had been in the pipeline for quite some time.

With more than half a million dollars in my bank account, I knew I would be free. I didn't have to stay in Manhattan, living in a threesome with an IKEA chest of drawers called Narks and a bedside table called Fluck.

I could go . . . well, anywhere.

I could retrain, go to college, study animal husbandry, or move to Maine. I could even travel the world. I could visit Maisie.

Or Geordie.

I could go to Pennsylvania and visit Karl.

This time I could disappear properly.

But what about Adam?

Of course he never contacted me. He never responded to my letter, never called, and never turned up, either on a white stallion or in a cab. I suppose I hadn't really expected that he would, but that frail hope that he might, just, one day, might, be there in the Mercedes sitting outside the house when I turned the corner, kept me going until the anguish of waiting, longing, dreaming, and continual disappointment obliterated it like Lysol does germs.

Why would he bother? I knew he had been in love with me, but we had no history, no family, no past, nothing but sex and hastily eaten pot roasts to hold us together—just a relationship built on lies and Knorr bouillon cubes.

I rang his house from a pay phone once but got only a mechanized voice on an answering machine that had obviously moved in when I moved out. I wondered if perhaps he and Gay had reconciled, and so I telephoned her apartment early one morning from the dental office courtesy of Dr. Goldmann. Her voice, as sharp and fruity as fermenting pears, piped down the line. I hung up.

The practice closed for Memorial Day weekend. Dr. Goldmann took his college-age kids to Miami and went windsurfing—I know, I was surprised too. You wouldn't think it to look at him, weedy little thing that he was. The divorcee went home to her widowed mother in Baltimore. The cat was, thank you, God, placed in a carrying case and transported with her on the back seat of her Honda Civic. Touchingly, she invited me along, having figured, by this point in my sad and lonely life, that I had no family and no friends. Krishna wondered if I wanted to go with him to visit another of his tribe of cousins in Toronto. Graham told me that he and his wife would be delighted if I would join them for a vegan lunch on Sunday.

To each, I said I had plans, which I did. I was happy to have the first weekend off in months and also to have the apartment, or, more important, the bathroom, to myself. In view of my soon-to-arrive riches, I had splurged on some bubble bath from Henri Bendel and had decided to go all out and buy my food at three times the price from a classy takeout place on St. Mark's. I then planned to heat it up in the verboten microwave that my landlady used to keep her bread in.

Woooo hooo, spring break.

On Saturday I sat on the fire escape to soak up the first few consumptive rays of sun that the year had just coughed up and ate peanut butter straight from the jar (low salt—defeats the fucking object, I say). On Sunday I had marshmallow fluff on white bread and, thus fortified, put on the by now grossly bloated black nylon skin of Lennie's coat and went to the reservoir in Central Park, where I mingled with the tourists, joggers, and dog walkers who had been my daily companions the summer before. It was strange being back on the Upper East Side. Strange and not altogether comfortable.

There was the same mix of high class and underclass, the groomed WASPy women in the stores being served by Spanish-speaking girls who have their kinky hair tucked up in barrettes, the African immigrants selling on carts on street corners, the restaurants where the wait staff couldn't afford to eat, the door openers and those for whom they automatically opened, the help pushing the wheelchairs and the strollers. I felt as though I were having the hair repeatedly waxed off my chest as I walked through the familiar streets. Everything was the same, except for me. I wasn't here anymore.

I forced myself to wait through three cups of watery black coffee in a diner before I allowed myself a ten-minute detour along Eightieth Street, past the house. I stood out of sight at the bus stop where I had waited for my interview, wishing Adam would walk out of the door. Even Lennie would have been a welcome sight. But the door remained closed, the house glassy-eyed and withdrawn, the tulips on the shutters like something that had long been abandoned and not loved much when it had been occupied.

Even the evergreen plants in the window box had withered and died, and not even a dandelion shoot reached for the light through the littered soil. The shutters on the dining room were pulled together. The lids on the garbage cans outside the basement apartment were upturned and pooled with water and dead leaves.

I toyed with the idea of knocking on the door. I even crossed the road and went as far as to put my foot on the bottom step but then retreated. Gay might once have answered the phone in her apartment, but that didn't mean she wasn't here now, or that he didn't have another woman who spent the night and shared his breakfast. If Francisco could manage to install an Agnes before the intermission, then it was certainly possible for Adam to have his own sequel during the second act.

The bus heaved itself up the hill. I let three go past before I had to admit defeat and board one. It was Memorial Day weekend after all. I could go to the parking garage and see if Adam's car was there if I was willing to make conversation with the guys who worked there, but even if it was, what did that prove? He was probably away somewhere that you couldn't drive to with the children, or a new girlfriend, or even Gay. The thought made me ill.

To fight the nausea, I went home and ate almost a whole box of Russell Stover nut candies; I nibbled around all the hazelnuts and threw them into the waste disposal to feed the rats—rules be damned. Dr. Goldmann had warned me about crunching down on anything too hard with my new white fillings. It was a pity he hadn't given me a similar warning about men.

What a fool I was. I was behaving just like a lovesick teenager, hanging around outside the house of the boy I had a crush on, hoping for a glimpse. Just like Kirsty and I had done with Dan Ponte, the bastard. The lucky bastard. I bet he was still running the café—almost forty now, married to some shrew, with a couple of kids with Italian names and Scottish accents, serving Parmesan and pesto with his French fries and tiramisu-flavored ice cream.

I went to bed, giving the futon the kick I usually reserved for the cat when it insisted on sleeping on my bed, and tossed and turned on the flimsy Scandinavian pine bed long into the night.

That was it. Exactly. A lovesick teenager. It had taken me long enough—one illegitimate child, two getaways, one husband, and too many bad bedfellows—before finally I scored my first proper, fully reciprocated love affair. Pity it had taken me thirty-seven years to get there. Pity I had to fuck it up.

By Monday I was longing for Tuesday and the welcome siren call of two hours spent vacuuming and swabbing floors in the dental office. It was almost enough to make me roll up my sleeves and tackle the hallway at home. Almost but not quite.

I didn't want to send myself into anaphylactic shock.

After swearing that I would never go back uptown again, I checked the paper and decided to visit the Guggenheim. I convinced myself that I was massively interested in the photography exhibition titled Women on the Edge, but of course I was fooling myself. I didn't even go to the museum. Instead, I got off the bus at Eighty-ninth as if I were, but made a loop through the backstreets, over to Madison, up to Ninetieth, along to Park, up to Ninety-fourth, across to Second Avenue, down to Ninety-first, then back to Fifth Avenue, looking at other people's shrouded existences, examining the doormen hiding behind the brass doors, dark-suited, butch figures standing in filigree entrances, imagining their lives the way I had once done before I married Francisco and coveted coupledom as though it were a kingdom to be forever denied me.

On the way to the Cooper-Hewitt I crossed the street to avoid a group of people standing on the sidewalk beside a large charter coach that was just pulling away from the curb. It was full of girls waving hysterically at their parents, who waved back with determined cheerfulness.

Even as they drifted back to the empty stomachs of their town cars and SUVs, their eyes still followed the back of the disappearing bus. A school field trip. Lucky girls. And then I realized where I was. Spence. Lennie's school. I had walked up here a couple of times to collect her when I needed to take her to the orthodontist.

Some of the women hung around chatting animatedly to each other, toddlers forked against their hips. They were all so glossy and beautiful, backlit by money. Lucky them. I turned back and stepped out into the road and looked to the right to see if it was clear to cross, but traffic streamed past the school. I stood and waited impatiently for the green man to clear my path.

A dark blue car nosed toward the junction and slowed to a stop as I waited, impatient for me to cross. Then I looked again, and hastily clutched around in the depths of my pocket, reaching for my inhaler while my lungs clenched like a fat girl's thighs around my windpipe. It was Adam's car. And there was Adam, alone at the wheel, staring at the traffic lights, his fingernails tapping out a tattoo on the dashboard.

Every time I walked home from work and turned the corner of my block I held my breath and imagined this car parked outside my apartment. And every day I turned the corner and saw the front of my building deserted. But finally, here it was. Outside Lennie's school. On Memorial Day.

His eyes flickered away from the light and caught mine.

Without thinking, I lifted my fingers in a feeble greeting. But when he saw me, the expression told me everything I needed to know. Alarm, distaste, embarrassment, fear even. And yet, still I stood there, not believing the sworn evidence of my own eyes. I might have said his name. I heard something come out of my mouth, several times; my two hands joined in an ineffectual wave until my palms pressed together beseechingly like one of those gypsy women who pull at your sleeve and beg for money on the subway.

His lips moved mutely; his head shook from side to side. His skin looked patchy, like marbled paper in sickly colors; he had bags under his eyes. His hair was rumpled and unkempt. Rain coursed down across the windscreen, the glass misted from the inside, his silent words hitting the window. I could see the shape of *no* through the beads of water.

The insistent beeping of the pedestrian crossing rang in my ears like the busy signal on a colossal telephone and then stopped abruptly. The light changed from red to green, but he sat with his hands clenched on the wheel, looking at me, until a car behind sounded its horn, and hastily he drove off.

I turned and watched him. He slowed beside the group of mothers on the sidewalk. My heart bounced and stuttered against my chest like pennies dropped from a great height. He was going to stop. He was waiting for me. I took one step forward until I saw a waving figure detach itself from the crowd.

Gay's metallic white head bent and opened the car door, her compact body jackknifed inside, and the last of my hope slipped away like water down the drain.

Stupid, stupid, stupid, I berated myself. He probably thought I had followed him there, that I had been waiting for him, that I was stalking him. I remembered sitting for twenty minutes on the wall at the bus stop on Madison the day before. He might have seen me there, hanging around like a bad smell that you just can't air out.

I felt drab and grubby and pathetic—wheedling for scraps like a refugee with a baby in a bundle of rags.

I walked away. Down Fifth all the way to the Twenties, where I hailed a cab and rode back to Brooklyn. It was only when I let myself into the apartment that I realized my coat was dry.

There were no damp footprints on the sea grass carpeting. My hair wasn't wet. It hadn't been raining. I had only imagined it.

I finished my candy and heated up some solidified sodium that claimed to be luxury beef consommé with sherry. I drank three inches of vodka with flat Diet Coke, and another inch straight up with an ice cube. When my landlady arrived home with the feline Helen Keller and offered me a piece of her mother's lemon pound cake, I pleaded a headache and went to my room with John Irving.

The next morning I didn't go in to work. I stayed in bed and pretended to sleep. I didn't bother watching out for the mailman.

He wasn't coming.

Nobody was ever coming.

24

AND THAT'S HOW I ended up here. Sitting in a black leather chair that looks like a chess piece while one of the professional sorry sits across from me, trying to look impassive, but not always managing. I can usually get a laugh out of him if I try, but I can't be bothered most of the time. I don't feel that funny.

His name is Irshad, and unlikely as it seems, given that they have nothing in common except skin color, he comes highly recommended by Krishna, who arranged the appointments. I would have expected to have had my nervous breakdown subcontracted out to another member of his extended family, but since they were all dry lawyers and accountants, in the case of madness the Indian mafia had failed him.

Instead, he had to resort to that good old standby: word of mouth.

One of his patients had taken her daughter to Irshad for treatment for anorexia, so when they realized I obviously wasn't eating but hadn't a clue what the root of my problem was, Irshad seemed as good a starting point as any.

I could have told them I didn't have an eating disorder. I had a waking disorder. I was finally cashing in on my sleep debt and had retreated to a semiconscious world where life went along nicely without me, and I slept.

I called in sick for the whole week after I saw Adam in the street, most of which was spent in bed with the yellow blinds casting a jaundiced light on the walls, while I floated in the shadows being visited by hybrids of the longed-for and the long dead. I simply didn't want to wake up.

I knew Adam was gone, but I dreamed of him, sometimes entreating me to come back, at other times screaming at me to go away. Both left me weeping when sleep departed.

I had a photograph of him, his head thrown back in delight, cut from the *New York Times* when one of his authors won the Pulitzer. Every now and again I took it out and looked at it, but it wasn't the same as the one in my head, with his crumpled smile, his generosity, his nervous laugh, and the smell of his skin all mixed up together. It was his Adamness that I summoned forth to comfort and taunt me.

But still I knew he was gone, as I had known from the beginning he would be. I had just nursed the hope like a sleeping baby that he might return while I got on with the business of life.

When I dreamed of him, though, he came back. I saw him as he was in life, and heard his voice, and felt his touch, and had another chance to make things right.

So, no, I didn't want to wake up.

But Krishna and Jocelyn had other ideas. They called a doctor, a real one, then dragged me off to his office to be stuffed full of happy pills. Then they threatened me with needles and potions in eyedroppers and boiled Chinese herbs that smelled of halitosis and wet dogs. I was touched by how much they cared, but I really agreed only because the effort of moving out of Jocelyn's apartment and finding another place where I could pine in peace was beyond me.

But Irshad is okay, I suppose. I see him twice a week, every week, whether I like it or not. Krishna claims he's very good. I take his word for it and hope his judgment with shrinks is better than with hat pins. I do feel a bit better, though, and it can't be the Prozac the psychiatrist gave me because I flush them down the john every morning with the homoeopathic tea. They take the edge off, but I like the edge. It stops me from falling off it.

Irshad's a rather solemn, low-key man, like a professional mourner at a funeral with no corpse who's very, very sorry all the time. He does this steeple thing with his hands, and I feel he might try to sell me a casket or ask me to pick out a floral arrangement. He's also big and broad, with the physique of a football player. His hair is a slippery sort of Grecian 2000 black, and he has blindingly white teeth that jump out of his ash-brown face. He always wears gray cords and either a charcoal-colored sweater or another in the shade of something that was once beige but put in the dark wash by mistake. No wedding ring. I asked him once why his clothes look like a uniform, but he just said, "What makes you think it's a uniform? Is that what you do, 'gnes—wear a uniform?" He does that a lot—hits the ball right back at you, leaving you stumbling, wrong-footed, trying to pick it up. I've never been much good at ball games. Anyway, I suspect it's to keep the "space," as he calls it, contiguous and neutral, so his patients remain calm.

"Analysand, not patient," he corrects. Sounds like something you put in your hair to keep your bangs out of your face.

That's one of the things that gets a smile, but then he asks, "Do you always use humor in a difficult situation?" He speaks with a clipped S'th African accent shorn of its vowels, that is, when he speaks at all, which isn't often. He mostly lets me ramble Vogonically on and on about the past. If I go quiet for too long, he asks me if I've had any dreams, so I usually keep talking. I don't want to talk about Adam, and anyway, now that he has stopped his nocturnal visits, my dreams are so dull that I answer e-mails in them. Sometimes I write stuff on my hand to prompt my memory, just to keep things rolling. If he's noticed, he hasn't said. I can't believe he's interested in listening to people recount the second most boring thing in the world, but I suppose he thinks I'm going to let something revealing slip on the royal road to the unconscious. But I'm not.

Irshad always manages to make me feel as though I'm walking around with my dress tucked into my underpants, an awkwardness caused by the fact that he is really quite good-looking, in a Bollywood sort of way. He has this slightly superior expression, as if he's indulging you but is willing to be patient until you stop fooling around. It's as if he knows what you're thinking. Well, hell, he does: you pay him to listen while you *tell* him what you're thinking. He's not as pretty as Krishna, but he has more of a presence, despite his attempt to seem ordinary so as to put us pathetic, drooling patients at our ease. He has the body of someone who's been enlarged to the point of distortion, so that the line of his nearly square jaw and the angle of his almost straight nose are just a little bit off. In my other life I would probably have slept with him by now. Oh, I know it's unprofessional, but when did I ever let that stop me? In fact, I would probably have slept with both of them, him and Krishna; hell, I'd have thrown in Dr. Goldmann, the dentist, on a three-for-two special offer.

I might have told him this in one of the sessions if it hadn't sounded a bit presumptuous, as if it were a boast of my powers of attraction rather than just my default setting. But what I would have done in the old days isn't relevant anymore. Times have changed.

There had only been one man since I left Adam. A one-night stand when I was working at the hotel, a surfer on his way to Maine where, unbelievably, he was going to brave the waves in the middle of winter. I thought that I could take a small maintenance dose of him, to get me through the night, but the minute he touched me I started to cry—always an effective libido booster, I find. Poor soul lost his erection and jumped off me as though I'd put a rat on his back. But it wasn't what he had done that made me weep, or who he was. It was who he wasn't. For the first time I found I couldn't just wipe out the memory of the last man with the next one. So why bother?

Now I don't even take all my clothes off to go to bed, I feel so cold all the time. I think sex must be one of those things that requires your inner thermostat to be set on high. My boiler just doesn't fire anymore.

This is my fifth visit. Krishna drops me right at the door, then I take the subway back. It's fucking expensive: falling to pieces doesn't come cheap. He's giving me a discount because of my low earnings—he doesn't know I'm half a millionaire—and the practice picks up a small percentage of the cost, the health plan half, and the rest comes out of the Agnes McBride Fuck-up Fund. I should add that my attendance was a collective, not elective, decision. The partners said it was a condition of my continued employment.

It's not good for the image of the wellness industry if the receptionist is barking and hasn't changed her clothes for a week.

But I don't mind. It's like going to the hairdresser's without having to talk about your vacations. It's not too bad.

However, the pockmarked anaglyphic wallpaper: now that is bad. And I'm not keen on the furniture, which is bulky and dark and has a lot of straight lines and corners, with nothing soft to rest your eyes on. Even the couch looks as hard as a dog biscuit.

You can just see the faint indentation on the pillow where the last person laid their head. But I don't lie. Well, not on the bed.

I sit on the chair and try to look him in the eye.

The first time I came he said he thought he should probably refer me on to a woman. He said he had a colleague who might suit me, but I told him, no thanks, and that I didn't get on with women.

"That's precisely why you should see one," he replied. But I had already resigned myself to him. So I stayed.

I think we're more or less up to date on My Life So Far. We've covered the absolute basics in the teenage pregnancy scandal—broad strokes, I think you'd say. I haven't told him any details, just that the father was a teacher at my school. Then we did Francisco, Adam, Mother, Geordie, and inked in the background of Gideon, Silvano, Karl, Ali, and the other member of the International Brigade of Bedfellows who once graced most of the back row of a Balfour College photograph, at least enough for him to get the idea. Some of their names I can't quite remember. I started to make a list, but it appalled me. Especially when I began writing things like *boy from the King's Arms.*

"Why do you think you've been involved with so many men?" he asked today.

I was startled. There was a cobweb in the corner above the door. It had been there since my first visit. Didn't anyone ever clean in here? His certificates were in frames on the wall behind his head. A spider plant sprouted untidily on a shelf.

"I don't know," I replied. "It just happened. They were there."

"You seem to think that you don't play any part at all in the progress of your own life, 'gnes," he said, snipping off the first syllable of my name as if it were the dead bloom on an ugly flower. "You don't take responsibility for the outcome. It all 'just happens.'" I was rather taken aback. First, by the unaccustomed speech, which was more than I had heard him say in weeks, and second by the criticism.

"But it does. I didn't ask to get pregnant at fifteen; you can hardly blame me for that."

He spoke softly, but his words fell on me like concrete dominoes, one after the other. "Of course not. I'm not blaming you for anything; I'm asking you to see how your own actions impact on your life. Yes, you had a child when you were still a child yourself in some ways, and the father was someone who was in a position of trust, who should have protected you, not taken advantage of you. I know the circumstances were very painful, but you have to remember that you didn't do anything bad or shameful. Teenagers have been having babies since time began.

"In some cultures children are married at this age. I know, I know"—he waved away my objections—"it's definitely not something to condone, but there is no shame attached to the act of giving birth to a child. You can't let it inform every single thing that happens for the rest of your days." I tried very hard to keep my face impassive.

"What I'm asking you to consider is that after your child was born, you ran. When your daughter came looking for you, you ran. When your husband came looking for you, you ran. When things became difficult with Adam, you ran. When are you going to turn around and face your demons? Are you going to go on feeling like a victim forever?" I was stung. Now, now, he turns into Chatty Cathy, and it's so he can have a go at me.

"Thanks."

"You see, you're being a victim now. Why are you thanking me for saying something that obviously upsets you? If you don't like what I'm saying, tell me so. Tell me to fuck off. Don't hold back. I'm not going to run away."

"Well, then, fuck off. Aren't you supposed to be supportive and sympathetic?"

"I'm supposed to help you. I'm not going to help you much by sitting here and saying, 'There, there, poor you.' Of course you deserve compassion and understanding, but, 'gnes, you have to look at the way you react to these events. There's no prince coming along to rescue you. You have to do it for yourself, so you can move on with your life."

I couldn't speak. My chest was tight, but it wasn't because of the asthma. The box of tissues on the side table was wavering in front of my eyes, but I'd be fucked if I was going to give him the satisfaction of weeping. A little pink wisp of paper protruded gaily from the serrated oval mouth, taunting me. What a frivolous color. How could he expect people to mop up their guts with a sheet of bubblegum-pink tissue?

"What do you suggest?" I said coldly.

"It's not my job to make suggestions. Ask yourself where you want to go and see if there is something you can do to take yourself there."

"I can hardly force someone to talk to me if they don't want to. Is that what you want me to do?"

"I assume you mean Adam?"

I nodded.

"Is that what you want to do?"

Jesus, I was getting tired of this. It was like one of those games you play where you have to answer every question with another. "Of course not. He knew where I was if he wanted to find me. He obviously didn't. When I saw him, he drove away."

"You knew where he was. Look at it from his point of view. You'd been living there for—what—six months?"

"Seven."

"Living there under an assumed name, and he'd fallen in love with you, or this person he thought you were, then pow—your supposedly dead husband walks in. Don't you think the onus was on you to make sure your voice, your explanations, your apologies, were heard?"

"He didn't want to hear."

"You know that for sure?"

I swallowed, mentally hissed at the tissues to piss off, and nodded again.

"Well, fine, so you just have to accept it and move on."

Silence.

"What about your daughter? Are you going to treat her the same way? You know where to find her, but you've made no attempt to contact her. Do you see that she could be forgiven for making the same assumptions about you that you're making about Adam?"

"But it's true—I don't want to see her. I would rather eat my own liver than speak to her. I have absolutely nothing to say to her." I was going to get this printed on cards and start handing it out to people. "Anyway, there's nothing good I can say to her."

"How do you work that one out?"

"I don't want to go over the past—I don't want to have to tell her about . . . all that old crap," I finished weakly.

"You could start by telling me."

"I can't."

"Okay, when you're ready. But you could still think about seeing your daughter. You only have to say whatever you feel comfortable talking about. Just as you do here."

"I suppose," I said. Yeah, right, I thought.

I sniffed and looked back at the corner where the cobweb hung suspended from the ceiling like a loop of saliva. Maybe it was like one of those dream catchers, but for misery. God knows the wallpaper looked saturated with the stuff.

"I don't think she's looking for me anymore, so it doesn't really matter." I waited for his response. It was his turn, but there was nothing.

Silence expanded to fill the room like the brown paper bags I used to blow up as a child just for the joy of hearing them bang when I slapped them. I felt as if I were suffocating, as if the quiet were absorbing all the oxygen in the room, and then, at last, Irshad coughed, the bag burst, and I could breathe again.

"Excuse me," he said, clearing his throat. He watched me very carefully, as if I might implode and leave nothing but a pile of scorched bones on his Eames chair. Maybe that's what the ashtray's for: incinerated patients that he's pushed too far.

"Obviously it matters or you wouldn't be here . . . What are you afraid of?"

"Letting it out and then not being able to push it back in again." I sighed. "You know, it's like I've been sitting on it all these years, hidden under a trapdoor, but if I stand up and move aside, it will just—erupt, uncontrollably."

"And do you think you can go on suppressing it? This could

be a safe place for you to examine these difficult feelings. Then you could walk out and leave them here. Pick them up again when you feel able."

"That's the theory," I said to him.

"That's the theory," he agreed. "You've been walking out and leaving things behind your whole life. Why not do it here, where it might actually help you?" I stole a look at his face. He was still wearing his fire-extinguisher-at-the-ready expression.

And so I thought, oh, what the hell, I might as well give him a controlled explosion.

I gripped the sides of the chair.

25

I DIDN'T WANT TO get out of the car, but Mr. Anderson just stood there in the open doorway, beckoning. Kirsty had gone inside. So, eventually, I had no choice but to unglue myself from the back seat and follow.

My face throbbed with every step. I longed to go home. I couldn't care less about what sort of trouble I would get into.

This was worse.

I stumbled across the threshold. There was a little porch, hardly big enough for the two of us to squeeze into. There was another internal door. He steered me through, with a pat that was almost a push, and then pulled the front door closed behind us.

Inside, there were only a few pieces of furniture, but it was bright as day. A long fluorescent strip light was suspended from the ceiling, dripping coils of electric cable like fat, white worms across the bare floorboards. The beams were exposed, sandwiched with wadding that spilled out like horsehair from an old sofa. The walls were bare. In some places there was striped wallpaper with dainty Dutch girls carrying milk pails at jaunty angles and clogging gaily up the blue ribbon bands; in others there was plaster, pink as new skin.

"I'm fixing it up. It needs to be gutted, but I'll have to wait for the better weather before I do the structural stuff," he said, smiling awkwardly at the strain of talking to us as though we were proper people, not kids at school, then urging us to sit down. "I camped here in the summer, but now I've moved back into my flat. It's a bit basic for the cold weather." Kirsty was already comfortable on the couch with a perky look in her eyes. Gloss had been applied to her lips. She was combing her hair with her fingers—I noticed she had taken out her ponytail and had crossed her legs. She was bouncing the top one, pointing her toe.

That left me the armchair, which even in my bloodied, grimy state I hesitated to occupy. It was worn and greasy with continental stains across the arms and seat.

"Aye, sorry it's not the Hilton, girls," he said.

I perched. He went into a lean-to at the back, and I heard water gushing out of a tap and hitting the aluminum of a kettle.

Gas hissed, and he made tea, while, behind his back, I made worried faces at Kirsty. She gave me a shrug of impatience and told me to shut up. We'd have the tea and I could clean myself up, then we'd go home, she whispered. Her mother would be comatose by now. She'd never miss us.

"Mr. Anderson," she piped up, "can Aggie use your bathroom?"

"Call me Bill," he said. "We're not at school now."

"Bill!" mouthed Kirsty with delight.

In answer to her question Mr. Anderson handed me a chipped enamel bowl full of steaming water.

"There isn't really a bathroom as such. At the back"—he gestured with his head—"there's a toilet and a sink, but no hot water. You'll get a towel in there, too."

"Oh, Bill." She giggled. "That's my dad's name," I heard Kirsty say as I opened first the wrong door, which led to some closeted stairs, and then the right one, leading to a tiny toilet.

"There's no light," I called, flicking the switch uselessly.

"No, the place isn't all wired up yet," he answered.

I washed as best as I could with the door ajar. My face looked like a butcher's block in the small, cracked mirror that hung askew above the chipped sink. When I closed the door to pee, it was like being in a coffin. The window was bricked up, and the only light came from the rim around the door frame.

Kirsty was drinking whiskey from a floral mug when I came back. I knew she hated whiskey. She was just showing off for the teacher.

"It's good for shock," he said, offering me some.

"I don't like it, so no thanks."

"Look, I'll put it in your tea; it'll do you good." He spooned in a few sugars, no milk. I sipped it reluctantly. It tasted rancid, but it was sweet and warm. I drank it anyway. It was a bit like the drinks my mother made when I had a cold.

"So you've been out on the razzle, then," he said. He was sitting next to Kirsty. A bit too close, I thought. His body was turned toward her, and she practically had to lever herself away in order to face him when she was speaking.

"Aye, Bill," she said carefully through a pert little smile. "Our Agnes here got in the middle of a gang fight in some lassie's house. Anything to be the center of attention, eh, Ag?" She lifted her eyebrows the way you do when you're talking about a baby that's not very cute. But I didn't have time to respond. The tea was making me gag. I rushed back to the toilet and retched again.

"Shut the door, Agnes," she yelped. "That's gross, listening to that puking." When I didn't move, she got up and did it herself, leaving me in the dark, where I hung over the side of the bowl, threading my hair behind my ears.

I could hear their voices burbling through the door, but the banging in my head drowned them out.

The water was tepid. I used the last of it to wash my face.

There was a sliver of Imperial Leather soap; the sharp, deodorized smell of it clung to my skin. I even rinsed out the inside of my mouth, replacing the acid taste with the sour tang of soap. I spat bubbles into the sink.

I got halfway across the room before my knees hit the floor for the second time that evening.

"Has she been drinking?" asked the teacher. They both jumped up and tried to get me back on my feet, but I could hardly stand.

"Leave me," I whimpered.

"Are you sure she hasn't been drinking?" he asked again.

"Maybe," Kirsty said airily, though she knew I hadn't had more than a couple of swigs of cider.

"She needs to lie down," he said. "There's a bed upstairs. Come on, give me a hand to get her up there."

"But I want to go home. I don't feel well."

"You can't go back to my house like this, Agnes, so go and lie down until you feel better," ordered Kirsty.

I managed to walk up the short flight of stairs and fell upon the bed. It was no more than a mattress with a pillow and tartan blanket on the top, but I closed my eyes gratefully. I couldn't fight the overwhelming desire to throw myself into the black.

I felt as if I had done little more than blink before Kirsty started pulling at me and pummeling my shoulders. It was as though there was a steel weight on my head. I could hardly lift it from the bed. Kirsty was shaking me and shaking me, her earlier arch flirtatiousness replaced by panic.

She was crouched over me on the mattress.

"Wake up, wake up, come awn . . . Agnes . . ." The toe of her boot kicked me hard on my hip. I squealed.

She reeked of whiskey. I barked at her to leave me alone, but she just dug her fingers into my shoulders and shook harder, giving me another hard kick.

We were in the dark, but there was enough light from the single skylight window in the roof to light the room. I could see the rim of the moon and a few stars, like sparks from a fire.

"He's gone away and left us here," she sobbed, throwing her soft, podgy arms around me and clinging to my chest through the blanket.

"How are we going to get home?" I forced myself fully awake and told her not to worry.

There was no problem; we could just walk. I told her that I was feeling better, which was a lie, but I would have said anything to reassure her. She was scaring me. Kirsty was supposed to be the one who knew everything and now she was carrying on like a silly brat.

"But he's left us. I came up here to get you and then I heard his car. When I went back downstairs, it was all in darkness. He put the lights off. Why would he do that?" she whimpered in a small, needy voice.

"We'll put them back on. Come on." I tried to push her arms away from me. It was like being in a straitjacket. "Put the light on in here and we'll see what we're doing."

"Don't be stupid, Agnes—there's no light." She was almost screeching, but she was right. I looked around the room and saw no dangling cord, no light switch, only the burned-down stubs of a few candles, an ashtray—or at least a tobacco tin that had been used as an ashtray—and bits and pieces of timber and plasterboard, a can of paint, some bales of roof insulation.

"Look, we'll light the candles, then. Where are your matches?"

"Downstairs, in my pocket."

"Well, go and get them."

"No, it's too dark; I'm feart. Come with me." I held her hand and raised myself up. The floor came up to meet me as I stood, but I took a few breaths and steadied my feet. "Come on, we can see where we're going; let's get the matches, sort ourselves out and get out of here. What time is it?" I looked at my watch in the moonlight. It had stopped and the face was cracked, but I knew I must have been asleep for hours.

I'd never been out this late in my life.

I picked up one of the candle stubs and led the way, holding Kirsty with one hand and feeling the way with the other as we descended down the dark pothole of the stairwell. The door at the bottom pushed open easily, but Kirsty wasn't exaggerating.

It was pitch black.

I edged round the side of the room, probing until I felt curtains, which I tugged open with a flourish, only to stand there perplexed when the room grew no brighter.

"There's no window," I said.

Kirsty started sobbing again.

"Don't have a fit—calm yourself. Just stand for a minute and our eyes will get used to it. There's a wee bit of light coming in from the stairs." I put my arm round her and sure enough after a few seconds I could make out the dark humps of the furniture, then the outline of the table, littered with mugs and papers.

"Where did you leave your coat?"

"Over there," she said, though I couldn't see where she was pointing. I walked over and flailed at the sofa.

"Why did you take it off, anyway? It's freezing in here." This sent her sobs into a crescendo. "He made me. He yanked it off. He tried to get my sweater off as well. He's a dirty pig."

"What?" I couldn't believe it. She probably stripped it off herself so she could flaunt her chest at him.

"He jumped on me. Tried to get his hands under my clothes and everything. I thought he was nice. I thought he liked me. I mean, he's a teacher. He's not supposed to be like that." Her words degenerated into wails. "That's when I came to get you, but you just wouldn't wake up, and then I heard the door shutting." I had found a bundle that felt like her jacket and gave it a shake. I heard the welcome rattle of matches, pulled the box out of her pocket, and sparked one.

The room flared into focus. "Gimme the candle," I said, and lit the stub. I sat down, holding it between my thumb and forefinger, yelping as hot wax ran over my hand.

The effort had tired me. My feet were cold. I realized I'd need my shoes before we could go. They must still be upstairs. I asked Kirsty to go up and get them, but she was afraid. She wouldn't leave me. Once again, we crocodiled up the narrow staircase, picked up my sandals and went back downstairs, where I wedged them on. They hurt. The straps pinched the blisters they had branded into my feet.

"Look, if I'm going to walk, I'll need to do something about my feet. Give me a minute." I started looking around downstairs for something I could wrap around the peeling skin underneath the holes my sandals had worn through the pantyhose, while Kirsty, gaining courage, let go of my hand.

"Put the big light on," I instructed. She played at blindman's buff in the shadows and eventually found the light switch, but when she pressed it, nothing happened. "It doesn't work," she said unnecessarily.

I was impatient. I stumbled over to the front door, listing three inches to the side with one sandal on, the other in my hand, and fumbled with the handle. "Just open the fucking door then, and let the light in." But the handle didn't move.

"Shit, it's stuck." I banged it with my hip, forgetting my bruises, and yelped with pain. "Don't just stand there—help me push it." Her little face was like a torn piece of paper in the glow of the candlelight. "Ha, you look like Caspar the scary ghost," I said, trying to lighten the atmosphere, and it worked in as much as she snapped at me to fucking shut up. But pissed off was at least better than petrified.

I counted to three and we both leaned on the door. It didn't budge.

Kirsty's voice was like a spent match, just before the flame gutters out. "I think he's locked us in," she said.

"Give the girl a coconut," I said under my breath.

I started shouting at her. "Why did you let him leave and lock the bloody door? Where was your brain? You're always that busy showing off."

"He was horrible to me. Called me names. I didn't know he was going to leave us here, did I?"

"What happened to 'yes, Bill, no, Bill'?" I muttered. But there was no point in arguing. We would have to try to figure out what to do.

It was a long night. All the windows downstairs were

boarded up. The ones in the kitchenette and the bathroom were filled with bricks. The skylight wouldn't open from the inside, and the door was locked. We found two new candles in a box in the kitchenette, but to save our meager supply, we sat upstairs huddled on the bed waiting for it to get light. We both slept on and off, our ears straining for the noise of a car, but when the sun turned its twenty-watt lamp on in the morning, there was still no sign of him.

We went downstairs to make tea. The stove worked on a small butane tank, so we could at least have a hot drink, but Kirsty was frightened we would set fire to the place and not be able to get out, and she stood there watching the kettle boil with a bucket of water in her hands. I tried to rationalize that we were more likely to suffocate on the fumes than incinerate ourselves because there was nothing to set fire to, but she was teetering on the edge, even then.

We were starving. There was nothing to eat, and the day crawled backward through the hours, but nobody came.

Maybe he was never coming back, said Kirsty, and we would die here, locked up forever. But I told her not to be stupid, that he wouldn't want two skeletons to explain away when his builders turned up to put on the new roof.

She didn't think it was funny. Neither did I. I didn't even think it was very likely. We could sit here and rot. He could dig a big hole and drop us into it and no one would be any the wiser. But when I thought like that, panic squeezed the air out of my lungs and stole my voice. Kirsty was freaking out enough for both of us.

When the sun went down, we sat there alone in the glow of a candle. And then it started to snow. That's when I felt the first waves of terror. With the snow covering our only source of natural light, we would be entombed inside the house. I kept tapping on the skylight, trying to stop it settling, until Kirsty told me to stop. If you break it, we'll get the snow in here and freeze to death, she said.

Of course, then it occurred to us. We could knock the glass out and climb onto the roof.

"Not in six inches of snow, we couldn't; we'd slip and fall and be dead anyway," said Kirsty. "He'll come back; he probably forgot he locked us in and thinks we'll just put our coats on and leave when we're ready. He was a bit drunk; I bet he just wasn't thinking straight." I agreed. But I was supposed to have swimming practice with him today. He could hardly fail to notice that I was missing.

"But he'll just think you're not well."

"My mother will be going mental," I said, picturing her at home, wondering why I hadn't come back from Kirsty's house before it was dark and then going up to see where I was.

"My mother is mental anyway."

"But she'll notice you're not there in the morning."

"Aye, but what will she do? She'll try calling my dad, and he's away golfing."

"But he'll come back when she tells him, won't he?"

"What the fuck do I know, Agnes? Anyway, she won't leave the house till he's back."

"Surely she'll call the police?"

"Not without telling my dad first. She won't put the kettle on unless my dad okays it. She might think I got up and went out again." We sat on the bed drinking tea as the night filled with snow.

We had just lit the second candle when we heard the hum of an engine. We nearly knocked each other over in our haste to get back downstairs, with Kirsty shouting at me, telling me not to drop it, not to start a fire.

Two keys turned in two locks, there was a click and then the light came on, almost blinding us. Another lock turned, and Mr. Anderson walked into the room with a couple of bags. He stamped snow off his shoes, and said as coolly as if he had invited us for the weekend and we had turned up early: "Ah, you're still here, then. I nearly couldn't get back. The snow has the road blocked and the plows don't do these back lanes till last."

Kirsty shouted at him: "We could hardly be anywhere else, could we? You fucking locked us in—in the dark." She ran to the door, opened it, and went into the porch, where she rattled uselessly on the outer door. "You've locked it again. I'm going to get the police on you—you pervert. What do you think you're playing at? Let us go. My dad will kill you."

"Shh." I held her arm, tried to hold her back when she started slapping at him. "Calm down. He's hardly going to let us out if you start threatening him. Be nice," I whispered into her hair. I stroked her arm through the coat and held her in a tight cuddle.

"Come on, we need to get home now; can you open the door, Mr. Anderson? Our folks will be worried," I said, linking arms with Kirsty, both of us clutching our handbags.

"Girls, you're not going anywhere in this weather. You're snowed in," he said, not lifting his eyes from the plastic bag that he was slowly unpacking in the back kitchen.

"No, we'll manage. They're probably out looking for us; just open the door."

"Nobody's looking for you," he said quietly.

Kirsty started crying, as she looked at me in horror.

So I tried a different tack. I begged. "I promise that we'll say nothing. Just that we got lost and let ourselves in here out of the snow. Nobody even needs to know that you even saw us."

"I'm telling. After what he tried to do to me."

He laughed. "Oh, you're telling," he mimicked in a singsong voice. "Are you not a wee bit old to be running crying to your mummy and daddy? Do you think anybody's going to believe you? Two lassies looking like that"—he nodded at Kirsty's low-cut T-shirt. "You're old enough to know what you're doing; you're not bairns. What are you going to say to convince anyone different?"

"You locked us in—you attacked me."

"Oh, did I? And how can you prove that? You've been throwing yourself at me for weeks—sitting down next to me at school in that little skimpy swimsuit—and now you're all coy. There're words for girls like you."

"I never did," she said.

"Oh, shut up," I screamed at her. "You're making it worse." We were both crying, but for different reasons. She was mad. I was worried. I could see that he wasn't bothered either way. He was crouched on the sofa, having carried the contents of his grocery bags into the sitting room. He'd brought a sliced loaf and cheese, a bottle of milk. There was a chocolate bar. Some bananas. "I thought you might be hungry," he said, smiling his funny smile. It was as if he didn't think he had done anything wrong. As if this were—well—normal.

I looked at the food. I was so desperate to eat something I would have done tricks for it, rolled over, played dead, given him a paw.

But Kirsty was defiant. She snarled that she wouldn't touch his filthy food, and neither would Agnes, daring me to say different. But I had my own ideas. "I'm starving, thanks," I said quietly, wiping away my tears. And I sat down next to him and folded two sheets of processed cheese into a soft slice of Mother's Pride and ate it. He poured milk into a mug, first throwing the inch of cold tea that was still in it onto the floorboards, where it soaked away in seconds. I hated milk, but I gulped it down. He looked questioningly at Kirsty, but she told him to go fuck himself.

"Okay, princess," he said, "suit yourself." He poured himself a glass of whiskey and started to roll a cigarette as he watched me eat. He took a couple of draws and passed it to me when I'd finished the sandwich. I puffed on it and coughed. It tasted vile.

"No, don't blow the smoke out, keep it in your lungs. You don't get the effect otherwise."

"I don't want any effect," I replied, worried again.

"Don't smoke it, Agnes, it's wacky backy. He's trying to drug you."

"Kirsty, sit down and shut up. Stop being so melodramatic," I spluttered through a cough, but I passed the cigarette back to him and shook my head the next time he offered it.

"Now then," he said, putting his hand on my pants, which were filthy with mud and blood from my fall the night before, "you go back up to your bed, hen. Me and the princess were having a nice wee chat last night, and we need to pick up where we left off."

Kirsty begged me not to go. "Don't leave me, Agnes—you promised."

He turned and gave me a look, then petted my cheek.

His eyes were a bit glassy. I thought—maybe he's stoned, maybe he'll fall asleep if he keeps drinking.

"It's all right, don't worry. I'll not go," I told her. I turned toward him. "Mr. Anderson . . ." I began.

"Bill, darlin'. I keep telling you we're not at school now."

"Okay, Bill." His name tasted worse than the soap, worse than the cigarette, but it came out of my bruised lips like a kiss. "Let Kirsty alone. Let her go up to her bed. I'll stay with you." Kirsty punched me on the arm. "What are you doing? I told you what he was like with me."

"Never mind, just go. I'll be fine. Don't worry about me—wait up the stairs." I pushed her away. "Go on. Go up and shut the door."

"But it's dark up there," she whimpered. "I don't want to be up there by myself."

"Go up the bloody stairs, Kirsty, and take the candles." This time she didn't argue but started weeping and sniveling as she stumbled up the stairs. I could hear her heels clumping through the floor.

Though why she thought she had anything to whine about, I don't know. I wasn't upset. Everything was fine. There was absolutely no need to get myself in a state. Not after my lip started to bleed and he let me do something else.

Then all I had to do was lie there.

26

"ARE YOU OKAY? Would you like a glass of water?" Irshad's skin has gone from ash to silver birch. I think he's the one who needs a drink, not me.

I nod, defiantly.

Of course I'm okay, I want to snap at him. It's not the first time I've heard the story. I lived it.

"I'm afraid our time's up for today," he said gently, as though he were calling in a pedal boat on a pleasure lake rather than stopping me halfway through my big finale. "But we can talk more about this next time." He pats me on the shoulder as he sees me out, and we walk past the other anonymous doors with their discreet brass plaques to the arthritic elevator at the end of the hall.

Hurriedly, I replace the demon on a high shelf at the back of my mind and leave it there to deal with later. It'll keep. It's kept this long.

"You know, 'gnes, if you feel you need to talk to me before we meet, you can always call me on the office number. Leave a message. I check them regularly. I'll call you back. Any time, day or night," he says as the elevator arrives and I slide back the metal grid that threatens to snap off my fingers in its mesh teeth.

I look at him as though he's a bit slow and thinks I need a note pinned to my lapel to remind me where I live. "I said I'm okay," I snap, but inside I feel relief. I haven't had anyone to call on for a long while. I want to collapse against him, but I keep my head high and my spine rigid as the elevator whirs and chatters manically and I sink through the floor.

I walk tall all the way down the block to the subway station, where I buy a packet of gum and chew piece after piece, spitting each out onto the platform the moment the sugar is gone. I hate the subway, but I have no choice. Just like my Woody Allen fantasy, Irshad's office is on Central Park West, up near Lincoln Center, and it takes me too long to get home if I ride the bus. I buy a *People* magazine that I won't read as I hurtle downtown and stride onto the F train, perfectly composed, until I get to Delancey Street. For some reason I always cry when I get to Delancey Street. I don't know why. It's not the worst stop on the subway. Penn Station—now that's what I call a shit subway station. Broadway-Lafayette's pretty dreadful as well, but—no—it's always Delancey Street.

I wipe the tears as covertly as I can and stare at my reflection in the empty subway window all the way to Fourth Avenue in Brooklyn.

Every time the train lurches, my face expands and contracts, my nostrils gaping like they've been devoured by some flesh-eating disease, my eyes and mouth converging into jagged lines on a television with bad vertical hold. There's another upside-down Agnes coming out of my head like a Siamese twin, who curls up across the roof until the glass stops her at chest height. Our hair stretches apart glutinously, as though the two heads have been stuck together with my chewed-out chewing gum, then flick back together into one broad forehead.

When I bend to rise out of my seat, I finally separate my head and pull away from her, leaving the reflection hanging there, ready to attach itself to the next person.

27

OVER THE NEXT weeks Jocelyn and I graduated to the intimacy of a shared midmorning beverage, during which she read aloud articles from *Holistic Health* and I counted backward from five hundred before excusing myself.

This morning I had returned from Jim Goldmann's office to find a brochure for Carnegie Hall laid out next to Jocelyn's plate of toast, the bread pocked and freckled with grain like an old man's back. My stomach sank when I saw its twin on my side of the table. The high-polyunsaturated-fat spread glooped ominously in a lake of jauntily colored plastic.

I sat down while Jocelyn splashed hot water over the tea bag in my cup. I had lost the war on white bread, but I had won the battle of Rose Red Tea. There was a letter waiting for me from Edelman, Singh & Kelly, which sounded like the beginning of a bad joke rather than my esteemed firm of attorneys. I regarded it with some trepidation.

Irshad was right. I couldn't go on hiding forever. When I

called Francisco to tell him what to do with the few personal possessions I had left in storage up in Cambridge, he mentioned that the girl had called him from England, wondering if he had heard from me. He didn't like lying to her, he said, and so had given her the address of my attorneys. A week later and they already had a letter from her. Whether I liked it or not, I was going to have to confront my past. I discussed it with Mr. Singh, who reminded me that I wasn't under any obligation to meet with her if I didn't want to. He suggested that he should reply saying that, at this time, I did not wish to have any contact with her.

"It's brutal, but it's better to be clear," he said in his toffee-flavored voice, managing to make it sound as if I would be doing her a kindness.

I opened the envelope and shook out the enclosure. It was a bill. I read the total at the bottom and tossed it aside with a deep sigh. Legal anonymity did not come cheap, but it was worth it. It was worth it to have this darn thing settled once and for all.

My attention focused on a stray cat hair curled in the sugar bowl.

I picked it out gingerly.

"It's incredibly bad for you, you know," said Jocelyn, as, fully satisfied the sugar had been dehaired, I added a large spoonful of it to my tea.

"What, cat hair? I know. It's a terrible allergen."

"No, sugar," she said with distaste, as though she should be throwing salt over her shoulder to deflect bad luck, except that salt wasn't allowed either.

I made no comment but kept on stirring, then separated the scalloped edges of the torn envelope and stared, overattentively, at the enclosed letter.

". . . really, little more than refined poison. It's the first thing I advise my clients against." Jocelyn was driving home her point with a Black & Decker. "Sugar, and alcohol," she added pointedly. "Especially spirits."

I began to wonder if I could get Mr. Singh to threaten Jocelyn with a gagging order.

"Sugar, alcohol, caffeine, wheat, hydrogenated oil . . ." She completed her litany of toxins and began to examine her brochure.

"Mmm . . . oh"—a small squeak of pleasure—"Shostakovich, 'Suite on Poems . . .'" she murmured, placing a little check in ballpoint beside a column. "That's in September. Would you like to go, Agnes? You could leave work early."

Months away. Who was that organized? I consulted my empty mental diary and hurriedly shook my head. I didn't want to think much further ahead than the next appointment with Irshad, and about Shostakovich I didn't want to think at all.

"What about György Ligeti? That sounds interesting, don't you think? That's a lunchtime concert. You could have a late start." Another check was added.

I started to count, 499, 498, while dropping crumbs of bread on the floor for the cat, which was dozing under the table. They skipped, unseen, within inches of its nose.

We skipped, check-less, through Mozart, Vivaldi, and Haydn, which would have been more to my taste. I prodded the cat, trying to draw its opaque eyes to the food, but it was blind, not dim-witted. 494, 493, 492 . . .

"Oh, drat. I forgot to tell you. You had a phone call. Not more than half an hour ago." I looked up from the still somnolent cat. The telephone ban had also been relaxed of late, so that Irshad and I could keep in touch.

"It was a man. He left his number."

"Was it Irshad changing a session?" I asked, slightly petulantly.

I needed to know these things so I could prepare myself. I had grown used to the routine.

"It might have been, but it didn't sound like him." Jocelyn looked around her, twitching her tiny nose, great fronds of dense, curly hair undulating around her face like a giant sea sponge, then reached behind her to where a row of numerals was printed in minute, homoeopathic handwriting on the top sheet of her "Road Less Traveled" thought-for-the-day calendar, which was still on the page for February thirteenth—IF AN ACT IS NOT ONE OF WORK OR COURAGE, THEN IT IS NOT AN ACT OF LOVE.

It had been a long time since anyone had called either of us.

"Please use the phone. It's a New York number." I took the opportunity to push a piece of toast into the waste disposal under the pretext of rinsing out my cup, then went into the sitting room, where I dutifully stooped to dial. Using the phone was one thing, sitting down on her ironed slipcovers quite another.

I didn't recognize the number, but Irshad practiced all over Manhattan and had an office at St. Luke's up near Columbia. He might have been calling from there.

The phone rang three times before being answered, tersely, by a bored male voice that sounded nothing like Irshad or his incongruously giddy secretary.

"Yup, Davenport, here." the voice said, just as Jocelyn slipped her head around the door and whispered with the exaggerated mouth shapes of a signer for the deaf: "I think it was someone called Adam?" Meanwhile, in my ear, despite my overwhelming disbelief, Adam Davenport repeated his name and had growled hello, twice, increasingly crossly.

I was mute with astonishment, too surprised to register either excitement or dread.

"It's Agnes," I finally croaked, before realizing my mistake. "I mean, Edith," I muttered after a cringing pause.

"Ah . . ." There was the muffled sound of a hand held over the receiver. Voices. Then more Adam. "Sorry about that; someone in the office."

"That's okay." I could hear him gulp while he obviously searched for something to say. "Um, this is awkward," he managed finally.

I began to answer and then realized I was holding my breath.

I inhaled hurriedly. "Yes," I agreed. "I hope I'm not disturbing you, but I had a message that you called. Maybe there was some mistake?"

"No, no mistake, I did call you, it's just, well, it's just, um, good of you to call back . . . You're okay?"

"Yeah, I'm good," I answered, holding my breath again for the uncomfortably long second of throat clearing that followed on the other end of the line.

"Um, Ed, Ag . . ." he began before abandoning all attempts to name me. "I've . . . I've been meaning to get in touch, and I'm sorry it has taken me so long, but, well, I guess I wanted to apologize. When I saw you last month outside Spence and I didn't stop . . . well, I couldn't stop. But, even so, it was shabby, really shabby of me. Unforgivably rude."

"No, not at all."

"No, it was. No excuses, but it's only that it was the worst possible day of days, and I felt so bad about it . . . I should have tried to get in touch with you months ago, but I didn't know how to find you, and then I went to London for the London Book Fair and after that I went to South Africa, and the weeks vanished, and—well . . ." He took a breath, as did I. A long, fluttering sigh of relief.

"Look, do you think we could meet? It's better than discussing things on the phone."

"Yes," I agreed.

"What about lunch today, tomorrow, any day this week? You could come here to the office. I mean, not to the office, but somewhere nearby." He began tossing restaurants all over the place like a card shark, trying to dazzle me. He succeeded. I hadn't heard of any of them. "Anywhere you like."

"I have to be at work at two o'clock."

"Oh. Yes, of course, I wasn't thinking. Where are you? Which part of Manhattan?"

"The East Village," I replied, promoting myself to a better area.

"Well, that's just next door. You can come to the Union Square Café or—no—it's a bit public. Look, I'll come to you. Today okay? There's a good French place on Bond Street."

I didn't even know where Bond Street was, but if he had asked me to trek to Machu Picchu, I would have been there by half past twelve. I agreed, and he hung up.

I held the phone to my ear, listening to the dial tone, afraid to break the connection.

My knees were trembling uncontrollably. I pulled my old cardigan around my bones and sank onto the arm of the nearest chair, dislodging the cat, which had followed me in. A small flurry of dander puffed into the air, accompanied by furious mewling. I was still sitting there, wheezing, absentmindedly, when Jocelyn came back, handed me my inhaler and led me, very gently, back into the kitchen, casting a wary eye over her hopelessly crumpled embroidered arm covers.

"I'll make you a nice cup of tea. Valerian tea," she said. "It's great for shock. Very soothing. Calms the nerves." She put her arm around me and patted me. "I hope it wasn't bad news, Agnes?" she inquired, handing me a cup of pale, straw-colored liquid.

"No, not at all," I said, smiling.

The tea tasted like horse's pee. Very tranquil horse's pee. But I drank it gratefully.

And then I put my arms around her and kissed her.

28

JEANS. I HAD gone down a size. They fell to my hips. I shrugged, sticking a safety pin in the back of the waistband. Hip-huggers were fashionable.

Hair. There was nothing I could do about that except wash it, brush it, or wear a hat. I didn't have a hat so I would have to put my faith in shampoo. I stuck my head under the faucet and lathered up.

Shirt. It was warm enough for short sleeves, which meant I could finally retire Lennie's coat, which threatened to hoist me aloft like a balloon in the Macy's parade every time there was a high wind. I put on a T-shirt that I bought in the kid's department of Gap.

Sweater. I smoothed out Gay's pilled heirloom cashmere sweater, used sticky tape to remove the cat hairs, and looped it round my neck like a Ralph Lauren ad, Brooklyn-style.

I was overly layered, but at least it padded me out.

I shaved, I filed, I pumiced, I moisturized. I dried my hair flat and spat on the wand of a dried-up mascara to spike up my eyelashes, and then I caught a cab to the restaurant, resisting the urge to run all the way there.

Even walking round the block three times and visiting an ATM to withdraw money, I still arrived twenty minutes early, loitering in the small forecourt surrounded by bay trees and a knee-high box hedge, trying to look innocuous. The whole way there I thought of reasons why he should want to see me. I didn't dare to think it was of the I-can't-live-without-you variety, but I allowed myself the luxury of an I-thought-we-should-clear-the-air.

What I hadn't expected was I-think-you'll-find-this-more-or-less-covers-what-I-owe-you, accompanied by a check, pushed across the table in a discreet white envelope.

Adam had also arrived early and was, even then, sitting on a banquette on the far side of the restaurant, leafing through a manuscript. It was one of those aggressively chic places, all chrome and black leather, like a French housewife at an S&M party, with round white-swathed tables arranged in rigid lines in the middle of the room like holes on a board of peg solitaire. I moved across the room toward him. He stood up as I approached but made no move to touch me. He looked terrible. Terrible and wonderful. His hair jumped in unruly curls from his forehead. His eyes squinted and blinked behind the Magic Marker rectangles of his heavy-framed glasses; his beautiful smile was held at bay, pinned down by long lines, tethered from his nose to his chin.

I dragged my eyes from his face to the check, as though a reporter from the *National Enquirer* would appear with a flashbulb should I dare to touch it.

"You don't owe me anything. I'm not taking it." I had sat

down but was still gripping my purse in my lap with two hands, as if it were a boisterous dachshund awaiting only a moment's inattention to bound away.

"Well, it's yours. You left without your wages, and I should have paid you some notice. I left it blank because I didn't know who to make it out to."

I picked it up and ripped it in two. "Don't insult me. I feel sick about what happened. If there's any debt here, it's entirely mine." My voice quavered like Jocelyn's version of Lotte Lenya in the shower. "In any case, you didn't need to come and meet me for this. You could have sent it to me."

"I didn't have your address."

"You did. I sent you a note. In February." He shook his head. His curls bobbed frantically, like a sea of drowning swimmers. I longed to catch them, smooth them down. I couldn't take my eyes off his lips.

The waiter came to take our order, but the rough-trade menus, with steel studs bolted into their leather spines, clenched their secrets at the side of the table. We hadn't opened them.

"We'll wait," Adam replied curtly. The waiter nodded and attempted to pour more ice water into our glasses before he noticed they were already brimming. What was he trying to do to us? Drown us?

"I didn't get any note."

"I sent it to the house. With my address in Brooklyn and my telephone number."

"I thought you said you lived here in the East Village."

"No, I'm in Brooklyn." He made a face that, right there, will tell you why people lie about their zip code. Adam was one of those people who thought you only crossed a bridge in New York if you were going to the airport. He unfurled and furled his napkin, leaving it like an unlicked rolling paper on his side plate.

"I can't understand what happened to it. February, you said? There was only Lennie in the house. I got a new woman to come in a couple of days a week to keep an eye on her. But she wouldn't . . ."

I agreed. Lennie would be more likely to steam open the letter and read it than to throw it away. I knew who would, but there seemed little point in voicing it. It didn't matter.

"So how did you get my phone number?"

"From your husband."

I was amazed. "But I didn't tell him." I had even given the practice as my home address on the divorce papers so he wouldn't know where I had gone.

Adam looked shamefaced. "I got Caroline to call him. She made some excuse about having borrowed something from you that she needed to return. But when I called the number he gave her, a guy answered. An Indian guy. I thought for one awful moment you were living with him. But then he said you worked there and gave me the number of your apartment."

Fucking Krishna. I loved him.

"It was Caroline who told me you hadn't gone back to your husband up in Cambridge. I assumed you had."

"No, that wasn't ever going to happen. When I left him, it was for good."

"Lennie and Ned both miss you. They kept asking me why you had left and wondered why you hadn't been in touch. I hope it's not a problem, but I just said that you'd had a family emergency and had to go away very suddenly." I nodded my head in assent, the all-too-familiar lash of shame landing on my back.

"Lennie talks about you all the time. Asked me why I didn't

go after you and bring you back." Lennie. Unexpectedly, my heart softened, the way prunes do when you soak them in Armagnac.

"How is she?"

"She looks like she should be hooking in Vegas, acts like a diva, sulks like a baby. Calls me 'daddy fucking dearest.' Even in front of my eighty-year-old mother."

I smiled. Yep, even steeped in fine French brandy, they're still prunes.

"That's nice."

"What? That she curses you out in front of your mother?"

"No, that you're smiling."

"I don't do it often. It's bad for the complexion. Gives you wrinkles. According to Lennie," I added.

Inspector Clouseau returned, this time with tiny bread rolls and a pair of silver sugar tongs. We waved him away.

I asked about Ned. He was fine. There were a few soccer stories, something about a trip to L.A. that Adam wasn't keen on him taking.

"Adam . . ." I began, when we had finished playing Twenty Questions. "I didn't get a chance to explain anything, to really tell you how sorry I am, how sorry I was."

"I didn't let you, did I? Throwing you out in the middle of the night like some kind of Victorian tyrant. I did try to find you. I went through the garbage looking for anything you might have left with an address on it, but everything was gone. I drove around Manhattan in the car half the day. I went back to the emergency room to see if you had given them a next of kin, but they wouldn't tell me anything . . ."

"You did?"

"I did."

He looked at me so long that I had to drop my eyes.

"Well," he said finally.

"Well," I repeated. Dear god, Dorothy freaking Parker had nothing on me. "Anyway, you didn't throw me out. I left," I protested.

"You have to have the last word, don't you?"

I smiled again.

"It's so fucking wonderful to see you. I can't believe you're really here. That day I saw you. It was nightmarish. Gay and I had been screaming at each other all morning. Then we had to put on this big show of solidarity for Lennie—she went on some school thing, I can't even remember where—and then, after months of wishing, praying, that I would get the chance to see you again, there you were, right there, at the side of the road. And I couldn't stop. It was like the whole universe was conspiring against me."

"I wanted to run after you, but then I saw Gay get into the car. I thought you were back together."

"God, no. She's got a boyfriend. In TV. Only thirty-two. Robert Frost—like the poet but no relation, obviously. He and Gay make quite the couple." He laughed easily. "He does those reality talent-show things on the East Coast that Lennie loves. She's delirious, of course; thinks she's going to go to Hollywood and meet all the stars. He's also worth a fortune, but Gay still feels I should be subsidizing and satisfying her every whim. They were planning on hiring a yacht in Cannes for the film festival this summer, and she wanted me to pay her half while Tricky Rickie paid the rest. So we were battling it out, all tight-lipped and heavy innuendo, then just straightforward yelling, and there you were. God, but I felt like a total bastard. You were crying. And you looked like shit."

"Compliments, compliments. I can see why you're in publishing; you have such a way with words." I laughed, or thought I did, but instead tears began running down my face and into the hollow of my throat.

"Oh, don't cry, please, I'm sorry. You still don't look well. You've got so thin. You haven't been taking care of yourself. You look pretty, beautiful, fantastic, un-fucking-believably wonderful, but not yourself. Don't cry." He stroked my hand, leaving little burn marks under his fingertips.

"I've been ill. Nothing serious. Just flu. Bad flu. But you don't look so hot either. What's your excuse?" I turned my palm over and held his hand for a second, then pulled it away when the temptation to press it to my face became too strong.

"Divorce. Bad divorce, but all better now."

The waiter hovered again. "Can I get you a glass of wine?" he asked.

"Wine?" Adam offered. I shook my head, giving my face a quick swipe with the napkin.

"I've had that too," I said.

"What?"

"Divorce, but not a bad one. Very civilized. Not unlike this, actually." I nodded at the torn envelope. "But I didn't rip his check up."

"So it is over?"

"It's been over for a long time."

"I'm glad. I mean, I . . . well, you know what I mean, don't you?"

I did.

His hand was lying flat on top of the menus, and he moved as though to pass me one, but I stopped him, laying my hand on top of his. I remembered the first time I touched him, in the kitchen in the Dutch house on Eightieth Street. Our eyes met again.

"There's such a lot to talk about, to tell you, to explain, I'm not even sure I can," I said.

"Edie, I don't want to hear it. Not any of it. I don't care. I've missed you," he said.

And I was back.

He was wearing a pale blue shirt and a tie, slightly loosened at the neck. A dark suit. Office clothes. The sort I used to peel off him, night after night. They would smell of his shower gel, and peppermint shaving cream, and other people's cigarettes. I couldn't stop myself from touching him. I moved my hand to his face, to his cheek, to his collar, stroked the knot of his tie, ran my fingers over the silky material.

"Are you really hungry?" I asked.

"I couldn't eat a thing." He reached for his wallet, from which he withdrew a fifty dollar bill, tossing it onto the table.

"What about the manuscript?" I asked as we reached the door.

It was still on the table, underneath the two halves of the envelope.

"Oh, forget it. I don't even know what it is. I just grabbed it off the slush pile so I would have something to hide behind."

I should have felt some remorse for the unfortunate author.

But who am I kidding? I didn't give a damn.

29

ADAM WANTED ME to move back into Eightieth Street immediately rather than commuting between the house and the apartment in Brooklyn, but I was cautious. I kept my job at the practice, despite failing to turn up for work at all that afternoon, but I gave up working weekends and found someone else to do my shifts.

I also said goodbye to Dr. Goldmann, who gave me a box of floss, a bottle of mouthwash, and a year's supply of toothbrushes as a farewell present. I don't quite know if he was trying to tell me something, but I left with the offer of free checkups for life, so possibly I didn't have the full ring of confidence that I thought I had.

In all other respects, my life went on pretty much as it had done before, but with sex: glowing skin, scraps of underwear in apricot silk bags (touchingly, two sizes too large for the more luscious woman Adam thought me, rather than the wraith I had become), white burgundy instead of vodka, and pesche al dolcetto from Dean & Deluca, which we ate with our fingers in bed.

During the next week Adam had a car pick me up every night after work, purportedly to take me out for dinner, though we never once made it to a restaurant. We spent our first weekend at the Pierre without getting out of bed except to answer the door to a guy with a tray in his hand or to run a bath.

I had urged Adam not to tell his children that we were back together. I didn't want them to know there was anything between us until I was sure that there really was, but he insisted. And the sky didn't fall, nor did the kids do more than shrug with possibly more embarrassment than they would have done if he'd told them he had syphilis.

Irshad had spread his palms in an I-told-you-so fashion and smiled as though he had arranged it all for me himself. I was gaining a little weight and my bones were padding out with contentment.

There wasn't a single cloud on my happy-ever-after horizon as the Lincoln dropped me off at Jocelyn's on Monday morning. There was a moving truck parked outside the building, so I got out at the end of the block, and I almost sang as I swept along the street. I was so carried away with my own remembered carnal pleasures, running blue movies through my head, that I had my key in my hand before I noticed that there was someone sitting on the steps.

It's funny how the weather can change from sun to storm in the blink of an eye.

A girl was leaning against the door of the lobby, stripping the withered, rust-ringed leaves from a rotting plant in the pot by the door. Her two large feet, shod in clunky all-terrain sandals that looked as though they should have had monster wheels, were planted on either side of the path.

She didn't need to introduce herself, but she did anyway. She leaped up at my approach, wiping the dust off her bottom with one hand and steadying a hefty knapsack with the other.

"Oh God, it's you. It's really you!" she said. I stared at her, stupefied. "I'm Cheryl—Cherry—Dawson," she said.

The demon had just climbed down from the shelf. Not the most fiendish of Satan's handmaidens, I thought at the time, but pretty hellish, nevertheless.

Of course I knew who she was. I would have recognized her anywhere. As Francisco had said, it was as if someone had drawn me on her face—but slightly off. She wasn't as skinny as I had been when I was her age, or indeed as I was now; nor did she have the same inbred, undernourished look from centuries of bad diet and no sun. Her body was broader, bulkier, exercised; but she had the sharp nose, the papery McBride skin, only photocopied with too much ink. She was dark like Bill Anderson and toasted a hardy, golden backpacker's brown. She also had his thick, dark hair scrawled untidily around the flush of high color on her cheeks, and his straight, unwavering eyes, gray, like flints.

Those eyes made me shudder. It was like being kicked back in time.

"I couldn't wait to see you, so I just came." She shrugged. "I spoke to your friend Jossy-something yesterday when I flew in and said I would come by, but nobody answered the bell when I rang it," she said, as I stood there, wishing I could rewind the tape, get myself back to the end of the road and stop before I got to the apartment.

"But . . ." Nothing else came out. It took all my resolve not to turn on my heel and flee. I thought of Irshad's words. Oh fuck off, I thought. Fuck off, all of you.

"I know I should have written and told you I was coming.

But I didn't think you'd mind." She explained that the adoption agency had told her there was a procedure. They had warned her to be careful because some mothers don't want to be found; that they may have made new lives for themselves with partners and second families who had no idea of the child's existence.

"But that isn't us, is it? You wanted to see me, or you wouldn't have got in touch."

"What—you flew here? From England?" I was stunned. "I thought my attorney told you that I wasn't ready to meet you yet," I stammered. "You did get a letter, didn't you?"

"Yeah, but it was only ever going to be a matter of time before we got together, I knew that, and I just couldn't wait any longer. I was that excited." The gray eyes held mine, daring me to contradict her. "I've been looking for you for such a long time. I registered with the adoption people when I was eighteen, and it was like a dream come true when I finally heard from you."

"From my attorney," I corrected.

"And so I thought, why wait, just get yourself on a plane, Cheryl. It couldn't have worked out better—my boyfriend and I had always planned, like, this big trip across America and then down to Mexico. We've been saving for years. And he's got rellies in New Jersey . . ."

"'Rellies'?"

"Yeah, his auntie lives in Metuchen so we're staying with them for a few days. But it's a dump though. Worse than Leeds." She had a dry Yorkshire accent, her vowels so flat they could have been ironed by one of the huge industrial pressing machines I had threaded with sheets in the off-off Broadway hotel. I could hardly take in what she was saying; I just kept looking at the rucksack and hearing the words *New Jersey.*

New fucking Jersey. How did she end up in New Jersey?

I felt like I was trapped in an alley with a Doberman at my throat.

"But you live in England, not New Jersey?" I said, willing it to be true.

"Yeah, but I just told you. We're *traveling.* We flew in on Saturday and the two of us came on the train this morning. And here I am." She paused. "And here you are. Finally," she said delightedly, the way you try to convince a child that it's not so bad that they wanted a pony for Christmas but only got a new set of underwear. "How great is that?" She smiled expectantly as though a royal herald were about to appear and sound the march triumphant, and I supposed some form of welcome greeting was in order. I just didn't know what to say. Then while I hesitated, trying to fashion my face into a rictus that could pass for an expression that wasn't horrified shock, she slapped two cobra arms around me and clapped my back, almost lifting me off my feet.

It was like being assaulted. I wanted to punch her and scream for help.

"I'm *gobsmacked*? I've imagined this moment for years, you know?" All her sentences ended in question marks, whether or not they contained any inquiry, and for someone who claimed to be lost for words, she had suddenly hit the mother lode. They followed each other so rapidly that it was as if she were firing them from a nail gun.

She told me she and her boyfriend "were planning on having a bit of a holiday?" as though I might not have come across the concept before. She was also "really glad to have finally caught up with me."

Oh, yessir, Bob's your uncle and Agnes is your aunt; I most certainly felt caught.

I wrested myself from her embrace and hugged my overnight bag to my chest like the baby I never wanted so she would keep her distance.

"I must have written you, like, about a gazillion letters?"

"Yes," I acknowledged doubtfully. "I've been traveling around a bit myself. Life has been sort of difficult lately," I said lamely, swaying the overnight bag to and fro, soothing it.

Words were dripping out of her mouth, on and on like a faucet with a faulty washer.

"I was worried that it might be a bad idea, you know, just coming here," she said, while I reeled at the understatement. "But I had this hunch, like, that it would all be fine? I just knew you would be as pleased to see me as I was to see you."

"It is a bit much to take in. Just springing yourself on me like this," I protested.

"Oh." She looked crestfallen. "I thought you would be excited too."

"Excited," I repeated in disbelief.

"I'm sorry about your husband and all. When I saw him the last time I was over, he told me he didn't know where you were because you weren't together anymore. I just came for a week that time, but now Lee and me have packed in our jobs. We got a six-month visa."

"Six months?"

"Great, isn't it?"

I shook my head.

"It was just so lucky that he was in when I went to the house," she said blithely. "I met his girlfriend too. She's a lovely woman?"

"Oh?" I could insert a mean question mark myself when it suited me. I waited to hear more about the "great girlfriend" who had been around since last year. The thought burned through my stomach like battery acid despite the fact that I myself had been fucking like I was training for a sex marathon.

"She's from Argentina. That's one of the places Lee and me want to go?" She stopped babbling and looked at me expectantly, as though waiting for me to do a backward flip. So I did.

"Hey, why don't we go and have a cup of coffee?" I suggested, turning around down the street.

She was disappointed. "Aren't you going to ask me in? It's just that this pack is really, really heavy. Couldn't I leave it inside and wash my hands? I've been up since seven o'clock this morning. I left Lee at the Empire State Building. Who knew that Brooklyn would be so far from the Penn Station? New York's that big. You could get lost here."

Oh no you fucking couldn't, I thought, as she chewed her lip, another gesture that had traveled from my mother's face, through mine, and onto hers.

I couldn't take her into the apartment. Jocelyn might come back and then there would have to be explanations. I would never get rid of her: she'd be in my hair, crawling all over me, and I'd never be able to comb her out. It was only good luck that there wasn't anybody home that morning. Jesus, I cringed at the possibility of finding Cheryl sitting in the kitchen with a chirping Jocelyn. I certainly didn't want her comfortably settled, with a cup of yarrow tea and an alfalfa carob muffin, spilling her guts to the homoeopath.

"Of course, leave your bag, what am I thinking of . . ." I lifted the haversack. It was heavy. I hoped she wasn't planning on staying. I unlocked the door, took her inside, and walked up the first flight of stairs to the apartment. The elevator, as usual, was broken, its metal gate hanging open.

In the apartment, I dumped her pack in my room, then showed her where the bathroom was while I stood in the hall with my hand holding the door ajar until she returned. I told her that it was my roommate's apartment and that she was a fussy old thing and that she didn't really like my having guests and asked if she minded walking up to Seventh Avenue to find a café.

After looking pityingly around at the dusty handmade pottery and shabby homespun tapestries from Jocelyn's various misguided attempts at community college arts and crafts, she agreed, walking beside me, looking at me out of the corner of her eye as if she were going to describe me later for a police sketch.

I glanced at her, too, covertly, in the window of the Corner Book Store.

She was half a head taller than me, and she made me feel small.

Very, very small.

The height and wide shoulders were Bill Anderson's legacy, and intimidated me, the reason I had never, until Adam, spent any significant period of time with a man I couldn't look in the eye in my stocking feet. I had liked to maintain the fiction that if it came to a fight, I could always knock them over. Though the idea of my fighting anyone was laughable. Hadn't I always just laid right on down for anyone who asked? She walked with a swagger, as though drunk, or recently disembarked after a long sea voyage, but then I realized her gait was caused by her repeatedly turning round to examine my face.

She pulled a strand of black hair out of her mouth, showing an uneven incisor, crossed as though for good luck over the tooth next to it. She had bony twiglet fingers, just like mine, and a diamond on the third finger of her left hand that was as tiny and as brilliant as a dust mote.

"You look almost as young as me," she said approvingly, as we reached a diner and pushed through the swinging doors. She sat, and I slid into as chair opposite her. "We could be sisters. You're so young, compared to my mother. My other mother," she corrected herself.

I twisted my lips into what was supposed to be a smile, wondering how much of my life I would have to rehash and serve up to her on a plate, but as I sat at my end of a Formica table decorated with a round plastic tomato, I realized my function was to listen, not to inform.

I should be charging for this, I thought, as she rattled out her potted childhood, the trajectory of her romance with a kid called Lee, her mother's job, her father's job, the house they had in the Yorkshire Dales, her training as a legal "secetary." On and on and on and on it went, while I nodded like a Japanese businessman. For the first time, it occurred to me that Irshad actually did earn his money. Listening was exhausting.

"Are you still in touch with my dad?" she asked, jolting me out of my fact-filled stupor.

"No."

"It's not your husband, is it?"

"What?"

"Your husband isn't my dad?" asked Cheryl. "He said he wasn't, though at first I thought he might be, 'cos he's dark like me, but he's a bit short to be related. Nice, though," she added apologetically. "Dead nice."

"Dead?" I was startled until I realized it was just an expression. "Yes, he's nice. But, no, he wasn't your father."

"Who was, then?" She was squirming, as though the question were being wrung out of her through a mangle.

I laughed. I did a good job of it too, full teeth, lips, head tossed to the side. "Oh, if I'd known the answer to that, life would have been a lot easier."

She looked puzzled. "You don't know?"

"I was a wild girl," I said. "It could have been anybody. I honestly don't have any idea who your dad was. It had been my birthday and . . ."

"Oh, when?" she interrupted.

"October the thirty-first." I waited for a Halloween joke, which was at least one of the reasons I hadn't mentioned it last year at Adam's, albeit not the most important one, but instead I got astrology.

"What's that, then? Libra?"

"Scorpio," I answered automatically, though it had been decades since I had thought of myself in terms of star signs.

"I'm Leo, the sixth of August, next month," she said, then giggled faintly when she realized that I would know this already, having been there at the time. "Sorry," she added, "you were saying?"

"So I had been to a big party, a weekender, in Glasgow. There were loads of people I didn't know there, and I got very drunk . . . speed, dope, mushrooms." Listen to me, I thought, the most exotic mushroom I'd ever eaten was a cep. "I couldn't even tell you what happened that weekend, let alone who I was with." She looked both dejected and queasy. "I know, it's not pretty. It's not a story you really want to tell anyone," I said ruefully, thinking that it was *Little Women* compared to the real one.

"Oh, well," she allowed eventually, "you were just a lass. I mean, people do daft things when they're young and don't know any better."

"But I did know better. I just didn't care back then."

"Oh, I'd never get away with that sort of thing. My mum and dad are strict. I was brought up right." I asked about her family. Both grandparents were dead, she told me, and she was an only child. Her parents were quiet people, Salvation Army, though Cheryl had rebelled against that.

But she didn't have many relatives, and no "real, blood ones."

That's what made me so special, apparently, and explained why this big, cold-eyed Colossus was so desperate to reattach all the family bonds that I'd quite happily cut decades earlier.

"I went up to see your mother, I mean, in the home? But she didn't have a clue who I was. The nurses say she hardly ever recognizes anyone. It's a real shame."

"Yes, it is," I agreed. and left it at that, while anxiety swirled round and round in my brain, picking up questions like a tornado wrenching parked cars from driveways. How had she found the home?

"Lee and I are getting married next March. After we get back to England?" I tried to look interested while thinking, March? She wasn't going home until March? "I'd really like you to meet him." I shifted awkwardly in the chair, as though the inoffensive pine seat had suddenly pinched me. I'd rather meet Stalin, I thought. "We're leaving next week, hiring a car, and driving down to South Carolina. Lee has a friend who's working in a restaurant in Myrtle Beach, and he says he can get him some casual work—he's a chef, did I tell you that?"

I didn't think it was included in the encyclopedia entry, but I perked up at the word *leaving.* "I'm not sure I'll be here myself much longer. I might be moving on myself soon?"

She looked disappointed. She pursed her lips, pouting with uncertainty, then she thought of something else and smiled at me, as if preparing me for bad news that could be worse. She had better teeth than me, apart from that one crooked tooth at the side. Dr. Goldmann would approve.

"Could I ask you something?" She was waiting for permission, so I nodded and waited for her to continue.

"Well, like, I know you were very young when you had me, but did you ever regret giving me up for adoption?" I didn't know how to respond. Strangely, I hadn't anticipated this question. I think this was the moment I was supposed to say that I still had the baby bootees and a pile of unsent letters and birthday cards in a drawer that I'd been saving up since her birth, but I was rescued from the need to invent something by a pair of white mugs set down on the table together with a bowl of sugar packets. Dear God, all this and we still had to drink the bloody coffee. It already seemed as if we had been sitting there long enough for dinosaurs to become extinct.

"You all set? Everything okay here?" asked the waitress, as though there were hidden nuances in the delivery of three-hour-old Kona coffee that she had, perhaps, overlooked. We both nodded our heads and tipped our chins in an identical gesture.

Undeterred, she went on: "My mother had three miscarriages before she adopted me, and she used to talk about them as if the kids were still around, as if they had been born and were playing in the other room. She even had names for them—our Jack, our Richard, our Edward. She used to say she couldn't understand how anyone could give away a baby." There was an awkward silence; or at least a silence even more awkward than the already hugely awkward ones that were milling around us like people waiting for trains.

"You know, this isn't going to work, Cheryl," I said, as she stirred and restirred her coffee.

"What isn't?"

"This. You and me," I blurted out.

"I don't understand?"

"You asked me if I regretted having you adopted, and I'm sorry, but I didn't. There was nothing to regret. Adoption was the only option open to me at the time. As you said, I was far too young for the responsibility of a baby and then there was the scandal. My mother couldn't have stood the shame of it."

"Scandal? What happened?" She looked offended. She was taking the shame as a personal affront. "Was it really that bad, having a baby?" I felt as though a blade had sliced through my head. It was hard to keep all these lies straight. I suddenly felt afraid that I had said too much. What if she went around digging up the past?

What if she went back to the village and started asking questions?

"Oh, people were very small-minded. And I already had a real bad reputation around the village. Getting pregnant was the last straw, as far as my mother was concerned. I was told to say nothing. I just vanished for a couple of months, had the baby adopted, and when I came back I was expected to pretend like nothing had happened."

"*Me* adopted," she corrected, reminding me that this wasn't just a faceless baby, but the real-life, grown-up person sitting beside me playing with her lips.

"It was what people did back then," I said, not mentioning that it had suited me fine, that I just wanted the thing out of me and gone. That I never gave her another thought that wasn't filled with dread from that day to this.

What could I tell her? That I felt guilty? I didn't. I just wanted things to stay the same as they always had been: with this girl far away and out of sight, if not out of mind, living the life that had been stolen from me. I wanted her gone so that every time I looked at her I didn't have to remember what had happened to me.

"I'm not complaining that I was adopted, like," she said. "I've got a brilliant mum and dad; you'd like them. I wasn't really bothered until Lee and I decided to get married. Then I thought it would be good to know what you were like, in case I had brothers or sisters, or if we had illnesses in the family, anything catching, you know—for when I have my own kids."

Damn, she had a lot of questions. But some of these I could answer. "Well, as for other brothers or sisters—you don't have any; and, as far as I know, there are no hereditary illnesses."

She asked what my mother was like before she lost her marbles.

"Kind," I said. "Funny and attentive and good-natured and cheerful."

"What about your father?"

"Overindulgent, jolly, always telling jokes, light-hearted, and helpful," I said. Then I colored in their golden haloes with stories of all their funny ways and amusing mannerisms and the dog we never had, and decorated my family with smiley faces, little gold stars, and hearts all around the edges of the paper. The pope would be calling any minute to sanctify them.

She asked about her birth. I wished I had suggested a bar instead of a café. But even I couldn't drink vodka at eleven o'clock in the morning. Then, I thought, why stop now? I was on a roll.

So I gave her a rose-tinted, soft-focus, hand-held version, leaving out the twelve hours of solitary labor, followed by mastitis and the weeks walking around with bandages strapped round my bullet breasts to stop the milk. I didn't tell her that even when I was living in the youth hostel in Oxford, and my stretch marks had faded from ugly red to silvery snot, I could still squeeze drops of sweet, blue-white fluid out of my breasts. I left out the forceps, the stitches, the gas and air, and the pethidine.

I passed over all that and filed the birth plan for *Rebecca of Sunnybrook Farm* while the reality had been more like *Bleak House.*

I STAYED AT the nuns' hostel for nearly three weeks before the birth, though in pregnancy time five minutes can seem like months, and adding nuns to the mix doesn't exactly speed things along.

As Irshad pointed out, teenagers have been having babies since the dawn of time, and there was a good representative sample of them at the hostel. There we spent the days having parenting lessons from a health visitor not much older than ourselves, who taught us how to bathe a stiff-limbed plastic doll in a bowl and instructed us on a variety of ways to pin diapers onto its unyielding asexual limbs.

Why, we dared not ask. Not one of us was planning on keeping her child. We knew there was a long line of baby-snatching parents with their gaze already fixed greedily on the nursery window, ready to whip our little cuckoos off and plant them in an instant, brand-new borrowed history that owed nothing to the circumstances of their birth. Nevertheless, we powdered plastic bottoms and burped plastic backs while little plastic eyes swiveled hither and thither, rattling in plastic faces that were permanently dimpled and never cried, giving them names, not all of them the sort of thing you would want to be calling out in the playground.

The girls and I cooked supper for each other under supervision from one of the sisters, and we slept all together in a dormitory, where we swapped sob stories about fathers who wouldn't marry us, and, in one case, a father who was already married to the girl's mother. I was the youngest in the hostel and subject to a bit of babying myself. One or two left in the middle of the night clutching their stomachs as if they were being eaten from the inside by a starving animal, but they never came back to tell us how their story ended, though we all knew, more or less.

My aunt visited as often as she could. She had warned me about the pain. "Don't let them give you any of that natural childbirth nonsense; be sure to ask for the injection or you'll be crying for your mother and begging them to put a gun to your head to save you from the pain." She was right about the drugs. But I didn't cry once for my mother.

"You be lucky," the midwife said, as I screamed in tandem with the woman in the next room. "You see, it all be over soon and it be like it never even happen." She gave my cheek a pinch with her sharp West Indian fingers. "Once you have that baby in your arm, Lord, you forget ev-er-y-ting." She was suffering from some selective memory loss herself.

She had forgotten I wouldn't be keeping the baby; it was going straight to social services. The family was already assembling the crib, hanging the mobile, airing the baby clothes, buying cans of formula.

"Where the baby daddy be?" she asked me toward the end, but I was too busy keeping the gas mask over my face to say that he was out on remand.

"I feel the Holy Spirit wit' me, praise the Lord. God bless you," she sang as she plopped the baby on my stomach. I didn't feel much like praising anything that didn't come at the end of a needle, but I held the baby for a few anesthetized minutes. She looked like a grub, a bloody, purple-faced wax doll, her head dented from the prongs that had dragged her out of me, her eyes squeezed shut, then blinking, then drooping back to a drugged sleep, dopey from the same stuff in her bloodstream that was also in mine.

"What you going to call her?" asked the midwife, lifting her out of my arms and carrying her away to a Plexiglas box, where she peeled back the blanket, pressed a stethoscope to her fluttering chest, and began to fill out a form.

"Girl," I remember saying.

"Yes, I know it's a girl, but what's her name, darlin'?"

"Just Girl," I repeated.

So she wrote Baby Girl McBride, her date of birth, and her weight and attached the tag to her wrist.

Well, it was better than Agnes, anyway.

The midwife dressed her in the little nightdress my aunt and I had bought in a baby store in Leeds and, without breaking either arm, expertly threaded her stringy limbs into the handmade baby sweater—my one and only attempt at knitting. It was a lurid shade of lime-green with gold flecks. My aunt had found the wool in a sale—it would have been great for a disco.

"What you think you be havin', darlin'—a frog?" said the midwife, chuckling. She put a cotton hat on her head—she looked like she was going to a Bar Mitzvah.

I held her again, wrapped in a papoose of blue thermal blanket.

Her little mouth opened and closed, and her tiny star-shaped hand wrapped itself around my finger, which was tipped with uneven purple sparkly nail polish. How could I have a baby when I couldn't even paint my nails without smudging them?

"You can feed her if you like; I can show you how, darlin'."

"No, I can't," I said, stroking the little face, marveling at the downy skin, soft like a peach.

"Course you can. It's the most natural thing in the world," said the midwife, now all gap-toothed, pink-gummed smiles, but I asked her to take it away until the woman from social services arrived. I said I didn't want to see it again, and nobody ever insisted I did.

Until now.

How had she turned into this strangely familiar person in chain-store denim and a sweat jacket? Yes, her hair was lackluster and black, her eyes fringed with lashes I would have, indeed almost had, killed for; but the thin, pointed chin, the cheekbones, the sharp bones at her narrow wrists, the collarbone like a coat hanger across the open neck of her T-shirt—it was like looking at myself, reversed in a mirror. But with Bill Anderson's eyes.

I couldn't stand it. I couldn't stand looking at her. I wound my feet round the legs of the chair to keep me anchored there.

"It must have been dead hard having a baby and being away from your family and all your friends? I'd be lost without my friends. My best mate, Pat, she's going to be my bridesmaid when we get married. We're that close, like sisters?" I nodded.

"Who was your bridesmaid when you got married?" The girl was gushing all over the place like a garden sprinkler.

You never knew where the next jet was coming from.

"He was called Karl."

"Carole?"

"No, Karl. It was a boy. I didn't have many girlfriends."

"What, not one? A bloke for your best maid? That's different."

"I guess so."

"So who was Kirsty, then?" I needed an air bag to protect me from these blows she kept raining down on me.

"Kirsty?" I repeated dumbly.

"The first letter I sent. To your old house in Scotland. I wrote to them asking if anyone remembered you. I got a nice reply from the people living there. Old folks. They said they remembered you when you were a girl. You and your friend Kirsty. They didn't know where you'd gone, but they gave me your mum's new address. That one got forwarded to her nursing home?" Her voice went up more emphatically than usual, as if I might not remember where my own mother was, though given the rarity of my visits that would, at least, have been an excuse for my continued nonappearance at visiting times.

"So what happened to her?"

"I don't know."

"You're really not a great one for keeping in touch, are you?" I gave her a level look. Did she know what she was doing? Did she know more than she was letting on? I had no idea who was living in our old house or what they had told her.

"No, you're right," I said baldly. "I don't believe in looking backward." I was running out of vocabulary. Clichés would have to do: "You have to look forward. The past is the past."

"So do you think you and your husband will get back together? I guess not if he's found someone else. Do you have someone else?" Dear God, it was like having a conversation with a squash ball.

I looked at my watch. It was two minutes later than it had been the last time I looked.

I didn't answer. Instead, I tried a question of my own. "How did you find my address?" I asked. "I didn't give it to you. I wrote to you through the solicitor." I had this creeping feeling of strangulated panic that the girl had put some sort of homing device on me.

"Oh, that was easy. It's not a secret, is it? I told you I was a legal secetary. I just called your attorney's firm from work and spoke to his secetary." Another missing *r*. Where do they all go, I wondered, moronically. Maybe there was a huge landfill somewhere with all her dropped *r*s, Irshad's vowels, and my *t*s.

"I gave her the name of my boss, said we were acting for you in England, and she told me your address. Sorted." She seemed to be expecting congratulations. I pictured the attorney's bill and stripped off all the zeros after the first digit.

Bloody Singh would be whistling for his money.

I could bear it no longer.

"I need to get going," I said, scrabbling to my feet. "Sorry, but I have to be at work by two."

"But it's only eleven thirty," she said.

"I know, I know, but I have a lot to do, and it's a long way away. I work in Manhattan; it takes me hours to get there. I didn't know you were coming, after all." I started to gather up my things before I realized I only had one bag. Instead, I lifted the torn sugar packets and crumpled napkins, dropped them into the inch of coffee in her mug, and carried them to the counter, where I paid.

"Lee's waiting for me, but we thought we might stay in town for a while, find a hotel or stay with you."

"I don't think that's a good idea. I don't have time to see you. And I can't have visitors. I also have work, and I work really late."

"Well, I suppose we could just go back to Metuchen. Couldn't I ride into Manhattan with you?" she asked.

"No, I'm miles away, Columbus Circle," I said, mentioning the first place that came into my head.

"But you'll keep in touch, won't you?" she asked apprehensively as I walked out into the street. It was already in the nineties out there and suffocating.

Jesus, this is why they leave kids to die on a hillside in China.

She wouldn't take the hint.

"I don't mean to be harsh, but, as I've already told you, I can't see you anymore. The letter that my attorney sent said that I didn't want to meet you. You shouldn't have contacted me, and you certainly should not have tricked my attorney into giving you my address. We've both got our own lives. It's better that we just leave things as they are."

"But I've come all this way. From the other side of the Atlantic."

"I didn't ask you to. In fact, I specifically asked you *not* to. I would rather be left alone."

"What, completely? Not even a card at Christmas, just so I know your news?"

"I won't have much news"—I struggled to spit out the name—"Cheryl. You're the one who's starting out in life, with all these plans to get married and travel. You're the one going across America on the big adventure with your boyfriend."

"Fiancé," she corrected.

"Fine, *fiancé*. You see—you'll get married, have your own family. Me, I'm not going to be doing anything very much different."

"So, I could tell you my news?" she offered.

I stopped on the sidewalk. "Look, I don't want to hurt you, but no."

"But I *do* want to see you again," she said querulously. "Sometime, like, if I had kids. Wouldn't you want to meet your grandchildren?"

"Well, we'll see. One day," I finally conceded. By then I

could tell her I'd emigrated to Zimbabwe or be "dead busy," as she might put it, or even just plain dead.

We walked back to the apartment, which, mercifully, was still Jocelyn-free.

"Will you show me the way back to the subway?" she asked.

Even better, I bundled her and her haversack swiftly into a passing cab and gave the driver thirty dollars, which was all the cash I had on me.

"Well, bye, then," she said, looking pitiful as she prepared to climb into the purring cab. I embraced my purse like a life preserver to keep her from hugging me.

I felt like the woodcutter, abandoning his children in the middle of the forest without even a paper trail to enable them to find their way home. I had hated that story as a child. Now I understood it perfectly.

"It was nice to finally meet you," she stammered awkwardly, as though it was a phrase that had been instilled in her since childhood, for birthday parties and visiting dignitaries.

I thought for one awful moment she was going to curtsy.

"Yes, wonderful." I waved, and smiled, and waved, and smiled, and waved, and smiled, and finally, after my lips had stuck to my teeth as if superglued, the cab drew away from the curb and lurched into the traffic.

Demon down. Buffy the Vampire Slayer couldn't have done it better herself. I felt relieved and dizzily, kick-ass happy as I walked back to Jocelyn's. It was over. I had done it.

Unfortunately, I had forgotten to drive the stake right into her heart.

That girl wasn't vanquished. She was just gathering her strength for the next round.

30

AND THAT'S JUST about it."

"Really?" Irshad is skeptical but trying to hide it.

He has been expecting that I would eventually feel relaxed enough to open up and tell him the rest of the story. He's been patient, session after session, while I have distracted him with the cat-and-mouse game I played with Cheryl, interspersed with selected chapters of *The Good Sex Guide.* But if he wants more, he's going to be disappointed.

"You don't feel there's anything else you'd like to bring to the space?"

I know what he means, but he's annoying me, so I look up from the tissue that I've been shredding and give him a baffled look. "'Space'?" I say, pretending not to understand him.

"Here, in the analysis."

"Oh, no. I don't think so." I have a sudden picture of myself dragging my feet round a department store with my mother in her black cape trying to interest me in a serviceable fawn school coat that I don't have the courage to tell her I hate.

He chipped away: "So how did things resolve themselves with your teacher?"

"Oh, eventually we found a way to distract him and I managed to get away. I was lucky. A car picked me up at the first crossroads, and the driver called the police and took me to the hospital."

"And Kirsty?"

"The police went back to get her. But she was in a bad way. Hysterical. He had slapped her around a lot too. I didn't see her again."

"Ever?"

"Never. Her parents blamed me. Quite rightly. They felt I had abandoned her, said I had led her astray."

"Why do you say 'quite rightly'?"

"I was the one who got away first."

"But it wasn't your idea to go with him into the house; it was Kirsty's. So why are you so ready to take the blame? How did your own parents react?"

"They didn't know what to believe. Kirsty and me . . . well, our stories didn't exactly match up. They were ashamed of me."

He waited.

"It was our word against his, and he was a teacher. He said that we had thrown ourselves at him, that we had been hitchhiking, and that he had only been trying to help us. He said we had begged him to give us a ride and then wouldn't go home because we were scared we would get in trouble with our parents. He made us sound like a pair of nymphomaniacs—with the stress on *maniacs*."

"And what did you say?"

"I could hardly claim that we hadn't gone with him. And we had been hitching. We went willingly, didn't we?"

"I wouldn't describe it as 'willing.' You didn't know what lay ahead."

"I guess, but there were other problems."

"I don't understand. You say that the two of you distracted him. You got away. You got help. You saved her, in a manner of speaking."

"I don't think anyone else saw it that way."

"And was the man sentenced?"

"At first they charged him with statutory rape—I was only fifteen—then with assault, but they couldn't make any of it stick. He'd hit Kirsty, threatened her with a knife, but she kept changing her mind about what happened. At first she said he did; then she claimed he hadn't touched her. She had all these old scars and a history of cutting herself. Not that I ever knew about that. It all came out later. They put my injuries down to being caught up in the fight at the party, and I couldn't say that he'd raped me."

Irshad tried to protest, but I kept on talking. "My parents didn't want me to press charges; they just wanted it dropped, especially when they knew I was pregnant. They told me to deny it. Kirsty's parents were furious with me, and then she got really ill. The police said they didn't have enough evidence to charge him without Kirsty's testimony. It all turned on its head. In the end he made it look like we'd entrapped him, the honest teacher. The Larksridge Lolitas, they called us."

Irshad shook his head questioningly.

"That's the name of the village. Newspapers. They like alliteration. He came out of it the much-maligned hero."

"But surely you had a good case against him. Why couldn't Kirsty testify? She would have backed you up."

"She wasn't there."

"I'm not following you."

"I mean, at first she wasn't there because she zoned out. They had her in a psychiatric ward for a while, doped up, electric shocks, the whole nine yards. She wouldn't talk, apparently. Then, after a couple of months, they let her go home and she really wasn't there."

He waited.

I closed my eyes against the picture of the rickety train whooshing out of the tunnel at the golf course, reeling down the two-track line on the perimeter of our village: Edinburgh, Galashiels, Selkirk, Hawick, Langham, Carlisle. When we were small we used to stand on the links and wave. But this time Kirsty hadn't waved.

"I mean, she jumped in front of a train," I said.

"My goodness." It wasn't often I got much of a reaction out of Irshad.

"I was in England by then," I added quietly, as though to excuse myself from any blame, which was, of course, impossible.

"Did you get any counseling at the time?"

I raised my eyebrows: "We're talking Scotland here . . . They give you a shot of whiskey in your tea and tell you to pull yourself together. No, but I did see somebody after we got away. An old doctor at the same psychiatric hospital they banged Kirsty up in. I was supposed to go back to him, but by then I had been sent off to have the baby."

"That's a great pity." He paused. "Wouldn't the pregnancy have helped your case?"

"Nothing would have helped me by that point. I think it would have made it worse. I woke up every morning surprised to find that I wasn't the one on trial. Anyway I didn't tell anyone."

"No one?"

"Who would I tell? It was hard enough telling my mother."

"It must have been so difficult for you. Keeping it all inside. Then and now."

I didn't respond. I realized I had shredded an awful lot of tissues. My lap was full of pink ribbons. I could see him looking at them. I waited for him to comment.

"What happened to the man, the teacher?"

"Anderson. *Mr.*"—I imbued the title with some sarcasm—"Anderson. He moved. Went to Canada as a sports coach for some school. My mother saw it in the paper years ago, before I was married: 'Troubled Teacher on Toronto Trail' or something. Actually, I think it was Saskatchewan."

"Is he still there?"

I shrugged. "I wouldn't know. I'm not exactly going to seek him out, am I? I never think of him."

"No?"

"No."

Irshad looked meaningfully at my lap. I scraped the tissues into a pile and threw them into the trash. I missed and they tumbled over the carpet like party streamers.

I couldn't think of anything else I wanted to say. The silence was excruciating. I searched my mind, desperately, for something, anything, that would move the session closer to completion. The hands on the clock seemed frozen, with ten minutes still to go.

I swallowed loudly enough to hear my gulp echo off the walls.

My stomach began to gnaw itself. Audibly.

Inevitably, it came: "Have you had any dreams you want to share?"

Dreams. Share. Like they were fucking Kit Kats you could tear into fingers and pass round. And then it came to me that I had had a dream. I'm hiding in the shed at the back of our garden in Scotland where we used to keep the coal. It was our favorite place for hide-and-seek. I was there with my cousin, "wee" Pamela—one of the lucky ones whose big sister got saddled with the A word.

Then this man arrives, fully grown and sinister, but unknown to me, black-faced like the person who used to deliver the coal, and tries to pull me out of our hiding place. I wrestle myself away and tell him: *don't take me, take Pamela.* So then he reaches back in and grabs Pamela's arm and pulls her out instead.

The dream popped into my head like a piece of mental toast.

I figured I could spread butter on it for Irshad, just to pass the time, but it was too risky.

"Yes, actually, I dreamed about my mother . . ." I said instead.

He signaled that I should go on. "I dreamed that she was dead." Okay, so it was a very short dream.

I wait for his response.

"What do you think it means?"

"I know what it means." I might be mad, but I'm not stupid. "It's wish fulfillment, isn't it?"

He said nothing, neither agreeing nor disagreeing. I wished I hadn't been as rash as to offer an opinion.

"And how did that make you feel?" he asked eventually.

"In a way, she's been dead for years. She's not the person she was—just this lost, pathetic shell."

"You haven't answered my question."

"Okay, well, actually, I was angry. Angry that she had removed herself before I had a chance to talk to her."

"Interesting choice of words: *removed herself.* Isn't that what you do yourself?"

I remained as mute as my mother used to when confronted with uncomfortable and leading questions.

"So what would you have said to her?" I shrugged like a sulky teenager.

"You obviously have a lot of unresolved issues to explore," he said, his face sweet with compassion.

I tutted impatiently. It all came back to bloody unresolved bloody issues and "exploring" things.

"I don't want to explore."

"Okay," he said patiently, "but 'gnes, you have to learn to forgive yourself. And maybe that's something I can help you with . . ."

Oh, yes, and maybe you don't dye your hair, I thought.

"It'll be all right; you'll see, we can work through it together."

That's what the police officer said when she came to take my statement. She gave me a hug when she got up to go. She said, "Don't worry, hen, you're safe now. Everything's going to be all right."

But I knew it never would be.

31

YOU KNOW, I might not have a row of certificates from the University of Durban, but I was right about one thing. It doesn't go back into the box once you've let it out. Your past arranges itself in the here and now, like your possessions in a hotel room. When you arrive, it's bland and anonymous—white sheets, clear surfaces, a white bathroom with the soap in a little wrapper—and then suddenly there's a hair in the sink and the pointy end of the toilet paper is flushed away. You put your dressing gown behind the door, your nightdress under the pillow. That's what happens with the past—it draws up a chair in the present and sits down with its feet on the table. It finds a place and stays there, like the guest who won't leave.

Though I've struggled for years to push him out of my head, the muscled bulk of Bill Anderson weighs down the other side of the bed when I climb into it at night. I feel the knotted string of the veins on his biceps pressing against my face and wake up, pushing tearfully at Adam's calming hands.

I've started to see him now and again, spread-eagled on the sofa when I watch television with my landlady; his eyes stare out at me from Adam's face while we're making love. I feel bruises on my arms. When I wake in the morning, Kirsty hunkers beside me on the floor, with a ratty tartan blanket over her shoulders.

It's her cold bare feet that really get to me, the chipped polish. Moscow Mauve. My fingers seem to stink of nicotine. I've started to crave cigarettes again.

I'm not just being brave when I say it wasn't so bad. I did then what I did a hundred times later, with tens of different men. It never worried me. It was my choice. Irshad thinks I see myself as a helpless victim; he says that what happened to Kirsty wasn't my fault—but what does he know? Only what I tell him.

I told him about the girl just turning up out of the blue. I told him about the liberation of finally having gotten the meeting over with. I told him that I had finally faced my past in the present.

He was pleased with me. It was progress, he maintained.

It was a nice theory.

And then the phone calls started.

There were two the first week when she was still in New Jersey, but even after she should have left for South Carolina, they still came once or twice a week. Of course I ignored them. Each time she would leave a message wondering when she could see me, which Jocelyn printed out in microscopic capitals on Post-it notes and stuck on my bedroom door. I peeled them off, but a few days later there would be another, and then another, until I felt as if I were being hounded by those damn yellow squares.

Meanwhile, Adam and I had been dating like teenagers,

going to the movies and leaving the theater halfway through the film to go home to bed.

He went in to work late so that we could sit around in our hastily donned pajamas reading the newspapers; we strolled in the park and had candlelit picnics in the backyard in the evenings. At the end of July we went to Cape Cod for the weekend and out to the Hamptons at the beginning of August, where we borrowed a little shack on the beach that belonged to one of his authors.

But, fun though it was to play Barbie and Ken, he was impatient for me to settle permanently into the Dutch Dream House.

The prospect was thrilling. The plan was that I would move in before we left for two weeks in Italy when the kids were back in school. I would come back from vacation, tan and rested, fully transformed from the bit on the side to the bit on the inside.

I imagined dissolving into Adam's life, my worries cushioned by money. I could sit on Irshad's Eames chair and empty my emotional purse until the leather molded itself to my bum. I could spend my days in the kitchen being Julia Child, burying my sins like chocolate chips in the double-fudge cookies, and my nights in the bedroom being Heidi Fleiss. He wanted to marry me. When my divorce was finalized, I could change my name again, this time legally, and fill Gay's bathroom, hell, fill *my* bathroom, with a smorgasbord of scented soaps. I could grow to tolerate Lennie and even like Ned. In two years' time she would be in college, and Ned was already away at school . Soon it would be just Adam and myself, alone in the house on Eightieth Street or wherever we chose to live.

I could be happy.

But how was I going to explain Cheryl to Adam without her bookmarking herself into my future? I simply didn't know how best to handle the situation. And then the situation began to handle me.

She turned up again soon after we got back from the Hamptons, just as I was leaving the apartment to have a haircut. God knows I needed one. I was combing out my bangs with my fingers, examining my reflection in Jocelyn's hall mirror, trying to flatten out the kinks, when the doorbell buzzed, but not the speaker phone at the entrance, the one beside the door. I squinted through the spy hole thinking it was the guy from the apartment across the hall, who had lost his key so often that he left a spare with us, but instead Cheryl stood in the doorway, holding a bunch of gladioli wrapped in soggy paper, drooping like a joint that has been passed around a lot of people.

"What are you doing here? How did you get into the building?" I asked crossly, barring the door with angrily crossed arms and ignoring the outstretched flowers. "You need to leave. I don't want to see you."

I half closed the door in her face and began to gather my things together, ramming stuff that I didn't really need into my purse as a shorthand for *I'm ignoring you, so fuck off.* But she obviously needed it spelled out for her because she didn't budge. Somebody must have let her in downstairs. Why didn't we have a goddamn doorman? I weighed up my options. Was it better to stay where I was, or should I leave and risk having her follow me out into the street?

I stayed where I was with my shoulder on the door, ready to close it.

"I just wanted to talk to you before I went back home. We're leaving next week. We're bringing our wedding forward," she said.

I reiterated what I had told her the last time. I explained that I couldn't give her the kind of relationship she wanted.

"But I only want to know a bit more about you," she pleaded. "You can't just blank me like this. You never take my calls. You're always out. It's not fair. It's my birthright. My history. It's not too much to ask after twenty-one years. You owe it to me."

"I owe you nothing, Cheryl." The name was getting easier to say. It flew out like an obscenity. "All I want from you is to leave me alone."

"I just want to know what your life is like."

"I'll tell you what it's like," I retorted. "Hell. Now let me burn in it by myself." The flowers flopped in her hands, and she laid them across the doorstep like a wreath. If she had cried, I wouldn't have been able to help myself—I would have relented and brought her inside to console her, but mercifully she grew irritated.

"But what about me?" she said in a raised voice, glowering.

"You have parents. You have a fiancé. You have a life. Go and live it," I said. "What part of 'adopted' don't you understand?" Her angry stare, her tight, bitter mouth, the black crow of her eyebrows, only made it easier to close the door.

I drew the bolt across and turned all three locks, then I went into Jocelyn's bedroom, where I watched from the window until, after an agonizingly long time, I saw her disappear around the corner at the end of the block.

My guts quaked and my legs shook, as if the carpet underfoot were heaving and buckling, but I still felt like a hard, heartless bitch as I watched the slow, reluctant clump of her sandals up the street, and I could hardly bring myself to touch the discarded flowers, which I hastily threw in the garbage shoot.

But then, the next day, she came back.

When I let myself in to the house in the morning, Jocelyn rushed out to meet me in the hall wearing a delighted expression and an equally unusual apron, and whispered, as thrilled as a debutante at her first ball, that we had company. I had a couple of visitors from England waiting for me.

I walked into the kitchen and found Cheryl sitting there with the cat on her lap, drinking coffee that I didn't even know we had and eating scones and jam that Jocelyn had actually gone out and bought for her.

This time she had brought her boyfriend. He was a raw, awkward, big-boned guy with blond leg hair and blue Band-Aids on his fingers, intimating that he wasn't as expert with his chef's knives as he should be. He was smoking, actually smoking, on the fire escape while Jocelyn *smiled.*

My face drained of what little color the sun had beaten into it as I apologized to Jocelyn for the intrusion and asked them both to go.

Poor Jocelyn didn't know what to do with herself. She had imagined she was being the perfect hostess and now I was marching the guests out the door. "I'm sorry, I thought they were friends of yours," she stammered, forlorn in her frilly apron, her cheeks, previously bright with excitement, now blotchy with embarrassment.

I patted her arm in apology and glared at Cheryl, willing her to leave with the poison darts I was shooting into her chest with my eyes.

But she merely rubbed her index finger under the chin of the cat, which closed its eyes in rapture. "Sweet," she said, making a kissy face and murmuring some sort of cat-baby talk, and still made no move to rise from her chair.

"It's okay." She attempted a smile, but it came out like a smirk. "I just wanted you to meet my fiancé. This is Lee," she said, as the boy clambered up the metal stairs, throwing the cigarette hastily at his feet, and came in through the kitchen door, wiping his blue-ringed hands as if to rid them of the smell of tobacco, obviously unnerved by the drama unfolding around him.

"Come on, Cherry, love, we should go," he said, flapping his arm as if he were fanning an already out-of-control fire.

Jocelyn glanced from my face to Cheryl's, then slowly scanned back to mine. It was like watching a slot machine roll through her eyes. I saw one bell fall. She caught my blind, animal-on-the-way-to-the-abattoir panic as the next bell spun and stopped.

"You know she's my mother, don't you?" said Cheryl, as the final bell racked up and *ding, ding, ding*; not only did the penny drop but it paid out the whole bloody jackpot.

"I think Agnes is right. You had better leave," Jocelyn said in a voice suddenly as steely as her hair.

Cheryl's boyfriend shuffled out into the hall. "Come on now, love, you don't want to be making a scene."

"You're not going to let my own mother throw me out?" asked Cheryl, her voice rattling like a box of little thumbtacks, spilling and skittering all over the ground, and me in bare feet, afraid to cross it. But Jocelyn was undeterred and escorted them out with a sharp jab of her finger in the direction of the front door, brooking no further discussion. "I'm the one throwing you out. This is my house, and if I want you to go, then you go."

I stammered some ineffectual thanks and a garbled explanation, but Jocelyn merely gathered me into her arms and held me in a viselike grip that could have been marketed as a weight-loss system. "Don't say another word, honey, it's absolutely none of my business," she said, giving me a brisk pat on the back that almost knocked my glasses off; then, unbidden, she made me another cup of valerian tea.

Unbidden, I drank it.

I was even getting to like the taste.

However, though I could tolerate the tea, it didn't do anything to solve the problem of Cheryl. The girl was shit on my shoe, and I was never going to be able to scrape her off. What homoeopathic tincture was strong enough to get rid of her?

"Get a restraining order," suggested Jocelyn. "I had to do it once when I had a patient who wouldn't stop harassing me, and then you can call the police if she comes back. Does Adam know about her?" she asked shrewdly.

I turned to her, shamefaced. "No."

"Well, I don't want to interfere, but you probably should tell him before she does."

"She doesn't know anything about him."

"She won't hear anything about him from me, but you need to watch out, honey; she doesn't look like the sort of person who gives up."

And she was right. Though I called my attorney and asked him how I could keep the girl away from me, before I could even get an appointment to see him, I had a telephone call from her adoptive mother, hoping that I could find it in my heart to get to know Cheryl.

My heart?

Fucking hell.

I didn't even have the zip code for it.

32

JOCELYN AND IRSHAD were singing from the same hymn sheet. He said I should think carefully about beginning a new relationship with another lie.

"It's not another lie; it's the same one," I snapped.

He didn't even dignify that with an answer, but gave me a long, reproachful, pursed look and held me to six squirming minutes of silence before I conceded defeat and admitted he was right.

I knew that I would have to tell Adam that I had a daughter.

She had me backed into a corner as surely as Bill Anderson ever had and once again, there was seemingly nothing I could do to escape. But I couldn't just produce Cheryl, then stand by while she picked away at me like icing on a cake, asking questions she had no right to have answered. I hadn't told Irshad everything, and even if she stopped coming to see me, she would go to somebody else; and, as well as gossip, there would be records, newspaper archives.

I screwed my fists into my eye sockets to wipe out the vision and wondered if there might still be something she could find out. It depended on how determined she was. On impulse, I called information and got the number for the *Selkirk Courier*, then rang Scotland when I figured the office would still be open. A woman with an accent so strong it made mine sound like the Queen's English answered on the seventh ring, just as I was getting ready to hang up.

I explained I was looking for an old copy of the newspaper and asked them how far back their records went.

"We've got the last few years in the office," said the woman. "What year were you looking for?"

"Nineteen seventy-four or thereabouts," I said quietly, as though I might be overheard. The line crackled and hissed.

"What?"

"Nineteen seventy-four," I yelled this time.

"No, we don't go that far back." She sounded a bit outraged, as if it the very idea was ridiculous. I breathed a sigh of relief. "You'll need to go to the library headquarters and get those on microfiche," she added.

Damn it. I explained I was calling from overseas and asked her if she had the number of the library.

"It's the funniest thing, hen," she said, "but you're the second person this week to ask that exact same question. An English woman. What a coincidence?"

I dropped the receiver as though it had grown teeth and bitten me.

It was no coincidence.

I hurriedly rang my cousin Agnes in Glasgow, but even if she managed to get to Selkirk and get her hands on a year's worth of newspaper records, there was bound to be something else somewhere. I had no choice. I would have to do what Irshad suggested. Instead of evading the past, I had no choice but to embrace the future, or at least nod at it across the room. I needed to tell Adam about Cheryl. As for Cheryl , there was little I could do to protect her if she was determined to dig.

I decided I would tell him when we were in Italy. Our trip was only a week away. Cheryl would be back in England. I could do it gently and only divulge as much as I wanted to.

In the meantime, I would move in with Adam right away and put some distance between Cheryl and myself. She didn't know where I worked, and she didn't even know that Adam existed. New York was a city of seven and a half million people, I could be as anonymous as I liked.

Jocelyn was sorry to lose me, but she agreed that I was doing the right thing.

"I know you're going to be so happy. I'm glad for you," she said, stroking the cat mechanically, sending clouds of hair into my face.

I sneezed and pulled the new red suitcase that Adam had bought me the previous week into the hall, where its wheels rocked to and fro on the woodblock flooring, sounding like a cricket with a strep throat. I had already taken most of my meager possessions to Eightieth Street and unpacked the few boxes of bric-a-brac which I had asked Francisco to send down from Cambridge.

Adam had found me a place in a copyediting course which I would begin in the fall, and the kids' basement sitting room had been cleared of teenage crap to serve as my study. A freshly photocopied manuscript sat on the desk placed underneath the barred window, and every time I walked into the room, I twanged the rubber bands holding the pages together with the same relish as a pervert would a stocking top.

Instead of CDs and magazines, the shelves held a motley collection of Colombian bowls, a painted wooden angel Francisco had bought me in El Salvador, and a sheepish collection of photographs, embarrassed in their new frames, of Maisie and her kids, and Adam, Lennie, and me, red-eyed and overexposed, taken at the Jersey shore one weekend. There was also a pot that Jocelyn had given me, which I had turned at an angle to hide the lack of symmetry, and a collection of matchbook altars from Brazil. The sofa had been recovered and was draped with a garish collection of magenta and bright-orange woven cloths that I had found in India when I went to a conference there with Francisco.

"Very cute and bohemian—it looks like a college dorm room," Adam had said approvingly when he saw it. I couldn't wait to really make it my own and get down to work, but first we had two weeks in Positano.

"I'm going to miss you," Jocelyn said, sniffing with what she claimed was a summer cold.

"I'll miss you too, Jocelyn," I said, surprising myself with the truth of the statement. "I don't know what I would have done without you. You've been such a support."

She went pink with pleasure. "Don't be silly, dear. It was nothing."

Jocelyn enveloped me in the old aunts' scent of lavender and mothballs and kissed my cheek. The cat mewled, crushed between us.

"We'll be lost without you at work. Particularly Krishna—he's taken such a shine to you."

"I'll come back and see you all after I get back from vacation. We can have lunch."

"Yes, but it won't be the same as having you there every

day." She followed me downstair, pulling the suitcase, and we stood together on the sidewalk.

A cab trundled down the street, and I walked out and stood waving my hand like a kid with the right answer until it stopped. Then, shouting over the squeal of the tires and an urgent sports commentator on a Hispanic radio station, I directed the driver to Eightieth and Madison and sat back, watching the meter tick off the minutes in twenty-cent increments, as he navigated his way across Brooklyn Bridge and drove uptown.

"Where do you want me to pull over?" he asked forty-five minutes later as we turned right into the street. I could hear the roar of an ecstatic crowd behind him.

"Just along on the left, anywhere you can stop," I answered, craning my neck as the houses repeated the two times table up to the red brick apartment building beside Adam's house. "This will do." He pulled into a gap between two parked cars.

My stomach lurched and dived with merry excitement, as though I had ridden a roller coaster and was just now coming up for the biggest dip.

I could hardly contain myself from jumping out of the cab and running up the Hollywood steps, knowing that Adam was inside, waiting to welcome me home. I pictured myself weeks into the future, day after day after day of opening the door, dropping my bag on the floor and turning my head up for Adam's lips. I could smell the meal I would cook later already bubbling on the stove, something with basil and garlic, I thought. I could taste the wine —crisp, Italian, maybe Prosecco, the bubbles tickling my nose—and see an armful of showy flowers waiting to be arranged in a vase. Adam's cheeks would crease into his little-boy smile; Lennie would be somewhere in the background, like white noise, laughing at something Ned had done; there would be gym clothes and school books spilled across the floor and crumbs on the table. I could see a novel turned facedown on the white sofa in the parlor and hear music playing in the dining room: the brand-new soundtrack of my brand-new life.

The cab door unlocked with a click and the driver swiveled round to face me. "Do you want a hand with your stuff?" he asked.

I dragged my rapt gaze away from the house where I had been placing myself like a store mannequin in a variety of fantasy panoramas: answering the door, weeding the window box that bloomed sedately with white tulips I had planted the previous weekend, kissing Adam goodbye, kissing Adam hello.

"That would be terrific, since there seems to be no welcoming committee," I said happily, a smile like a standing ovation on my lips and a fifty-dollar bill in my hand from which there would be no change. I handed it the driver as I got out of the cab and walked round to open the trunk. I watched him disappear as, momentarily. the world turned yellow, and I heard the case being lifted onto the sidewalk. I slid across the seat telling him that I would get it from there and then the words dried in my mouth.

Out of the corner of my eye there was a figure sitting on the wall by the bus-stop at the end of the street. I leaned back, flattening myself against the vinyl seat. My skin stuck to the upholstery. I turned and looked properly. Black hair, a sleeveless shirt, freckles across the back of her rounded shoulders.

"No, wait a minute," I gasped, shrinking back and closing the door. "Can you keep going? Just up to the end of the block. Slowly . . . Pull in at the corner, by the traffic signals, after that garbage truck."

The driver tutted and started to mutter about the case that stood on the sidewalk.

"Leave it. It doesn't matter. Just drive on," I hissed.

He shook his head, as though women, capricious, willful creatures, were something he would never be able to understand, revved the engine with a sound like loose change in a tin box, and restarted the meter as he crawled down the street.

A car behind honked impatiently and a voice yelled at us to move.

I glanced anxiously behind me as the figure rose and turned at the noise. Cheryl stepped hurriedly out onto the road, watching perplexed as my cab drew away, taking a few urgent steps toward down the street.

Fred came through swinging doors of his apartment building and waved at one of the guys who was washing windows at Ann Taylor, then, as though on cue, stuck a cigarette in his mouth.

Fuck, fuck, fuck. Please, let him not talk to her. Just for once, let him mind his own damn business. What was she doing here? I ducked down, my skin making sucking sounds like a Band-Aid being ripped off, cowering till I was almost flat on the back seat, hoping she hadn't seen me.

"Is this all right, lady?" the driver's voice interrupted. His eyes met mine in the rearview mirror. I could see he thought the crazy freak was in the back of his cab instead of standing in the middle of the road watching us. He pulled in obediently in front of the U-Haul.

I risked another glance out the back window and saw Cheryl cross the street. She seemed to hesitate, then walked over to my suitcase and pulled it up the steps to the door beside the tulips, and pressed her palm to the bell.

"That's gonna be another fare," said the driver.

"Never mind, just keep driving," I whispered as I saw the front door swing open.

He swore under his breath. "Make your mind up, lady. I just can't sit here all day waiting. Where do you wanna go?"

"I don't know," I answered. I craned my neck anxiously toward the house. Adam appeared on the top step. They exchanged a few words, then Cheryl handed over my suitcase and pointed down the street.

"Uptown or downtown, you gotta give me a clue." The cab driver hesitated on the hump of the intersection at Park as the lights turned to green. The engine stuttered like an old sewing machine on overlock.

"Just drive. Now. Go. Anywhere," I said, so softly I had to repeat it twice before he heard.

"Hey, are you sure you okay miss, *miss*?" His voice came over the intercom in stereo because the window between us was wide open. It was loud and tinny. Somebody, somewhere, scored.

I nodded in reply. I couldn't speak.

I glanced at the meter. I only had another twenty dollars in my wallet and I already owed him four of those. If I was going to go any distance, I would need to stop at an ATM.

I would also need clothes. I still had my purse, but everything else I had in the world was in the house on Eightieth Street.

Everything.

Irshad would have told me to get out and explain. As far as he was concerned, it was just a simple matter of filling in the details.

But that's where the Devil is. In the details.

And, as I said, I didn't tell him everything.

33

"You have to talk about it," said Irshad, whose talking cure made confession the answer to every problem. And so I had told him about Kirsty's depression and suicide, but I couldn't revisit the inquest to which I'd been summoned as a witness after the baby was born. I didn't tell him about the list of injuries she sustained after the train crushed her that, for years, I heard like a poisoned whisper in my brain, or the note she left saying I had betrayed her, or the way her mother looked at me and cried. I didn't talk about how afraid I was that Anderson would come after me when they released him, even when I heard he moved away to Canada—not that Irshad wouldn't have understood those fears, but some things are too great to admit, even to yourself. So, I didn't tell him everything

The hardest part was the nights. Sitting awake when time seemed to hang suspended in the suffocating darkness, after he'd locked us in again and gone. I had begged him to leave the light on, but it was almost worse sitting there in the harsh, flickering glare of the fluorescent tube than it was in the dark. So we moved upstairs, with the door open, and squatted on the bed like two stray mutts, covered with our coats and the blanket. Kirsty ignored me at first. She was disgusted that I had let him touch me, so disgusted that I didn't tell her what he'd made me do. I couldn't. She made me feel dirty and ashamed.

I assured her that it had been fine. I said it was nothing. I said that I didn't mind, which I hadn't. Not really. I told her I liked him. It made me feel less vulnerable to her scorn. I was terrified of him, I might have said. Strangely, both were true. I couldn't understand why she, who had been the one who had droned on at length about how good-looking he was, how much she fancied him, was now revolted at the thought of touching him, and appalled at the idea of him touching me.

"Did it hurt?" she asked eventually.

"Nah. For a second—but my bones are sore from falling down. That hurt."

"I've never done it. Not even with Dan." That was news to me. "And I'm certainly not going to let that pervert touch *me*. It was horrible. He tried to force me," she spat, the emphasis on *me*.

"He was going to force one of us—it was either me or you," I reminded her.

"You didn't take a lot of persuasion," she said, loftily. She maintained that she would rather be dead than do anything with him. I didn't point out that this was still a distinct possibility.

After all, he hadn't let us go.

Kirsty was like my mother: she did it all for show. In her case, however, it wasn't the house she covered in ornaments; it was herself she put on the mantelpiece. She liked to flirt; she liked to display herself, but hadn't let either of her last two boyfriends have more than a furtive, fleeting grope of her breasts. Not even I had seen her naked. She hid herself in a big housecoat and long nightgowns whenever I visited and was careful always to lock the bathroom door when she changed.

She was still a virgin. We had both been. But whereas Kirsty, at least, had the guidebook for the world of sex, I hadn't even had a boyfriend. I'd hardly been kissed. There were things I had done with Mr. Anderson that I hadn't even known existed.

Kirsty said she was saving herself. For what, I wondered, a shallow grave? I couldn't see how we were going to get out of this house alive except through persuasion.

I warned her that she would have to stop threatening him or he would never let us go. I told her to be sensible—why would he let us out if we were going to tell the police that he'd abducted us? That would get him into trouble. "He's not going to let that happen, is he?" I said. I reminded her that she had got into the car, and that she had wanted to go to his house—that it had been her idea.

But no, it was my fault—I had got knocked out. I was the one who knew him, who had trusted him, who had let her believe he was safe. I was the one who had thrown myself at him. I was just a slut.

I slapped her.

She wept and I wept, and she wept more.

I told her to shut up or I would slap her again. I needed to think.

She snored and snuffled and took most of the blanket. I stared at the white felt rectangle blocking out the light on the roof and tried to think of a plan.

To this day I don't like skylight windows.

I went through everything that he had done when he came in.

He had unlocked two doors. I heard three bolts. He had put a big key in the inside pocket of his coat. I heard the metallic chink of it as it hit something else, but I hadn't seen him use another key. He hadn't taken his coat off, not even when he was on top of me.

Maybe I could sidetrack him next time; hit him on the head with one of the planks of timber. I could lock him in the toilet.

But, no, it opened from the inside. So did the door from the stairs. I could smash the window or the milk bottle and stab him. But none of these would work. I knew that. He was huge.

I couldn't overpower him, and any attempt to hurt him would only madden him and make it worse for us.

If I could persuade Kirsty to knock him out while he was on top of me, I thought. That might work. But, no, she was in no state to do anything. And then he might lose his temper and strangle me or something. He hadn't been too rough the night before, but he was strong. His arms were wider than my thighs.

Anyway, I couldn't rely on Kirsty. She just whined and rocked and cried and ranted at me.

The next morning when the sun shone through the rectangle of snow and lit up the room, I coaxed her down onto the sofa and made her some toast by holding it up to the gas flame until it was brown. She wouldn't eat the first piece, which I had burned. I smashed banana on top of it with the heel of the milk bottle—there was no knife. I heated the milk and made her a cup of coffee. I'd torn up a dish towel and strapped a strip on to my blisters with masking tape, while Kirsty was still wearing her new boots. I persuaded her to remove them, telling her she'd be more comfortable without them digging into her flesh. She was reluctant, but I insisted, and eventually she peeled them off, the zippers leaving long indentations on her chubby calves, her pink toes naked like small, blind animals blinking in the light. She had a thin scab on the inside of her thigh, like a line of dead ants, and, beside it, a crisscross of little lines, like snail trails but straight, almost geometric. She thumped me when I asked her what they were.

"None of your fucking business," she snapped.

I thought she was embarrassed—perfect Kirsty with some sort of scabby rash.

She made some snide remark about my freckles and the mole on the back of my neck looking like a spider, which was supposed to shut me up.

It did.

After agreeing to keep a bucket of water by the fireplace in case the house burned down, I got together a broken picture frame and some splintered wood, rolled up some newspaper, and lit a fire in the grate. I could see daylight up the chimney, so I hoped I wouldn't choke us out. Maybe someone would see the smoke and investigate.

I read her bits from three-month-old copies of the *Scottish Daily Record* to pass the time, but she wasn't listening. I found a pencil stub and did the crossword. They held that against me afterward. What kind of girl being kept prisoner sits and does a crossword? his lawyer said.

He didn't come back in the evening, although since snow was covering our only window, we had just a sketchy idea of the time.

It was either dark or it wasn't. And now it was.

As darkness fell and Anderson failed to arrive, Kirsty became alternately hysterical and catatonic. I fed the fire by jumping off the stairs onto planks of timber and breaking them into smaller pieces. It kept her warm. I fed her cheese on the crust of the loaf until the combination of the heat of the fire and the whiskey I added to her tea put her to sleep. When she dropped off, I tried on her boots. Her feet were smaller than mine, and I had to struggle to get them on. They pinched my toes like pliers, but I decided that I could probably get them on, although the torn strips of dish towel that I had wound round my blisters would make it difficult.

I cuddled up on the sofa next to her and tried to warm myself so I could get some sleep, but she pushed me away.

It felt as though I had lived through three lifetimes by the time he came the next day. I'd just scraped the carbon off the toast I'd burned the day before and given it to Kirsty with the last of the cheese. He brought fish and chips this time, and lemonade and beer. I almost bit his hand off as he passed me the newspaper-wrapped parcel. I would have danced on my hands for them.

The smell of vinegar was intoxicating. Kirsty said she didn't want any, but I put some on her knee, and she ate it in tiny bites without looking at him.

But he was jittery. I tried to appear unruffled and asked if he would let us go home now, but he replied in an almost casually detached voice that, no—it was too late for that. His eyes darted all over the room as he told us that it had been on the news that we'd disappeared and not been seen since the party. Our picture had been on the TV and was in the morning paper. The police had been to school that day and asked questions. They'd taken some boys who'd been at the party away for questioning.

"So there you go, then," I said breezily, as if it was all a fuss about nothing. "Nobody knows we're here. You said it yourself. Who would believe us? We'll say you haven't done anything wrong. If you could just not lock the door, we could make our own way home," I rationalized.

I swore that I wouldn't say anything—and that I would make sure Kirsty wouldn't either. I even told him that if anything came out, I would take the blame, say that I was the one who'd wanted to stay and that I'd forced her to remain. I'd say that he didn't even know we were in the house. I'd call her a liar if she said anything different, but he didn't respond. Instead, he paced.

"It's a problem, hen," was all he said.

It was still snowing; his coat was flecked with snow and it was melting into little pools on the floor. Kirsty, roused by the food, began to threaten him again. She railed at him until he reached into his coat and produced a penknife, which he fanned out slowly until he found a hook to flick the top off his beer. The blades winked in the light as he bent them back into the sheath.

I watched him slip it back inside beside the key. Maybe I could get my hands on the knife, but first I had to force her to keep quiet, for her own good. I sent her to the bedroom, forcibly ramming her up the stairs, pleading with her to shut her mouth and let me handle it.

"But, Agnes," she whined, "I don't like being up here without you. Don't leave me. You promised that you wouldn't leave me."

"Yes, yes, shush, I promise, cross my heart. Where am I going to go? I'll be right here and I'll sort it out, okay?" Then she wanted her boots back on. Her feet were cold, she whimpered. I took off my jacket and threw it after her. "Wrap them in this—come on, now—go away before he gets nasty." I waited until I heard the match fizz and saw the candlelight dance across the rafters, then I pulled the stair door closed. His eyes had followed me, but it wasn't me he wanted to see; it was Kirsty. Even after three days without a bath and with her hair tangled, she was beautiful. My shoulders shrank into two curls of defeat. It always came back to Kirsty.

I sat down next to him and smiled brightly, or as brightly as I could with a bruised eye and a busted lip. His eyes switched from me to the closed door. He still had his heavy outdoor coat on.

I smoothed my hands over the lapels.

It was soaking. I said, "Is it still snowing outside?"

"It's turning to sleet," he answered. "But it's going to freeze. The roads will be bad, and there's already a foot of snow out there. I don't know when I'll get back again."

"Never mind," I soothed. "But your coat. You should take it off. The fire will dry it." In answer, he looked at the grate and told me I shouldn't be burning any of this stuff.

"It was for Kirsty," I replied. "She was cold."

"She's a lovely-looking girl, isn't she? What a figure. That hair." I agreed, though it felt like I was coughing up scissors.

He wanted to know everything about her. Where she was going when she left school, how old she was, where she lived, what her father did. I answered him, but monosyllabically. I didn't want to get drawn into a Kirsty love fest when I was the one who had spent the day holding her hand, spooning food into her mouth, and wiping her nose.

He smoked a joint. I pretended to smoke it too, but I held the smoke in my cheeks and puffed it out. I told him his coat was soaking me and making me cold, and he finally took it off and laid it on the back of the armchair. He got down beside me.

"You're really skinny, aren't you?" he said, looking at my ribs appraisingly. I crossed my arms protectively across my chest.

"Your bones are sharp." He put his large, spade-like hand on my hip. "You could use a bath," he said.

"Aye, well, there's a shortage of towels in this hotel," I replied.

Then he asked me about the boys the police had picked up. Was one of them Kirsty's boyfriend? I sighed. I was lying there spread open in front of him. He used me, but he didn't see me. I was just the stand-in, the inferior body double for the main star, who was upstairs, curled into a ball, sucking her sleeve.

"Oh, she has loads," I said, puffing out my cheeks, though this time there was no smoke to pad them out.

"Really?"

"Ever since she was wee—her first boyfriend was seventeen, and she had him when she was thirteen."

"Hah, that's not the way she tells it. She's a bit of a stuck-up little cow, isn't she? Thinks she's something special. Mind you, she is something special."

"She's spoiled. Her father gives her everything she wants—she's used to getting her own way with everybody. Especially boys. They all fawn over her."

"So lots of boyfriends, you say?"

"Definitely," I replied. "She's always been a bit loose. Plays them off against each other. You don't want to believe the little miss prissy act. She's just having you on. Whose idea was it that we were walking home the other night? Why do you think we were even at that party?"

He went quiet, and so did I for a while. I had my eye on his coat. I was sure the key was in the pocket. I felt around his pants; there was nothing there but some coins.

"You should go upstairs. Don't listen to her. All that shy stuff—it's all kid on." He sat up, lifted the bottle of whiskey, unscrewed the cap, and drank from the bottle.

He wiped the back of his mouth with his hand. I was

bleeding again. I could see it on his cheek and on the tail of his shirt.

"Go on," I whispered. "I'll not say anything. She likes you. She used to fancy you. She told me. It was her who wanted to come here, wasn't it?" Keeping a grip on the bottle, he stood and pulled his pants together and, with barely a glance at me, walked toward the stairs. I held my breath, but then at the last minute he doubled back and picked up the coat.

Damn, damn, damn, I wailed. I was so tense I thought I was going to wet myself.

I sat on the sofa and wiped myself with newspaper. Then yanked my clothes back on as swiftly as I could.

The stair door was open. I could hear Kirsty telling him he was disgusting and to go away and leave her alone.

I darted around the room as quickly as I could. I grabbed Kirsty's boots, opened the porch, and threw them inside.

Kirsty was roaring now. Crying and screaming at him to stop.

"Agnes," she was shouting, "Agnes, help me." I heard the slap of a hand against something hard as I crept up the stairs, holding my breath. He was hissing at her, telling her to be still, to shut up, but she kept on struggling and fighting until there was another hard slap and then she just sobbed, in muffled gasps. He had his hand over her mouth.

I saw the coat: it was hanging over the little banister at the top of the stairs. The candle was guttering wildly as I stood on my tiptoes and tugged at the hem. Slowly, it slid into my arms, making a soft *thunk* as the collar landed on the wood. I froze, but the steady movement on the bed continued with Kirsty's strangled cries. I walked backward, my feet feeling as though they were floating on air, but the minute I got back into the room, I sprinted to the front porch, pulling the coat onto my shoulders. It was massive and kept slipping off.

My heart was beating so loudly that I could hear it above Kirsty's crying while my hands raked through the deep pockets.

I couldn't make my fingers work. There was no penknife, but I felt the key. There was only one—it was huge and old-fashioned, and I grabbed it tightly in my fist like a spear. I closed the porch door as slowly as I could bear, jammed the key into the lock, and turned it. Please, God, he hadn't heard it. I shot a look at the wall. There was a fuse box with a big handle that I knew would put the house into darkness. I pulled it. That would hold him up a little longer. I drew the bolts, then I grabbed the boots, tossed them out into the snow and went out into the bitter black night, locking the outside door with the same key.

I sat for a minute tearing the wadded masking tape off my feet, pulling strips of skin that had bled and hardened, adhering to the cloth. My fingers were covered with bright, scarlet blood.

Then I screwed my feet into the boots and zipped them halfway up, where they jammed on the bunched-up material of my pants. The zipper pinched the bare skin of my leg, but I ignored it, stood up, and slipped and lurched across the driveway. The wheels of the car had compacted the snow into cursive loops and scribbles, like a big mistake.

I looked inside his car, checking behind me to make sure there was nobody coming, irrationally thinking that there could be another way out of the house that we hadn't found. He'd left the car door unlocked and the keys in the ignition. I took them out and held them for a second in the palm of my hand. Then I threw them across the snow into a hedge.

Behind me there was a muted banging on a door coming

from inside the house. Mr. Anderson was yelling and swearing. "You fucking bitch, I'll kill her if you don't come back, ya fucking whore, open the fucking door." I could hear Kirsty screaming my name, saying *don't leave me, Agnes, don't leave me* . . . but I didn't hesitate. Not for a second.

I pulled the coat together and never once looked behind me. I ran and ran and ran.

I ran, and I never stopped running.

34

I GOT AS FAR as Lexington before I told the driver to go back around the block and drop me off outside the Carlyle. As we swung round the corner of Madison, the wall beside the bus stop was deserted, but when the cab pulled up outside the revolving doors of the hotel I still couldn't drag enough air into my chest to speak. I felt like I was having an asthma attack, but even after I scrabbled around in my purse for my inhaler and puffed it into my mouth, my lungs wouldn't work. I handed over my last twenty and walked unsteadily up to Eightieth Street, looking around me furtively as though Cheryl was going to step out of a shop doorway at any second and tap me on the shoulder. I couldn't see her anywhere, But that didn't make me feel any safer. Wherever she was, she would be back.

When I reached the house, I squinted through the glare of the dining room window hoping she wasn't already inside introducing herself to Adam. I had no idea how she had found out about him. Who knew how she had discovered his address, or what she had told him, but there was only one way to find out.

I had to do this.

I walked up to the door, fished my keys out of my pocket, climbed the stairs, and unlocked the door.

It swung open to silence.

The hallway was empty. Tentatively, I called out Adam's name, but my voice just bounced lazily around the walls, the echo following me as I walked slowly through the dining room into the kitchen, listening for footsteps, my ears sucking the space for sound. But I heard nothing above, nothing below.

The AC hummed gently in the background like a contented housewife getting on with her chores, and I shivered. Chills prickled up my arms and across the back of my neck, but it had nothing to do with the cool air. Upstairs in the parlor, everything was in its place, the upholstery on the sofas as smooth and taut as the face of a Hollywood legend retouched for a closeup, the gaudy bunch of parrot tulips snaked out of the vase I had arranged them in a few days earlier, and the rows of photographs bared their teeth as smugly as ever on the top of the piano. It was like the whole house was holding its breath, bracing itself for a blow. I crossed over to the bay window, hid behind the drapes, and glanced up and down the street through the curlicues of wrought iron. A woman in tiny shorts and jogging shoes walked her dog along the sidewalk, but no other figure lurked nearby.

I found my suitcase abandoned in the middle of the bedroom, where it dug its wheels into the deep carpeting. Surely that was a good sign, I decided. He wouldn't have dragged it up two flights of stairs if he was going to throw me out again. I rapped on his bathroom door and turned the handle. Nobody.

Only Adam's study showed any real disarray. Apart from the

usual confusion of manuscripts and Post-it notes, his desk was strewn with upturned boxes of paper clips and rubber bands, their ugly, toothless mouths open in pain. A ceramic jar of pens had spread its inky fingers across the blotter, and his top drawer was ajar. The small pillows on his sofa, as their name suggested, though probably for the first time in their lives, were scattered and thrown across the floor, and the seat cushions upended. It looked as though he had been searching for something in a hurry. I rearranged the sofa, remembering the feel of its rough, shredded-wheat texture on the back of my thighs the last time I sat there, a memory I didn't want to pursue, and refolded the plaid blanket that Lennie wrapped herself in when she felt sick. I wished it would work for me now.

I checked the street again from the guest room, but the silver foliage of the sickly birch tree planted at the corner obscured my view of the bus stop. Fred, if he was there, was sheltered underneath the green canopy shading his doorway. Cheryl could be there too, I realized, and panic slipped its arms around my rib cage and thumped me in the chest like I was choking.

I needed a glass of water. I went back down to the kitchen, turned on the faucet, but then couldn't swallow more than a sip without gagging.

And then the door slammed. There was the jangle of keys, the soft, animal-paw pad of leather on the table, and a loud keening as a chair drew its heels across the dining room floor. I held my breath and waited . . . but heard only one set of footsteps.

"Edie, *Edie*, is that you?" Adam cried, catching sight of me backed against the sink. He strode across the room, leaving his jacket to swoon off the back of the chair and fall limply on the floor. He grasped my arms roughly as though to shake me, then pulled my body against him.

I couldn't move for a second, but like the steps of a familiar dance, my hands slipped around his waist and my face buried itself in his neck.

"Where the hell did you go?" he said, his voice a mixture of exasperation and relief. "I ran up the street after you and then I got in another cab to follow you, but didn't have my wallet and I had to come back to the house and pay the fare when I didn't even go anywhere. Then I thought I'd drive, but I couldn't find the damn keys, and the guys in the garage took about ten minutes to get the fucking car out. So I just kept walking round, looking for you. Why did you leave? Why did you just leave your suitcase out on the street like that? Are you crazy? What's going on?" The relief had gone. Now he was just mad.

"There was someone I didn't want to see," I whispered into the linen of his shirt, rubbing my cheek against its dampness, crushing it under my skin.

He sighed, then stared at me regretfully, as though he were the one with the secret, then drew out a chair and gently pushed me into it, his hand stroking my shoulder and my hair and the side of my face. He was tan from our weekends at the shore, but now his skin just looked sickly.

I sat obediently, grabbing his hand in mine, and held it fast: "Adam, listen, I've got something to tell you and you're not going to like it," I blurted out urgently. "The girl . . ."

"Ah, the girl . . ." he said sadly, and it wasn't a question.

I closed my eyes for a second and then looked at him full in the face, but now it was his turn to drop his gaze.

"Oh God, what has she . . . ?" I wailed. "Please . . ." I didn't know what I was begging for. I just wanted to make it all stop.

"Wait a minute," he said very quietly.

"No, this can't wait," I insisted, my voice reedy and shrill with panic. "Adam? *Please*, don't go . . ." I called to his back as he walked out into the hall. I rose to follow him, but he came back a second later, holding his wallet.

He opened it and took out a worn scrap of paper, which he carefully unfolded and handed to me. On it, in Francisco's heart-monitor handwriting, was Cheryl's name followed by a telephone number.

"I guess this is the same one." He still wouldn't look at me.

My spine melted into ice water. "How did you get this?"

"That night your husband came here. He left it on the dresser, and then I found it thrown in the trash in the bathroom. I'm sorry. I kept it."

"You're sorry?" Disbelief made me stupid. "What do you have to be sorry about? I'm the one who should be sorry . . ."

"I meddled. I didn't know where to find you. I thought it might be a relative or something."

"Did you call her?"

He didn't answer.

"Adam, did you call her and ask about me?" I insisted.

"Once—maybe a week after you left," he admitted. "I asked for Edith Lutz and left my number in case there was anyone there who knew you. A few days later the girl called back, said she was looking for her birth mother. I told her I couldn't help her and that there had just been some sort of mix-up. That was the end of it."

"I wish," I said and shook my head in disbelief. "You've known about her all this time?"

"I didn't know anything, Edie. I still don't. I just found the piece of paper and kept it. I thought if it was important you'd mention it eventually. I didn't want to scare you away again—like that all worked out *exactly* according to plan," he added, wryly.

We both sat in stunned silence.

"So that was her? At the door?" he said, eventually.

I nodded.

"She looks a lot like you."

"Yeah, so everybody keeps telling me. What did she say?"

He shook his head. "Not much, honey—something about finding the suitcase on the sidewalk. I don't think she even knew it was yours. Of course I recognized it. And then I recognized her."

But she knew all right. I don't know how, but she wasn't waiting out there on the street corner by accident.

He lowered himself into another chair, taking both my hands in his, kissing one, then the other. "So what's going on, Edie?"

I pulled away from him, gripping the edge of my chair so tightly I could feel the varnish splinter under my fingernails.

"Come on, whatever it is, I want to know," he said, and I noticed his hand shake.

"I'm afraid it's not a good story," I said.

Then I licked my lips, took a long shuddering breath, and screwed my eyes closed while I tried to figure out exactly which one to tell him.

Acknowledgments

Authors always offer profuse gratitude to their editors and agents, but anyone who has ever been involved in producing a book will know that this is more than a polite gesture. So a sincere thank-you to Toby Mundy, who introduced me to George Capel, who, together with her assistant Rosie Apponyi, were tirelessly supportive. Thanks also to Jenny Dean and everyone at Penguin in London and to Claire Wachtel, Julia Novitch, and all at HarperCollins in the United States for believing in the book.

My children, the best part of my life, have kept me positive through the worst of times and deserve a greater debt than can be expressed in a few lines. Thank you, Nel, for being my perfect imaginary audience, and thanks also to dear Alex Kitroeff, Eduardo Posada-Carbó, and Luis Mora who patiently helped me with some background details, though they cannot be blamed for my inaccuracies. Other friends—Maria, Julia, Sarah, and Yvonna, especially, were also a great help, as was Judith Corrente, who put up with me and put me up when I needed her, and aided in the Americanization of Agnes.

Finally, I want to thank Christopher MacLehose, whose kindness, interest, and help kept me going.

Getting a book published is the result of a long chain of random acts of encouragement and the goodwill of strangers. Editors who have commissioned me; readers who have responded to things I have written; Miranda; my sister, Lesley, and brother, George, mercifully not like those in the book; and others who have been loved and lost along the way have all played their part.

I'm only sad that some of them are not here to see the book.